MW01057702

Going Back

A Tom Novak Thriller

by Neil Lancaster

Burning Chair Limited, Trading as Burning Chair Publishing
61 Bridge Street, Kington HR5 3DJ

www.burningchairpublishing.com

By Neil Lancaster
Edited by Simon Finnie and Peter Oxley
Book cover design by ebooklaunch.com

First published by Burning Chair Publishing, 2020
Copyright © Neil Lancaster, 2020
All rights reserved.

ISBN: 978-1-912946-14-3

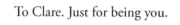
To Clare. Just for being you.

1

The gates of Centralni zatvor, Belgrade's Central Prison, opened to allow through the small blue prisoner transport van. It was closely followed by a marked Skoda police car as it swung out into the residential streets surrounding the massive, ugly edifice that was the city's major correctional facility.

'How far to Padinska Skela?' asked Zoran, a hugely overweight uniformed guard who sat in the passenger seat, biting into a chocolate bar.

'Thirty minutes. Do you never stop eating? You will give yourself a heart attack,' said Ljubo, the driver, shaking his head.

'All muscle, my friend,' Zoran laughed, patting his massive belly.

'You are revolting,' Ljubo shook his head in disgust.

'Why the police escort? We don't normally have cops with us when transporting prisoners to other jails.'

'You've not heard of Babić?'

'No. Should I?'

'Yes,' scoffed Ljubo. 'Maybe if you spent more time doing your job and less time stuffing your face, you'd know something about the scum we've got. He's a dangerous bastard. Ex-Paramilitary, and he's now a crime boss, a really major criminal. He has been causing nothing but problems in the short time he has been here; that's why they're sending him to *Padinjak*.'

'So why are we not in an armoured van, then? Rather than this piece-of-shit Fiat,' Zoran said, knocking a fat fist against the dashboard's flimsy plastic.

'Ask the Governor. How should I know?'

'We won't be missing him, then. We have enough problems with the filthy addicts and the gangs,' Zoran said through a mouthful of candy.

'Stop with your spitting, man. It's disgusting,' Ljubo said, screwing up his face as he watched the flecks of food splatter the dashboard.

Zoran let out a bellow of a laugh, as he reached out and turned up the radio, so that the other man's words were drowned out by the music blaring out of the tinny speakers. Ljubo just shook his head at his oafish colleague's terrible manners.

The traffic was light as they headed up to the main junction leading onto the E70 and north to the Pancevo Bridge over the Danube. The morning sun glinted off the wide expanse of water, shimmering blue in the brilliant sunshine.

Zoran yawned. 'How was that little lady you were taking out last night, Ljubo?' he asked as they drove alongside the dark, imposing steelwork that supported the huge bridge.

Ljubo didn't answer immediately, his eyes locked on the dark van in front of them. It was slowing, without any explanation. It was a dark, anonymous vehicle—not old, not new—with blacked-out windows at the rear, and the licence plate was so filthy as to be illegible. 'What is this fool doing?' he muttered as the van slowed even further. He checked his mirrors and was reassured to see the liveried Skoda police car immediately behind him. But he could feel that something wasn't right.

Suddenly the other van's left-hand door was thrown open wide, revealing a masked figure in dark clothing clutching a strange-looking, dark plastic implement. It was like a firearm, but at the same time totally different, with what appeared to be a torch head attached to the front. The masked man heaved the large, matte-black weapon to his shoulder and pointed it directly at them. There was no barrel, nothing to give the impression of it being a gun of any type, so what the hell was it?

Whatever it was, it wasn't good. There was only one conclusion: they were under attack.

'Attack, attack!' Ljubo screamed into the radio on his lapel, his heart racing as he stamped on the brakes. The unrestrained Zoran flew forward, his head crashing into the windscreen.

'What the fuck, Ljubo?' yelled Zoran.

The confined cabin was filled with a feeling of mild heat and the faint smell of ozone. Then the van stopped dead. The digital radio was suddenly silent, the readout went black, and the engine cut out as if it had been switched off with the key.

'Ljubo, what's happening? Why has the van stopped?' Zoran asked.

His question was answered suddenly and terribly, as the remaining door on the attacker's van flew open. Three masked men in dark combat clothing dived out of the van, all clutching sub-machine guns. The lead man charged past them without giving them so much as a glance as he raised his weapon to his shoulder, sprinting past them towards their police car escort. The thunderous, cracking report of the assault rifle was deafening as automatic gunfire was poured into the Skoda.

Ljubo didn't try to look behind, being more concerned with the stocky, intimidating-looking gunman who was now stood directly in front of him, his weapon levelled at their windscreen. Panicking he reached for the van key and violently wrenched it, but the van was as dead as if the battery had been completely removed. Through his panic Ljubo was sure he could detect a strange smell, almost akin to the charged, ozone smell that often preceded an electrical storm.

The last gunman was stood to the left of the van, his legs planted wide, the barrel of his submachine gun pointing unwaveringly at Zoran. Ljubo felt the weight of his pistol in his belt but knew that any movement towards it would only have one outcome, and that would be bullets crashing into him through the windscreen of the flimsy Fiat. His hands instinctively shot upwards in a gesture of surrender as the unseen gunman behind them continued to stitch the police car with gunfire. He didn't give the police officers a single thought; his only concern was for his own immediate future.

'Get out!' commanded the gunman closest to him, pale blue eyes blazing beneath the eyeholes in the ski-mask. Ljubo's hand scrabbled for the handle and, trying not to panic he opened the door. He stepped out, his hands aloft. 'Please, please, I have a daughter,' he babbled in terror.

'You have one chance to let the prisoner out, or you die,' the attacker growled in a pure Belgrade accent. He risked a glance at their police escort vehicle; it looked now more like a colander than a car and the inside of the vehicle resembled an abattoir. The two officers inside were broken shells, their chests studded with bloodied holes. The bottom half of the driver's jaw had been blown off and the top of the passenger's head was missing completely.

'I don't have the keys, he does,' he said, his voice wobbling as he looked at Zoran.

'Keys,' the other attacker, a much smaller man, said.

Zoran was already out of the van and scrabbling in his pockets for the keys.

'Quicker! Fucking hurry up,' the smaller man shouted.

Zoran located the keys in his pocket and held them out.

The smaller man gestured with his weapon. 'Open the back. Now. We are taking Babić. If you resist or try anything, you both die here and now. Do you understand?'

Zoran nodded rapidly. He turned towards the back of the van and out of sight of Ljubo, who just stood with his hands aloft as the attacker kept his firearm trained on his chest. Ljubo kept his eyes away from him, not wishing to antagonise the man at all. All he wanted was to get home to his wife and kid. Babić could go free, as far as he was concerned.

There was silence for a brief moment, followed by the sound of the van's rear doors being opened.

'Handcuffs. Take them off.' Came a deep voice from the rear of the van. Ljubo recognised Babić's voice, bringing back memories of the one time he had crossed swords with that nasty, intimidating thug inside the prison over a minor infraction.

And then he was there, stood in front of Ljubo, a small pistol in his hand. Babić was surprisingly short but stocky, with a thick beard and a pale scar bisecting his forehead. His dark, flashing eyes glittered with menace.

The first gunman passed them without pausing and got back into the van, sitting next to the man who was still clutching the strange weapon which had started this whole nightmare.

'I remember you. You disrespected me in the jail in front of my men. That was a mistake,' said Babić, a blank, evil look on his meaty face.

Ljubo said nothing and just closed his eyes, consumed with abject terror. He just wanted to live, to see his family again.

'Please, don't kill me,' he whimpered, with no pretences at anything other than utter capitulation.

A slow, unpleasant smile stretched across Babić's face. 'You think I am an animal? I'm not going to kill you, so don't piss your pants,' he sneered.

Ljubo let out a small exhalation of relief, hope rising in his chest. Babić lowered the pistol from his chest, pointed it at Ljubo's knee and then the gun cracked and bucked. A 9mm bullet smashed into his patella and he collapsed like a falling tree, screaming as the jacketed round tore through the joint.

Babić nodded and both men jogged off to join the others in the back of the van. The doors slammed shut and then there was a screech as the van sped off in a cloud of acrid smoke.

*

Babić looked across the rear of the van and smiled at the twins, Risto and Milan, who had both pulled their masks up to reveal big, heavy faces swathed in sweat.

'You did well,' said Babić. 'I am glad to be away from that shit-hole.' He pointed at the slim man with a small moustache, who was still clutching the large, strange looking weapon. 'Who is this?'

'This is Cerović. He is the man I talked to you about when you managed to call me from the prison a while ago. He is the creator of this weapon; it stopped the van as if by magic.'

Babić looked at the bulky plastic-covered weapon with interest before turning his attention to Cerović. His dark eyes glittered like a snake stalking a rodent as he appraised the man.

'Thank you. You did well.'

'You're welcome,' Cerović said in halting Serb laced with an American accent.

'You're American?' said Babić in good English.

'I was born in Kosovo, but I was raised in New York.' His voice was light and nasal, with a distinct New York drawl. His movements were nervous and staccato as he shifted from side to side in his seat. He held up the weapon. 'It worked a fuckin' treat, right?'

'Indeed. Like a fucking treat,' repeated Babić, his face darkening. 'Can you make more of these?'

'Sure thing. As long as the price is right. I'm an electronics man and I can make anything you want, dude,' said Cerović, his confidence visibly rising.

'Show me?' Babić said. Cerović handed over the weapon. It was about the same size as a sniper rifle, but much bulkier and covered in a crude, hard plastic. There was a simple trigger mechanism and a rough sighting device, that seemed to have been fashioned from a monocular. The weapon had a cone-type appendage at the end that resembled a large flashlight. It was heavy, at least twenty kilos. 'Hmm. We will speak of this again, Cerović.'

'Sure thing, buddy,' smiled Cerović, beaming with pride.

'Did you make contact with the arms-dealer we spoke of, Risto? We need to begin operations again, immediately,' said Babić, not taking his eyes off Cerović. He was not used to being addressed so informally by someone he had just met.

'Yes. Ex-Bosnian army man,' said Risto. 'Seems reliable. He got these submachine guns for us; they are pretty good. He is saying he can get anything we want, no problem; he managed to get us military spec batteries for this device as well.'

'I want modern weapons, Risto. No old Bosnian garbage. With

what I have planned we want the best.'

'He claims he can get Western weapons; says he has a reliable source.'

'Where did you locate him?'

'Dark web. Turns out Cerović has some computer skills, as well,' Risto said.

'What's his name? I want to meet him soon.'

'Pavlović.'

'Then make the arrangements,' said Babić.

'As you wish. It's good to have you out again, my friend,' Risto smiled.

'It is. You did well but, for now, I need a beer. You have a safehouse?'

'Not in Serbia. Too dangerous and you are too well-known,' said Risto.

'So, where are we going, then?'

'We are going to Sarajevo.'

2

Davud Babić stood in the middle of the disused and decaying industrial estate, projecting pure menace at the wiry form of Goran Pavlović.

It was a look he had perfected over many years, from being a member of *Arkan's Tigers*, through his time in the Serbian special forces, and later when he managed to get a hold on crime in Belgrade and beyond. He had spent the last few months staring down the scum of Serbia in the Central Prison and had always prevailed. He feared no man; particularly not this unknown, skinny pencil-neck who, despite his comparatively diminutive stature, returned his hard stare with an underlying trace of humour.

Babić was angry: really angry. He did not appreciate being ripped off, especially when it was his own people who had made the deal possible in the first place. One thing was for sure: if Pavlović thought he was paying the full price for those machine-guns, then he was sadly mistaken.

'Do you have the merchandise we agreed?'

'Yes. It's all here, just as you ordered, do you have the funds ready to transfer?' Pavlović had a flat and yet resonant tone with no discernible accent.

Babić stared at him, failing to understand how the little shrimp was so relaxed; he was used to people being far more intimidated by his presence and, unbelievably, Pavlović had come alone. His Ford van behind him sagged tellingly at the rear, indicative of the weighty cargo it carried. Babić feared no man, but there was no way that he would hand over thousands of dollars' worth of military hardware without some degree of support. For his part, he knew that the reassuring presence of Risto glowered from the driver's seat of his own pickup.

His world was a dishonest one, and many men would have cheerfully just shot Pavlović and taken his merchandise without a second thought. But there was something about the arms dealer that gave Babić pause. It was the way he conducted himself; it took a great deal of self-belief to carry oneself with such utter confidence, almost bordering on arrogance, when meeting a man with Babić's reputation.

Babić stared hard at the arms dealer, his anger rising. 'So, Pavlović, when were you going to tell me that it was the American— no, *my* American—that tipped you off about the location of these weapons?'

Pavlović's face didn't register even the slightest flicker of surprise. 'Babić, it is a problem for you if your people are holding back information from you. I took all the risks to acquire them the merchandise; they are mine to sell,' he showed his stained teeth in a cold smile.

'You disrespect me at your peril, Pavlović,' Babić snarled. 'This was *my* source, not yours, and yet you conspire to cheat me. You are making a big mistake by crossing me. I have a long memory and I do not forgive easily.'

'You should control your people better, or maybe pay them more: then they wouldn't cheat you. Now, do you want the guns or not because—I tell you this—you won't find MP5's like this anywhere else.' Pavlović chuckled.

Babić's face darkened at the slightly jeering tone. 'You ought to be more careful, Pavlović. This is a violent city and many men would cheerfully just steal your merchandise and leave you dead in the gutter. I am almost insulted that you feel able to come here to hand over so much military hardware without any backup.'

'What makes you think I have no backup, Babić?' Pavlović replied in a soft, curious tone, his face relaxed and almost amused.

Babić smiled and looked around the industrial wasteland in which they stood. Piles of rubble lay strewn on the rough semi-cleared space. It had once been a thriving, if shabby, estate of small businesses and manufacturing outlets. Over the past few years a developer had been preparing it for clearance, ready for a shiny new shopping and leisure centre, but cash flow problems had left it a barren wasteland, a perfect place to hand over bulky and dangerous contraband.

'I see no one, Pavlović. I picked this location as there is nowhere to hide and nowhere for prying eyes to loiter. It's just you and me.'

Pavlović just smiled and sniggered. 'You bring your big ugly friend in the car, Babić. What, you are not confident in your abilities?'

Babić returned a mirthless smile, feeling a jolt of irritation at the little wretch's insolence. 'You should be careful of your words, Pavlović. You must know of my reputation.'

'I know all about your reputation, old man. It is widely known throughout Serbia and beyond. A man in your line of business would do well to keep a lower profile. However, I know for a fact that you know nothing of me, which pleases me a great deal. I assure you I would not come to an exchange like this without a little insurance,' he smiled again once more and scratched the top of his head.

In that instant, a red laser dot appeared on Babić's chest. Babić looked down at the laser sight marker, and smiled, almost imperceptibly. Seeing this, Risto leapt out of the car, reaching for the gun at his waistband.

'That would be unwise, my friend,' said Pavlović without looking up, his voice eerily calm. 'Look at your own chest before you concern yourself with your friend.'

Risto froze and looked down to see an identical red dot dancing on his denim jacket.

'Now, Babić,' Pavlović continued, 'I am not an unreasonable man. I can see why you may be a little disappointed as to your relationship with your source, so, in the spirit of goodwill I am willing to reduce the price a little. Shall we say a ten percent reduction?'

Babić sighed and looked over at a tall, semi-derelict building, about four hundred metres away, the only place where the two snipers could be hidden. He realised he had little choice: he needed those weapons and he needed them now. And the price was still cheaper than anywhere else. Pavlović's time would come; revenge was a dish best served cold, after all.

'Okay. We do the deal, but at a *twenty* percent discount,' Babić growled.

Pavlović paused, and then nodded. 'Excellent. All is fair in business: you understand this. You would do the same in my position.'

Babić said nothing, his face twisted in a smile which could be mistaken for a grimace. He swore then and there that, one way or another, he would kill Pavlović. Very soon.

3

On the tarmac directly in front of Inverness Airport's small terminal, Tom Novak sat inside the Learjet on a leather chair facing Mike Brogan. Having read the email from the Commissioner authorising his secondment to the FBI, he handed the iPad back to his friend. Tom was tired—really tired—as the events of the last few days began to hit home.

'So what do you need from me?' he asked.

'I take it that's a yes?' Mike asked, showing his teeth in a typically American smile.

'I owe you everything, Mike. What do you need?'

'We need you to go back to Sarajevo.'

'Sarajevo?' Tom's stomach lurched a little, his mind reeling at the prospect of returning to his place of birth.

'The very same. Look, man, this is a short-notice assignment that has taken us by surprise. The computer and thumb drive you liberated from the recently-departed Zelenko has caused a furore in intelligence circles, and we need to take action urgently. I don't know if you heard, but your friend Zelenko was tragically murdered at the hands of the Ukrainian mafia. I'm sure this news comes as a shock to you,' Mike stared straight at Tom, who met his gaze unflinchingly.

'It's a jungle out there, Mike,' Tom said, flatly.

'It clearly is, Tom. It clearly is. Still, before I go any further, I need to know that you are ready for this. We only have parts of the puzzle so it could be a very dangerous assignment. This is voluntary. You don't need to stay on this plane—you can get off now and go home to Cameron and Shona—but you do have some unique qualities and skills that we need,' Mike said, earnestly.

Tom only hesitated for a moment. He had saved Mike Brogan's life years ago in Basra, Iraq, when he was deployed as an operator with the Special Reconnaissance Regiment. Mike had very much returned that favour, with interest, when he saved Tom and his foster family's lives in Scotland last year, and then more recently when helping him bring down a far-right terror group. It wasn't a difficult decision.

'I'm in. Whatever you need. But the FBI?'

'Just a cover, don't need too much info being out there. Anyway, that's fantastic. Leo?' Mike said, turning and raising his eyebrows at the agent that Tom had mistakenly disabled just a few minutes ago in the airport terminal toilets.

A remarkably relaxed Leo stepped forward with a brown manilla file marked *"Secret"*, which he handed over to Tom. 'Non-disclosure agreement and terms of your secondment. You wanna read?' Leo handed over a heavy and expensive looking pen.

Tom glanced at the file headed with the crest of the FBI and the header *"Detective Sergeant Tom Novak: Terms of Secondment"*. Tom signed at the bottom of the page, giving the contents only a scant glance before handing it back to Leo.

'So when do you want to do this?' Tom asked, already knowing the answer.

'Now. If you're good with that?' Mike replied.

'Yep. Let's do this.'

Mike flashed his dazzling smile once again. 'Welcome to the team, Tom. Buckle up. We are getting airborne right away; we have a very narrow window on this. You'll notice that the FBI crest is all over this, but you will be working directly for me on this operation.' The engines began to whine as Leo pulled the steps in and closed the aircraft door. The aircraft began to edge forward.

'There is some coffee here. You want a cup?'

'Sure,' nodded Tom.

Within a few seconds, Leo had passed a Styrofoam cup to Tom, who took a sip. 'This coffee sucks, by the way.'

'What do you expect on a Government jet?'

Tom shrugged. 'So why am I here?'

'A few months ago, a prisoner was broken out of a prison transport van in Belgrade,' Mike said, staring at Tom. 'Are you familiar with the city?'

'Possibly,' Tom said guardedly. He had travelled to Belgrade a while ago to exact revenge on a paramilitary criminal who had murdered his father during the Balkan War and who had, coincidentally, become central to a major plot that Tom was investigating.

'Well, whatever. Basically, this prison van was completely disabled by a weapon of unknown type and origin. The guards reported that the vehicle had a complete power outage and simply glided to a halt. Armed raiders then sprung the prisoner: a nasty bastard called Davud Babić who was being transferred to another prison. This was a brutally efficient attack during which they killed the escorting cops and maimed one of the van drivers. There was no explanation for the power outage, but you could explain it by a vehicle fault. What can't be explained was the fact that both guards' cell-phones were also fried, the radio was wrecked, and all the vehicle's electronic circuits were completely disabled. Local police have never seen anything like it, so they reached out to some experts who alerted us. We offered the Serbs some expertise and access to our specialists and they accepted. We've had our tech people look over the van and the guards cell phones and they are completely scratching their heads. Someone thought electromagnetic pulse, maybe; but the scientists are all arguing about it, and opinions are split as to whether a small device as described would have the power or capability to cause the sort of damage done. All the tests on man portable EMP and other energy weapons have been way too underpowered to cause this sort of catastrophic failure. It has the boffins worried.'

'Anyone see anything?' Tom asked, his detective's mind starting to tick over.

'Guards saw nothing before the attack. There were three

attackers all armed with automatic weapons, plus one other who remained in the van with something that was described as looking like a rocket launcher or similar. No one has been able to clearly describe it, but then that's understandable as they had plenty on their hands with the gun-toting raiders. Guards report the attackers as Serbian, from their accents, apart from the man with the device, who did not speak during the incident. By all accounts, a highly professional team, clearly of military origin. This attack was ruthlessly efficient. One of the guards was recognised and was kneecapped by Babić; purely out of malice, from what we can gather. The other cooperated fully after that and Babić was handed over. He has not been seen since.' Mike was in full briefing mode at this point. 'Questions?'

'Anything on the prisoner?'

'Davud Babić. A particularly nasty former member of the Special Operations Unit that was formed out of *Arkan's Tigers*. Are you familiar with this?'

Tom said nothing, but nodded gravely, his mind reeling at the familiarity of this. *Arkan's Tigers* were a paramilitary group from the Balkan war, headed up by the now-deceased Raznatovic Arkan. They were incorporated into the Yugoslav Army but were later disbanded after several members of the Special Operations Unit were involved in the murder of the Serbian Prime Minister. The two most murderous of the Militia groups were Arkan's Tigers and The White Eagles who had murdered Tom's father. A dull ache settled in Tom's abdomen. This felt far too familiar.

'I take it there is more?' Tom said, flatly, his eyes impassive.

'Yeah, a little. The scientists are very worried about this weapon that they used. Mostly because they didn't think that anything with such a capacity should exist. Various agencies have tried to build something like this in the past but, so far, no one has managed to make it powerful enough or reliable enough to consider taking it further. We hadn't really worried about it before now, but this situation has us concerned. The way it instantly disabled the van and destroyed pretty much all the circuits within is a real worry.

Imagine if it could be scaled up, particularly in the hands of well-organised ex-paramilitaries.'

'Such as a plane?' said Tom, a knot forming in his gut.

'You got it. Imagine a terrorist stood close to a runway, just as Air Force One is taking off?' Mike let the sentence hang in the air.

'Jesus,' said Tom.

'Jesus indeed. Up until now we were sure that there was no one, outside of the major arms manufacturers or aerospace engineering community, with anything like the capacity or ability to develop something as potentially destructive as this.'

'Now you think there may be?'

'It seems so,' Mike said, a worried look in his blue eyes.

'I'm taking it you don't know who that is, right?' Tom raised his eyebrows.

'Not for sure; but we have a lead, which is where you come in.'

'I'm listening.'

'The intel that you liberated from Zelenko has thrown us a lifeline. We have had a whole raft of data experts look into it and it has been quite enlightening. It would seem that our recently departed Oligarch was investing in this very project. Several wire transfers have been traced to a bank account that we are pretty sure is in the control of Davud Babić. Babić has also recently transferred some funds into a bank account in the Bahamas, that we are almost certain belongs to an individual named Stefan Cerović. Which is particularly interesting.'

'Why so interesting?'

'Several reasons. Firstly, he is a Serb like yourself. Also, like yourself he was a refugee. But he settled in the USA, lives in Manhattan. Want to know the interesting bit?' Mike asked, a half smile on his face.

'I was getting interested anyway, but carry on.'

'He studied electrical engineering at NYU, gaining a first-class degree. Bit of a genius, apparently. Worked for a major tech company developing the protection of their server banks. Seems he was going rather well, but then got fired after an employee drug test. He was fairly upset about it, apparently.'

'That is interesting. What do you want from me?' Tom said, already suspecting the answer.

'I'll get to that in a moment, but it's best I give you the full picture. Now the bank transfer data you secured was hugely complex, but we have some serious analysts who have managed to cut through the fat to the meat of it. We have followed the money from Babić to accounts linked to a Sarajevo-based arms dealer called Goran Pavlović. As well as weapons, we believe that he had also been looking to procure some military grade batteries to supply to Babić and his gang. Pavlović was coincidentally arrested just a few days ago when local police stopped him driving his car and found a number of stolen pistols in the trunk. This has left the gang still needing these batteries, but without a supplier. This opens up an opportunity for us.'

'I'm seeing where this is going, but I don't understand one thing,' Tom said. 'Why so much effort? This is surely a comparatively small time, and non-American, problem.'

'We haven't told you everything, Tom.'

'Why am I not surprised?'

Mike nodded gravely. 'We think that Zelenko was just one of a series of hugely wealthy investors in this project. The trail is complex, but there are large sums of money being moved. The feeling is that there is no way that these investors would be spending such cash without expecting a return. They are trying to procure military-grade batteries, so we are really concerned that they won't stop with just one single weapon. They could build many of them, or they could be planning to build a massively powered one. We can be sure that if the investors are throwing these large sums around, it won't be for no reason. We are worried, Tom; hence you being here now.'

4

The flight took just under four hours, during which Mike spent most of the time at the rear of the small aircraft speaking in hushed tones into a laptop on what seemed to be a conference call. Meanwhile, Leo had handed Tom a tablet computer loaded with a detailed briefing presentation, which in turn contained a reasonable amount of detail on Babić, Cerović, and Pavlović.

The lion's share of the intelligence was on Babić. He had a violent and ruthless past, initially as a member of *Arkan's Tigers*, a violent militia during the Balkan conflict. Following the war, he served with the Special Operations Unit in the Serbian Army before being discharged with disgrace when the unit was disbanded following the assassination of the Serbian Prime Minister. From there he descended further and further into organised crime and was suspected of multiple murders and kidnappings. He had been imprisoned recently for his part in the shooting of a rival gang member and, since being sprung from the prison transport, he had fallen off the radar completely.

Tom studied the man's photograph, noting the deep-set, dark eyes, the scarred forehead, and contemptuous facial expression. The look was one that Tom had witnessed a number of times during his life beginning with the *White Eagle* paramilitaries that murdered his father in 1992. It was a look of sheer, unadulterated cruelty.

The photograph of Cerović was a complete shift: a slim man who looked much younger than his date of birth suggested. A weak mouth and pencil moustache were contradicted by blue eyes that shone with intelligence and cunning. Reading his biography, Tom was unsettled to note that Cerović had a similar background to his;

he was a refugee who had fled to the US from Kosovo in 1999, aged ten, after being orphaned. Raised in New York by a foster family, he excelled at school and studied electrical engineering, at which he seemed to be supremely gifted. After graduating he worked for various tech companies, including his roles in protecting servers against EMP attacks. Homeland Security reports showed that Cerović had left the US six months previously, after a failed random employee drug test destroyed his career. His last known location was in Belgrade.

Finally, Tom studied the photo of Goran Pavlović. He was an anonymous-looking man, a little younger than Tom. A forgettable face with dark, short hair and icy blue eyes stared out at him, emotionless and unfathomable. There was very little intelligence on Pavlović. He had lived through the devastating siege of Sarajevo that Tom had fled in 1992. He was orphaned during the war and was cared for by the authorities before eventually being conscripted into the army in 2003, when Bosnia and Herzegovina were rebuilding. He served for two years but there was little information on file about this service. Following that, there were some reports of the young Pavlović having been involved in the illegal arms trade using contacts made during his conscription, but nothing concrete. There was unverified intelligence from telephone intercepts that he had sold a stolen Serbian anti-tank rocket as well as mortars and grenades in the last few months, but again this was not confirmed. The CIA analysis concluded that he was an independent arms trader who was utilising the dark web to ply his trade to criminal groups.

'Time to land. Buckle up please,' Leo's voice interrupted Tom's train of thought.

Mike came and sat opposite Tom once again, and smiled.

'So, what's next?' Tom asked.

'As soon as we land, we head straight to the US Embassy. We are working on computer and phone data seized from Pavlović, so hopefully we should be able to finalise a plan very soon.'

Tom nodded and stared straight ahead as he secured his seatbelt.

Looking out of the small aircraft's window he could see the densely packed streets of Sarajevo, the city of his birth, far below. Vivid memories and a sense of foreboding swept over him as the Learjet descended into the city that he had fled as a child.

*

Tom and Mike were met by a large SUV, driven by a wordless driver who wore an earpiece and dark sunglasses to shield against the fierce Balkan sun.

The journey through the Sarajevo streets was confusing for Tom. He recognised some of the landmarks, but the extensive rebuilding that had occurred since the conflict made the streets both familiar and unfamiliar.

They pulled up outside the US Embassy and Tom looked with interest at the white, sprawling three-storey building, a feeling of anticipation building in his stomach. A large US flag gently swayed in the breeze, standing out against the cobalt blue sky. The building was peaceful and almost serene, a vivid display of purple blooms decorating the garden at the front.

'Impressive, isn't it?' said Mike. 'It was opened in 1994, after the US formally recognised Bosnia and Herzegovina.'

'I guess. America knows how to build an embassy, that's for sure.'

'How does it feel to be back in Sarajevo after all these years?'

'A little odd. So much has changed, but so much is the same,' Tom said, showing none of the disquiet he was feeling.

'You okay, bud?' there was a touch of genuine concern in Mike's blue eyes.

'I'm all good,' Tom said flatly, staring at the flag that danced gently in the breeze. 'I'm ready when you are.'

They alighted from the SUV and moved into the lobby, where they were met by a short, stocky man with a cropped haircut and twinkling, humorous eyes. His face lit up when he saw Mike.

'Mikey, Mikey! Been too long, Buddy!' he said locking Mike

in a tight hug and slapping his back. Mike returned the quick embrace before both men broke away.

'Good to see you, Rudy. When was it last?' Mike said, a wide grin splitting his face.

'Five years, at least. Afghanistan, right? Man, that was a tough gig.'

'Sure was. Can I introduce my good friend, Tom? Tom, this is Rudy O'Shea, who is Second Secretary at the Embassy. Basically he does nothing much for his money.' In spite of what Mike said, it was clear to Tom that Rudy was a spook of some sort.

'Good to know you, Tom,' said Rudy, shaking his hand. 'Mike has told me nothing about why you're here, and I ain't asking as Mike wouldn't tell me, in any case,' Rudy guffawed and slapped Mike on the back.

'No problem,' Tom smiled.

'Okay, Rudy,' said Mike. 'Enough of the gushing; let's get this show on the road. You got a room?'

'Sure, we are all set up and ready to go in the conference room. The defence attaché knows you are here, and he will probably come and say hi.'

They set off at a good pace along the glistening corridor towards the rear of the building, their footsteps echoing on the polished marble.

'Who's the D.A.?' Mike asked Rudy.

'Colonel John Havers. Nice guy but a little nervous. He asked me why you are here, and I told him the truth: that I have no idea. You arrivin' on someone's turf tends to have that effect, bud.'

Mike chuckled, 'I know John. He can be a wuss. Don't worry about it; the DOD has our backs.'

They came to a solid-looking wooden door, which Rudy pushed open to reveal a large windowless conference room containing a long central table bedecked with US and Bosnian flags. A large screen was erected at the end of the room, and a petite bespectacled young woman with a short, choppy, dyed red haircut sat in front of a battered-looking laptop that was festooned with stickers, the largest of which proclaimed, *"Trust me, I'm a programmer".*

'How did I know you'd be here, Pet?' Tom smiled, his stomach lurching just a touch at the sight of his friend.

'Someone has to keep you out of trouble, Detective,' she smiled, her face lighting up in a dazzling smile as they hugged warmly.

'You've had your hair done. I like it,' Tom said.

'You know me; I like a change.'

Pet often worked for Mike when complex, off-books computer problems needed solving. Tom had worked with her on a couple of occasions, and there was nothing she couldn't do with any type of IT. She had been caught as a teenager successfully breaking into the CIA mainframe for no reason other than to see if she could. No computer was secure enough to keep Pet out; she had a way with technology that was as much about instinct and feelings as sheer technical skill. Tom was surprised at the immense sense of relief he felt at seeing her in that room at that particular moment.

There was a brief knock at the door before it swung open to reveal a slim, wiry and tanned man in his early forties. He was smartly dressed in an impeccably tailored suit and blinding white shirt with no necktie.

'Hey, if it ain't Mike Brogan,' he said, showing white teeth in a beaming smile.

'John, good to see you, man. Tom this is Colonel John Havers, the defence attaché at this joint,'

Colonel Havers smiled at Tom and then nodded at Pet.

'I'm on my way to a meeting Mike, but I just wanted to say hi before I did, I have to check in with the ambassador, who let me know earlier that he wants to chat with you as soon as we can arrange; he has a few questions. Can you do that?'

'Sure thing, John. Let me finish up here and then I'll check in, okay?'

'Great. I think Mr Shriver just wants some reassurance from you.' Havers turned to Rudy, an eyebrow raised. 'Rudy, can we speak?'

Rudy nodded. 'Gentlemen and lady, I'm gonna run and leave

you to it; sounds like I am required elsewhere. Shout me if you need any resources, okay?'

'Thanks, Rudy.' Mike said as the big man left the room with Havers.

'Rudy not part of this gig?' Tom asked.

'Not at the moment. This is very early stages, and I am applying the need-to-know principle right now. Rudy is cool with it, although I suspect that the ambassador will be a little more searching,' he chuckled. 'Perhaps I should have mentioned that I have asked Pet along. When the Bosnians arrested Pavlović we needed to get into his computer and phone data urgently and Pet was available, despite a busy period helping you out in Ukraine,' Mike said, a half smile on his face.

'Very much appreciated,' said Tom.

'Okay, let's get moving as we don't have a huge amount of time,' said Mike. 'I have brought Tom up to speed on the background, but we both need updating on anything new, and we then need to formulate exactly how we do this. As I understand this, we are expected to make contact soon, right?'

Pet cleared her throat and spoke, her soft German accent tinged with an American lilt. 'First off, how we linked the late Zelenko to the issue at hand. Zelenko had transferred a reasonable amount of funds into a network of accounts and offshore companies a few months back, before the Belgrade incident. The trail of money was complex, but we managed to unpick it using some of my software and linked it to a number of identifiable accounts. Some went into a New York account in Cerović's name via a circuitous route, and some to an unidentifiable numbered-only account in the Bahamas. Cerović then wired about half of his money into a money transfer bureau in Belgrade and immediately withdrew it. We then much later see two payments from the numbered account in the Bahamas, half to a bank account we have managed to trace to an alias for Pavlović and half into a Bitcoin account that we now know is controlled by him as well. With me so far?'

Tom nodded.

'Okay. Two days ago, Pavlović was arrested, purely by chance, and local police found a number of stolen pistols on him that had all been liberated from the Serbian Army a few years ago. They seized his computer and smartphone, downloading his data using conventional law-enforcement software. This copies all the data but won't break encryption. CIA have a contact on the Sarajevo Police Department, who shared the downloaded data with us without the knowledge of their employers. Pavlović is careful, but not careful enough. He has encryption on both devices, but it was easy to break and I found that he had been using an *onion router* to access the dark web, where he has been communicating with Cerović. It seems that Pavlović had set himself up as an arms dealer on *Alpha Bay* selling stolen military hardware. Unfortunately, this part of Europe is awash with misappropriated military hardware.'

'Sorry. *Alpha Bay*?' queried Tom.

'You heard of *Silk Road* on the dark web?' Mike asked.

'Sure. FBI shut it down, right?'

'Yes,' said Mike. 'But it only takes a spotty student with a laptop and a decent server or two to reinstate it. There have been a few other attempts on setting up dark web marketplaces, such as *Farmer's Market* and *Silk Road 2.0*, but they never really took off. Or were not using Bitcoin, which kinda goes against the point of using the dark web if you have to use your *PayPal* account. *Alpha Bay* seems to be the latest iteration. FBI is constantly trying to shut it down, but this one keeps staying a step ahead.'

'Sorry for my ignorance. Carry on, Pet,' Tom smiled.

She nodded. 'Anyway, Pavlović was advertising a number of items of military hardware, including weapons and explosives of some variety. To be honest, it wasn't clear exactly what he was offering. The computer trail seems to suggest that a single military grade battery was purchased as a trial and supplied via an unknown courier: as Cerović confirmed he had received it, hence the transferred funds. The timing suggests that this battery may have been used in the Belgrade prison van attack. The chat between Pavlović and Cerović then turned to a requirement for further batteries. These messages were discussing the size and capacity of the batteries and charging profile, which Pavlović didn't seem to know too much about. Pavlović did confirm that he could lay his hands on what they needed, although he said it could take some time to procure. And then, unknown to Cerović, Pavlović was arrested,' Pet paused to swig from a bottle of mineral water.

'So do we think that they are now looking to build more of these mysterious weapons? Possibly to sell, or deploy more widely?'

'That's our current theory,' said Mike.

'Okay,' said Tom. 'So what's next?'

'With Pavlović being out of the game, Cerović is still seeking top-spec batteries, so, we baited a trap for him. We have put an advert on *Alpha Bay* using an avatar name of *"Tarzan"*, saying we can supply military-grade equipment at good prices. We haven't been too prescriptive but have used terms that may appeal to an electronics expert like Cerović. In short, he has bitten: almost immediately and rather amateurishly, to be honest. If I was guessing, I would surmise that he is managing this part of the operation independently, as I can't see Babić being this slack. He is asking about what inventory we have, and more specifically whether we have military-grade, high-powered lithium-ion batteries.' Mike paused for a moment to let this sink in.

A silence descended in the room as the reality of the situation sunk in. This was nothing like a traditional undercover police infiltration. Tom was used to being deployed against drug dealers, money launderers and contract killers, with the whole aim of gaining evidence to convict serious criminals. This was different: he was being drawn into top level Black-Ops. This stuff was deniable, and he had no idea what would happen if he blew out. He wasn't even sure how officially sanctioned this was; he knew for a fact that Mike had a certain amount of autonomy within his organisation, but how much swing he would have if he got arrested by Bosnian police, he didn't know.

One thing was clear: he was going to be deployed undercover, in a sovereign nation, without official sanction. They knew very little about any of the individuals, and Tom was being asked to convincingly play the part of an arms dealer in a foreign country with no back story and only a scant legend.

'How do we proceed?' Tom asked in a level voice.

'Simple,' said Mike. 'We reply to the last message from Cerović and say that you want to discuss his requirements and meet to arrange a deal. He has shared his cell number—we've checked, it's an untraceable burner—and we have been communicating using a secure messaging app. I know that it is shooting in the dark, but we will arrange the meeting in a public place nearby and we can play it by ear, right? You can find out exactly what he wants and we can then take it from there. We have to do this; they cannot be allowed to succeed.'

'Okay, fine. Let's get on with it. How about a legend?'

Mike threw a battered brown leather wallet across the table. Tom looked inside finding a sheaf of banknotes—Euros and Bosnian Marks—a driving licence in the name Marko Delić bearing Tom's photo, and a selection of bank cards.

'You guys work quick, right?' Tom said admiring the documents.

'No time to jerk about, buddy,' said Mike, smiling.

'You were obviously sure I would agree.'

'Awesome. Pet, you ready to send the message?' Mike said.

'Sure. Whenever you're ready,' Pet said, picking up a new-looking smartphone.

'Any suggestions on a meeting place?' asked Mike.

'Needs to be something obvious and specific,' said Tom, 'as we are not supposed to know what each other look like yet. Will we have the use of a surveillance team?'

'No. We need to keep this really tight. The local police are notoriously leaky, and we just don't have the resources on the ground here.'

Tom sat and thought for a moment, his mind wandering back to his childhood and the regular trips to Sarajevo Old Town. A slow smile spread across his face, 'Can I see the phone, please, Pet?'

Pet slid it down the table. 'The app is open. Last message was seven hours ago.'

Tom looked at the screen. *'When/where can we meet? Need to discuss capabilities and requirements before we agree price.'*

Tom quickly composed a brief message. *'Steps of Sebilj, Bascarsija 8pm.'*

'The old fountain in the Old Town square. Always busy, plenty of people so easy to follow him from there. Twenty-hundred hours gives us plenty of time, right?'

Mike and Pet nodded.

Tom pressed *Send* and the message whooshed.

'What now?' Pet asked.

'We hope he responds. I need to spend some time getting to grips with the contents of Pavlović's phone and computer so I am fully up to speed with what they have said to each other, and so I can see how an arms dealer conducts himself.'

'How about wearing a wire?' Mike asked.

Tom shook his head,' The guy is an electronics whizz; we can't be sure he won't have scanning tech and we have no idea if he is going to be alone. First meeting, I go in cold. Just me.'

The phone vibrated on the polished tabletop. Tom picked it up and opened the app to see the reply. *'Fine, 8pm it is.'*

'He's bitten,' Tom said as he composed a reply, *'How will I know you?'*

The reply came back almost immediately.

'NYU blue sweatshirt.'

'We're on,' Tom said.

5

Ambassador Shriver's office was a spacious room, with floor-to-ceiling windows, polished marble floors and a huge mahogany desk that was only sparsely occupied with a leather jotter and a brass table lamp. A ten-gallon hat sat on a sideboard which had a small confederate flag on the side of it.

A large photograph of the ambassador shaking hands with the president was affixed to the wall and the US flag hung limply behind an oak and leather chair in which sat the ambassador himself. He was a middle-aged man, thick set, with a shock of grey hair and a disdainful look on his face. His cheeks were flushed a deep red, and there were broken veins, like a road map across his bulbous nose.

Shriver's greeting to Mike was perfunctory and bordering on rude, but Mike remained his normal charming self as he sat, showing not even a slight trace of discomfort at the other man's pugnacious attitude. Rudy O'Shea also seemed to be finding the whole encounter a little amusing; unlike John Havers, who was twitchy and nervous.

Havers cleared his throat. 'Mr Ambassador, this is Mike Brogan, who holds a senior position in the CIA. As I understand it, the DOD has been assured by the US Foreign Service of our full cooperation in facilitating his presence.' Havers paused to allow a response but was met by a long and uncomfortable silence as the ambassador stared directly at Mike, a contemptuous look on his face.

Mike remained bolt upright in his chair, showing not even a trace of disquiet at the ambassador's attempts to elicit discomfort.

Instead, Mike smiled warmly at Shriver.

Eventually Shriver broke first, 'Mr Brogan. It is true that I received word of your arrival, but no mention of the nature of your operation was forthcoming. I think that it would be courteous if you could enlighten me as to what the CIA are doing here? I have worked hard to build trust and good relations with our Bosnian hosts.' He paused, taking a sip of water.

Mike's smile remained fixed, his eyes showing a trace of amusement at the ambassador's supercilious attitude.

'Mr Ambassador. I am here on the instructions of the Director of Defence on a fact-finding mission. I understood that you had been informed of this?'

'Only those scant details, Brogan. I think that, as ambassador, I am entitled to know a little more so that I can be prepared to liaise with our hosts, if necessary,' his face began to flush even redder.

'I am afraid that I am not at liberty to be any more specific at this time, Mr Ambassador,' said Mike, the smile not leaving his face.

'This is highly irregular, Brogan. Highly irregular.' His accent was pure Texas, pronouncing the word *'highly'* as *'haaleh'*, which made his attitude seem all the more ridiculous.

'If I may interject, Ambassador,' blurted Havers desperately trying to mediate, 'I was not given any prior notification; but when I queried it, I was given a missive from the DOD office requesting that we would cooperate.'

'And we will cooperate, Havers. But I am responsible for this region. Me.' Shriver thumped his chest. 'Anything happening on my turf, I need to know about. It is in my nature, Mr Brogan, we are a polite bunch in the South.' He pronounced *'polite'* as *'powlaate'*.

Mike sat back in his chair just a touch; still smiling, still saying nothing.

The desk telephone erupted with a peal that made Shriver jump, almost imperceptibly, before he picked up the receiver, not taking his eyes away from Mike.

'Janet, I said no calls,' he barked, his face almost scarlet. After a moment, his face changed from anger to capitulation.

'Director-General, my apologies, I had no idea it was you. Yes. Yes. Brogan is with me now. I appreciate that, Margaret, but I would expect to be kept—' He paused, and a tinny voice was almost audible from the phone handset.

Finally, he sighed, 'I understand, Margaret. Yes, of course. Every assistance, of course.' He replaced the handset, a contemplative look on his face.

'That was the DG of the Foreign Service. Please let us know of any assistance you require Mr Brogan. My staff are here to assist you in any way you require.' He stood to indicate that the meeting was now over.

*

'How the hell did you manage that?' chuckled Rudy as he, Havers, and Mike walked back down the corridor.

'I heard that Mr Shriver can be a little parochial,' said Mike, 'so I told one of my contacts of our impending meeting. It seems like they thought the DG of the foreign service may be able to mediate.'

'Well thanks a bunch, Mike. He will take this out on me, you know,' said Havers, his voice tight.

'He'll get over it,' said Mike.

'You do have a certain reputation, Mike.'

'All rumour and conjecture, John. All rumour and conjecture.'

6

Stefan Cerović tried to push away the slight tingle of nerves as he squared his shoulders and upped his pace just a little through the square at Bascarsija, which was busy with the hustle and bustle of evening revellers touring the ancient bazaar and cultural centre. He was feeling jumpy and anxious at the prospect of this meeting, probably not helped by the fat line of cocaine that he had snorted before he had left home. Mostly, though, he was excited about meeting the new contact from Alpha Bay who he only knew by his Avatar name, *"Tarzan"*.

Cerović had been struggling to find batteries with sufficient capacity for his requirements. The single test unit Pavlović had provided was as close as he'd managed, and it had worked perfectly in the Belgrade operation. It was therefore not only worrying but also frustrating that Pavlović had suddenly gone silent; so when he saw *Tarzan* advertising military-grade equipment on Alpha Bay he was immediately interested.

He needed as much power as he could lay his hands on. As he still didn't know where he would be using the weapons, he wanted all-climate capacity as well, something that many of the commercially available cells just didn't have. All of these had been promised by Tarzan, but Cerović really needed to physically see and examine the contact's stock of batteries so he could be sure of buying the correct ones. And the sooner the better: Babić was a scary bastard who was starting to get frustrated with Cerović's lack of speed in building the new units.

'Cerović, we are paying you well. You are supposed to be an electronics genius, so we need much more power. Make it happen or I may think that you are becoming a liability. Do you understand me?' Babić's deep set eyes had drilled into Cerović as he spoke to him in that sinister, heavily-accented English accent.

Babić's implied threats were, frankly, terrifying; so Cerović decided that the best solution was to source the batteries on his own initiative. He could tell that Babić held him in low regard, despite the fact that it had been Cerović's weapon that had secured his release from prison. He knew that he often irritated people, but being a bit annoying in an electronics company was nowhere near as dangerous as being irritating to murderous paramilitaries.

He picked up his pace as he entered the square and walked towards the imposing and well-lit wooden fountain known to all as *"Sebilj"*. He walked up the four steps and leaned against the wall of the pseudo Ottoman monument, just next to the drinking trough. He looked up at the structure's ornate roof, festooned with what seemed like a thousand grubby pigeons all settling down in the balmy night air. Despite living near Sebilj for the last few months he had never taken any notice of it, but looking at it now he had to admit that it was a striking monument, despite all the pigeon shit.

His sudden and unexpected interest in the ancient monument was interrupted as a scruffy-looking boy, aged about ten, tapped him on his shoulder, a gap-toothed grin splitting his grubby face. He said nothing but simply handed over a small, cheap-looking phone. 'Man pay me ten euros to give you this, NYU,' he said in Serbian, cackling as he pointed at the old university sweatshirt Cerović was wearing. The boy turned and ran off, clearly delighted to be ten euros richer for such a simple task.

The phone buzzed in his hand and he answered it. 'Hello?'

'Walk along Telali down towards the river. I will call you back in four minutes.' The voice was flat and emotionless, with an indistinct Sarajevo accent.

'Where are you? Is this Tarzan?' he replied in his broken Serbian.

'Just do it. Stand by the river and wait for my call.' The line went dead.

Sighing with frustration, Cerović did as the voice had

commanded, walking steadily south along the busy street towards the river Miljaka. He looked all around as he walked but noticed nothing. If Tarzan was there, he was blending in very well. The journey only took a few minutes and he was soon crossing the busy main road and waiting by the river wall. The phone buzzed once again in his hand. 'Yes,' he said, a slight stutter in his voice.

'Walk left towards the green space two hundred metres in front of you. Go to the bench at the far end of the space by the river wall and wait there.' The beep in his ear told him that the call was over.

He did as instructed once again, feeling more and more nervous as to how this was turning out. He dearly wished he could stop and have another line of cocaine, just to up his confidence before meeting Tarzan.

Finding the bench, he sat down heavily. Reaching into his pocket he felt the small paper wrap containing the cocaine that he had purchased just a few hours ago. He really needed to get a grip on his coke habit. It had cost him his job back in New York and had been the indirect cause of him being in the situation he was now in. Not for the first time, Cerović felt way, way out of his depth. Looking around and seeing nobody, he dipped his apartment key into the wrap and quickly snorted a small pile of the drug. No big deal, he thought. Just a toot to keep him sharp before Tarzan arrived. He felt the familiar rush as the drug was absorbed through his mucus membranes. He sniffed deeply, feeling the confidence surge back in him. He was ready.

*

Tom watched with a little amusement as Cerović raised the key to his nose and sniffed, loudly.

'Cocaine is bad for your health, you know,' he announced suddenly from where he was stood, leaning against a tree a few metres away.

Cerović jumped in alarm. 'Jesus! You scared the fuckin' life out of me!' he exclaimed in his New York drawl, turning to look at

Tom with a look of alarm on his face.

'You're American?' Tom asked in thick, Serb-accented English.

'No. I'm from Kosovo but lived in the US for years until recently.' Cerović was breathing heavily, his pupils enlarged with a mix of alarm and the cocaine he had just snorted.

'I'm not doing deals with a cocaine addict. I'm leaving.' Tom spoke suddenly and emphatically and turned as if to walk away.

'Wait, wait. Look, I was just a little nervous. We need to talk, man, please.' Cerović gabbled, a touch of panic in his voice.

Tom stopped and turned, eyeing the other man, blankly. 'People who take cocaine are unreliable. I need reliable people to do business with.' Despite his harsh tone, Tom sat on the bench next to Cerović.

'I am reliable, I promise.'

'What's your name?' Tom asked.

'Stefan,' Cerović said, relaxing a little. 'What do I call you?'

Tom ignored the question. 'So, my little cocaine friend. What do you need?'

Cerović smiled. 'Batteries. Smallest possible size with maximum output. Military grade, as in the type I can't buy from a shop.'

'I have a good range of batteries. Military batteries for torpedoes, military vehicles, drones. You won't find these in a shop, not without lots of paperwork, anyway.'

'I don't want any paperwork, which is why I have come to you.'

'What do you want them to power?' Tom asked.

'I can't tell you. But they need to be light as possible.'

'I need to know a little. I have batteries that weigh very little and I have some that weigh one hundred kilos. Unless I know something then I don't know how I can help you. What will it power, how long do you need the life to be? You tell me the basics and I can tell you if I have them. Otherwise, maybe you find someone else with stolen military-spec, high powered batteries.'

Cerović stared at the fast-flowing river, deep in thought. 'I'd like a range of cells; I can pay whatever you like.'

'Not much help to me. Look if you tell me what you actually

need, maybe I help you. If not, I'm going home.' Tom stood, an exasperated look on his face.

'No. Don't go. Look… I need a number of batteries for different purposes. If you tell me what you have, I will be interested in all of them. Money is not a problem.'

'Okay. Well I can help you then,' Tom smiled broadly, playing the part of a typical trader realising when he has a sucker on his hands.

'That's cool. If you get me a list of what you have,' Cerović smiled nervously.

'Always good to have a customer like you, my friend.'

'Someone like me?' Cerović frowned.

'Someone who wants merchandise I am supplying for an illegitimate purpose. Look, I don't care why you want batteries. If you can pay, you can have.' Tom barked a coarse laugh as he stared at Cerović's glassy and dilated eyes. He made an immediate decision.

The ability to make a sudden decision and change the plan whilst in the middle of a deployment was the difference between an undercover operative and a good undercover operative. Tom now recognised the opportunity that was before him, so the original plan was instantly canned. 'How about a drink?' he smiled.

7

Cerović raised his glass to his lips, saying 'Ziveli', the Serbian traditional toast.

'Cheers,' said Tom in accented English as he sipped his Ojusko beer, which was cold and clean as it slid down his throat.

Cerović continued gulping his drink until the glass was almost empty, banging it down on the table when he was done.

'The beer in Sarajevo is good, no?' Cerović said.

'Clearly,' Tom said nodding at Cerović's almost empty glass.

'No offence, man, but you make me nervous. I'm not used to meeting arms dealers,' Cerović said, belching.

'I'm just a trader, my friend, and keep your fucking voice down.' Tom couldn't help noting the bleary, slightly unfocused expression in Cerović's eyes. The man was high as a kite.

'Sorry, I get a little excited, sometimes.' Cerović let out a long, irritating cackle, causing Tom to wince at the overly loud noise. There was no doubt that Cerović was out of his depth, and his nervousness was palpable.

'The cocaine won't help with that, will it?' Tom asked.

'Livens me up, man.'

Tom nodded, deciding that a change of tack and a little bonding session may be worth exploring. 'Well, Steff,' he said, a smile splitting his face. 'Fancy sharing a little of your Columbian marching powder?'

'Sure man, sure. The stuff over here is wild man.' Cerović rummaged in his jacket pocket and handed over a small wrap of paper to Tom.

Tom smiled and took the package. 'Back very soon.' He stood

and moved away into the bar and towards the toilets. Pushing his way into the grimy cubicle he locked the door behind him. Looking at the small wrap in his hand he took a fat pinch from the white, flaky powder and dumped it into the sink. Running the tap, he quickly washed the cocaine residue from his fingers and re-folded the paper. He used the toilet and then returned to Cerović, who was sat with a fresh beer in front of him.

'It's good gear, my friend,' Tom said, holding out his hand to Cerović, the cocaine wrap hidden in his palm. Cerović shook his hand, a wide smile on his face as he accepted the palmed cocaine and returned it to his pocket.

'You know it, Tarzan, my friend,' he chuckled. 'In fact, I may go and have another little toot now. That motherfucking stuff is fab-u-lous,' His speech was pure Manhattan brogue delivered at an ever-increasing pace. He stood and made his way away in the direction of the bar toilets.

Tom sighed and shook his head a little as he pulled out his phone from his pocket and quickly dialled.

'What gives, my friend?' Mike Brogan asked.

'The guy's a junkie,' Tom said quietly into the handset. 'He's high as a kite so I have come to a bar with him, as it looks like he wants a friend. It may be a good opportunity to learn a little more, and I've a feeling this may present a new opening. I'm going to run with it.'

'Cool. Go for it, but don't take any risks. We just need to supply those batteries.'

'Okay. He is an unusual character; in fact I am surprised they have let him come on his own. I'd better go, he will be back soon.' Tom said as he poured half of his beer into Cerović's almost empty glass.

'Sure thing. Be careful.'

'Always careful,' Tom said and hung up.

He saw Cerović appear from the toilets, moving quickly with his jaw grinding and his eyes red-rimmed and wide open.

'Whoa! Man, you must have had a decent pinch,' said Cerović.

'It's great stuff, right, but it's nearly all gone. Wow, man, you must be bang on for it. I'll need to get some more. I've some back at my place. We can get some more later, right?' He spoke with machine-gun rapidity whilst glancing from side-to-side, his face split with a wide grin. Tom noted some white residue under his nose.

'You may want to wipe your nose and maybe calm a little. Finish your drink, I'm thirsty.' Tom said, smiling widely as he tapped his glass.

Cerović threw back his head and bellowed with laughter as he cuffed his nose, completely unaware of the disapproving looks from the nearby tables. He picked up his full glass and finished it in one hit, slamming the glass down on the table with a thump.

'Another!' he cried, his voice just slightly slurring, his cheeks flushed and eyes even more glazed.

The taciturn waiter approached the table with a disapproving look on his face and two more glasses of beer in his hands.

'You know why I'm here in Sarajevo, Tarzan?'

Tom just shrugged.

'Right now I'm drunk and high, but I am a fuckin' electronics genius. Which is why I want your batteries so I can build bad bastard shit that will make me a fucking fortune, dude. Can you get me the batteries?'

'Sure, I can get whatever you need as long as you can afford it.' Tom replied, smiling widely and slurring his own speech slightly to give the impression of an impending intoxication that he wasn't feeling in the slightest.

Cerović threw his head back and guffawed as if Tom had just said something hilarious. 'My friend, the people I am working with are dangerous fucks, but they are *rich* dangerous fucks. If I can come up with the right batteries that give us the power we need, they will realise just how fuckin' awesome I am and pay me more.' He giggled drunkenly.

Tom realised that he had to play this carefully; he wanted to loosen Cerović's inhibitions so that he would open up a little more, but not so much that he would end up getting arrested.

'How much more of that coke do you have back at your place?' Tom asked.

'I have a couple of grams and a bottle of 176 Degrees Balkan Vodka. Let's get some food and get drunk and wasted at my place so we can talk without being overheard.'

Tom had tried the legendarily strong Bosnian vodka before but, at eighty-eight percent proof, it was far too strong and fiery for his taste. However, he could spot an opportunity when it was offered.

'Sure, why not. I've nothing else planned.'

*

Cerović's place was only a few streets away from the bar and they walked through the cobbled, twisty streets pausing to pick up a couple of bureks, the meat filled traditional Bosnian snack. Cerović was a little unsteady on his feet as they negotiated the walkways and he spoke loudly as they walked.

'I'm gonna make a fuckin' fortune, man. They need me as I am so fuckin' amazing with electronics, they are all luddites. They look down on me because my Serbian ain't so good, but I can show them. I'm still a fuckin' Balkan, even if I don't sound like one.' He laughed uproariously and Tom couldn't help but reflect that, if he behaved like this in front of Babić too often, he could find himself in a world of pain.

He really was the epitome of an arrogant cokehead, but Tom realised that this was offering an opportunity right here, right now.

'Come on, let's get back to your place. I need some more of that coke, Steff,' Tom said, affecting a bawdier than normal tone.

'You know it, brother. Couple of lines, eat these bureks washed down with the mean vodka, then maybe hit a club I know later. I've been a few times and the chicks are awesome. Bosnian chicks rock, man,' Cerović said, clapping Tom on the back.

Tom inwardly groaned at Cerović's crass attitude. He had no intention of going to any club with him; not if his plan came to fruition.

*

Cerović lived in a small and messy one-roomed apartment above a convenience store, with a small kitchenette and tiny, filthy bathroom. The glass coffee table was strewn with circuit boards, wiring, and disassembled electronics items, but Tom also couldn't help but notice the white powder residue evident on the surface. Clothes littered the floor and a small TV set sat in the corner. A large, cracked leather couch had a duvet untidily thrown across it and clearly doubled as the only bed in the place. It really was a shithole and looked to Tom like every junkie's place he had ever encountered in his police career.

'I know. It's a dump, but it's cheap and anonymous and they didn't need references or any shit like that. I just use it as a base whilst I'm doing what I'm doing. You want a line right away man?'

'Sure. Cut me a fat one, Steff. And where's that vodka?'

'Man, you're a wild dude. I thought you arms dealers were all quiet and dangerous,' Cerović said delightedly as he produced a small plastic bag from a carved wooden box on the coffee table. He expertly tipped out a small quantity of the white, flaky cocaine onto the glass surface and began to cut and chop it into four fat lines. Cerović loudly snorted two lines, one up each nostril, through a rolled dollar bill.

'Whoooo!' he exclaimed, his eyes watering and shiny. 'Man, you get serious quality coke in Sarajevo. Comes from Albania and is real pure. But if you want the best quality product, then it's the heroin you want to try, my friend. Sarajevo is on the Balkan route, so we get the best, uncut stuff from Afghan before it gets cut to shit. You want to try some? I got a little here, works fantastic with the coke?'

Tom paused as if thinking it through. 'I'll just do the coke and booze. Heroin isn't my bag.'

'Your loss, man. Best feeling ever, heroin. Like a warm blanket when it's good stuff. I'm gonna take a piss, help yourself to a line and have some vodka.' Cerović banged a bottle down on the table before disappearing into the bathroom whilst singing *"Mustang Sally"* in a loud, tuneless wail.

Tom quickly swept both lines of cocaine into one hand and took the bottle in the other, taking them over to the sink where he dumped the powder into the plughole. Taking two tumblers from the drainer, he filled one to the brim with the vodka and the other with water from the tap. Inhaling the raw spirit, his head jerked back at the powerful, acrid smell. He rinsed his hands and quickly dried them on his jacket. One of the tumblers he placed back on the table, while the other he held onto as he sat on the sofa.

Cerović returned to the room and saw the glass on the table. 'Man, that is a savage measure of vodka. We are gonna get really fucked up!' he whooped.

'That's amazing coke, Steff. Ziveli!' Tom smiled, holding the glass high and downing a glass of Sarajevo's finest water in one gulp. He affected a cough and wheeze as the water slid down his throat.

'You are a fucking savage, Tarzan. Ziveli!' Cerović cried and downed the neat, powerful vodka. He erupted into a paroxysm of violent coughing as the pure, neat spirit attacked his throat. His eyes streamed with tears. 'Woo hoo!' he shouted, laughing.

'So, how many batteries do you need then, Stef?' Tom asked, a broad grin on his face.

'Many as you can get, my friend. As many as you can get. More you get, more bad shit I build, and more money I make. Those fuckers think I am useless, but when I suddenly show them the power with your batteries, they'll fucking respect me.' He was drunk now, the raw, almost pure alcohol assaulting his bloodstream.

'But these batteries are all rechargeable. You could just reuse them.' Tom said.

'What, you don't want our money?'

'Of course I do. I'm just curious.'

'I love you, Tarzan. You're the dude!' Cerović was fully slurring now. 'I'm building shit loads of weapons, dude, and with the extra power I can make them do shit no one will be able to believe. With what we've got planned, we need plenty. We are gonna fuck some shit seriously up. The people paying me are nasty, dangerous ass bastards. Man, I am racing here, feels like my heart is gonna explode out of my chest. I need a little come down. You interested?'

'In what?'

'A little brown blanket, my friend. A little Afghani hug!' Cerović's face was flushed and sweating and his eyes were like saucers. He was jittering and his movements were staccato.

'I'm good. But you go ahead.'

Cerović went back to the carved box and pulled out another small plastic bag, this one containing a quantity of brown powder. Sitting on the far end of the sofa, he tipped out a little onto a small square of foil. He flicked open a Zippo lighter and applied the flame to the underside of the foil, before using a straw fashioned out of yet more tinfoil to greedily suck in the smoke that began to swirl up from the liquifying heroin. Tom watched as Cerović moved the foil, allowing the molten drug to dribble along and leaving only a faint trail behind. He recognised the absence of a black residue as an indicator of purity.

Cerović snapped the lighter shut and emitted a deep, deep sigh as he relaxed like a deflating balloon. 'Man, that's the stuff. Cocaine is great, but this is the stuff. Like nothing you've ever felt, buddy. Sure I can't tempt you?' his voice had changed noticeably into a long, slow drawl, a complete contrast to the rapid-fire New York tones of a few minutes before. He leaned back into the cracked sofa with a sigh of contentment as if he was relaxing on an expensive, Egyptian cotton covered bed. His eyes closed and he yawned. 'Sorry, Tarzan, but I don't think I am gonna be good for a club now,' he slurred. He picked up a remote control from the coffee table and fiddled with it for a second before loud, trippy music filled the room.

Tom wrinkled his nose against the unpleasant vinegary smell emanating from the heroin. It was really distinctive and immediately took Tom back to previous drug busts when, whilst undercover, he had burned heroin to test its purity.

The prone form of Cerović was now breathing deeply and evenly. 'Steff,' Tom said. The man didn't even stir.

'Cerović?' he said louder. There was still no response. Tom stood up and went over to the sleeping form. Shaking his shoulder gently he called his name a few more times, but still the man slept. Tom pinched Cerović's earlobe with his fingers but the man didn't even alter his breathing. Tom felt for a pulse in the man's neck and was reassured by the feel of a regular, slow rhythm. He was truly out of it, fully sedated by the powerful drug.

Tom pulled the unconscious figure down onto the floor and placed him in the recovery position. He needed him alive and not choking on his own vomit, given that he was their only active link into the gang.

He reached to Cerović's waistband and removed a smartphone from the leather case attached to his belt. Tom stifled a little smile, he had often associated those who wore their phones on their belts as being a little geeky, and this just proved him right. Pressing on the screen he saw that it was locked and was requesting a six-figure code. Sighing, he tried each of the man's digits on the sensor, but none of them unlocked the handset either. He clearly hadn't activated the finger scanner on his phone and instead relied on a PIN code, or possibly he had added extra layers of security.

Sat on the floor next to the prone Cerović, Tom saw the end of something that had been pushed beneath the narrow gap between the sofa and the floor. Pulling it out he was not surprised to find that it was a sleek, new-looking laptop. He examined it but decided against trying to gain access; he had no idea what level of defence that Cerović may have put on it, and he didn't want to initiate a memory wipe.

Reaching for his own phone, he dialled.

'How are you getting on, Tarzan?' Pet asked, the usual hit of sarcasm detectable in her German / American accent.

'Interesting, to say the least. He is possibly one of the most irritating people I have ever met. Are you far away?'

'Well, as I've been tracking you on your phone, no. In fact, I am watching your GPS beacon flashing away on a screen right now. Is that Cerović's place? The one above the nickel-and-dime joint?'

'Yes. Walk up to the door, I will come and let you in. Have you got your bag of tricks with you? For an iPhone and a laptop, possibly with some security on both.' Tom whispered into the handset.

'Sure. Gimme five.' The phone went dead.

Tom took the duvet from the sofa and covered Cerović completely. As certain as he was that he was out for the count, it struck him as wise to make sure he couldn't see what was going on.

Tom left the apartment leaving the door wedged open with the mat and descended the stairs. Opening the door to the street he saw Pet's diminutive figure walking towards him, a beanie crammed over her red hair and a beaming smile on her face, carrying what looked to be a heavy rucksack.

'What gives?' she asked.

'Cerović is snoring upstairs; he has over-indulged a little. How quickly can you download the contents of his computer and an iPhone?'

'Depends on the level of security and how much data, but not long I imagine. If you just want them imaged for later examination, then even faster.'

'That will do. He's a blabbermouth, but I can't believe that there won't be some leads on his IT.'

'Blabbermouth?' she chuckled. 'You English are so cute,' she had a mischievous look in her green eyes as she handed him a pair of nitrile gloves.

'I'm not Eng—' started Tom in a Scottish burr.

'I'm playing with you, Detective. Let's go see this gear.' She eased past Tom and they both quietly headed up the stairs. Tom raised his finger to his lips as they entered the apartment, relieved to see that the duvet had not moved aside from a gentle rise-and-fall in time with Cerović's breathing.

Tom snapped his gloves into place, picked up the phone and laptop, and handed them to Pet. She took them in her already-gloved hands and sat cross-legged on the floor. Rummaging in her bag she came out with an aluminium-cased device about the size of a large paperback book, along with some cables, and then busied herself with Cerović's laptop.

While she was doing this, Tom began to carefully and systematically photograph all of the circuitry laying around the apartment. None of it looked particularly interesting, but he felt he ought to document what was there. There were very few possessions in the place, Cerović seeming to live quite a spartan existence. The wallet that was on the coffee table contained just a thin sheaf of banknotes: euros, US dollars and a few Bosnian marks. There was also a Bosnian and Herzegovinian driving licence in the name of Benjamin Ahmic that bore Cerović's photograph.

Suddenly there was a crashing and thumping at the front door and an indistinct voice bellowed from outside.

They froze as Cerović began to stir beneath the duvet, mumbling and murmuring incoherently. Tom looked at Pet and pointed at his watch with a questioning look, mouthing, 'How long?'

She held up one finger and continued typing silently on the rubberised keys of her custom built laptop.

Tom went to the door and said in Bosnian, 'What is it?'

'Turn the fucking noise down, you American fool,' barked a rough voice from outside the room.

'Sorry, sorry,' slurred Tom in a rough approximation of Cerović's accent. Moving quickly to the table, he picked up the remote and reduced the volume down to a far more acceptable level. Cerović didn't stir, and once more his breathing became rhythmic and regular. Tom exhaled in relief and sat back down to wait for Pet to finish her work.

After a few seconds Pet nodded at Tom and tossed the smartphone to him, which he caught and set back down silently on the coffee table next to the wallet. Pet packed her laptop and download device into her bag and then stood, handing Cerović's laptop back to Tom, who silently slid it back beneath the sofa.

Pet nodded at Tom, pointed at her watch, and crept silently out of the apartment.

Tom sat down on the sofa to collect his thoughts. It was fortunate for him that Cerović seemed to have such a big problem with narcotics, but it seemed very sloppy. A major team of international criminals had an out-and-out junkie at the centre of their organisation, and it just didn't seem right.

Tom quickly scrawled a note, *'Steff, you passed out, so I went to nightclub without you. I'll call you.'*

8

Pet was sat in a new-looking Ford Kuga parked just around the corner from Cerović's apartment, her eyes glued to the screen of her laptop.

'That was quicker than I expected, Pet,' said Tom as he climbed into the passenger seat.

'You know me, Detective. My genius knows no bounds.'

'Of course, and humble, too,' Tom smiled. 'How did you get on?'

'Pretty easy, although I still have work to do to maximise the results. He was only PIN-code protected on the iPhone, which took just a few seconds. It downloaded but there isn't much on it; however I have implanted some malware on his phone, which means we will have pretty much full remote access to it. We will see all his messages, emails and SMS and I am hopeful that we will be able to remotely access his microphone and camera, but I need to work at that a little.'

'Amazing stuff. How about the laptop?'

'He had protected that a little better. I haven't broken the encryption yet but I am confident that, with a little time, I will be able to. There is obviously something on it of value to him, as the system had a wipe function on it designed to totally destroy all the data if the computer was booted up without going through certain steps. I didn't have to boot it up, as I bypassed those sequencers and I have imaged the drive so it's now stored safe on my external hard drive. There is a protected file within the main drive, so that may be interesting; I just need to break the encryption. My brute force attack software will help, but we could do with finding some social media or more personal information. I will check further once I get back to the Embassy.' Tom could sense some frustration from Pet. She was an absolute genius with computers and the fact that she had not immediately gained access to the data would be really bugging her.

'I take it there is no trace of your presence on his phone or Mac?' Tom asked

'Nothing that he will find. He thinks he's clever, but he's not clever enough or I would have never got into or downloaded the data so quick.'

'Fair enough. Why don't you go back to the Embassy and make a start on the decryption? I want to have a look at Pavlović's place; something doesn't feel right about him. Do you have the address?'

'Sure, it's pretty close. But why?'

'I'm not sure, I'm just not buying the situation entirely. It all feels a little easy, I mean, was he an arms dealer, or just selling stolen batteries and other kit? It doesn't feel right, and I can't quite put my finger on why.'

Pet scrawled down an address on a post-it note and handed it to Tom. He entered the address into his map application and noted that it was just a fifteen minute walk away.

'You have a pen-knife?' Tom asked.

'I have a Leatherman multi-tool,' she replied.

'Can I borrow it?'

'Sure. But why?'

'Best I don't tell you; you don't want to be an accessory,' Tom smiled.

Pet handed the multi-tool over, shaking her head. 'I don't want you doing anything nasty with it. I'm attached to my Leatherman; my dad gave it to me, and I know what you're like.'

'Scout's honour.'

'I can guarantee you weren't a Scout, Detective.'

'Why?'

'Not prepared enough.'

'I take it you were?'

'Damn straight: Girl Guide, Bavarian Lodge.' she smiled and raised the three fingered Scout salute.

Tom laughed, 'I'll see you later.'

'Be careful,' she said.

'Where's Mike, by the way?'

'Embassy, I think. He had meetings and I think he said the ambassador wanted a briefing. He said we should all meet up later.' Pet snapped her computer shut and tucked it away in her bag.

'Okay, I'll make my way there. I'll catch up later.'

Tom got out of the car and made his way in the direction of Pavlović's apartment, an uncomfortable feeling in his gut.

*

Pavlović's apartment was a small place in a small apartment block. The chipped and worn door was solid enough, but it was only secured with a simple pin-tumbler lock. Tom went to where the block's rubbish bins were located and, within a few moments, had found what he was looking for: an empty two-litre plastic Coke bottle. He quickly extended a blade from the Leatherman and cut around the circumference of the bottle at each end, leaving him with a plastic tube. He then cut along the length of the tube and flattened it out on the ground to create a rectangle of flexible, pliable plastic. Returning to the door, Tom pushed against the top of the door to make it bow inwards just enough for him to slide the edge of the plastic sheet in between the door and the jamb. He then worked the plastic down until it caught on the lock bolt. If the door had been deadlocked, he would have had to think again, but he felt immediate movement as the plastic slid between the door bolt and popped the mechanism open. Tom smiled. The old burglar's trick, known as "loiding", was still effective on a spring mechanism door.

The apartment was sparsely furnished with minimal home comforts and no obvious signs that he was involved in criminality. The contents of the rooms had been strewn about after a police search, with most of the drawers turned out and their contents emptied on the floor.

There were no photographs and very little that would suggest that it was anything other than a crash-pad, and offered no real insights into Pavlović himself.

Tom sat, suddenly very tired, on the futon bed that was flush against the wall, yawning deeply. It had been a really busy time with a ridiculous amount of stress, and he realised that he needed to sleep. Feeling his eyes begin to droop slightly he sat back up quickly, shaking the fog from his head. There was nothing to learn here, he realised; it was time to go back to the Embassy and then on to somewhere for a full night's sleep.

As he stood and made his way towards the door the tip of his boot caught on a wrinkle in the rug, causing him to stumble slightly. Cursing, he looked at the wrinkle in the worn, patterned square of carpet, and then frowned. The imperfection in the rug's surface was caused by an uneven floorboard. Feeling a prickle of anticipation, Tom went to the edge of the rug and pulled it back to expose the smooth, varnished floorboards. The edge of one was just a little higher than the ones adjacent. Tom squatted and looked at the screws that secured the board in place. The slots on the screw heads were burred and the brass showed through the varnish. They had recently been interfered with.

Tom slotted the Leatherman's screwdriver attachment into the screw and turned. It gave immediately. He quickly removed all the screws and then slotted the screwdriver edge into the crack between the boards and levered up. The twelve-inch-wide board came away easily and smoothly, revealing a crawl space underneath. Tom took his phone and switched the torch on, shining it into the void. A small leather attaché case lay beneath the boards on its side. Tom reached in and pulled it out. It was a tight squeeze but, with a tug, it came free of the gap and into Tom's grasp.

It was fairly heavy and made of scratched and worn brown leather; Tom couldn't help but liken it to a doctor's case. His hands moved to the brass clip at the securing buckle, and he was about to open it when a shadow fell across him. Turning to the door he saw a figure looming above him, a large kitchen knife in its hand and a look of suffused fury etched across Slav features. Icy blue eyes surveyed Tom with barely concealed hostility. Recognition flashed in Tom's mind. It was Goran Pavlović.

'Who the fuck are you?' asked Pavlović in a deep, sonorous voice. His eyes were flinty and hard, his jaw set in grim determination.

'Police,' Tom said in Serbian whilst standing up.

'Show me your badge,' Pavlović said, his eyes not leaving Tom's. His eyes were intense and knowing but Tom recognised something in those hard eyes. There was no panic, no confusion, and no fear.

'Put the knife down, Pavlović,' Tom said.

'Fuck you. Show me ID. If you're a cop, why are you in my fucking place?'

'Finishing the search. What's in the bag?' Tom asked, trying to take the initiative, even though he knew it was pointless. He began to mentally prepare himself and plan for what was about to happen, relaxing his body and allowing a reassuring smile to spread across his face. 'Goran, I am a cop. I was finishing the search. I didn't know you had been released, no one tells me anything.'

Tom saw straight away that Pavlović was not buying this at all, instead stiffening his grip of the weapon, a large-bladed kitchen knife that Tom had noticed on the drainer when searching earlier.

'Cops told me it was all finished,' said Pavlović. 'No charges. You're no cop. Why are you here?'

'Goran,' Tom began, but the words died in his throat as he saw what was about to happen. Tom always recognised these situations earlier than others; some primitive part of his brain allowed him to see things quickly and he could see what his opponent was going to try almost before the aggressor. He saw it in the change in Pavlović's grip on the knife handle: just a stiffening, the fingers moving slightly. He saw the tensing of the man's core, the almost imperceptible planting of the rear foot to provide stability in the attack that was about to begin. Mostly though, it was the eyes; those cold Baltic eyes flashed towards Tom's chest, the intended target for his knife.

Right on cue, Pavlović thrust the knife forward and with terrible force towards Tom's torso. If successful it would have driven straight in between his ribs and into his vital organs. However, Tom saw the passage of Pavlović's arm almost in slow motion as he moved with lightning speed to his side, slapping the onrushing wrist in a wide arc away from his body. Pavlović's momentum caused him to overbalance and stumble into the futon, falling over in a heap.

Tom stepped back. 'No need to do this, Goran. I'm not your enemy,' he said in a calm and reassuring tone, totally at odds with what had just occurred.

Pavlović leapt to his feet, the knife still clutched in his hand and held at waist height. His eyes were wide and full of hatred but his stance was steady, and he was breathing evenly. Tom could tell that the man had been well trained and was an opponent not to be under-estimated.

Pavlović slowly circled around the futon, edging closer to Tom while switching the knife between his hands with a practised ease. With a surprising flash of speed, he leaped forwards, the knife swinging upwards in a powerful underarm strike, aiming for Tom's midriff. Tom jumped back and the knife flashed in front of him; he felt the disturbed air as it whistled past his face.

Pavlović recovered his balance and switched his grip, his underarm strike moving seamlessly into a downward overhead stab aimed at Tom's head and shoulders. Tom thrust his right arm up straight over his head, deflecting the arm bearing the knife and sending it sliding downwards, the momentum propelling the knife towards the floor and embedding the blade into the boards.

Pavlović reset his stance and tried to pull the knife free, but the blade had bitten in deeply and he had to alter his grip to gain the required purchase. Seizing his opportunity, Tom kicked Pavlović's hand away from the knife, propelling the man's limb up towards the ceiling and exposing the arms dealer's torso. Tom's hand flashed forwards, its fingers expended like a blade as they drove into Pavlović's throat, crushing the cartilage of his trachea.

This was quickly and instinctively followed by a palm strike to the side of the man's neck.

That was it: game over. Pavlović clutched at his throat and then fell to the floor, the nerve branch in his neck temporarily interrupted, which caused the lights in the man's eyes to go out. In his semiconscious state, he realised that no air was getting to his lungs and he started to paw at his ruined throat, his face turning a deep shade of scarlet. Tom watched the struggling Pavlović; he was going to die very soon unless something was done. Much as Tom had a somewhat ambivalent attitude to death and killing, now was not the time.

Tom went to the knife buried in the floor and, with some effort, pulled it clear from the floor. 'You've one chance to live,' he told the writhing figure. 'Stop struggling and stop panicking.'

Looking quickly around the spartan room Tom saw a cheap, plastic ball-point pen on the work surface. Grabbing it quickly, he removed the nib and ink strip and placed it on the floor. He picked up the Leatherman, ignoring the rising look of panic on Pavlović's face as his disrupted central nervous system began to recover in order to deal with the more urgent problem of no air getting into his body.

'Your windpipe is crushed, and you are going to die unless I cut a hole in your throat. It's going to hurt a lot, but the alternative is that you die here on the floor. Do you understand?'

Pavlović nodded, the fear palpable in his eyes as his chest heaved ineffectually in and out.

'Keep as still as you can.' Tom didn't hesitate, he took the razor-sharp Leatherman blade in his hand and using his finger he located the space just below the Adam's apple.

He had to push surprisingly hard before the blade pierced the cartilage with a sudden pop and blood trickled out from the wound, followed by a hiss as air rushed into the man's starving lungs. Reaching for the ballpoint housing, Tom slid it into the wound. The rapid whistling of Pavlović's breathing was a relief for Tom to hear. Nobody was dying today. A body, right here, right now, would be something of an inconvenience.

'Right,' Tom said as he stood up and reached for the attaché case. 'You'll live but you will need some proper medical attention straight away. Wait five minutes and then call for help.' He quickly rinsed the blood from his hands and the Leatherman in the sink, before closing the blade and tucking it in his pocket. Before leaving the apartment he took care to also gather up his makeshift "loid", ready for disposal somewhere safe and far away.

How the hell had he not been told that Pavlović had been released? What the hell was going on? Tom's mind was racing as he shut the door behind him.

Producing his phone, he dialled Mike. After a couple of clicks the phone fell completely silent. No ring, no automated message. Nothing. Tom frowned.

As he left the block, he dialled Pet. The phone was answered immediately.

'Tom?'

'Pet, where are you?'

'At my hotel. I needed to use some of the kit I had here.'

'That's fine,' said Tom. 'Who booked the hotel?'

'I did; earlier on.'

'Who knows you are there?'

'No one yet.'

'Is Mike there with you?'

'No,' said Pet. 'Mike asked me to book rooms for us two; he was staying somewhere else. I haven't spoken to him for a few hours.'

'Okay,' said Tom. 'We have a problem: Pavlović has been released. I've just had an encounter with him at his apartment.'

'What? What type of encounter?'

'Don't worry; it's the type where he is not dead. He will be out of action for a while, though.'

'That's something, I guess.'

'So where's Mike?'

'He was at the Embassy when I last spoke to him, when he sent me out to support you.'

Tom looked at his watch, it was just past midnight.

'Okay. pick me up, will you? I'll be outside the Sacred Heart cathedral in thirty minutes.'

'I'm leaving now,' she said.

9

Pet was as good as her word and was pulling up in a street just adjacent to the nineteenth century Gothic cathedral only a minute late.

'You okay?' she asked, as Tom climbed into the front seat of the Kuga.

'I'm fine.' Tom said as he fastened his seat belt and handed her the Leatherman. 'Thanks.'

'You're welcome. Did it do whatever it was you needed it for?'

'And more, Pet. I must get one.'

Pet eyed him suspiciously.

'Best not ask,' said Tom, tucking Pavlović's attaché case in the footwell. 'Now let's get out of here and get off the street. Does Mike know what's going on?'

'I can't get hold of him; his phone keeps hitting voicemail.'

'Is that usual?'

'Not generally, but he was with Rudy and they were supposed to be meeting the ambassador at some point this evening. Signal can get sketchy, so maybe he is just out of range.' Pet didn't sound convinced.

Looking at his watch, Tom saw it was almost half-past midnight, 'Will anyone still be about at the Embassy?'

'It will just be minimum night staff by now, but I can't see where else Mike would be. Maybe he went out with Rudy or some other employees. He seemed to know a few people there.'

'I guess,' said Tom. 'Look, I see no point going to the Embassy now, a few hours won't make any difference. Let's go to the hotel. I have barely slept for days and my brain isn't working as it should;

I am just going to make mistakes if I keep working. We can start fresh in the morning; I'm sure Mike will have surfaced from wherever he is by then.'

'Sure. Let's go. Mike has probably just turned in; he's had a real busy few days as well; he has spent the last few days on planes.'

The journey to the mid-priced chain hotel was short and, within a few minutes, they were both sat in Pet's room.

'Tea?' Pet asked.

'Sure. British thing, right?' Tom smiled, filling the small kettle and switching it on. Pet drank tea more than any Englishman; it was almost a religion to her.

'Any luck on the encryption on the laptop download?' he asked her.

'I've not started yet; I was going to do it at the Embassy.'

'Maybe shelve it till the morning. It can wait. It seems that we have a little control of the timeline.' Tom gave Pet a full blow-by-blow account of the evening's events, from the meeting with Cerović all the way through to an abridged version of his encounter with Pavlović.

'So… Hold up, let me get this straight,' said Pet. 'Pavlović came from nowhere, right?'

'Yep.'

'I thought he was in custody.'

'You and me both,' Tom said with a shrug.

'So how?'

'That's what I am hoping Mike can tell us. Police released him, but we don't know why. One thing is sure though,' Tom paused, pouring water into two mugs with tea-bags in.

'I'm listening,' Pet said.

'Pavlović was more than all the intel suggested. He was calm and collected and clearly knew how to fight. We need to find out more about him.'

'You managed okay, right?'

'Sure, I disabled him, but he was a tough cookie. Luckily, I managed to surprise him.'

'Luck? Okay Detective,' Pet shook her head, disbelievingly. 'He's in hospital now, right?'

'I am assuming so. Can you check?'

'Maybe. Let me see.'

While Pet opened her laptop and switched it on, Tom reached for the attaché case that he had liberated from under the floorboards at Pavlović's place. He unzipped the worn metal fastener and emptied the contents onto the bed. Four thick bundles of US dollars fell onto the linen along with a new-looking pistol and a spare clip.

Tom let out a low whistle as he picked up and leafed through the bank notes. 'Check this out, Pet,' he said. The notes were crisp and new, and secured in bundles with paper wraps. All were hundreds, with about a hundred bills in each bundle.

'If my maths is correct and those bundles are the same, we have forty grand here, in new US bills. How the hell has a minor military contraband dealer got his hands on this kind of money?'

Tom picked up the pistol: a new-looking Beretta M9, both magazines full. 'This doesn't make sense,' he said.

'Why? Can't be too surprised that an arms dealer has a gun,' Pat said.

'Agreed, but this is a US Beretta M9. Standard US military issue handgun. I would expect a Bosnian arms dealer to have an Eastern European pistol, one of the millions littered across the whole region. He was found with a boot load of them just a couple of days ago, for Christ's sake. It doesn't make sense that Pavlović would have a stolen US military pistol. I mean, the odds are just so far against it.' He turned the weapon over in his hands. It was well cared for with a sheen of gun oil on the working parts, and a line of deep, machine-cut grooves on the side of the weapon where the serial number should have been.

Tom sat looking at the firearm for a few moments, wondering what all this meant. He looked at the full spare clip, a total of fifteen rounds of 9mm ammunition, then ejected the magazine from the M9 and found that it too was full. A total of thirty rounds of ammunition. He slid one of the rounds out of the magazine and held it between his thumb and forefinger to examine it. 9mm x 19 hollow points. Nasty: they would spread on impact and cause devastating injuries. He recognised the NATO cross on the base, meaning that the weapon was Western in origin.

He picked up the attaché case and checked the various pouches on the worn brown leather case. All were empty apart from one on the inside where Tom found a US passport that bore Pavlović's photograph but listed his name as Goran Rastoder. Tom had a reasonable amount of experience in detecting forgeries in travel documents, but this passport bore none of the hallmarks of a forged document, with all the security features looking legitimate. It looked genuine and was crisp, unmarked and, in fact, brand-new.

Tom frowned, deeply. 'You know what this looks like, Pet?'

'Tell me?'

'A man planning to run. Forty Kay in US dollars, a US pistol and ammo and what, to me, looks like a genuine US passport.' He tossed the document to Pet who studied it briefly.

'I can look into this. In fact, I have lots of things to look into, right?'

'How the hell did he get a US passport? This stinks, Pet.'

'I'll check; hold up.' Pet turned to her computer, her fingers flashing across the keys. After just a few minutes she said, 'It's genuine. It was issued a couple of weeks ago at the US Embassy in Sarajevo. I can't tell much else behind how it came to be issued as it's just listed as a replacement following a loss. I'd need better access to the database than I can access remotely. Nothing on the name Rastodor, that I can access.'

'Okay, don't worry about it. But it tells us one thing: whoever is controlling this has the clout to get a genuine US passport issued. That can only come from a high level.'

'You want me to keep digging?'

'Let's wait until tomorrow. I'm knackered, and I am sure you are,' said Tom.

'Sure thing; but you want to know about Pavlović in hospital?'

'What, you found out already?'

'Sure, it was pretty easy. I'm just getting the entry translated now. Goran Pavlović was admitted to Sarajevo University Clinical Centre just a while ago with a damaged throat. He has been admitted and surgery is expected tomorrow. Apparently, a good Samaritan gave him an emergency tracheotomy after some kind of accident. A nice clean and neat job, the records state.' Pet paused and looked at Tom.

He smiled and yawned. 'I'm gonna hit the hay.'

10

Tom woke early the following morning, then showered and dressed in the previous day's clothes; a visit to a cheap clothing outlet was going to be one of the day's jobs. He left the hotel and headed to a coffee shop he had noticed the previous night to buy two coffees and two breakfast bureks: more of the buttery, flaky pastry, this time filled with some type of fruit.

He jogged back to the hotel and knocked on Pet's door. She answered wearing a voluminous hotel gown, her hair secured in a towel, fresh from the shower.

'I bought coffee and bureks,' Tom smiled. 'Good morning, by the way.'

'I'm glad you're here,' Pet smiled, accepting her coffee and looking a little suspiciously at the burek. 'Your friend Cerović is up and about; he has been searching the internet on his phone, messaged someone in the US, and has just received a voice call. I can't listen in on the call, but I am working out how to activate his microphone so we can at least listen to his half of the conversation. Good morning, as well, by the way.'

'Can we see the number called or calling?'

'Sure; the screen is mirrored to me so I should be able to see everything. It was a cell phone number that called him. I'm running it through, but it may take longer than normal as it is a local airtime provider. It's not so easy as being back in the US or UK.' She sipped her coffee and sat back down on the bed, her fingers drumming on the keyboard.

'Any luck with his laptop?' Tom asked, munching his greasy burek.

'Not yet. The brute force algorithm is working, but it may take a while. I found an old Facebook profile, but he has not used it for ages. It may help narrow the parameters, but the encryption is more sophisticated than I thought.'

'How about activating his camera on the phone?' Tom asked.

'That should be easy, but I don't want to activate it unless I have to. I can't be sure whether it will have any visible impact on the handset from his end. If I'd had a little more time last night, I could have been more certain.'

'Well, listen. I need to contact him soon in any case, why not use that opportunity to test what the capabilities of the malware is? I could do with checking in and giving him some story about sourcing and laying hands on the battery. I need a burner phone, though.'

'Hold up, Detective. Girl Guide: I'm still always prepared; I have one in here.' She reached into her computer bag and produced a basic mobile phone.

'What type of SIM?'

'Local, most popular network.'

'Cool. I'll message him now on the secure app and see if he wants to give me a number. We are buddies now after last evening's debauchery.' Tom chuckled as he tapped out a brief message on the secure messaging app.

'Are you awake, we need to talk. Give me a number, Tarzan.'

'Why did we pick Tarzan?' he asked Pet.

'Mike suggested it when I created the profile on Alpha Bay. Maybe Tarzan was a Serb?'

'I don't know about that,' said Tom, 'but Johnny Weissmuller, who played the first Tarzan character, was born in Mejda in Serbia.'

'Whoa, you are really boring,' Pet shook her head, smiling. 'That's the most boring thing anyone has ever said to anyone, ever.'

There was a buzz as the phone indicated a received message: a phone number flashed up on the screen. Tom showed it to Pet, who noted it in her book as he was dialling before clamping a pair of sleek headphones over her ears.

'Hey buddy. Man, I feel like a dead guy today. How about you?' Cerović's voice was thick and gummy.

'Not too great. I thought we were going to club? Lots of girls you said.' Tom said, his Serb accent strong.

'Passed out, dude. Slept like a baby, though. You are a fucking animal, man.'

Tom just barked a short laugh. 'What we were discussing. I am going to inventory my items today, then I will call you tomorrow.'

'Sounds great, man. My people are giving me pressure, they've already messaged me wanting an update this morning. I've assured them I have the right batteries coming, don't let me down Tarzan.' Tom could hear the man yawning.

'Sure thing. I'll call later.' Tom hung up.

'Sounds like you guys had a blast last night, Detective.' Pet said, a smile creeping across her face.

'You've no idea,' Tom said, shaking his head. 'Microphone okay?'

'Clear as a bell, but only his side of the call,' Pet said.

'Better than nothing. In fact, better than expected. Let's call Mike; we need to get this moving.' Tom picked up his phone and dialled.

There was nothing; no ring tone, no voicemail, no clicks or buzzes. Just silence. 'That's strange. You try, Pet?'

Pet picked up her phone and dialled, her face a puzzled frown as she got the same result. 'Maybe in an area with no phones allowed?' she shrugged.

'What, in the US Embassy? He's a senior spook. Something isn't right. Come on, let's get there and find out. I can't believe he would be out of contact this long.'

*

They parked the Kuga in a multi-storey car park at the Alta shopping centre, within a short walk of the Embassy.

The Embassy lobby was just as Tom recalled it the previous

day, a wide open space with a shiny marble floor, an immaculately turned-out US Marine guard stood by the metal detector arch behind a lectern just inside the door. The Marine stood straight and bolt upright, staring directly ahead. 'May I help you?'

Pet smiled and held out an Embassy pass for the Marine to examine.

'This is a temporary pass, Ma'am,' the guard said. 'It expired at midnight yesterday.' He turned to Tom, keeping hold of Pet's pass. 'Do you have a pass, sir?'

'I was escorted in by Mike Brogan yesterday and my pass was left with him when I departed.' Tom said. He had left his temporary pass behind, on the basis that carrying a US Embassy pass when deployed undercover would be a daft idea.

'Brogan, you say, sir?' the Marine said formally with no warmth.

'Yes, Mike Brogan. He's a senior employee of the US government.' Tom said, a rising feeling of unease creeping up in him.

'Your name, sir?'

'My name is Novak.'

'Are you a US citizen, sir?'

'No.'

The Marine looked down at a computer screen in front of him. 'Sir, I have no Mr Brogan listed as being a member of Embassy staff.'

Pet interjected. 'I was sponsored yesterday by Rudy O'Shea, who *is* a member of staff here. Please check; it's urgent we see him or Mike.'

The Marine looked at Tom and Pet in turn, a hard look in his flinty eyes. His head tipped forward to appraise his screen, once more.

'I have no record of a Mr O'Shea at the Embassy either, ma'am. Are either of you employees of the US government? Do you have any official form of identification?' His gaze once more flicked between Tom and Pet, a look of suspicion on his strong features.

'No. Neither of us are employees of the US Government, but

both of us are providing officially sanctioned services to Mike Brogan.' Pet's normally cheery voice had slipped a little. 'Just put the call in and let them know we are here.'

'As I said previously, ma'am, neither man is listed here.' A slight trace of frustration tainted the guard's formal delivery.

'Look can you just get the CIA representative down here?' Pet said, matching his frustration.

'Sorry ma'am, do you have an appointment?'

'Christ's sake, you know I don't.' Pet said, her voice hardening.

'Please take a seat,' the Marine said, politely but in a way that made it obvious that it was not a request, and indicating to a line of plastic chairs close to the door.

'Tell them it's urgent,' Pet said as they sat down.

'This isn't right,' Tom said, flatly. 'Something is wrong.' He took out his phone and dialled Mike once more. Nothing. Dead and silent.

The Marine fixed both of them with a hard stare whilst he spoke conspiratorially on the phone. His gaze only briefly flicked away from them to look at Pet's Embassy pass.

'Mike's phone is still silent. Literally nothing. This is fucking weird, Pet. Have you tried calling Rudy?'

'I don't have a number for him. I'd never met him before yesterday.'

Tom exhaled a deep sigh.

'I'm worried, Tom,' said Pet. 'What's happened to Mike?'

'Let's see what the spooks say. They must know what's going on,' Tom said, but the sinking feeling in his gut told another story.

The Marine beckoned them both over once again.

'There's no one available to see you. Neither of you are US citizens. I must ask you to leave the Embassy.' His voice was flat and invited no further comment.

'What? What do you mean there is no one to see us?' asked Pet.

'Please leave immediately, ma'am, or I will have to have you removed,' he said, his eyes unyielding, almost daring them not to comply.

Pet opened her mouth to argue, but Tom took her elbow and said, 'Come on, let's go.'

They walked out into the morning sunshine, the streets already bustling with commuters, shoppers, and sightseers. Rather than turn left back towards the car park Tom walked with long strides straight ahead towards the main road.

'Tom, wrong direction,' Pet said, struggling to match his pace.

'I know. Keep walking; I think we can expect company,' he said. His head was fixed straight ahead, but his eyes swivelled left and right, scanning around them.

'Who from?'

'Someone from the Embassy. That was all wrong. All of it. Just stick with me; I am going to see if I can flush anyone out.'

They hit the busy road that consisted of two lanes of traffic in each direction with trams running down the middle. Tom led the way as they came to the kerb and halted as if waiting for a gap in the heavy traffic. Looking in the reflection in the window of a shiny Mercedes stopped in front of them, Tom could clearly see a lone figure behind them, wearing mirrored shades. He looked military in his cargo pants and polo shirt and his hair was closely shorn. Without a doubt he was following them, but the amateurish approach made it clear to Tom that there was no team backing him up: just a lone follower pulled out of an office at short notice. He'd be easy to lose.

'We're taking a tram. Hold on a second, see if this dude follows us further. Don't look around,' Tom said, his lips barely moving.

'Who?' Pet said, her voice tainted with concern.

'Blue polo, grey cargo pants, mirror shades, left the Embassy just after us.'

'Is he following?'

'Yes, and very badly. I'd be fuming if I was his surveillance team leader.'

A red and white tram slowly and steadily came into view.

'Move when I say, Pet.' Tom said, pulling his phone out of his pocket and pretending to look interested in it.

From his peripheral vision Tom watched the tram doors slide open and the half a dozen passengers begin to file on. Just as the last one jumped on Tom said, 'Now. Normal pace,' and they both got into the vehicle.

'Two single rides,' Tom said in Serb to the driver.

'Three marks sixty,' the grizzled driver said.

Tom handed over a ten mark note and waited for the change. They walked to the rear of the packed tram, Tom looking away from their follower.

'Is he still there?'

'Yes, he's on his phone. He looks a little stressed, like he doesn't know what to do.' Pet whispered.

'Amateurs. Is it just him?' Tom replied as the doors hissed shut and the tram glided away.

'I can't see anyone else. Why are they following us?'

'I don't know. I need to figure this out. And look, we have another incompetent watcher.' Tom nodded towards the sidewalk, where a similarly-attired agent had joined his team member looking in the direction of the tram. One was touching his finger to his ear, the classic sign of an amateur surveillance operative. Confusion reigned between the two. They were clearly expecting them to head for a car; did they know about the Kuga?

'Who would know about the Ford and the hotel?' Tom said.

'The car was hired by Mike's people, but I arranged the hotel. Why?'

'What audit trail will there be?'

'Car is through company Amex. I did the hotel through my own expenses fund as I couldn't get hold of Mike. I use an untraceable account, as I'm paid via an unconventional route. I'm deniable so I like to be a little difficult to pin down. I move money about plenty, so I'm sure the hotel is safe.' Pet looked ahead, her voice barely a whisper.

'Okay. We leave the car where it is; there is nothing in it we need. Let's get our gear from the hotel quickly and relocate. I don't want to take the risk that they can trace it, so we'll move hotels whilst we figure out what the hell is going on.'

'Is that necessary?'

'Maybe not, but it's not worth the risk. We'll find a cheap place and pay cash. We need to stay off the radar for a while so I can think.'

'What the hell is going on, Tom? Where the hell is Mike?'

'To be honest, Pet, I've no idea.'

*

They rode the tram into central Sarajevo and dived into a small, empty coffee shop. Tom decided that they needed to pause a moment to gather their thoughts before they made the next move.

'First thing, we need a new car. We can't use the Ford as it's too traceable. Is there a second-hand lot nearby?'

Pet picked up her phone and began tapping, swiping and scrolling.

'There's one not far from here, but why don't we just hire one?' she asked.

'Too much of an audit trail. I want to be anonymous and, as we are cash rich with Pavlović's stash, we may as well use it. He tried to kill me, so the least he can do is buy me a car.'

'Seems fair,' Pet smiled. 'They have plenty of cheap stock. What are we looking for?'

'Just cheap and anonymous; anything will do.'

'Well this seems to be the place to go then. Let's get our gear from the hotel and get a cab there.'

11

They ended up with a twelve-year-old Skoda estate car in an anonymous, faded grey. It had almost three hundred thousand kilometres on the odometer but it was clean, had good tyres, and seemed in reasonable order. It also had a powerful two-litre engine that felt strong and smooth. Tom didn't intend on getting into any car chases, but he figured he would rather have a powerful car, just in case.

The dealer, a grimy little man, didn't turn a hair when Tom offered him two thousand dollars for a car that was advertised at sixteen hundred euros, and he had a relaxed attitude to any paperwork which suited them just fine. As always, wherever you went in the world, people were always happy to accept Uncle Sam's dollars and, within thirty minutes of entering the grimy office, they were driving back out onto the Sarajevo streets.

'Right, hotel next. Any suggestions, Pet? Same criteria: cheap and anonymous, and preferably relaxed attitudes to paperwork.'

Pet searched on her phone for a few moments. 'In or out of town?'

'Maybe just out. We need some time to plan our next move, and I'd like some breathing space. We don't know if we are being looked for by anyone; in fact we don't know anything at all. We can't locate Mike or Rudy. I don't like any of this; we need a base so you can do some work on trying to find Mike.'

After a few more minutes Pet nodded. 'Okay, here is a place. Head to Krupac, south of the city, and I'll direct you. I'll reserve a room online.'

'Krupac?' Tom said, something in his voice.

'Sure. Problem?'

'No. No problem. I just remember it from growing up. There was a small wrestling club there; my father took me there for lessons and practice a couple of times. I know the way, I think.' Tom said, his voice flat.

'Is that okay? I can find somewhere else,' Pet looked at him with a touch of concern.

'It's fine. It's very quiet there.' In reality he felt some unease, vivid memories beginning to seep into his consciousness despite the passage of almost thirty years. He had been concentrating on matters at hand until now, but travelling out of the city towards his childhood home, a place that held so many memories—both good and bad—was beginning to resonate. It didn't feel like home; it felt odd and remote, despite the seething memories of a childhood spent here.

The traffic was heavy in central Sarajevo, but began to thin as they exited the city towards Krupac. Memories assaulted Tom at almost every mile as the scenery flew past, becoming more mountainous as they left the city. He searched his mind, trying to gauge his feelings about returning to such a familiar landscape after all those years. Nothing had changed apart from the fact that there were more cars and less tanks and military vehicles. As was often the case, he felt blank and empty. Was this normal? he wondered. How could visiting his homeland after all those years away evoke no emotions in him? He shook his head to remove the thoughts; they were pointless.

Twenty minutes later they pulled off the main road towards the edge of a forest, where they found a quaint guest house that resembled a cuckoo clock, nestling on the side of a steep hill. A small swimming pool lay to the front of the property on a terrace that stretched out towards a stunning view of the distant mountains.

'Man, this is nice! How can it be this nice and this cheap? It's only thirty euros a night,' said Pet.

'It's a bit off the tourist trail. People can't forget the war yet, despite the passage of time.' This had occurred to Tom as he travelled through the lush, verdant countryside leading up to the mountains. Bosnia was a stunningly beautiful country, but memories were long and the passage of time was short. How long would it take before tourists saw Sarajevo for what it is, not what it once was?

'Maybe soon, Tom.'

'Come on. Let's get in there, we have work to do. Maybe let me do the talking, if I stick to Serb with her it may attract less attention.

'Best we look like we are a couple, then. There was only one room left, so we are sharing,' Pet said, taking Tom's arm.

'I guess so,' Tom said, feeling a slight prickle of unease at her touch. He had to admit that, if they wanted to arouse the least attention, then posing as a couple would be the most normal situation to present.

The owner met them at the door with a beaming smile. She was a gamine, slim and attractive woman in her forties with smiling eyes and a short, choppy haircut.

'Hello and welcome, I am Emina and this is my place,' she said in halting English. 'I am pleased to have you here. Can I have someone take your bags?' She nodded towards the rucksack and shoulder bag that Pet was lugging.

'Thank you, but we can manage fine. We travel light,' Tom said in Serbian

'Ah, I thought you would be from England from the booking form. You are lucky as we have only one room left; it is our largest so should be suitable. Are you on honeymoon?'

Tom smiled. 'No. Just touring a little. We are from Mostar,' he said, referring to the Bosnian City two and a half hours away.

'Mostar is so beautiful. Why Sarajevo?'

'Many things to see. My wife wants to do some shopping and to see *Tunel Spasa*,' Tom said smiling broadly, every inch the tourist. In reality Tom always thought that it was a little vulgar that the Sarajevo war tunnel had become such a major tourist attraction. It always struck him as voyeuristic when tourists took selfies at the scene of such horrors.

Emina was clearly hugely proud of her little guest house and showed them into the clean, spacious room with a flourish.

'I'm afraid that you have missed lunch, but I can arrange for some sandwiches,' she said.

'Thank you, but we are fine. We may eat here later, however.'

'Well, dinner is from seven until nine pm.' She smiled widely again and left the room.

'I can't believe you said no to sandwiches; you know how hungry I get,' Pet said in a mock irritated voice. Tom was always amazed that, despite Pet's waif-like frame, she had an enormous appetite.

'Stop moaning. There's a kettle here and some biscuits, I'll even let you eat mine. We need to get moving on finding Mike, and I didn't want her coming back up here for a while. Let's get cracking,' Tom said, filling the kettle with water and switching it on.

'First let's try the obvious. He may have his phone back on.' She produced her own phone and held it to her ear. The shake of her head indicated that the other line was still dead.

'So when did we see or hear from him last?' Tom asked.

'About seven last night. I left him at the Embassy, and he sent me a message a short while after saying he would be there for a while and to book rooms for me and you. There could be a simple explanation,' Pet didn't sound convinced.

'Maybe, but nothing I've seen so far makes me feel good about the fact that we haven't heard from Mike for eighteen hours or so. I also don't like it that all knowledge of Mike or Rudy was denied by the Embassy guard. What checks can you perform, and who can we safely conduct to try to find him? Do you have any friendly contacts within the CIA? The reaction at the Embassy earlier tells me that something unusual is happening, so we need to be a hundred percent sure that whoever we contact is reliable.' Tom had a very uneasy feeling about the whole situation. He had no idea who was aware of his and Pet's presence in Bosnia and Herzegovina.

'I only spoke to Mike about this. Remember: I am a freelancer,

I am not employed by the CIA, and Mike likes to keep my areas of operation 'off-book'. I have access to most databases, but I don't know who knows about me and my role. I have no idea how to proceed, here, Tom. The whole thing feels weird. How do we know that, if I call someone, it won't be the wrong person? Will it make it worse?'

'I think that our best bet is to use your skills to give us some clues as to where the hell he is. Maybe start with his phone, I didn't recognise the number he was using; was it a new one?'

'I thought that as well. He gave it to me at the start of this operation and told me not to use his usual number for the duration. I didn't think it odd at the time, but on reflection it's unusual. I've only ever used one number for Mike. He said he didn't have his normal cell with him.' Pet opened up her hold-all and produced her battered, sticker-festooned laptop.

Tom chewed this over in his mind. Why would Mike use a completely new phone for this operation? He hadn't given it a thought when Mike had given him the new number during the flight, but Tom had also only ever used the one phone number for contacting Mike. It often diverted elsewhere, but that was the only point of contact he had.

'Pet are you using a secure internet connection here? Can anyone—local law-enforcement or CIA—trace what you're doing now or, more importantly, where you are doing it from?' Tom felt an overwhelming desire to be careful.

'Well I was going to use my usual route of access, but now you are speaking to me in that suspicious voice I may use a different method. Hold up.' Pet dug deeply into her cavernous bag and came up with a small, oversized, scratched and battered metallic dongle that she connected via a USB port. She began to tap away at the keyboard at lightning speed.

'I won't bore you with the details, but this will allow me to piggy-back onto another server elsewhere and will firstly obscure where we are. Secondly, and more importantly, it will look like another member of the CIA is accessing the databases. It's a little insurance policy that I have that uses a fake employee profile I created as an experiment a while back. Fortunately, the employee has a decent level of systems access, although not as good as my usual one.'

'Nice. I like that,' Tom said admiringly.

'It pays to have a backup plan,' Pet smiled.

Tom busied himself making the teas whilst Pet stared at the screen, a look of utter concentration etched across her fine features.

He deposited a mug of steaming tea on the bedside table next to where she sat, cross-legged on the bed staring intently at the screen.

'Right. Mike's new phone was active and making and receiving calls and messages up until about ten last night. Then it dropped off the system altogether and it has been dead ever since.'

'Where was it when it was last on the network?' Tom asked.

'Hold up. System is sticky here.' She continued to tap away at the keyboard. 'I'm gonna overlay it onto a map for the preceding hours.' She continued tapping at the keys before turning the laptop round to face Tom. 'Here. All the calls and sent and received messages are marked on the map.' Tom looked at the screen, where he could see a number of dots, all with times alongside. The main cluster of times were located on and around the US Embassy.

'Where was the final activation on the network?' Tom asked.

'This one.' Pet pointed to a dot just a few centimetres from the main group.

'Do we know exactly where this call was made from? As in, how tight a location can we pinpoint?'

'These are just cell tower locations. I can narrow it down by looking at signal strength and trying to triangulate but that may only give us a search area of a few streets. What are you thinking here?' Pet asked.

'I'm thinking that if we get a final location, we may be able to locate some CCTV and see if we can get a clue as to what happened.'

'Probably not from cell sites. It's too broad to do historically, but I have another option.'

'What?'

'You know about *"Find My iPhone?"* Pet asked.

'Sure. Log into your phone account and look at the GPS signal. Ties it down to a few feet, but surely that's a bit basic for you?'

'Why make things complex? Promise not to rat me out to Mike?'

'Where are you going with this?'

'It's possible I may know his password for his cell phones,' Pet said.

'How?' Tom asked.

'Despite being a senior CIA man, he has a terrible memory for passwords. I was always giving him grief for his poor security, but he just brushed me off.'

'Will this allow us access to his phone contacts, so we can see who called him at the relevant times?'

'No reason why not,' said Pet.

'Well crack on then; I won't grass.'

Within seconds Pet had opened up the Apple website and was working on the login screen. Her first two attempts failed.

'He isn't very imaginative, so I have another one to try.' She tapped at the keys again and smiled. 'We're in.'

Within a few seconds she had the final location of the phone up on a map. The blue dot pulsed in the centre of a small street, what appeared to be a short walk from the Embassy.

'What is on that street and is there any available CCTV nearby?'

Pet began working the keys again, that familiar mask of concentration on her face.

'Okay, right. This ain't good. Last GPS pulse the phone emitted was at Omera Stupca, a short walk from the Embassy. It seems to be a residential street and, coincidentally, a street where several of the senior US Embassy staff live. Mike said that he was going to stay at the Embassy, I guess this is what he meant.'

'Where does Rudy O'Shea live?' Tom asked.

'What, the elusive Rudy who wouldn't come and see us earlier on today?'

'The very same.'

'Short answer: I don't know. All I can find is that there are three houses next to each other for senior staff. I could probably find out, but it would take time we don't have.'

'You're right. Time is not our friend. Who was the last person to speak to Mike?'

More tapping. Then, 'His wife at about 9:45 last night.'

'Another thing: where is Mike's usual phone?' Tom asked, suspecting the answer.

'Hold up.' Pet's fingers danced across the keyboard. 'By the look of it, on his desk at CIA headquarters. Also, by the look of it, with a divert on it so he would still receive calls whilst away from it.'

'Who was the last call from?'

More tapping before Pet paused and looked at Tom. 'Last call to Mike, on his usual number which diverted to the one he's been using in Sarajevo, was at nine-fifty and was from Rudy O'Shea.'

Tom paused. He turned it all over in his mind but couldn't see through the fog. Why had Mike left his phone back in Washington? Where had he gone? Why were the Embassy seemingly unaware of Tom and Pet's role? Was this a maverick operation? Tom's mind seethed.

'The Rudy that security denied worked at the Embassy...' he said quietly.

'Yep,' Pet responded.

'Let's get out of here.' Tom said.

'Don't you want me to look for any CCTV?' she asked.

'Not at the moment. You can use that whilst we are mobile, but many CCTV systems won't be online so we will be luckier if we use the "Mark One Human Eyeball", as we used to say in the Corps.'

'So, you're using analogue methods in a digital age, right?'

'I prefer to call it old-fashioned police work. Let's go.'

12

Omera Stupca was a wide, straight, and affluent-looking road with large, detached properties on either side. Pet remained glued to her laptop as they drove steadily along the quiet, well-kept road. Tom scanned from side to side, looking for any obvious CCTV cameras either on the street or within the boundaries of each of the properties.

'Okay, this is the spot that Mike's phone was at when his GPS was last on the system,' Pet said, her eyes not leaving the screen.

Tom slowed up a little. 'Can you ascertain his direction of travel?'

'Sure, he was eastbound, so coming from the general direction of the Embassy.'

'So do we assume that Mike was heading to the staff accommodation?'

'That would make sense. The Embassy properties are at the far eastern reach of Omera Stupca.'

'How far down?'

'About two hundred metres from the last GPS.' Pet's fingers continued to tap at the keys before she continued. 'There are no municipal CCTV cameras listed that I can find. The Embassy properties will have cameras, but they are too far away to cover where the phone dropped off the system.'

Tom sighed slightly before pulling to the side of the road, 'Take over driving. I'm going to have a walk to see what I can see. I need to be on the street to get a feel for it. Can you drive past the Embassy properties? I'll call you.'

Without waiting for an answer, Tom got out of the car and

began walking away from the car, his head down, eyes scanning left and right. He heard the car note change as it drove off.

Tom walked steadily: not fast, not slow. Just a normal guy going about his business. The properties on both sides of the street were all large, double-fronted, spacious dwellings. Most had gates and sweeping drives, many with prestigious cars parked on them. Tom noted with interest that at least fifty percent of them had some form of alarm boxes and many had visible CCTV cameras facing out onto the drives, and thereby the road, presumably protecting valuable vehicles.

Tom walked to about fifty metres away from the last GPS pulse from Mike's phone, before crossing the road and making the return journey, walking a further fifty metres. One property was in the perfect spot, number forty-six. It had a smaller drive than the others, but was of a similar size. It was an attractive red-brick with stuccoed windows and a wrought iron fence to the front. The vehicle gate was wide-open, and the drive was empty of vehicles. There were three modern-looking cameras, each with antennae mounted on their tops. One was covering the front door, one covered the drive entrance, and one the front garden area and presumably the front windows too. Between the three cameras, Tom was certain that they would have captured all activity on the road, including the exact spot where Mike's phone had last emitted a signal.

He continued walking at his normal pace, putting his phone to his ear, and calling Pet.

'Detective?'

'Pet, I'll walk to the end of the road where we turned in. There is a shop just opposite the Saudi Embassy; pick me up there?' Tom hung up and upped his pace, a plan forming. He needed to see what the CCTV had captured, but he wasn't risking knocking on the door just yet.

Pet pulled up in front of the small convenience store. 'Detective, we have to work on your social skills. You can be very abrupt, sometimes. Did you buy me candy from the shop?' Her smile through the open window did not add any resonance to her firm words.

Tom smiled back, 'Candy soon. There is a house just back there, number forty-six. Can you find anything out about it?'

'Not whilst I'm driving,' she said, shuffling across to the passenger seat. Tom opened the driver's door and climbed in, driving straight off.

'The house has three cameras facing the front. If they are recording, and Mike did walk down here, they will have captured him. We need to see what is on that footage for last night. Is there any way you can find out the best way of doing that remotely, or am I going to have to break in? I don't want to do that; it looks pretty secure and alarmed.' Tom spoke quickly and efficiently, all business now.

'Okay, I can do some checking. Drive back past it so I can get a better look at it,' Pet said, picking her phone up. 'I want some coffee, as well. And some food; I'm hungry,' she smiled.

'I've never known someone eat so much and not be fat, how do you do it?'

'Fast metabolism. Hurry, hurry. I need coffee.'

They drove past the house at a steady pace: not too fast, but not so slow as to look suspicious.

They pulled up a few streets later at a petrol station. Tom refuelled the car and then went into the shop, paid for the fuel, and bought two large coffees and two sweaty-looking muffins.

Getting back into the car he passed the coffee to Pet and dumped the muffins on the dash. 'How are you getting on?'

'You expect me to operate with crappy gas-station muffins and coffee? Jeez Detective, it's like you have never worked with me. You owe me a big dinner,' she bit into the muffin and screwed her face up. 'This muffin sucks. However, I can tell you that the house is privately-owned and mortgaged to— as far as I can tell—a normal-looking family, although I am not digging. The alarm box is for a defunct company and an image search on the cameras lead me to believe that they are web-based Wi-Fi cameras that stream the images to either a computer or, more likely, a phone. You know the types, right?'

Tom nodded. 'So can you intercept the images being sent?'

'If we can identify their Wi-Fi, then almost certainly. Whether I can access historical images depends on if they have hard-drive or cloud-based storage. The model they have, which is quite new, offers both.'

'Okay. So what do we do?'

'We go sniffing,' said Pet, rummaging in her bag.

'Pardon?'

'Man, get with the times. We need to get back there, and you need to get me as close as you can.'

*

They sat in the car directly outside the property, feeling horribly exposed.

'This is a bit close for comfort, Pet. How long do we need?' Tom asked. His surveillance experience had taught him that you always needed a reason to be in any particular place, in case you were challenged. At this stage, they had nothing.

'Not long, hold on.' Pet produced a small white box with a couple of antennae at each corner, which she plugged into her laptop.

'You want to tell me what the plan is?'

'I'm looking for their signal. I'm using a Wi-Fi sniffer and WireShark to analyse their router, it should give me everything I need. Now hush, Detective, I'm concentrating. How long do I have?'

'As little time as possible,' said Tom, looking into his mirror.

'Bear with me. Typically, they are using the factory-set password and the cameras are definitely transmitting across the net. Okay, I am capturing their live packet data, right now. Jeez, would it hurt some people to put a little security on their computers. If I was a criminal, I'd be a millionaire.' Pet was almost speaking to herself in little more than a happy, sing-song mumble.

'Okay, done,' she said. 'Let's go, we can finish this off away from here. I have all the packet data dumped and I don't think it's encrypted, so should be easy to get what we need.'

'What is it we actually need?' Tom asked, as they pulled away.

'Just three things: the cloud address for the storage of the footage, the username, and password. It's all in the packet data dump so I just have to extract it. As long as we have that it won't take long to isolate, and we should be able to access it. Let's find somewhere quiet; this won't take too long.'

Pet's fingers tapped across the keyboard as Tom drove.

'You still hungry?' Tom asked.

'Always,' said Pet, not looking up from the laptop.

'McDonald's? There's a drive through not far from here.'

'I love you, Detective. Let's go.'

The journey to McDonald's took just ten minutes as Pet continued to work on the data. There was only a short queue at the window. Tom turned to Pet. 'What can I order you?'

'Big Mac, fries and Coke.' She said, not looking up from the laptop.

Tom gave the order and, within a couple of minutes, they were sat in a nearby parking bay each clutching a burger.

'How long will it take?' Tom asked.

'Should be soon. I have a programme looking for the information we need. Where do we go next?'

'Depends on what's on that film.' Tom replied through a mouthful of fries.

'And if there is nothing?'

'I'll worry about that as and when it happens, but there will be something. Absence of evidence is not evidence of absence, Pet.'

'Sounds like a cop thing to say.'

'It is, and it's accurate. We have to find out what happened to Mike. Whatever has happened, it has to have something to do with this conspiracy he has brought us here to assist on. Is Cerović up to anything?'

Pet tapped at her keys, once again. 'Not moved, as far as I can see. Your session with him yesterday has finished him off for the day, by the look of it.'

'We can revisit that once we know more about Mike.' Tom screwed up his burger wrapper and tossed the packaging into the back of the car.

'It's done. Hold up, I'm accessing the camera cloud storage.' Pet turned the screen slightly so Tom could see it as the browser loaded up. She clicked on the previous day's link, which loaded three camera thumbnail icons showing the area around the front door of the property, the parking area and drive, and the street heading west. The images were high quality and pin sharp.

'I will set the time parameters to run from the time of Mike's last call at 9:45 last night.' Pet clicked her mousepad and they both watched the three windows on the screen. The streetlights lit the area well and the cameras' night vision system seemed to be effective showing the quiet street and drive of the property. Pet speeded up the footage to three-times speed

As the time stamp hit 22:10 hours, they saw Mike. He was walking briskly along the footway adjacent to the house, a small bag over his shoulder. Just after he passed the closed iron gate, a dark blue van pulled up alongside him. The side door slid open and three dark, hooded figures exited the vehicle with urgency, one raising a bright yellow, pistol-shaped object. Mike froze, his hands raised in front of him as the two red dots of the taser shone bright on his torso, exaggerated by the image-intensifying night vision camera. Mike stiffened as if suddenly frozen solid and fell, rigid, like a falling tree. The three men quickly scooped him up, still twitching, and bundled him into the van with practised efficiency. The door slid shut and the van drove off.

'Holy motherfucking shit. They've got Mike,' Pet said in a hoarse whisper.

Tom just stared, his face blank giving no visible sign of the turmoil he felt within.

13

Risto Stefanovic left the farmhouse and emerged blinking into the strong sunshine. He produced his phone and dialled, a little pensive at the conversation he was about to have. He was a hard man and not much scared him, but he had served with Babić in the military and more recently on their more recent enterprises, and the man was, frankly, terrifying.

'Yes,' said the voice in his ear.

'We have him.' Risto said bluntly.

'Excellent. Did he give you any trouble?'

'No. It was simple. He was where your contact had said he would be.' Risto had not questioned Babić's information: a simple text message that contained a photograph of Brogan together with a simple message giving a location and a time. From there it had been simple: Risto and the others were already just a short journey from the location provided. They'd seen Brogan walking confidently along the backstreet and it had been child's play to pull over, taser him, and bundle him into the van.

'Good. Has he said anything yet?'

'Claiming to be an entry clearance officer for people wanting to travel to America. We are going easy on him at the moment: the boys have had a little fun, but other than a few bruises he is fine. He is clearly well-trained; he is sticking to the resistance-to-interrogation handbook so far.'

Babić guffawed, a hoarse and unpleasant noise that was full of phlegm. 'Entry clearance! Is that the best he can do? I'm assured that he is CIA and that he is over here to stop us. My source doesn't know any other reason he could be here, and it seems Brogan only goes where the most serious threats are present. We must know exactly what he knows, and who else knows it. With our plans being almost ready to move to the next stage, we cannot afford any obstacles. The weapons must be ready soon and any countermeasures they are planning, we must be able to navigate. Step up the pressure on Brogan.'

'I understand,' Risto said. 'But I must caution: if he has been trained as we suspect, then the usual violent methods will not work. We need to break him down a little more first, if we are to get beyond his cover story.' Despite being a brutal thug, he was well trained in interrogation and counter-interrogation and was well-versed in the resistance-to-interrogation training that Western forces deployed. A more subtle approach was often more effective in the long run.

'Sadly, you are probably right. Maybe break him down for a while longer, I would rather wait a little for accurate information. How close is Cerović to completing the devices?'

'I spoke to him earlier. He says that he has located a supplier for the appropriate power sources we need. He hopes to take delivery of them soon.'

Babić gave a snort of derision. 'Can he be trusted to procure them?'

'I would hope so; he has found a supplier. They're only batteries, it's not as if he is obtaining explosives or weapons. I don't have the technical expertise to ensure they are appropriate. Now we have Brogan we don't really have the manpower to babysit him. He is a wretch, but we need him to complete the devices. Once he has done this, he is expendable.'

'Well, proceed carefully. The sooner the devices are ready, we can arrange for their transportation. Are the operators ready?'

'Yes. They will require a final brief on their operation before deployment, in case of any differences. The operators have been training and all are reporting that they are ready to deploy as soon as the devices arrive at the locations.'

'That is excellent news, Risto. We just need to know what

Brogan knows of our plans before we can proceed. Once the devices are completed, I want us to move as soon as possible. The investors have placed huge funds in certain positions to benefit from the chaos we will cause, and we need to be ready to ensure we all benefit from this.'

'I understand.'

The phone clicked in Risto's ear and he re-joined the others in the barn. A hooded figure was sat on a chair that was bolted to the floor, his arms and legs shackled with metal restraints. Two guards stood either side of the figure, both of them clutching assault weapons. One of the guards was identical to Risto.

Risto nodded at his twin, indicating for him to join him in the corner of the barn, where he spoke in a low voice.

'Milan, we move to a full tactical questioning routine. Stress positions, and don't let him move or sleep. No food, no water and, if he needs to piss or shit, he does it in his pants. All day and all night, we will then try again with the questioning. Understand?'

Milan nodded, a nasty smile on his face. 'White noise? There is a big stereo in the farmhouse.'

'Good thinking. Babić wants us to move fast. No let-up: we will break him down very soon. But he is a professional: usual methods won't work, so we must behave as we would have in Special Operations, okay?'

Milan nodded and returned to where Brogan sat, barking orders at his fellow guard. They swung into action, professionally and efficiently. Brogan's shackles were released, his hands instead secured to the front and he was forced onto his knees. Brogan didn't resist, behaving as they knew he would: as the "grey man." His heavily shackled arms were forced aloft by the guard and his ankle restraints were secured to the bolted chair by a length of galvanised chain. Soon, they knew the weight of his shackled wrists would become painfully heavy, and the pain in his legs and back would become intolerable, and he would begin to slouch. He would then be vigorously returned to his stress position. This would go on for hours, the intention being to break his resistance and make him malleable and ripe for tactical questioning.

Risto smiled at the scene before him, which would only become more surreal once the stereo came in and the deafening white noise, or thrash metal music, began. The mix of pain from the stress positions and sensory deprivation of being hooded and deafened would soon have Brogan begging to tell them everything. They all did eventually: it was just a question of when.

14

'Can you get a licence plate number?' Tom asked in the low, even voice that Pet knew so well. They were still in the McDonald's car park, the remains of their meals strewn in the footwell of the car.

'Hold up,' Pet said, zooming in tighter to the image of the van on her screen. The licence plate was visible at the rear.

'There it is. It'll take a while to access the local systems, but I will be able to get a match.'

'They'll be false. They knew they'd be seen on camera and they know who they are dealing with.' Tom's voice was full of certainty, even though its pitch didn't shift.

'I'll still check. If they are stolen plates it will still be worth knowing.'

'Right.' Tom exhaled deeply and scrubbed his face with his palms. He was tired. 'This is all about the weapons plot. It has to be. Also, one thing is absolutely certain: there is a mole. Is there anyone you can trust who you can reach out to?'

'I work almost exclusively for Mike. We just don't know who is feeding these guys. What do we do? What about Rudy?'

'We can't trust him. We don't even know where he is; he could be part of it, he could be dead. We don't have any information. I know one thing, however: we need whoever is behind this to think that we have fled Sarajevo. In fact, we need them to believe we have fled Bosnia altogether.'

'How do we do that?' Pet asked.

'Simple. We take the passports that Mike gave us for this trip, and we cross the border into the Schengen Zone. Once we are there, they will think we have fled, and they may relax a little. Before we do this, I need you to find out what has happened to Pavlović. I need to speak to him; it was too convenient him being released from jail and coming back to retrieve his cash and passport, just as I was at his apartment.'

'What, even though you nearly killed him?'

'Won't know until we try. He did try and stab me.'

'Well you had broken into his home; I'd be a little pissed if I were him, too.' Pet said, an eyebrow raised.

'Well possibly. We have to try, though, and I have almost forty thousand reasons he will want to speak to me. I also need to know what Cerović is up to. I don't think he suspects anything, as he has contacted us independently; I am sure that the dots haven't been joined up yet by the bad guys. Thinking about this, they've snatched Mike to find out what he knows. Whoever the mole is clearly suspects that Mike is out here looking into the weapons, but I don't think they know what he was planning with the undercover infiltration and contact with Cerović. Remember: Cerović initiated contact with us, and I think he is genuinely looking to get these batteries.'

'Are you sure about this? It feels a little reckless.'

'Maybe, but we have to explore it. We are the only ones looking out for Mike. I have to do this, Pet; Mike needs us. You get back to the hotel, I need you to find out exactly what Cerović and Pavlović are up to. We need to be listening to whatever Cerović is saying to the gang. We have an edge here, Pet. Let's use it.'

'What are you going to do?'

'I have an idea. It may not pan out, but I need to try.'

'Where are you going?' Pet asked, staring directly at Tom. 'I've seen that face before, and it worries me. It generally means that bad shit is going to go down.'

'I'm going to look for an old friend.'

'Okay…' said Pet.

'Do you have any clue as to what has happened to Pavlović?' Tom asked, quickly changing the subject.

Pet paused for a full second before turning to her computer and tapping at the keys. 'He discharged himself after he had some minor surgery to tidy up your inexpertly-performed attempt. Apparently, he refused to listen to staff, and upped and left just a while ago.'

Tom paused, considering this information for just a moment before he opened the door and said, 'Right. Go back to the hotel and start on the research. Look into the registration on the van, and we need a detailed look at what Cerović has been doing. I'm going to need to make contact with him as soon as possible to arrange something. He holds the key to this. If we keep tabs on him, then we find who is controlling this and then, by default, we find Mike. He must be alive otherwise why would they taser him rather than just slotting him?' He turned to look at her, holding out his hand. 'Do you have your passport?'

'Sure. Why?' Pet said, pulling a US passport from her bag and handing it to Tom.

'See how it goes, but I may be able to come up with something. In surveillance we used to talk of "painting the picture" by acting in a certain way.'

'You're being obtuse, as usual.' she said.

'Only because it may not work out. Look, I'll call you. Okay?'

'Sure thing. Be careful.'

'Am I ever anything else, Pet?' Tom smiled and picked up the attaché case, still containing the remainder of the cash and Pavlović's passport.

'Often. And it worries me when you have that look on your face.' She shook her head.

Tom smiled before striding out the door, slamming it shut behind him.

15

Tom sat inside a small, scruffy café, sipping a surprisingly good cup of coffee as he looked through the grimy window towards the residential block that housed Pavlović's place. He had been there about thirty minutes thinking through the whole situation. None of it felt right. There was clearly more to Pavlović than the intelligence picture suggested: the money, pistol and passport obviously suggested outside help, most probably American. Also, the paucity of the intelligence held by the Americans on Pavlović just didn't ring true. The fact that Pavlović had discharged himself from hospital was also telling, bearing in mind the serious injury Tom had inflicted. It all smacked of desperation; but desperation for what? To leave Bosnia? To go to America?

All he could do was to plan his next move, which meant talking to Pavlović, even if he didn't particularly want to talk.

Tom's mental gymnastics were interrupted by the sight of Pavlović descending the apartment block stairs and emerging onto the main street. He looked terrible with sallow skin, a laboured, shuffling gait, and sagging, desolate shoulders. His transformation from fearless and focused fighter to this shambolic wreck was remarkable.

Pavlović began walking away towards the rear of the block in a slow, pained fashion, his hand moving up to his throat as he walked, a grimace of pain on his face.

Tom dumped a banknote on the table and left the café, falling into step behind Pavlović, who was showing no awareness of his surroundings at all. Tom remained about fifty metres behind him as he crossed a car park in the middle of the quadrangle of apartments that led up to a small row of lock-up garages. As Pavlović approached the garages, Tom lingered at the window at a small newsagent, making a show of examining a row of handwritten cards advertising rooms to rent, massages, and other services. He used the reflection in the glass to observe Pavlović's movements as he used a key to open one of the garages, lifting the up-and-over door and disappearing inside. Tom circled the car park, keeping a view on the garage premises and using the cars as cover. In the middle of the car park was a small playground, about fifty metres from the garage, that comprised of a swing set and slide, a couple of young kids about eight years old playing happily on the swings.

Perfect cover, thought Tom as he sat on the chipped, dilapidated bench close by, peripherally watching the garage. To any casual glances he would be taken to be a parent watching out for his kids. As always, having a reason to be in any space was a crucial rule of surveillance. Tom took out his mobile phone and began casually scrolling through the apps, just like every other bored parent often did as their kids played. Opening the camera app he snapped a couple of shots of the open garage door. Zooming in, he could see that the space inside seemed to be fairly full of anonymous boxes, one of which Pavlović was currently sorting through.

After a few minutes, Pavlović appeared back at the door. He paused and turned to lower the garage door and snap a hefty padlock at the bottom on a hasp. Straightening up painfully, he then began a slow walk back towards the block, not looking about him at all, oblivious to his surroundings. From his unsteady gait, Tom couldn't help but think that he was still suffering the effects of anaesthesia from his recent minor surgery.

Jesus, thought Tom. *How desperate, or scared, must he be to want to get away in the state he's clearly in?* Tom remained seated, watching peripherally whilst seemingly looking at his phone, as Pavlović walked aching slowly back the way he had come.

The blip of an engine to Tom's left made him look up from his scrolling. A battered old motorcycle swung into view from a small intersection further up the road. It had a rider and pillion, both helmeted with dark visors. Something flashed in Tom's mind. This wasn't right. The timing wasn't right, and they didn't fit the environment. In Iraq, they'd have called this a "combat indicator" that something was wrong.

Tom stood and quickly followed Pavlović, closing the distance to about thirty metres as the motorcycle began to slowly move along the road, just behind him and on the opposite side of the road. A quick glance back revealed that they were showing no interest in Tom, instead totally fixated on Pavlović.

Pavlović turned left along a small one-way street, heading away from the quadrangle. The bike sped up and roared straight past Tom, turning sharply into the alley behind Pavlović, both occupants looking straight ahead, as the bike moved out of sight. Tom's stomach lurched and, fearing what was about to happen, he broke into a run, following the bike into the alleyway. As he rounded the corner, he immediately realised he was too late. The motorcycle was about thirty metres ahead, the pillion passenger's arm extended as the bike pulled up alongside the shuffling and unaware Pavlović. A pistol barked twice in the confined, narrow street, its report echoing off the walls of the buildings on either side. Pigeons took flight as Pavlović fell, dead before he hit the ground, all life snuffed out by the two slugs that had blown the side of his head clear off. Blood, brain, and skull fragments exploded from the exit wound and hit the wall in a Dali-like mess. Pavlović slumped to the floor like a collapsed pile of clothing, a widening pool of gore under his head.

The motorcycle turned quickly and roared as it accelerated out of the street and out of sight, followed by a brief, deep, impenetrable silence.

Tom quickly walked up to Pavlović's prone form, keeping away from the mess that was now the side of his skull. He knelt by the corpse and quickly located the bunch of keys in Pavlović's pocket, and then stood and walked away from the ruined body, heading away from the main road, his head down.

Picking his phone from his pocket he dialled Pet, who answered immediately. 'Talk to me Tom.'

'They got to Pavlović. They shot him dead, two on a motorbike. Can you meet me in an hour? There's someone I need to see.'

'Hang on, back up. They've shot Pavlović? Why? Are you okay?'

'Yeah, I'm fine. I just need to go and see someone, and I need to get away from here; police will be swarming all over this place soon. Can you see if you can find out what is going on? Monitor news and anything you can find out from police channels. I followed Pavlović to a lock-up a few hundred yards from his apartment; I need to see what's in there, but not at the moment.' Tom's voice remained level and even.

'Jesus, Tom, this situation is getting worse every minute.' Pet sounded shocked.

'Tell me about it. Look, I'll call you back but get to the city in an hour.' Tom rang off.

He and Pet needed fresh identities, and he had an idea who would be able to help them out. He delved into his mind and dredged out a memory that he had tried, many times, to banish.

Tom began walking, briskly; his mind focused, a plan forming.

16

In a city where so much had changed, what was remarkable was that, in this quarter of Sarajevo, nothing had changed. As he walked along the shabby side street, memories flooded and almost threatened to overwhelm his senses. Tom felt a strange sensation in his stomach, one he was not used to experiencing: a gnawing, fluttering hunger, but somehow different. It was nervousness.

The dreary side street was poorly repaired, with large potholes and uneven pavements. A dingy-looking bar was the only other occupied premises that seemed to have any sign of life. Then he saw it. The same glazed window, with the same neon sign, slightly askew in the window that simply said *"Cab"*, with a telephone number in peeling stickers on the grubby window. A lone elderly Mercedes sat in front of the building, bearing a yellow sign on the top that read simply, *"Sarajevo Taxi"*.

Tom was immediately catapulted back to the last time he had walked on this street, holding his Mama's hand as they went to meet the man who was to help them flee Sarajevo for Great Britain.

Tom took a deep breath and stepped through the open door into the dim and dingy office premises.

Everything was different, and yet everything was the same. Different linoleum, yet still sticky and cracked; the same chipped, wooden desk, but bearing a modern radio microphone and a computer terminal. Even the same ancient wall clock ticked rhythmically on the wall, the only noise pervading the cloying, intense silence.

The young woman sat behind the terminal looked at Tom with bored, suspicious eyes. She was familiar, of the same heavy build as the woman who had sat in the same chair on his last visit. Her face bore the same lines and the same heavy make-up. She was the same, yet she was different.

'You need a taxi?' she said in a thick Sarajevo accent.

'No. I need to speak to Braslav.'

'Who are you?' asked the woman, a sneer stretching across her face.

'An old friend.' Tom's voice remained low and even, despite the gnawing feelings of anxiety that this place was giving him. The last time he had been in this cab office was over a quarter of a century ago. He didn't even know if Braslav was alive, but something had compelled him to find out. He owed Braslav everything. Braslav was the reason that Tom had experienced the life he had, smuggling the twelve-year-old Tom and his Mama out of Bosnia after his father had been murdered by paramilitaries. Tom needed Braslav to be there.

'Why do you come here to see Braslav? Why do you think he is here?' The woman's voice was harsh and gravelly and the deep wrinkles around her mouth marked her out as a heavy smoker.

'This is Braslav's place. Please, tell him I am here.' Tom was convinced that Braslav would be here. The fact that the place had barely changed made it inconceivable that anyone other than the old man owned it.

'Name?'

'My name is Tomo,' said Tom, using the Bosnian variant of his name.

'Wait.' The woman sighed heavily, a scornful look on her heavy features. She pulled herself to her feet with a groan and disappeared through the open door shielded by a beaded curtain that Tom remembered from all those years ago. The beads clacked and clattered as she pushed through them, coughing a phlegm-laden hack as she moved from view.

Tom looked at the clock, his mind flashing back to his last visit. The cracked and stained old timepiece showed that it was just after 3pm. His mind went back to that date all those years ago, remembering his tearful Mama, newly widowed and desperately seeking help to flee what was to become the siege of Sarajevo. Tom remembered his confusion, his sense of loss, and his fear. Especially the fear.

The rattle of the beaded curtain jolted Tom away from his reverie.

Braslav stood looking at him, confusion etched across his meaty face. Like the cab office, Braslav was the same, but different. He was older, with a heavier build and with less hair. The monstrous moustache still bisected his face and the bright eyes still gleamed from behind the spectacles he now wore. He was dressed as before in a crisp shirt and pressed trousers. The same, but different. He leaned on a dark walking stick as he surveyed Tom. Despite his advanced age, his eyes shone with intelligence as realisation began to creep and a broad smile began to stretch across the rugged face, the silver moustache bristling.

'Tomo! Can it really be you?' he said, a tone of astonishment in his rich voice.

'Hello, Braslav. Yes, it's me.' Tom smiled, broadly advancing and holding out his hand, which Braslav took and shook warmly. He clapped Tom on the shoulder, showing teeth which were too white and even to be anything other than dentures.

'Little Tomo. Come through, come through. Ema make coffee for my friend, Tomo,' Braslav said to the woman at the control desk. She scowled as she heaved herself to her feet once again, shaking her head and muttering to herself.

Tom followed Braslav into a back office, where the old man sat behind a heavy desk heaped with papers, a grunt and a look of discomfort on his face as he did so.

'You must forgive me, Tomo. My mind remains strong, but my old bones are complaining as much as Ema does. It is good to see you, my boy, after all these years. You must tell me everything. How is England?'

'England is fine, Braslav. Life is good, thanks to you.'

As a twelve-year-old, Tom had not given a thought to how

Braslav had managed to get him and his Mama out of Bosnia during what must have been a really challenging time to do such a thing. He had just been grateful to be away from the bombs and shooting, and to be safe with his Mama so they could grieve his Papa in peace. Over time, especially once he had become a police officer, he had realised that Braslav had been some kind of "fixer".

'It was nothing my friend. Your father had done many favours for me, God rest his soul. How is your Mama? Is she...?' He left the sentence hanging in the air.

'She died not long after we arrived in England. Cancer.'

Braslav paused, sadness in his blue eyes. 'Oh, my boy, how tragic for you. First your father at the hands of those murderous paramilitaries and then God sees fit to take your Mama. I am so sorry. Aishe was a fine woman. So much misfortune for one so young, Tomo.' Braslav shook his head.

'It was sad, my friend, but I have been lucky, too. I was raised by wonderful foster parents and I have had a good life.' Tom smiled.

'Maybe God has a plan for you, then, Tomo. Anyway, what brings you to Sarajevo?'

Tom was about to answer when Ema shuffled into the office carrying two small cups filled with thick, dark liquid. She deposited the cups on a part of the desk not piled high with papers and left without a word.

'I need some help, Braslav. I am guessing that you are a man with many contacts.'

Braslav smiled as he picked up the coffee cup and took a sip, smacking his lips appreciatively. 'Ema is a complainer, but she makes the best Bosanska coffee in Sarajevo. Try it.'

Tom picked up the cup and took a sip of the strong, dark and bitter coffee. It reminded him of Turkish coffee, and it was heady and delicious.

'It's good coffee.'

'So, what can I help you with? I have been working in this city for decades so, yes, I know many people.'

Tom paused a moment. He suspected that Braslav had

connections to organised crime, but he didn't know to what extent. He needed his help, but he didn't want to explain the reasons why. One thing was sure: he couldn't tell Braslav he was a cop, and he certainly couldn't tell him the truth.

'I urgently need to procure passports for myself and a friend. European, preferably EU. I was hoping that you may know who to approach.'

Braslav paused and sat back in his chair, appraising Tom. 'I take it that the fact you are approaching me suggests that you cannot use a traditional method of obtaining a passport?'

'Yes. I would really rather not talk about why we need the documents. It's probably safer if you don't know, but it is urgent.' Tom returned Braslav's stare.

'What manner of trouble are you in? Maybe I can help in other ways, too?'

'Just the passports, Braslav. They need to be good quality. Good enough for me to cross borders with, and I need them as quickly as humanly possible. Preferably within hours, not days.'

'Is this trouble with the law?'

'Kind of. It's better I don't say, Braslav. I have the money to pay.'

Braslav stroked his moustache, clearly turning the situation over in his mind. 'Why do you approach me for this, my boy? What makes you think I have these connections?' A hint of a smile on his broad face suggested a little levity.

'Braslav, you managed to get my mother and me out of Bosnia when gangs of opposing militia were rampaging across the region. I didn't think about it at the time, but if my father sent us to you to make it happen, then I am assuming that he knew you were resourceful and had the necessary contacts. Let's not play games; can you help me?'

Braslav let out a guffaw of raucous laughter, his moustache twitching. 'Of course I have the contacts, my boy. I know everyone in this city. It can be done but will be expensive. I have influence so I will ensure you are not cheated, but I suspect for a good EU passport with photos put in and the electronic chip altered to match it will cost at least three thousand euros each.'

'That's fine. What do you need?'

Braslav, scrawled an email address on a piece of paper and handed it to Tom. 'Email photographs that you want to go on the passport to this and I will get it done. Then wait for my call. When I call, come with the cash and I will have the passports ready for you. I have a relationship with the best forger in Sarajevo and he will produce them quickly if I ask him. He owes me many favours as I supply him with much of his custom.' Braslav chuckled again. 'You are a smart boy, Tomo. All the years that pass and you know who to approach when you are in difficulty in this city. You are also clearly a good judge of character.' He chuckled once more.

'I know a fixer when I see one, Braslav,' Tom smiled.

'I prefer to be known as a "facilitator". I am a man who is adept at making and keeping friendships and relationships. Everyone knows that Braslav is an honest broker in a dishonest world.' He scribbled a phone number down on another scrap of paper which he passed to Tom. 'Call me later and I will confirm progress, okay?'

'I'm grateful, Braslav.'

'Be careful, Tomo. Not everyone in the underbelly of this city has my attitude to collaboration. Many would kill in a heartbeat just for a small amount of money.'

'Braslav, I'm always careful.' Tom stood.

'Even though I worry about what you are up to in my City, I wish you well, Tomo Novak.'

Tom walked out of the office and smiled as he passed Ema who was, once more, sat scowling behind her desk.

Back on the street again Tom dialled Pet's number.

'Tom.'

'Right, can you email passport photographs for both of us to the following email address?' Tom read the email address from the scrap of paper Braslav had given to him.

'Sure. I will get them from the databases easy enough. Why?'

'A very old contact is sourcing replacement ones for us.'

'Cool idea. I'm in the city again. What next?'

'Come and meet me. I want to check something; we then need to see what Cerović is up to.'

'He's still doing nothing since I last checked. I think your session last night has knocked him out.'

'He's a lightweight. All he had was beer, over-proof vodka, cocaine, and heroin.'

'I know. These kids, right?'

'No stamina. Okay, can you meet me as soon as possible, I'm at…'

Pet cut in. 'I know where you are. I can see you on a map: I'm tracking your phone, Detective. Someone has to look out for you. Stay where you are, I'll be there in ten,' Tom could hear a smile in Pet's voice.

17

'Okay, where to?' Pet asked, as Tom climbed back into the car. 'Head north. Pavlović had visited a lock-up garage just before he was shot. I want to see what is there,' Tom said. Pet had mounted her smart phone on the vehicle's dash with a cheap bracket. Tom moved the map to the location of the lock-up and dropped a blue electronic pin on the location.

'Follow the satnav, but we need to take care for police activity before committing to entering. I doubt they've connected the garage to him, especially as a passer-by removed the keys from him before anyone arrived.'

'Your good self, I take it?' asked Pet.

'Possibly. He wasn't carrying a bag when he left, so whatever he took would be pocketable. I'm very keen to get into the lock-up before the police do; I'm still convinced that there was far more to him than met the eye.' Tom stifled a deep yawn. He was seriously tired, but they needed to find some leads to get hold of Mike. Tom was convinced that he wasn't dead; the nature of his abduction wouldn't make sense if all they wanted was to kill him. He knew that Mike would have extensive training in resisting interrogation, he just hoped he could hold out long enough for them to get to him. Cerović was the key, of that Tom was sure.

The journey was quick through the fairly light traffic, and soon they were turning into the quadrangle and passing the street where Pavlović was shot. A small knot of ghoulishly interested passers-by stood at the entrance to the alleyway behind a line of police tape fluttering in the warm breeze. A lone cop stood, looking bored, at the boundary of the line and a couple of forensic-suited CSIs seemed to be inspecting and photographing the scene. A single white forensic tent was erected where Pavlović had fallen.

'Keep driving past the entrance and head beyond the lock-ups over there,' Tom pointed to the row of garages. 'Pull over into that one,' Tom said indicating to a vacant space in a small row of parking bays.

'What now, Detective?' she said, turning to face Tom as she switched off the Skoda's engine.

'We search Pavlović's lock-up. For an arms and military hardware supplier he had little in his apartment. Let's see what is in there.'

'What, now? With the cops just round the corner?'

'Yeah. I don't think for one second that there will be anything linking Pavlović to the lock-up. We don't have the luxury of time to wait for them all to leave.'

They both got out of the car and walked the thirty metres to the garage door. One of the benefits of Pavlović's recent demise was that anyone lurking in the area was more likely to be at the cordon observing the proceedings as the police worked the murder scene. Sarajevo, despite its violent past, is a comparatively safe city, so a homicide was rare enough to capture the attention of a curious public who were all now experts on procedures after watching countless episodes of CSI on American cable TV.

Tom felt for the keys that jangled in his pocket. The door was an up-and-over that seemed to have been heavily beefed up. Wrought iron bars had been secured into the concrete walls either side, and the door had been well reinforced with sheet metal over the flimsy garage door. The heavy padlock and hasp were fixed to a steel loop that had been firmly concreted into the ground. The key was a complex design but slid easily into the well-oiled padlock and turned smoothly, opening with a soft click. Tom removed the lock from the hasp and heaved the door up with a grunt. It was much heavier than he had expected.

'Looks like Pavlović cared about security.'

'I was just thinking the same thing,' Pct said, her eyebrows raised behind her dark spectacles.

The sunlight flooded into the garage revealing metal shelves all full of wooden crates, cardboard boxes, and a few hessian sacks. Tom located a light switch and flicked it on, quickly closing the door behind him. A box of nitrile gloves was positioned on the floor by the entrance: clearly Pavlović was forensically aware and very careful. Tom was always amazed at how lax many criminals were about forensic matters, so clearly Pavlović had been a cut above the average. Something as simple as a pair of gloves would prevent fingerprints and DNA transferring onto firearms, ammunition and any other contraband used by criminals.

Tom plucked two pairs out of the box and tossed one to Pet. 'Glove up. No need to leave anything behind.'

He stood and surveyed the garage with a detached, professional eye. This was meat-and-drink to Tom: searching premises for evidence.

'Okay. You start this end, I will do the other, and we will meet in the middle. I want to be out of here as soon as we can.' Tom said, snapping a pair of the blue gloves on his hands.

'What are we looking for?'

'Anything that looks bad. Anything that gives us a clue as to who Pavlović is.' In reality, Tom didn't know what they were looking for, but his instinct told him that Pavlović was not who they thought he was.

Tom lifted the lid on the first crate, which was empty apart from dense black foam with pistol-shaped cut-outs. The next crate contained tightly packed boxes of 9mm parabellum ammunition. Tom whistled through his teeth. There were thousands of rounds in there, all US manufactured, in red and white boxes.

'Check this out,' Tom said. Pet joined him.

'Jesus. That's thousands of rounds of ammo. By the looks of it all from US manufacturers. How has a low-grade arms dealer gotten his hands on this? Another thing: why the hell isn't he flagging up more on intel systems?' she said, her eyes wide.

'Let's keep going. We don't have long, and we really don't want to be caught here by the police.'

The next crate's lid was loose on the top and, at first sight, appeared to be empty with a pile of polystyrene chips littering the bottom of the crate. Tom dug his hands down into the chips and immediately stubbed a finger on something hard and metallic. Stifling a curse, he gripped the metallic object and pulled it upwards, revealing a Heckler & Koch MP5SD, with a bulbous integrated silencer.

'How the hell has he got hold of this?' Tom said, removing the empty magazine, racking the slide, and checking that the firearm was unloaded. The weapon had a light sheen of oil and looked brand new. He wasn't surprised to see that the identifying number had been removed, a deep, rough groove where the serial number should have been.

'What is it?' asked Pet.

'A Heckler and Koch MP5SD, the silenced version of the MP5. It has an integrated suppressor that turns the 9mm supersonic ammo into subsonic and cuts most of the noise down. It even had an aftermarket low-light optic fitted and, even more unusual, an underslung sure-fire torch secured on a bracket at the front with a remote-control cable secured front handgrip guard.'

Tom pressed the rubberised pressel and a beam of white light flooded out from the LED torch. 'This gets more interesting, Pet. This is a top quality and really expensive weapon system. Special Forces use them, and they are seriously hard to come by. I've never seen one on the black market. More to the point, there was clearly a whole crate of the bloody things and there's only one left. This means that whoever we are facing is armed with reliable, modern weaponry that your average criminals definitely can't get hold of. Just who are we dealing with, and who provided these weapons to Pavlović?'

Tom looked at the weapon admiringly as he extended the telescopic stock and raised it into his shoulder, looking along the iron sights. He had fired countless rounds at various ranges in the past through identical weapons and he knew how effective they were. Handling the submachine gun almost gave him a comfortable feeling, such was his familiarity with it. He closed the telescopic butt with a snap and lay the MP5 on the ground, reverentially.

He dug down again into the crate and pulled out a black canvas magazine holster that contained three empty thirty-round magazines for the weapon, which he placed on the ground with the MP5.

The next two boxes were empty, save for some packaging, but the next, a stout wooden crate, was nailed shut. Tom found a crowbar hanging neatly on a nail on the wall and quickly prised the lid off the crate. Six rectangular batteries, all brown/grey in colour and encased in ruggedized military looking plastic. Each was marked with the brand name *"Saft"*, and had metal fold-down carry handles on the side.

'I've seen batteries like this before,' said Tom. 'Can you search the web for *Saft* 28-volt battery boxes? If my memory serves me well these are used as part of missile systems that we once had a presentation on when I was a Marine.'

'Hold up,' said Pet scrolling at her smart phone before saying, 'Your memory does serve you well, Detective. Saft Industries, 28-volt lithium battery box. Used on US Army target acquisition systems. Preferred option owing to its low weight and being maintenance-free and an ability to work in all temperatures. And only available to military. You think this could power a directed-energy weapon?'

'How much do they weigh?'

'Specs say fifteen kilos.'

'I'm sure it could but that's really heavy for a man-portable weapon. Let's see if there are any more.'

They continued searching the various boxes, and it seemed that most were empty apart from two. One contained a ruggedized pelican case that contained a label with the logo *"Saft McEc2"* and a red and black charging lead both rolled neatly within the lid.

'Bingo. Here is the field charger. I've definitely seen this type of thing before. They'll charge different types of battery and all operate in poor conditions.'

'So at least we know what we can supply to Cerović, then.'

'Yes. But you know what worries me?' said Tom, scratching his face.

'What?'

'The empty crates. All these empty crates suggest that Pavlović had already supplied a significant amount of arms and ammo to these guys. I'm also very curious as to how a supposed small-time Bosnian arms dealer managed to get his hands on a significant quantity of US-made or supplied weapons and ammunition.'

'You think the MP5 is US-supplied?'

'Definitely. Same erased serial number technique. We can be sure that these weapons are supplied by Uncle Sam, if indirectly.'

'Well that's a nice thought.'

'Isn't it.' Tom said, mustering as much sarcasm as he could.

'What are we going to do with this stuff?' Pet said, indicating towards the firearms and batteries.

'Leave them here for now and lock up tight. I take it all your research found no link between Pavlović and this lock-up?'

'Nothing at all.'

'My guess is that whoever stores this type of weaponry in a garage won't register it to himself. We don't want to be driving around with all this kit until we absolutely have to.'

'Who are we dealing with here, Tom? This kind of weaponry—American weaponry and ammo—shouldn't be in the hands of a minor, low-grade arms dealer from Sarajevo who advertises on the dark web.' Pet's face showed confusion and concern.

'My guess: it all came from an American. What we need to know is who and why.'

18

They sat in their hotel room, Pet staring at the screen of her laptop intensely as Tom made tea.

'Any luck with the decryption of Cerović's data?' Tom asked handing over a steaming mug.

'He's more careful than I gave him credit for. I won't bore your techno-averse brain with it, but the encryption was of a far more complex type than I first imagined. The first layer was real easy, but the subsequent ones are far more challenging. If I had more processing power it would be quicker, but I am being careful which servers I am accessing remotely.'

'Fair enough. How about his phone?'

'He's still not moved from his apartment. Looks like he's down for the day; I guess hard narcotics and liquor does that to a dude.'

'Any phone activity?'

'Not really. I have downloaded his call data, but I've not had a chance to analyse it yet, we've been on the move so much.' Pet stared intently at the screen and it was clear that the challenge of the encryption on Cerović's computer data was frustrating her.

'Okay. We need to prioritise here as to what is actually going to give us the best chance of finding Mike. I think we can be clear that these weapons are central to this. Nothing else makes sense, agreed?' Tom asked, sipping his tea.

'Sure, but what else do we know?'

'It's clear that no one knew for certain why he was in Sarajevo. Rudy didn't seem to know, that's for sure. But it is really odd that Rudy seems to have disappeared from the Embassy as well.'

'Do we think the bad guys have him as well?' asked Pet.

'No way of knowing, but my instinct says no.'

'So, what next?' Pet asked, turning back to her screen.

'We need to stir this hornets' nest a little. I'm going to call Cerović and let him know that I have batteries. Let's see what that prompts. He will have to call the rest of the network. He is just there for his electronics expertise, there is no way that he is the brains behind anything else. Get ready to monitor his phone. I think that we should risk activating the microphone on his phone so we can hear half of any call he makes after I tell him I have the batteries.'

'Sure. I'm ready when you are,' Pet said, clamping on a set of headphones.

Tom picked up his phone and dialled. Cerović answered almost immediately. 'Hey, buddy, I've been waiting for you to call. You got something for me?' his nasal New York drawl echoed down the handset.

'I have six items for you. I think they will be suitable for your requirements,' Tom said, flatly. Pet signalled with a thumbs up, a smile, and a nod. That was good; the microphone monitor was working.

'Awesome. What type and what spec?'

'*Saft* battery box, 28-volt, lithium-ion. Used by the Americans for missile target acquisition systems. Can be used in all climates. I have a field charging system as well.'

Tom could hear a tapping of keys in the background and he could imagine Cerović furiously researching the batteries online as they spoke.

'Man, they look perfect, if a little heavy. Fifteen kilos but lots of reserves and the charge profile looks adequate. When can you get them to me?'

'Tomorrow?'

'Tomorrow is good, my man. How about tonight, you and me go paint this town red again? Try and get to the night club if I don't pass out again, you motherfuckin' animal?' He guffawed and Pet winced at the irritating, high-pitched sound. It made Tom realise that, however this situation turned out, Cerović's days were numbered if he was this irritating when in the company of brutal militia criminals.

'I can't tonight. Maybe tomorrow after I deliver batteries.'

'Man, I'm gonna be busy once you hit me up with them. I will have lots of work to do and my people won't want me going missing with you,' he laughed uproariously, once more. Tom couldn't help notice Pet shaking her head at the noise in her ears. Tom smiled, at least the microphone monitor was working.

'I'll call you in the morning to confirm a time and place. They are heavy and there is six of them plus the charger so you will need a car.'

'I have a car, don't worry about that, dude.'

'I mean, they are in a big crate, with a suitcase-sized field charger. It can't be a Smart car.'

'It's cool, I have an SUV: plenty big enough. How much?'

'A thousand euros for each battery and five hundred for the field charger.'

'Okay, that's cool.'

'I'll call you tomorrow,' Tom said and hung up.

'Jesus, that man is really annoying,' Pet said, pulling her headphones off her head and unplugging the cord. A hiss erupted from the laptop speakers and a tapping of keys could be heard accompanied by a muffled coughing. The sound of a TV could be heard in the background.

'You should try spending a few hours with him,' Tom said.

'I'll pass, thanks.'

Further clicking sounds erupted from the computer screen and then the sound of a phone number being called was audible.

'He's making a call. I'll run the number and see what comes out,' Pet said, that familiar look of utter focus on her face as half a conversation began to come from the speakers.

'Babić, it's Stefan. Yeah, I have sourced the batteries, through a contact… Six of them… Yeah, I know we need eight but it's all he has… I'm sure he can get more, but this gives me something to work with. They're military spec and will be perfect. No way could we get these by conventional means… Tomorrow… Not sure… I'll be fine… Don't worry, Babić, I can handle this… it's only batteries, he's just a dude off the dark web, no need to have him see your face… Man, you worry too much… Dude, I negotiated a great price, ten thousand euros… I have the dough to pay him here and you can reimburse me. I will bring them to the farm as soon as I have them. I want to get straight onto integrating them. Okay. Laters, my man.' The phone clicked as it was set down on a hard surface.

Pet snorted a chuckle, 'I think our friend is definitely gonna get whacked. He's ripping them off.'

Tom paused for a second before speaking, a perplexed look on his face. 'Fifteen kilos is really heavy for a battery powering a man-portable weapon. If it's shoulder-launched then maybe, but if the battery alone is that heavy, the whole weapon is going to weigh a ton. I'm not sure this makes sense.' Tom paused for a second, the cogs turning, before he shook his head and continued. 'I think we can chalk that up as a worthwhile exercise. We now know there are eight weapons, they are being built somewhere near Sarajevo on a farm and that Babić won't be present at the handover. We also now know for a fact that Cerović and Babić are the key. This gives us all sorts of options. A farm would also be a pretty good place to hold Mike if they want to keep all their resources in one place. Can you tell where Babić is?'

Pet screwed her face up as she looked at her screen. 'I'm struggling to access the cell site database. The phone is a burner predictably but the CIA intelligence profile I am piggybacking doesn't have the correct access levels. I could try to hack the cell phone company, but that would be using a lot of time that we don't have. I could use my own profile, but it risks exposing us.'

'Don't bother. We don't need to take any risks; Cerović will take us to them. Do you have any surveillance kit with you?'

'What are you thinking?'

'GPS tracker?'

'Won't his phone suffice? I can monitor that in real time,' Pet said.

'I don't want to risk that he doesn't take it, or that the group has enough operational security procedures that he has to switch off. We can't afford to lose him, but we also can't follow conventionally into a rural location without showing out.'

'I have nothing with me, sorry. Minimal kit only was Mike's brief.' She shrugged.

Tom paused, the cogs almost visibly turning. 'Okay, no worries. I'm sure I can come up with something.' Without waiting for a response, he picked up his phone and dialled.

'*Zdravo?*' Braslav's voice was rough down the phone.

'Braslav, it's Tomo.'

'My boy, good to hear from you. Good news: your passports are ready now. I have them ready for you at the office,' he said, sounding particularly pleased with himself.

'You work fast, my old friend. I figured you were well connected but coming up with passports in a few hours is impressive.'

'To reach my age in this city, my boy, you need contacts and influence. When will you come?'

'I'm coming now.' Tom looked at his watch: it was 5:30pm. 'I'll be with you by six.'

'Be careful, my boy. A man who needs two passports in a few hours has enemies, and Sarajevo is a small city. There are eyes on every street corner.'

'I'll be there soon.' Tom hung up.

'What now?' asked Pet.

'We go and get our new passports and then we head out of the country.'

'You make it sound simple, Tom. Why do I get the feeling that it will be anything *but* simple?'

'It *is* simple. Come on, bring your computer and internet access but we'll leave anything we don't want to take over the border here. Last thing I want to take is thousands of dollars and a pistol. Come on, let's get going. We need them to think we've fled like rats deserting a sinking ship.'

'Why is it, Novak, that any time we hang out together it is trouble? One day, let's just go out for dinner and a show,' Pet shook her head and sighed.

'Pet, I promise you that after this we'll have the best dinner and musical in the West End.'

'Musicals suck. I was just joking. Let's get Mike back.'

19

Pet drove the Skoda as they made their way back to Sarajevo, Tom directing her to stop briefly at a large pet store in a small trading estate on the outskirts of the city. He disappeared into the store briefly before returning clutching a bag.

'I'm sure you have a good reason, Detective, but try as I might I can't think of why now would be the time to visit a pet store, beyond some weird English pun about my name.' She looked quizzically at the brown paper bag from which Tom produced a blister pack, which he then began to open.

'You know me, Pet. I'm improvising. We often had to make-do-and-mend in hostile environments when I was in the military. This is no different: I'm just thinking ahead. I also needed a couple of things from the hardware store in there, too. Head north and turn left soon.'

'It looks a little like you just bought a dog collar.'

'You would be mostly correct. It's a GPS dog tracker. No one likes to lose their pooch; I thought with a bit of adaption we could secure it to Cerović's car, and it would be as good as a vehicle tracker. It uses GSM and I got a SIM with it, so I can't see why it won't work.'

'Cool idea. You're just like the *"A-Team"*. What's next, building a tank from rudimentary materials whilst imprisoned in an improbably well-stocked workshop?'

'You're too young for the *A-Team*. Improvise, overcome, adapt: what we used to say in the Corps. Do you have an adapter, so I can top the charge up using the car cigarette lighter port?'

'Sure, there will be something in my bag in the side pocket.

I pity the fool that messes with my bag man,' Pet made a poor attempt at a deep gravelly voice.

'That is the worst Mister T impression I have ever heard,' Tom sniggered.

Tom reached into her computer bag and found an adapter. He plugged the charger cable into the adapter and plugged it into the cigarette lighter port. The green light on the side of the small rubber-covered GPS monitor blinked to indicate that it was charging.

'Nice one. Once fully charged it should be good for a few days: more than enough for us.'

'As always, Detective, I'm impressed.'

'Simple stuff, Pet. Right, pull over here. I am going to go and see a man about some passports. He's probably the shy type, so can you wait here? Maybe keep working on the decryption, or something.'

Pet sighed. 'Tom, I understand that your contact doesn't want any unknowns, but can we ease up on the patronising tone, maybe? The decryption is currently running remotely using a server bank I have access to. I am probably one of only a handful of analysts capable of decrypting this type of encryption with the facilities I have available. I am giving it everything I have.'

Tom sat back in his seat and looked at Pet, suddenly deflated and embarrassed. 'Look, I'm sorry. I know you are the best out there at this kind of thing, and I can't do this without you. I'm just a little anxious that we get to Mike as soon as we can. I owe him my life and that of my foster-family.'

'It's fine, Detective. I owe Mike plenty as well, but right here, right now, I can't speed up the decryption.'

'I know. I'm sorry.'

'It's cool. Stop apologising and go do your thing. I will run the number that Cerović called Babić on, see where that takes me,' Pet said, reaching into her bag and pulling out her laptop.

Tom opened his mouth to apologise once more, but the word stuck in his throat once he saw that Pet's face was set in the familiar frown of deep concentration.

He slammed the car door and strode off towards Braslav's office, just one street away. As he walked, he thought deeply, trying to come up with a cogent plan. He was woefully under-resourced, so mounting a rescue by storming wherever they were holding Mike just wasn't an option. He needed Babić and his men to relax, which meant him and Pet appearing to leave the country.

Walking into the office he nodded at Ema and said, 'Braslav is expecting me,' as he walked straight past her desk into the back offices. He found Braslav where he had last seen him, sat at his desk with his face glued to an iPad that Tom could see was open on a news feed.

'Tomo, my boy, you are punctual,' he said without looking up.

'How did you know it was me?'

'Eyes everywhere, my friend. I don't know why I read this thing. All bad news, murder and mayhem. I read here about a gangland execution just close to here. A young man shot dead, in what police call "a mafia-style gangland hit". Apparently, the victim was armed with a pistol himself. Tragic.'

He looked up from his tablet and fixed Tom with a hard, searching stare through thick-lensed spectacles.

'It's strange, Tomo. I know most of what goes on in this city, and yet none of my associates have any knowledge of such a gangland-style assassination. Normally I would have heard rumours.'

Tom shrugged. 'Out of towners, maybe?'

'My police source say that the victim was a gun-runner who had links all over the Balkans, but no one in my extensive network has any idea who is responsible.'

Tomo just shrugged once more.

'Anyway, to business. I take it you have the necessary funds?' Braslav smiled widely.

'If you can take dollars. I'd rather not change it for euros or marks right now, if that's okay?'

'The US dollar is always welcome with me, Tomo. Shall we say three thousand five hundred dollars to allow for the exchange rate?'

'Fine by me.' Tom reached into his pocket and counted out thirty-five hundred-dollar bills, which he deposited on the desk in front of Braslav.

Without looking at the currency, Braslav reached into a drawer in his desk and flipped a brown manilla envelope at Tom. He caught it and opened it to find two brand-new looking German passports. Flipping to the bio-data page of the first he saw the picture of Pet with the name *Greta Schmidt*. Turning to his he found that his given name was *Hans Graumann*. Flipping through the passports, Tom was impressed with the quality. All the relevant security features were present and if he didn't know better, he'd be convinced that they were genuine items.

'These are excellent, Braslav.'

'Of course. I only work with professionals, Tomo. Both are genuine, using the details of Germans who died in infancy. My contact has the ability to directly input the photos and the bio-data chip will work as would be expected. I can assure you will have no difficulty crossing borders. There is even a border stamp showing you entering recently from Croatia. Your passage out of Bosnia and into Europe will be smooth, you have my guarantee.'

Tom nodded his thanks before sitting back in the chair. He realised that now wasn't the best time to be asking Braslav, but he also knew that this may be his last opportunity to ask a question that he had wanted answering for some time.

'Braslav, can I ask you a question about my father?'

Braslav surveyed Tom from behind his huge, bushy eyebrows. 'Of course, my boy.'

'A little while ago someone said some things about my father, and I need to know if they are true.'

Braslav took off his glasses and polished the lenses, his discomfort obvious. This was clearly a topic he had been hoping wouldn't arise. 'What type of things?'

'This person told me that my father was a killer. That he used to work for Tito before the fall of Yugoslavia, eliminating his enemies,' Tom eyed Braslav closely as the question hung in the air, like a fug.

'Some things are better left in the past, my boy,' Braslav said, his eyes clouding a little.

'Braslav, I have to know. I deserve to know. I have spent my whole life not knowing who I am,' Tom's voice quivered, just slightly, his teeth clenched. Ever since the dying paramilitary had made the allegations about his father, he had needed to know if this was true or not.

Braslav sighed and rubbed his face. He paused for what seemed an age. 'Your father was a loyal servant of Tito, this is true. We both were.'

'That doesn't answer my question, Braslav.' Tom's voice was firm and determined

Braslav closed his eyes and sighed, the pain was clear in his eyes when they reopened.

Tom knew. In that moment, he knew, beyond all doubt. The silence in the room was deep and cloying

Tom stood and left the dingy cab office without a backwards glance.

20

Davud Babić sat at a small scruffy table in the farmhouse and opened up the tablet computer, his face a blank mask. He clicked an icon and opened up the secure messaging app that his lead investor had insisted they use for all communications. He had no clue as to the identity of this investor, whoever they were, and in reality he didn't want to know. As long as the money kept appearing in his offshore account or bitcoin wallet, he really wasn't bothered.

There was a soft buzzing for a few moments before the call was answered with a digitally altered voice.

'Yes.'

'You requested an update.'

'Go ahead.' The voice was mechanical and projected no emotion or intonation whatsoever.

'All eight weapons are built, and we are just waiting for the power sources, which Cerović is in the process of procuring.'

'Timings?'

'Very soon.'

'Excellent. Will they be adequately powerful for our purposes?'

'Cerović assures me they will.'

'What of the American?'

'He is claiming to be a low-ranking Embassy official. He is being interrogated as we speak.'

'That is good. We need to know what he knows or suspects of our plans. We cannot afford any interfering. My co-investors have placed very large sums of money into the appropriate funds. We must stick to the timetable. Do you have enough men in Sarajevo?'

'Yes. Most of my men are currently in the theatre of operations, ready to deploy immediately once we are ready to proceed. We do not need many operatives in Sarajevo, they are better served at the objective.'

'What does your contact at the Embassy know?'

'Little. Brogan is some kind of trouble-shooter, but he is powerful and only used in high-threat situations. I'd prefer to know what he knows before we move the weapons.'

'Very well. Proceed.' The line was suddenly dead.

The door opened and Risto stepped inside the farmhouse kitchen.

'Anything?' Babić asked.

'No,' Risto never used any unnecessary words.

'Sticking to his cover story?'

'Yes. Despite several hours of tactical questioning.'

'He has clearly been well trained, which is more evidence that his story is nonsense. Entry clearance officers are not trained in resistance-to-interrogation. Continue for the time being; it hasn't been long enough yet and we still have some time before we have to move. I want to know what he knows. Step it up: worse stress positions, louder music. You know the routine; we have completed enough interrogations together.'

'As you wish, Babić.'

21

Tom climbed back into the Skoda and tossed the passport to Pet. 'Here you go, Greta,' he said in a flat voice.

'Everything okay?'

'Everything's fine. Best get familiar with the passport, you should know who you are,' he said, putting on his seat-belt.

'Sure you're okay?'

'Pet, I'm fine, seriously,' Tom managed a smile, but it failed to reach his eyes.

Pet stared at him, a concerned look on her face for a moment. Realising there was little point in asking further, she said, 'So, I'm still a German. That's convenient, although I don't like the name. Schmidt is far too common and, boy, Greta is the least fashionable name, ever. This looks like a good passport, by the way,' Pet said, leafing through the document.

'Do you know, I don't even know your surname, Pet.'

'We all like to keep ourselves mysterious in the intelligence world, Novak,' Pet smiled.

'Embarrassing name, then?' Tom said, returning her smile, which offset the clouds that seemed to have taken up residence in his eyes. He looked at his own passport. 'I'm Hans Graumann, by the way.'

'Man, that's a dull name, in fact, could we have been *given* more boring, old person names?' asked Pet.

'You still haven't told me your real name.' Tom persisted.

Pet didn't reply, just shook her head a little.

'Come on, I won't laugh.'

Pet sighed deeply once more. 'This is the reason I have very

little to do with my folks anymore. My name is Petra Von Trapp.'
She looked directly and piercingly at Tom, with a withering look
as if daring him to mock her.

Tom's face remained deadpan, 'Oh. Is that it?'

Pet's voice remained flat as she stared at Tom, her eyes narrowed.
'You don't get it?'

'What?'

'The name. Von Trapp? My youth was miserable because of it.'

'Why?'

'You're taking the piss, Novak.'

'Sorry, Pet, I don't follow.'

Pet stared at Tom, her eyes flinty. 'Okay. What now?'

'We take a little road trip.'

'Where?'

'We're going to Croatia; Dubrovnik, specifically.'

'How far to Dubrovnik?' Pet asked, a tone of resentment in her
voice.

'Four hours or thereabouts.'

'So at least eight hours in the car travelling overnight. Thanks,
Detective. You will be on top form when handing the batteries
over to Cerović, tomorrow.'

'I will just look tired and dangerous.'

'Come on let's get going, Detective. I hope your banter is going
to improve if I have to spend hours in the car with you.'

'Come on, Pet, I'm the Archbishop of Banterbury.'

'What?' Pet raised her eyebrows.

'Sorry, a saying I nicked from Buster. Probably best you get
some sleep. We've had a busy few days and it is only going to get
busier.'

A muffled ping emanated from the vicinity of Pet's bag.

'Let's swap seats, Detective. That tone is indicating that the
encryption on Cerović's computer files has been broken. Either
that or my battery is about to die, and I am about to have a very
red face.'

'I'm sure it's the former; I have absolute faith in you.'

They quickly swapped positions and Pet settled into the passenger seat, digging into her bag and pulling out her laptop while Tom settled behind the wheel, adjusting the seat backwards.

'Bingo,' said Pet, a smile spreading across her face. 'We're in. That jerk thinks he's so clever, but his encryption couldn't keep me out.'

'Anything interesting?' Tom said as he pulled away from the kerb.

'Nothing is jumping out immediately but hold up, I'm only just in. I'll need some time to run this through e-discovery software. He seems to have lots of schematics.' Her fingers danced across the keys, her face set in a mask of rapt concentration.

'Okay. I also have the schematic for some kind of energy weapon, talk of electromagnetic and microwave energy waves. Shit. Lots of circuit diagrams, I'm scanning, but we will get more out soon. This will be awesome evidence. This really is a silver bullet.'

'Unfortunately, I doubt that,' Tom said shaking his head.

'Why? It's all here.' Pet looked genuinely flummoxed.

'We are off-books. I doubt Mike told anyone about what we were going to be doing, and this was all gained by irregular surveillance and data interception. We would probably end up in as much trouble as Cerović. Our only objective is to get Mike back; that's the only reason for what we're doing.'

Pet sighed deeply and shook her head as she typed. 'You want to know something worse?'

'Probably not,' Tom said with a sinking feeling.

'There is an email trail here. It is a little cryptic, but there is talk of eight devices and he is planning to build more. He just needs the power sources then he is good to go. The email exchange talks about high value targeting, and effects on stock and currency prices. Jesus. Just how big is this?'

Tom stared straight ahead, his jawline set. 'Do we know where the first targets will be?'

'No. It could be anywhere. So, what next?'

'We carry on as before. We travel to Croatia and you keep

analysing that data. We need to know where and when they are planning to deploy them. We then deliver the batteries to Cerović, get Mike back, and stop them doing what they are planning.'

'But how?'

'By any means necessary. Whatever it takes, Pet.'

*

The journey through the setting sun to the border crossing at Ivanica and into Dubrovnik went smoothly. The unsmiling border guard paid them scant attention as they left Bosnia, and the guard manning the post on the Croatia side barely looked up from his screen as he pressed each of their CIA-issued US passports against the electronic reader.

'Purpose of visit?' he asked in bored-sounding English.

'Travelling to Europe,'

'Enjoy your trip,' he said, handing the passports back, already looking for the next person waiting in the queue.

Once they had cleared the border they headed towards the old city of Dubrovnik on the coastal road, Tom still driving. The journey had passed quickly enough, Pet still running checks on her laptop trying to data mine the depths of Cerović's stolen data. Very soon it became acutely obvious that Cerović was far more careful than she had originally given him credit for.

'What now, Detective?'

'We head up the coast road to Neum where we cross back into Bosnia on the German passports, we got from Braslav. It probably wouldn't be wise to just turn round and cross back into Ivanica on different passports. Even the bored-as-bollocks border guards may raise an eyebrow, and we could do without the grief. Can you book us on the next ferry to Bari? Use your CIA credit card and the Identities on the two US passports. We need to be firmly on the radar, so that whoever is feeding info to Babić and the others will think we are on our way back to the Schengen Zone. Once there they won't know where we have gone and will hopefully relax a bit.'

'Sure. But can we be sure they'll know to look for those names?'

'We can't be, but they are the only identities we entered Bosnia on, and someone would have had to record us as entering the Embassy on those passports with Mike. If they have us flagged, which I'm betting they have, we will raise a big red flag. You using your credit card may just confirm it enough for them to switch off a little.'

'Okay, I'll book them now. There is no ferry until 10pm tomorrow; is that cool?'

'That will be perfect. Means they have nowhere to look for us; they will assume we will be keeping our heads down in Dubrovnik until the ferry leaves. There are so many small guest houses that they wouldn't be able to even begin to know where to start searching. If they do try, it will just waste loads of time and resources when we will actually be travelling back to Sarajevo.'

'Okay, done. Are we heading back now?'

Tom nodded. 'I don't want to waste time, so we will cross the border as soon as we can. We need fuel soon, so we will have a quick stop for some food and then cross. It's almost two hours to Neum and then under four back to Sarajevo so we need to crack on.'

'Awe-some,' Pet enunciated every ounce out of the word, her voice thick with sarcasm.

'Such devastating sarcasm, Petra,' Tom said, stifling a smile in the gloom of the car's interior.

'I'm gonna punch you in the face in a moment, Detective.' She paused to assess the impact of her words which only drew a puckish grin from Tom. 'Anyway, kindly refer to me as Miss Schmidt.' She enunciated both words harshly, but Tom could detect the humour that lurked within the vowels and consonants.

'Sorry, Greta. If I buy you a late dinner will you forgive me?'

'Unlikely. There is a rest stop in a kilometre, let's stop there.'

They stopped briefly for fuel and a pile of junk food that Pet selected.

'Okay, let's go. We have a way to go and I need to call Cerović,' said Tom as they returned to the car.

'It's real late. Will he be up?'

'I don't care. I need to present as the ruthless arms dealer who has been sourcing expensive military spec power cells. I don't mind waking him up; I want to keep the initiative.'

'Can we have our coffee over there at the picnic tables before we set off? Be nice to drink it in slightly nicer surroundings than an ageing Skoda.' Pet pointed to a picnic area on a stretch of grass that led towards the sea. It was a pleasant and clear evening with a warm, gentle breeze and Tom could see no harm in doing so.

'Sure. Ten minutes won't make much difference.' They walked over and sat down, Tom yawning as he did so, a sudden weariness overcoming him.

'You tired?' Pet said yawning along with him.

'A little. It's been an intense few days, to say the least.'

Pet yawned deeply once more, rubbing her face with her hands before looking at Tom slightly quizzically.

'Why don't you catch yawns?'

'Pardon?'

'I've been with you loads recently. I'm really tired and have been yawning loads, but you never catch them. I've never seen that before.'

Tom simply shrugged, but he knew exactly what she was talking about; his friend and colleague Buster had made the same point recently. It was an evolutionary and empathic response in social groups for yawns to be catching: for one person's yawn to spread to others. Tom had a bit of an issue with empathy; it was an area of his psyche that he preferred not to delve too deep into. It was disturbing and was the reason that his foster-father's code of "always do right, boy" was how he had found a moral compass.

'I need to call Cerović,' Tom said, brusquely.

'Way to change the subject, dude,' Pet said, sipping her coffee with a half-smile touching her face.

Ignoring the comment, Tom pulled out his mobile and called

125

Cerović.

'Man, I wondered when you were gonna call. Hold up, I need to get out of this bar or I won't be able to hear you.' Cerović shouted over the deep thump of heavy dance music.

After a moment, the background noise faded. 'Tarzan?' Cerović's voice sounded slurred.

'Yeah. I'm ready to deliver the batteries to you. Tomorrow okay?'

'Sure, buddy, sure. I'm always ready.' He hiccupped just slightly and the thick, gummy sound in his voice told its own story. Cerović was clearly indulging in his favourite pastime.

'You don't sound ready. I need to get rid of these batteries tomorrow, I have another trip planned to get some more power-cells and my contact won't wait. I need to meet you tomorrow morning. Do you have the cash?'

'Sure, man. Six-five like we agreed, right?'

'Yes. You need to leave the bar and go home now. I will call you in the morning and I need you ready to receive the merchandise within half an hour of calling. Understand: no more drink or drugs. I have others who want to buy.'

'Sheesh, whadda you, my mum?' Cerović let out a high-pitched laugh and Tom could tell he was high.

'Stefan, I just need you to meet me tomorrow. I am leaving Sarajevo straight after meeting you tomorrow, as my contact wants me to collect more batteries tomorrow afternoon. If you're late, the deal's off. We can go out and drink again once our business is complete, understand?' Tom's voice was hard and, he hoped, had an intimidating quality. He wanted Cerović on the defensive.

'Sure. Sure thing, buddy, I'm leaving now.'

'Wait for my call tomorrow.' Tom hung up. He turned to Pet. 'He is stoned and drunk and clearly out clubbing. He will be a mess tomorrow, but I may be able to turn that to our advantage.'

'How so?'

'Well, let's say he won't be paying the greatest of attention to what we are doing. Come on, let's get moving; he may make a call now and I want to see who he calls.'

Pet sighed. 'I was enjoying my coffee. You are a hard task master; I feel sorry for people who work for you.'

'They all love me, Pet. Come on.'

They both drained their lukewarm coffees and got back in the Skoda, Pet already opening her laptop, her fingers flashing across the keys.

'He's not making any calls quickly. I suspect he is back in the bar, despite his BS to you. In fact, scrub that: he's not moving anywhere. If I was a guessing girl, I'd say he's in The Underground Bar at Marsala Tita in central Sarajevo,' Pet said as she studied the screen where a blue dot pulsed on a map.

'Not surprising. He has the breaking strain of a Kit-Kat,' Tom smiled.

'Huh?'

'You not heard that one?'

'Man, I mostly hang with Americans. They don't have your cute version of our language.'

'No idea what you are talking about; my first language is Serb.'

'Yeah, right.' She shook her head with a smile. 'Nothing on the phone, in fact no calls in or out since his last one to Babić. I'll keep looking through his data while you carry on with the most boring journey I have ever been on.'

Tom snorted in amusement as he pulled the Skoda out from the car park and back onto the coast road.

They drove in silence, the radio quietly on playing pop tunes for about ten minutes before Pet suddenly spoke. 'This is interesting.'

'What?'

'A semi-secure folder within a subfolder held in a portion of the hard drive you wouldn't expect to find it. It is password protected, but my algorithm is making short work of it; presumably as it's similar to the main drive password. It should only take a minute.'

'Does it have a file name?'

'No, just a number. I can't see why he'd protect it within a secure file like this when the main drive was so well protected.' Pet sounded puzzled.

She continued to tap at the keys before suddenly exclaiming, 'Man, what's this. Hold up I'm screenshotting.' She paused for a second, before her voice turned to panic. 'Shit, bastard. We have a wipe programme, it's automated and it's wiping the whole fucking drive.'

'Can you stop it?'

'I'm trying! Jesus it's a powerful one. I've not seen anything like this, it's so fast.' Her hands were flying across the keyboard, but the rows and rows of numbers began to fall away from the screen like cascading rain. The ones and zeros then dropped from the screen to be replaced by a crude image of a smiling face and the words: *"NOT THIS TIME. MOTHERFUCKER!"*

Pet let out a strangled scream of frustration. 'The bastard got me. He had hidden an auto-destruct in the sensitive file. I couldn't see it from the outside, there was no obvious sign. The whole drive is now corrupted; thank God I used an external drive for it, or it would have totally fucked my laptop.' She let out another growl of anger. 'I'm sorry, Tom. We've lost the lot, all of it.' She banged her hand down repeatedly on the dash.

'No back up file?'

'No. With the rush deployment, I only had the one external drive with me that was big enough, and with my current access levels I wasn't uploading anywhere else. Sorry, Tom. It's gone.'

'Hey, it's cool. Forget about it. At least we had sight of it; at least we know more than we did before. Don't beat yourself up.'

Pet sighed deeply as she disconnected the ruined external drive from the laptop.

'Is everything gone?' asked Tom.

'I have some screenshots of schematics that I uploaded onto a cloud drive and one or two documents, but not a great deal.'

'Then don't sweat it. Is your computer safe?' Tom's voice was calm and even.

'Yes. Thankfully, I always use safety measures to protect my own server and hard drive.' Tom could hear the relief in her voice.

He didn't like to think of the reaction if her precious laptop had been ruined.

'We still have Cerović's phone hooked up?'

'Yes, still quiet as well. I imagine he is ripping it up in a club right now.'

'Then we are fine. We will figure it out, don't worry about it.' Tom smiled at Pet.

'You're not angry?'

'Not your fault that he is better at computer shit than you, Pet.' Tom's voice turned mischievous.

Pet didn't reply. Instead she balled her fist and delivered a short, sharp punch to his thigh.

Tom yelped in pain. 'What was that for?'

'Some things you just don't say, Detective. Not about a ninja-level computer nerd with no sense of humour about her abilities. I've never been defeated before; tell me we are gonna nail this motherfucker.' Her face was a mix of humour and embarrassment, all tinged with just a little anger.

'Pet, I guarantee you that we are going to nail this motherfucker.'

'Then drive and don't talk; I am going to sleep.'

22

Mike Brogan was stood, his knees bent at ninety degrees, his hands shackled behind his back held as high as they would allow. The pain in his shoulders and thighs was intense: the stress position he had been forced into had long since taken effect. His hooded head was held low, his shackled arms extended out, his shoulders and thighs screamed with pain. He tried to ignore the uncomfortable feeling of a soaked crotch where he had been forced to urinate in his trousers. This was what felt like the umpteenth stress position he had been placed into by his, so far unseen, captors. Every time he slumped, unable to hold himself in the position they had forced him into, they would roughly return him to the torturous pose. There was no overt violence, just ruthless, assertive manhandling by the silent, unseen guards.

Their tactics were straight out of the interrogators' handbook that he himself was completely familiar with, and this gave him some degree of comfort, despite the seriousness of his predicament. He had used the same tactics himself on many occasions whilst carrying out interrogations across the world with captives from various wars, conflicts, and incursions. Some regular, some irregular.

The rationale was simple. Deprive the captor of any sense of time, overload his senses, no food, no drinks, no sleep, no toilet breaks. The constant, varying stress positions were designed to sap will and make a prisoner malleable. Ensuring that the prisoner had to soil or wet himself ripped any dignity away from him, adding to the feelings of helplessness and humiliation.

He had been forced to his knees, leaning forward. Leaning

against the wall, knees bent or standing on one leg, or his arms forced up as high as they would go. On one occasion his shackles had been moved to the front and he had been forced to stand, his arms straight out in front of him with what felt like a bicycle tyre in his hands. At first it wasn't too bad, but after a while it began to drop which resulted in a hard slap against his hooded face. A similar blow followed every time the weight of the tyre made his arms drop, even just a little. His throat was parched and he was desperate for water.

Mike knew that the intention was to break him down completely, so that the captor could almost become the rescuer when calling a halt, even if temporary, to his discomfort. His captors would become all powerful, the givers or relievers of pain, humiliation, thirst, and hunger. The subjugation would be total.

The sensory attack that he was experiencing was exacerbated as his hearing was overloaded by the thumping thrash metal that pounded out of the big speaker just a few feet away from him.

Mike tried to work out how long he had been held in this fashion but was unable to cogently come up with a reliable figure. He knew that captives almost always over-estimated when in situations as he was right now. He thought that it was about sixteen hours, but he was realistic enough to accept that it could be significantly less. It was unlikely to be more. Despite his situation, Mike felt oddly calm. The use of well-practised tactics meant that killing him was not the objective; not yet, anyway.

When he had first arrived, they had launched into a rough interrogation—demanding to know who he was and why he was in Sarajevo—but he had stuck to his cover story. He was seconded from the US as an entry clearance officer, interviewing those who wanted to visit the States on a work visa.

They hadn't bought it, even a bit, and he had taken a beating, which he had expected and was ready for. Soon he was bruised and bloody, his ribs ached from being kicked, but he stuck to the cover story which only seemed to enrage them more. He had played on his injuries, pretending to be in far more pain than he really was. He had been hooded the whole time, even during the interrogations, so he had no idea of his surroundings beyond the unmistakable smells that told him he was on a farm.

Then, all of a sudden, the beatings had stopped, and the next phase had begun. Rather than being relieved about the respite from the minor violence, Mike was more disturbed than ever as they moved into what he recognised as planned tactical questioning, beginning with the first stress positions and the arrival of the thumping, pulsating music played at a terrible volume, so high that the speakers distorted the wailing guitars and driving beats. Mike was a music fan, with a penchant for heavy music, but having Slayer interspersed with long periods of white noise played over and over again at an ear-splitting volume was just a little too much.

All of a sudden, the cacophony stopped, only to be replaced with a deep, cloying and impenetrable silence, only punctuated by Mike's own rasping breaths.

'Mr Brogan. Please relax, just a little. Sit on the floor for a moment.' The voice was rough and harsh, the accent thick.

Mike sighed as he sat on his backside, his thighs burning with pain.

There was another minute of silence before he felt hands on his arms lifting him gently up. He was led a few feet to the front, whereupon he was sat down once more on what felt like a hard chair.

'Mr Brogan, your blindfold is going to be removed. Be assured that you have no chance of escape and my men are armed. If you resist, you will be shot. Do you understand?' The voice spoke once more; measured, ruthless and rough.

'Yes,' Mike said, his voice cracking, his tongue sticking to the roof of his mouth.

Blinding light replaced inky blackness as light assailed his eyes. He clamped his eyes tight shut, letting out a soft cry at the sudden pain.

'Open your eyes, Mr Brogan. You will soon become used to the light.'

Mike blinked his eyes open once more, squinting against the harsh light from an overhead bulb, which hung from a pendant in the middle of what looked like an agricultural barn. Loose straw littered the floor and sacks of animal fodder were piled in one corner. There were no windows and the large double door directly in front of him was shut tight. The room was gloomy and depressing.

Three men stood in front of him, all wearing ski-masks and black and white combat clothing. Two of them clutched submachine guns, and the one in the middle wore a pistol in a holster on his belt. He was clearly the leader. He was short, stocky, and muscled and even through the mask Mike could sense the man's presence.

Through the fog of pain Mike couldn't help but notice that both guards were cradling Heckler and Koch MP5 silenced submachine guns. This caused interest and concern in equal quantities. How the hell had they got hold of sophisticated weapons like those? With the plethora of illegal Eastern European guns flooding the region, it struck Mike as odd that they would have such modern Western guns.

'Mr Brogan you have been with us some time now. Perhaps the time has come to tell us the truth as to why you are in Sarajevo?' The man's voice was low and even, but the menace was obvious.

'Can I have some water please?' Mike replied, his voice rasping. His throat was like a cavern of fire.

The leader didn't speak, but instead nodded to someone behind Mike who appeared from out of his peripheral vision and held a plastic bottle to his lips. Mike drank deeply from the bottle, feeling his morale lifting with each drop of liquid that made it past his raw and parched throat.

'Now, Mr Brogan. Why are you here? We know you are not an entry clearance officer. We have this information already, but it will demonstrate some trust between us if you could dispense with this nonsense and tell us why you are here. We know already from our source at the Embassy that you are CIA. We have shown you respect by removing your blindfold and allowing you to drink; please now afford us the respect of telling us some truths. The consequences of further prevarication will be unpleasant.' The same level voice still carried the same degree of menace.

Mike knew that to continue with the same cover story would probably result in a beating and further hours of sensory deprivation, but he needed to buy some more time for Novak and Pet to try to find him. It was time to release a controlled piece of information. He didn't know if it would work, as it looked like they were as familiar with the playbook as he was.

'Okay. I'm CIA, from Washington,' Mike spat, enunciating every word as if he were in significant pain and distress. 'Sorry, I am really confused, I was just doing the right thing in not saying I was CIA. I'd get fired if I told you; I was frightened.' He blinked repeatedly, a confused look in his eyes.

'Thank you, Mr Brogan. A little trust. A little quid pro quo if you like. We know this already, so please. Why are you in Sarajevo?'

'I am here to perform a risk assessment on security at the Embassy. My bosses are concerned that there may be further terrorist attacks similar to the one in 2012.' This was a calculated risk. The Embassy had been attacked in 2012 by a lone gunman, Malvid Lazarevic, so it was conceivable that the risk of such an attack would be on the minds of the CIA in the light of current Islamic extremism. They wouldn't believe him, of course, but the stage of tactical questioning he was at almost certainly would mean that he would be subjected to several hours more sensory deprivation if they felt he was still holding out. His extensive training meant that he could cope with that, and he needed to buy Novak time. If he told the truth now, all that awaited him was a bullet in the head.

The leader sighed deeply and shook his head, 'Mr Brogan. You disrespect me and my attempts to treat you with respect. We will speak again later.' He nodded at his men, turned, and left the barn.

The hood was roughly thrust back over his head and Mike felt a vicious slap connect with his ear. The pain was immense and he cried out in agony as he was dragged from his chair and forced into a new stress position. Stood up with his backside against the rough wooden wall, his legs bowed, and his body bent over at ninety degrees at the waist. It wasn't immediately uncomfortable, but the beginnings of a twinge in his thighs and shoulders were warning enough of the agonies that were to come.

Mike jumped as Megadeath exploded out of the speakers which had been moved so that they were almost so close that Mike could have touched them, if his hands weren't shackled.

23

Tom was exhausted. He yawned deeply as he opened his eyes; his phone alarm was buzzing on the bedside table, signalling that they had only had four hours sleep. He looked across at the single bed adjacent to his, occupied by Pet's sleeping form. Her childlike face was set in a relaxed dream-like state, the covers rising and falling as she breathed deeply.

The journey back from Dubrovnik had been remarkable only in how dull it was. He had stuck religiously to the speed limits and driven carefully and steadily, arriving back at their hotel at 4:30 in the morning just as the grey tendrils of dawn were beginning to appear on the horizon. They'd crept back into their room, keen not to wake any other occupants.

Tom threw back the covers and jumped out of bed, filling and switching on the kettle in the corner of the room and dumping teabags in two cups. He quickly showered and dressed then made tea.

'Morning,' he said, smiling at Pet as she looked up through bleary eyes, screwing her face up as the shafts of light struck it. She looked weary and tired. Reaching across to the bedside table she fumbled for her glasses, which she tiredly jammed on her face. Shaking her head to clear the fog she looked at him and yawned. 'Why is it that when we get together it is always in situations like this, Detective? Why can't we just one day go for a nice meal and have some fun? Maybe go to the cinema or a show. Why is it always guns, kidnaps and evil criminals?'

'Someone has to fight the monsters, Pet. Drink your tea; we will be moving soon.'

'Sure thing, sure thing. Fight monsters? You quoting Nietzsche now? Remember the rest of that quote? Why so pretentious, Detective?'

'"Take care lest you yourself become a monster", yada,' Tom smiled.

Pet groaned, picking up and sipping from her cup before screwing up her face. 'UHT milk. I fucking hate UHT milk. It tastes disgusting and ruins a nice cup of tea. Whatever we are doing today, we are not doing it before we have had breakfast and at least three cups of decent coffee.' She glanced up at him. 'Man, you are in good shape. You could turn a girl's head, Tom. Or a boy's, for that matter. If you weren't so weird, that is,' she added, dampening the compliment just a touch.

Tom felt his cheeks colour just a little as he realised that Pet had never seen him shirtless before. 'I like working out. Not recently though. Anyway, enough of that. We need to get moving soon. We need a change of clothes or Cerović is going to think that I am too scruffy to be a dangerous arms dealer. I've been in the same clothes for days, now.'

'You and me both, bro. I suspect that my underwear would be able to walk to the launderette on its own right now.'

'A little too much information, Pet. Get in the shower, breakfast here, then we are on our way. I want to make a stop for clothes and a few supplies, and then we will call on Cerović. We need to get this moving.'

Pet sighed and yawned, before throwing back the covers. Standing, dressed in a t-shirt and underwear, she stretched, yawned once more, and then headed to the bathroom, having picked up her discarded clothes from last night. 'Still not catching yawns, Detective? Man, you are a little weird,' she said, disappearing into the bathroom.

Tom smiled at her retreating back, ignoring the jibe as he quickly dressed in his now distinctly funky-smelling clothes, beginning to mentally prepare for the coming day. Despite the urgency of the situation, a little preparation was required to give them the best chance of success. He was acutely aware of the old military mantra: *"Eat and drink when you can, as you never know when your next opportunity may arise."* A big breakfast was required, but first he needed to call Cerović.

Pet emerged, fully dressed and smiling, with her short hair damp against her scalp. 'Breakfast. I'm starving.'

'Soon. I want to try to call Cerović now, and I want you to monitor and tell me where he is first.'

'Sure thing, dude,' she said, reaching for her bag and pulling out her laptop.

'Is he at home?'

'Sure looks like it. No activity on the phone overnight, but his GPS puts him in his place.'

'Can you tell what time he got back there?'

'Hold up, just checking,' Pet said, focusing on the screen. 'Ah man, what a little liar. He didn't get back to his place until almost 4am. I'm gonna go out on a limb and suggest that he will still be a little drunk.'

'You think?' Tom said sarcastically.

'Sure, man. I have a sixth sense for this shit.'

'Perfect. I'll call him now, then.' Tom picked his phone up and dialled. Predictably, the phone rang repeatedly without being answered. Tom smiled just a little as he composed a message on the secure app. *'I have items for delivery. Will be in city soon. Call me when you get this message.'*

'Come on: let's get breakfast and go, we need to make some progress.'

'But if he's not answering, what are you going to do?'

'Improvise, Pet. But it's time for us to take the initiative,' Tom said with a wink.

'Your improvisations make me nervous, Detective.'

'No idea what you're talking about,' Tom said, blank-faced.

'You know what I mean. You improvise, bad shit goes down.'

'I hope so. Come on. You're not the only one who gets hungry.'

24

Stefan Cerović's head pounded as he stirred, the pressure on his bladder forcing him from his bed towards the bathroom. His lip was sore and cut after a minor altercation with a bouncer in the club the night before. He had to admit that he had been extremely drunk on vodka and high on about a gram of really pure coke... but he hadn't been that bad, had he?

True, he had got a bit over-familiar with the bargirl, who had persuaded him to buy her drink after drink at an eye watering cost. He thought he was nailed-on for some action with the surgically enhanced beauty called Alina. She had seemed really up for it, especially when he made it clear that he had cash to pay her. She had handed him a scrap of paper with a cell phone number on it and a little heart scrawled underneath. Cerović had felt himself harden a little at the prospect of a few hours of sex with the beautiful Alina, but the management obviously didn't encourage staff and client encounters beyond their control. The bouncer had materialised out of nowhere and Cerović had been unceremoniously thrown out. His drunken remonstrations had only resulted with the powerful punch that had floored him to the damp pavement.

So, he had given up and staggered home in the early hours, collapsing into his bed unconscious until the urge to piss forced him to leave his bed. Looking at his phone, he saw that it was 10am. He then noticed the missed call from Tarzan and, more worryingly, the message on the secure app.

'Fuck!' he exclaimed, panicking just a little. He had to get those power cells, or Babić would go crazy. With trembling fingers, he called the arms dealer back. The phone rang repeatedly with no reply. 'Fuck, fuck, fuck,' he muttered.

He began to compose a reply with his shaking hands but the urge to urinate was just too strong. He quickly rushed to the bathroom where he relieved himself as nausea began to creep up from his lower stomach before sweeping over him like a sickly tide. Suddenly a spray of vomit erupted from his mouth, most into the toilet, but some onto the surrounding vinyl flooring. He retched and coughed as spittle and bright orange vomit dripped from his mouth. Jesus, he thought. He needed to lay off the booze and drugs for a bit, certainly with everything that was going on with Babić. He needed to bring his "A" game, or he had no doubt that Babić would have no hesitation in putting a bullet in him. He really was a scary motherfucker.

Cerović splashed his face with cold water and took a deep drink from the rusting tap. Feeling just a little better he made his way back to the main room. He had to get hold of Tarzan; if he didn't deliver the batteries and start integrating them today, he didn't want to know what may happen to him.

He blearily walked back into the room and almost jumped out of his skin. Tarzan sat on the sofa, dressed in new-looking black jeans and a dark sweatshirt. A hard yet amused look was etched across his dark features, his face a mask of sardonic amusement

'Hello Steff. I thought we had an arrangement.'

'Holy motherfucking shit! You scared the crap out of me, man.' His heart was pumping wildly in his chest with the shock.

'I want to help you, man, but you're not making it easy for me. I have others that want these batteries if you don't.'

'I want them, I really do. How the fuck did you get in here?'

'You have tin-shit locks. You should be careful, there are some bad people in this city.'

Cerović's head swam, a combination of the alcohol and drugs and the shock of seeing Tarzan in his apartment. He slumped down on the sofa with a sigh.

'I'm sorry, man. I tied one on a little too much last night. I'm feeling a little shit, you know. Look I have the cash here, we can still do this deal.'

Cerović found himself flinching under Tarzan's gaze. The man's dark, almost shark-like, eyes projected absolutely nothing. Cerović had been dealing with some very bad people recently but, despite Tarzan's sociable and friendly nature, he had no doubt that he was also dangerous and ruthless.

Tarzan sighed, his dark eyes glittering. 'Where is your car? The batteries are fifteen kilos each and there are six, so I hope your car can cope with that.'

'It's fine; I have a Land Cruiser.'

'Where is it?'

'Car park out back of the building. Ah man, I'm gonna hurl again,' Cerović leaped to his feet and rushed back to the bathroom where he vomited again, coughing and spluttering as the thin bile hit the bowl.

After a minute, he wiped his face and re-joined Tarzan, his deathly pale face beaded with a muck sweat.

Tarzan shook his head, a trace of sympathy on his face. 'Look, get the cash and I will load them up for you, you're in no fit state. There are six of them: all Safts, all brand-new, you know they'll do the job. I want them gone today and I can't wait for you to be fit to move them.'

Cerović paused for just a second, knowing that he should test the batteries before parting with the cash. 'Can you bring just one of them up here and load the rest? I'd be grateful man. I can do some tests on the one in here before I transport them. That will give me enough time to get rid of this fucking hangover. I need to get them away in a couple of hours.'

Tarzan shook his head once more. 'You take big liberties, my friend, and if it wasn't for the fact that we are drinking friends I would tell you to fuck off. Give me your car keys.' He held out his hand.

'Ah, you're my buddy really. I owe you a load of beer and some of the best coke you'll ever find.' He tossed him the Toyota key.

25

Tom returned to the Skoda, which was parked in a small car park a short walk away from Cerović's place. He quickly dialled Pet, who was ensconced in a nearby café. 'I'm about to transfer the batteries to him, as I thought he is totally mashed and incapable of much so I'm loading his car up for him, aren't I nice?'

The journey from the hotel had been swift and they had gone straight to Pavlović's lock-up to retrieve the batteries, weapons, and ammunition before heading to Cerović's apartment.

'You're so considerate, Tom. I'm monitoring his phone, so all is good. He is not calling anyone, and I have his microphone open in case he starts using other means to call anyone.'

'Nice one. Sit tight.' Tom hung up.

He quickly drove the Skoda around into the car park at the rear of Cerović's block, where a new-looking Toyota Landcruiser sat in one of the bays. Tom pulled in next to the vehicle and blipped the fob, opening the car. He quickly transferred five of the batteries into the rear of the SUV, along with the field charger.

Once the final one was in, Tom took out the GPS dog tag from his pocket and, making sure it was switched on, secreted it under the seat, tucking it up into the foam rubbers so it was secured within the main body of the driver's seat.

He quickly composed a text to Pet, *'Tag deployed. Visible?'*

Her answer came back immediately with a single thumbs-up emoji. *Excellent*, thought Tom. He was aware that they may be able to use Cerović's phone to track him, but he also knew that phones lost signals, lost batteries, and that Babić was professional enough to insist on phones being switched off for security reasons. The tag gave them a degree of certainty that they could keep close enough tabs on Cerović.

Leaving the Skoda parked where it was, he lugged the final battery, holding it by the two carry handles. He was sweating by the time he entered Cerović's apartment, dumping the heavy power cell on the floor by the sofa.

'Thanks, man. I owe you,' said Cerović.

'You certainly do, this is heavy. Six and a half thousand euros, if I recall.'

Cerović said nothing but handed over a bundle of crisp new euros, all hundreds. 'Sixty-five hundred, count it, it's all there, man.'

Tom counted the sixty-five hundred-euro bills, as he would have been expected to. It's only in movies that criminals say, *'I trust you, bro.'*

Tom pocketed the bills and then threw the key towards Cerović, who only saw it coming too late and fumbled it, dropping it onto the sofa.

'Man, you need to sort your shit out, or you're not going to be able to do anything, especially not complex electronics'.

Squatting by the grey and green battery box, Cerović whistled. 'Man, I won't need to bring my "A" game here. These are perfect, integrating them will be a cinch. In fact, I could probably do it drunk.'

'Nice doing business with you, Steff. You still want more?'

'Can you get more?'

'Maybe.'

'I will take any you can get, stay in touch. You want a toot before you go?' Cerović produced a self-seal baggie from his pocket, containing white powder.

'Shit, man. You need to give it a rest. I have business to attend to. I'll call you later.' They bumped fists and Tom walked out of the apartment without a backwards glance.

As he returned to the street, he pulled out his phone and called Pet.

'Talk to me, Tarzan,' her distinctive German/American twang crackled down the line.

'He has the merchandise; he is looking very peaky indeed. I'm wondering if he will be going anywhere at all, which isn't so great.'

'I think he will. He's been muttering to himself. He even shouted at himself to "Get a fucking grip, man".'

'We need to hope he does. Every minute that passes is another minute away from getting Mike back. I'll pick you up in five minutes, we need to go shopping.'

'We've *been* shopping, I am wearing some very cheap clothing and have lovely new pants on, and you are wearing your *"Man from Milk Tray"* outfit.'

'Not clothes shopping; I need some kit. If this gig goes the way I suspect it may, I will need some essential items.'

'Detective, you've enough supplies to start a small conflict. What else could you need?'

'I'll see you out the front of the café in five. Keep monitoring Cerović's phone; we have to know when he is about to move.'

'I'm on it,' Pet said and hung up.

Tom jogged round to the car park and jumped into the Skoda, gunned the engine, and pulled out into the busy stream of traffic.

*

Pet jumped into the Skoda, wearing her new pink hoodie and a blue baseball cap, which they'd purchased, along with Tom's black jeans and sweatshirt, from a cheap clothing store an hour earlier. She had headphones clamped on over her head, a cable snaking into her laptop bag.

'No call yet, he's still stumbling around his apartment and he's just hurled again. Sounded repulsive; he really is a piece of work, right?'

'Right. If it wasn't for the fact that they need him at the moment, he would be dead in a ditch somewhere.'

'Understandably so. I've not met the guy, but I want to shoot him myself.'

'Is there an outdoors store nearby? Fishing shop, something like that?'

Pet pulled out her laptop and tapped briefly. 'There is one at a shopping mall only ten minutes from here, pretty close to the Embassy, in fact. You not worried about being spotted?'

'Not by those clowns; they couldn't spot shit. Let's stop in there, I just want to be prepared for any eventuality I can.'

'Proper Planning and Preparation Prevents Piss Poor Performance, right Detective?'

'Absolutely, Pet.' Tom engaged the gears and drove off towards the Embassy.

*

The shop was a fairly small place, which seemed to mostly cater for the burgeoning ski market that was beginning to gain traction around the mountains that overlooked the city. With it being firmly in the off-season, the shop was clearly attempting to diversify into the hunting and shooting markets, which Tom hoped would suit his purpose. Having only visited a similar store in Lviv in the Ukraine just a few days before, he couldn't help but wish he had hung onto some of the equipment he had purchased there, but he hadn't fancied flying with tasers, night sights and CS gas.

Tom selected a Gerber multi-tool with a leather pouch for mounting on a belt. He had a similar item at home and knew that it was an invaluable piece of kit, comprising of pliers, wire snips, mini saw, various screwdriver attachments, and a razor-sharp three-inch blade. It was similar to Pet's Leatherman, but of a higher quality. He realised that he could have just borrowed her multi-tool, but he had an ominous feeling about the hours ahead and didn't want to lose her precious bit of kit. He also located a cheap pair of image intensifying night vision binoculars. They didn't appear to be the best of quality or highest specification but, with 3x20 zoom and an infrared capacity, he hoped they would suffice for what may lie ahead.

He browsed quickly through the rucksacks in the hiking section before selecting a small, compact, and ergonomic pack with integrated camelback water bladder.

A short hunt in the ski section found the last item on his mental list: a lightweight black ski mask. He was now sorted, and ready for whatever may come up.

He paid the friendly cashier almost four hundred euros for the items, using the crisp euro notes that had been given to him by Cerović just a short while ago. He stuffed all the items into the new rucksack and left the store, jumping back into the car with Pet.

'Anything?' he asked, eyebrows raised.

'Yep. I recorded it; you need to hear this.'

'Do it. How long ago?'

'Just finished the call now. To the same number as before. Pretty sure it was Babić at the other end. Hold up and I'll replay it for you.' Pet busied herself on the laptop once more before the hissing and crackly sounds of half a conversation came from the speakers.

'Hey, man, it's me?' Cerović's nasal New York drawl sounded huskier than normal, probably as a result of his hangover. 'Yeah, I have them. Six of them, they're perfect, I reckon I could have them all integrated in a few hours. Shall I come now?' A pause, then, 'Sure, same place?'

There was a longer pause during which there was a faint sound of almost, but not quite, audible conversation. Tom would have loved to hear what Babić was saying, but all that was discernible was a faint, tinny muttering.

'Trust me, man. They'll work. Haven't I proved it already?' Cerović had a touch of indignation in his voice as the unheard voice continued.

'Where?' Cerović asked. Then, 'What I need to know is, as soon as they are ready, where are we going?'

A pause. 'But I will need to know,' Cerović sounded indignant.

Another pause. 'Because I will have to programme each one, that's fucking why.'

The muttering from the other end took on a flintier tone and Cerović said quickly and in a more conciliatory tone, 'Okay, sorry, sorry, man. These things are my babies, you get me?' He was clearly shaken by some degree of threat following his petulant outburst.

'Sure, well, yeah. I'm ready to go, man.'

'Yeah sure. I get paid once this shit goes down, so of course I'm ready, but can it be done with just the six ones we have power for?'

'Okay. I'll be a couple of hours or so. I want to run some tests here before I make the journey, just to make sure they will work.'

There was a brief silence before Cerović added, 'No reason they shouldn't, man, but I want to make sure before I make the journey. Sure, I'll be there soon.' There was a click as the call was ended and the phone was placed on a hard surface.

'Holy fucking shit, this is getting real,' there was a deep, audible sigh that, even through the tinny speakers, Tom could tell was a mix of fear and anticipation.

There was a brief silence in the car as Tom and Pet stared at each other.

'What do you make of that?' Pet asked, her voice trembling just a little.

'It doesn't feel right. We are missing something,' said Tom, his brow furrowed in thought.

'What doesn't feel right?'

'They are about to move these weapons, but for some reason Cerović wants to programme them. Babić clearly won't tell him the location. Why would that matter? This just doesn't sound right. If they are just energy weapons, why is there an issue with where they are headed?'

Pet simply shrugged. 'Problem with only getting half of the conversation.'

'It's a whole load better than getting none of the conversation. It doesn't change what we do, in any case.' Tom shrugged and smiled before continuing, 'Anything on Babić's phone?'

'It's a burner, Bosnian-issued SIM, but I can't access the cell site information without putting myself on the map, which would destroy any of that element of surprise we spent all night creating.'

'Such is life, Pet. We have an advantage now. We will know where Cerović is going and they think we are somewhere in Schengen Europe, so they won't be expecting us. The odds are against us, but we are still in the game and we're ready to go.'

26

Babić strode into the barn where Brogan was being held, feeling the frustration rising in him as the thumping drums and wailing guitar noises assaulted his senses. It was intolerably loud and the fact that Brogan had been experiencing it for hours non-stop surely meant that it must have been having an effect.

Brogan was sat in the middle of the straw-covered floor, shackled to the rear now and on his knees, his head almost touching the floor. Babić knew that he would be in excruciating pain as the stresses in his thigh and back muscles began to bite more and more.

After the call from Cerović he was now aware that the weapons would be ready, probably within a few hours. Once ready, they couldn't afford to procrastinate a moment more. There were hurdles to overcome and large amounts of money had been deployed to ensure that the devices got where they were needed. Bribes had been paid and palms greased, but there was a time limit on how long those individuals could provide their irregular service. He desperately wanted to accelerate the American's interrogation but he knew that, for a man of his skills and experience, it would probably be counterproductive.

Pulling a ski-mask over his face he nodded at the masked guard, who immediately silenced the pounding thrash metal music. *If you could call it music*, mused Babić. The contrast from ear-splitting, discordant, and disorientating noise to utter silence was almost palpable. Brogan's hood was ripped from his head, leaving him blinking in the harsh light.

No one said anything whatsoever for a full three minutes, and the only audible sounds were those of the American's ragged and laboured breathing. He sounded stressed and frightened. *Perfect*, thought Babić. It was time to up the pressure.

'Mr Brogan.' Babić paused, his rough voice attempting to sound smooth and reassuring. 'I hope you have reconsidered your position. Do you appreciate that you are helpless here, that there is no help coming, and that your future lies completely on what you say in the next few minutes? I will very soon ask you a very simple question. Now, Mr Brogan, I already know the answer to this question, so it would be, perhaps, a demonstration of trust if you answered truthfully. The consequences for you should you not tell me the truth will be, shall we say, unpleasant.' The tone in Babić's delivery, whilst measured and calm, did not hide the menace that lurked in the Serb's rough voice.

Brogan said nothing, just closed his eyes in an extended blink that seemed to take an age. Confusion and fear emanated from his smooth face and his blue eyes were dull and lifeless. He coughed dryly, his lips adhering to each other.

'Water, please,' he said, and the act of speaking seemed to be a real effort.

Ignoring the request Babić simply said, 'Why are you in Sarajevo, Michael Brogan?' His eyes shone with hatred from behind the ski-mask.

Brogan opened his mouth and tried to swallow a gasp of air, but his gummed together lips made it difficult and he coughed once more. Babić nodded once more at the guard, who picked up a bottle of water and held it to Brogan's lips briefly, allowing him to take just enough of a sip to lubricate his parched mouth enough to speak.

'Mr Brogan. An act of kindness, yes? Allowing you water despite your continued refusal to be truthful. Now, why are you in Sarajevo.' His voice hardened.

Brogan hesitated, a glint of intelligence behind the tired and scared eyes, 'I... I told you. I am here to perform a ri—'

Brogan could not finish the story as Babić, in a sudden outburst of fury, strode the four steps across the floor and delivered a wild, uncontained open-handed slap across his face. It made a sound like a pistol shot as it connected with the CIA agent's ear, sending him flying from his chair to land in a heap on the straw. His restrained wrists meant he was unable to break his fall, and his head connected with a sickening thump as it struck the concrete floor that was barely cushioned by the thin layer of animal bedding. Blood flowed from a gash in his temple and he lay still, knocked out clean from the blow.

Two of the guards dragged Brogan to his feet, dumping him back onto the chair. The guard took the bottle of mineral water and splashed the contents liberally over his head and squirted the remainder into his face. Brogan shook his head, coughing and spluttering as he tried to clear the daze from the impact. He was conscious, but only just.

Babić moved almost nose-to-nose with Brogan and screamed at full volume into his face, 'You tell us the fucking truth, you American pig or, by God I will remove one of your fucking eyes with a blunt fucking spoon.' His earlier calm approach now fully eschewed, his body language emanated unrestrained fury.

'We know everything, we know it all. We know you are senior CIA. You fucking tell us all or you will be sorry.' A fleck of spittle flew through the mouth hole in the ski-mask and his deep, brown eyes blazed with hate.

Brogan's eyes widened, but he said nothing, a look of confusion on his face.

'You tell us everything,' Babić said, recovering his composure, once more.

Brogan paused, his dazed eyes clearly working through the variables. He was stunned and concussed, but he was clearly aware of what was happening.

'I told you, I promise. I am CIA, but I am here to do a risk assessment on the Embassy. Please, you have to believe me, I don't know what else to tell you. Please.'

Babić held up a hand. 'Mr Brogan. This can all end now, simply tell us the truth and we will let you go. You have my word on this, but we know already you are lying. I don't want to cause you more discomfort, but if you persist you will leave me little choice.' Babić sighed deeply and shook his head, displaying insincere sorrow.

Brogan's haunted eyes swivelled from side to side, his face a mask of blood from the freely flowing head wound. He paused as if assessing his options before saying, 'I don't know what else to say. I am here to inspect Embassy security measures and report back to my superiors in Washington.'

Babić interrupted simply by raising a laconic hand, once more. He turned to the guard and said in Serb, 'See to his wound, then continue as before. No water, no toilet. If he moves from positions, cause him pain when returning him. More intense from now on, understand?'

The masked guard with the submachine gun simply nodded.

Babić turned on his heel and, without another word, he left the barn. Brogan's heart sunk as the guards moved menacingly towards him. It was about to start again.

*

An explosion of violently loud music filled the air as Babić walked away from the barn. He needed an update from his source at the Embassy. He pulled out his phone from his pocket and composed a message on the Wikr secure messaging app. It was totally secure, and, more importantly the messages had a "burn on read" facility, leaving no evidence if the phone fell into the wrong hands. Perfect security.

I need an update. Brogan is not cooperating,' Babić typed.

The reply came back immediately. *'Unsurprising. He is a pro.'*

'What of the man and woman who arrived with him?' Babić typed.

'Looks like they've fled. They passed through the border into Croatia last night. Probably freelancers Brogan uses all the time. He doesn't trust anyone and prefers to use his own people. Now is not good time. I'm at Embassy.'

Babić frowned at the petulant reply. *'Don't piss your pants, we are paying you well, so you have to keep your end of the deal. I need regular updates; we are about to move and I cannot afford any unforeseen problems. Has Brogan been missed yet?'*

'Not yet. He operates to his own rules, and only reports back to Washington. No one in the Embassy will know or even care where he is. How much longer will you hold him?'

'Not long.'

'Good. Then get rid of him and make sure he isn't found.'

Babić smiled as the last message disappeared, as if by magic, from the phone. Brogan wouldn't be found; he had hidden dozens of corpses over the years, and none of them had ever been found.

27

'What now?' Pet asked, yawning deeply. They were still sat in the car outside the store.

'I want to check out of the hotel, and I want to test the kit we have. By the sounds of it we have at least a couple of hours before Cerović moves, and we have him covered with his phone and the GPS bug on his car. He can't move without us knowing,' said Tom.

'Test again? Mr Boring OCD.'

Tom chuckled, put the Skoda in gear, and moved off.

Their time was now tight, Tom thought ruefully. They needed to get their kit out of the hotel and he really wanted to check that the Beretta and MP5 were in good order. The last thing he wanted was to mount a rescue wherever Mike was being held, only to have a stoppage at the crucial time. He would have dearly liked to have test-fired the weapons, but being in unfamiliar surroundings he didn't feel safe doing so. It would just be a clean and inspect, and then trust that the legendarily reliable weapons would work when required.

Once at the hotel they speedily cleared their room of their belongings. There wasn't much: mostly it was Pet's computer gear, the cash, the Beretta liberated from Pavlović, and a few items of clothing. They quickly paid the bill in euros to the still smiling Emina, who swelled visibly with pride when Tom assured her that they had had a wonderful stay.

'Thing is,' Pet said to Tom as they left, 'it really is a lovely place here. I'd love to come back when people weren't trying to kill us.'

'Me too. Nice little gaff. Maybe in the ski season. The snow here is amazing, and yet it's not fashionable to come here.'

'Looks lovely. I love to ski. Everyone in Bavaria skis. It's in our blood.'

'Well let's get this crap out of the way, and we'll come back to this hotel as genuine tourists, not desperate people running from corrupt CIA and ruthless militias.'

'It's becoming a theme, Detective.'

'Takes one to know one, Pet.' Tom smiled.

'Okay, Jonah. Where to next?' asked Pet

'Jonah?

'Unlucky Old Testament dude, you not hear of it?'

'Wasn't it something about the whale?'

'Kinda. You not read the classics?'

'I only read stuff with exploding helicopters on the cover.'

'So uncultured, Detective.'

'Meh, come on. I need to find somewhere quiet so I can check all the kit over and make sure we are all ready to go.'

'You sure about this?'

'What?'

'Charging off on your own, rescuing Mike. Why don't we take a moment to think?'

'About what?'

'Alternatives,' Pet shrugged.

'I'm all ears. Mike is in deep shit. I don't think he is dead yet, as I am certain they would want to know what he knows, and that will take time for someone as experienced as him. If they'd wanted him dead, they'd have shot him dead on the street. As soon as they have what they want, they will kill him. I'm not letting that happen, Pet. I owe Mike too much. We call this in, and we have absolutely no idea who will overhear or become aware of what is going on. That happens and Mike is a dead man.'

'I guess. I just worry about you.' Pet's voice had a tone of genuine concern.

'We don't have time for this. We have to be ready for when Cerović moves the batteries. I'm betting that Mike is wherever they are as well.'

'Okay.'

'What, just okay?'

'What did you expect?'

'An argument, or you convincing me that killing lots of people won't solve my multiple character flaws and lack of empathy and, in the long run, it will leave me unhappier.'

'All valid points, Tom, very well made. But Mike is in a shit situation and, if it wasn't for him, I would probably be in some US state penitentiary wearing orange trousers and fighting off predatory inmates who think I look cute.'

'Good point, well made, Pet. Let's get on. Put the radio on, I want to hear the sound of music,' said Tom with a straight face.

'Say again?' Pet whipped her head round to face Tom like she'd been slapped.

'You know, radio. Sound of music?'

'Oh ha. Big funny man, Detective,' said Pet, delivering a short, sharp punch to Tom's thigh.

'No sense of humour, Ms Von Trapp,' Tom grinned. 'Anyway, don't you have work to do?'

'Absolutely. I have a few irons in a few computer fires I can work on,' Pet smiled her crooked grin.

'That is the worst and most geeky metaphor any human has ever used in the history of the universe,' Tom said, chuckling.

'Geek and proud, Detective. Let's go.'

They drove away from the hotel and, after about fifteen minutes, Tom turned off the highway and along a small track that led into a forest clearing, where he pulled over. It was peaceful and the late sun cast dappled shadows into the car as they sat.

Pet's eyes remained glued to her screen, the glow reflecting in her spectacles as she concentrated.

'Keep your eyes about,' said Tom. 'I want to check the weapons over.'

'Sure thing. Don't forget our food stop, though,' she smiled, still not looking up.

'As if,' Tom said as he popped the boot and got out of the car.

The MP5 was in a hold-all in the boot, and Tom was comforted to heft its familiar weight. It was a supremely balanced weapon that he had fired on countless occasions. It was a superb close-quarter weapon and Tom had always been a top performer when using it in training with the SRR and later the police. He quickly disassembled it, almost intuitively such was his familiarity with it. He checked each component carefully and found that his first impressions of it were correct; it had clearly never been fired before. The handgrip and silencer were free of carbon or any type of dirt or rust, and the thin layer of oil had clearly kept it in top condition. Looking down the barrel he saw no dust or debris. The weapon was good and ready to fire.

Reaching back into the hold-all he opened some of the 9mm parabellums, all of which looked in perfect order. He quickly loaded the three magazines with thirty rounds each and slapped one of the magazines into the MP5, then racked the slide, injecting a round into the chamber. He removed the magazine and added another round, taking it back to its capacity of thirty rounds. It seemed overkill, but that one extra round could always make a difference. He ensured that the safety catch was set before filling the other three magazines with the parabellums and slotting them into the holster. He fastened the webbing belt around his waist and cinched it in so it was secure, adjusting it until he was satisfied that it was in the best place for speedy reloads. A few quick practices, removing the incumbent magazine then returning it, convinced Tom he had the best possible positioning.

He extended the butt and shouldered the weapon, pressing the retrofitted optic to his eye. It was very low magnification, and Tom hadn't worked with that type of optic before. He made some minor adjustments, making sure that it was centred on a tree. As much as he wanted to, he couldn't really test fire the weapon: he wasn't in known territory and the last thing he needed was cops being called or, worse, a stray round going where it wasn't intended. He pressed the rubberised torch switch and, even in the daylight, there was enough shadow cast by the trees for the torch beam to be visible against the tree. He noted that the beam was slightly off-centre and checked the adjusting screws on either side of the torch mount. He found his newly acquired Gerber and, using the screwdriver attachment, he made minor adjustments until he was satisfied that the torch beam was central on the sight aiming point. That was perfect, as long as the zeroing wasn't too far off with the sight. He just had to shine the beam on a target and the bullet should hit dead centre.

He made some fine adjustments to the weapons sling until he was content that it was at the correct slackness so that, if he needed to let go of the weapon for whatever reason, it would drop to an appropriate position.

Finally, he pulled out the Beretta and quickly disassembled it, again checking each component. It too was well-maintained and looked like it had been recently cleaned. The Beretta, he knew, was a bullet-proof and reliable pistol and, as long as it was well cared for, would always reliably fire. He quickly unloaded and reloaded each of the three magazines before slotting one into the handgrip and racking the slide. Again, he removed the magazine and inserted a parabellum to replace the one now in the chamber, giving him sixteen rounds immediately available. The pistol was held in a pancake holster with a metal retention clip. It fitted on the webbing strap that held the MP5 magazine pouch just perfectly. The other two magazines he tucked into the box-pockets on the side of his black combat trousers. He clipped the Gerber back into its leather case and attached it to his trouser belt. Picking out his rucksack he deposited three boxes of ammunition into it along with his binoculars, making a mental note to fill the water bladder as soon as possible.

He unclipped the webbing belt and tucked it back in the boot along with the MP5 and the rucksack and covered all the items with the sweatshirt he had been wearing before his shopping trip.

He climbed back into the driver's seat and looked at Pet. 'Anything?'

'No, he's still faffing about. He's obviously picking up a bit, he has been whistling whilst doing whatever he is doing. It's actually rather annoying, but then again so is everything else about this guy.'

Tom chuckled as he gunned the engine. 'I'm all set and ready to go. We are in Cerović's hands now, shall we get some scran?'

'Scran?' asked Pet

'Sorry, Marine slang. Food?'

'Now you're talking, man. Let's go.'

*

They found a small diner just off the main road back into Sarajevo. It was a pseudo American style place with bench booths, plastic menus, and a flashing *"Coke"* sign outside. They sat opposite each other; Pet had a single earbud in her left ear so she could continue to monitor Cerović's phone. Her smartphone lay on the table with a map open and a pulsing blue dot in the centre of the screen in the middle of Sarajevo. As soon as Cerović moved they'd know.

The diner was empty apart from a dour waitress who bore a badge that stated her name to be *"Thelma"*. 'What can I get you good folks?' she said in heavily accented English, a bored smile on her brightly-painted lips. Her hairstyle was a Dolly Parton bubble perm that simply had to be a wig.

'Burger, fries and a Coke, please, Thelma,' said Tom, a broad grin splitting his face.

Thelma cocked an eyebrow in the direction of Pet, her mouth gyrating with some unseen gum.

'Same please,' said Pet.

'You want Mom's special apple pie too?' Thelma said without a trace of irony.

'Why not,' said Tom.

Thelma turned without a word and returned to the counter where she bellowed the order out in Serbo-Croat to the unseen chef.

'I know I'm going out on a limb, here, but I am going to hazard

159

a guess that her name isn't Thelma,' grinned Tom.

'Wow, Detective, I can see why you get the big bucks. Is this place for real?'

'Perfect for me. I could murder a burger. I hope it's good.'

'So, are we ready?'

'As we can be, bearing in mind we have no idea what is coming next. I have weapons of a quality I'd probably struggle to get back home, which I didn't expect, if I'm honest. I still don't understand that angle or how Pavlović came to be in possession of them. It doesn't make sense.'

'They're American-owned and they were stolen from a store in Bosnia. US advisers have been helping train Bosnian security forces. All part of the US helping Bosnia and Herzegovina improve its security and counter terrorism capabilities.'

'What? You're just telling me now? When did you find this out?'

'When you were testing the kit in the woods.'

'So why now?'

'You mentioned food. Plus, it doesn't make any difference right now. Also, I can't be absolutely certain, but there were definitely a number of MP5SDs with attached optics and Sure-fire torch mounts stolen.'

'Evidence enough for me. Anything else?'

'Just a load of 9mm parabellums from this particular raid.'

'Stolen from where?'

'A secure transit store not too far from here. They were being transported to the Bosnian anti-terror police for a training detail after they had all been modified with the torches. Someone broke into the store with explosives and stole the lot.'

'How many?'

'Twenty-five. Plus, a whole shit-load of parabellums.'

'What else?' Tom asked.

'What else from where?'

'You said from this particular raid. I take it from that there have been others,' said Tom.

'There have been a few thefts or misappropriation of military equipment over the last year, between here and Serbia.'

'Such as?'

Pet sighed. 'A load of night vision goggles went from a base near Mostar, some sniper weapons at an army base in the north of the country, a consignment of grenades that were due to be decommissioned, and apparently the Serbian military police were really worried about a single Bumbar that was unaccounted for after a major exercise.' She frowned and looked up. 'Bumbar? What the hell is a Bumbar?'

'It's Serbian for bumblebee. It's a Serbian-made wire guided anti-tank weapon,' Tom said, flatly turning it over in his mind and wondering how it impacted their situation.

The arrival of the food stopped any further conversation, as big and appetising-looking burgers, piles of fries and two large glasses of Coke were brought to their table. It smelled divine.

'This looks awesome,' Pet said as she bit deeply and with satisfaction into the burger, chewing appreciatively.

'Not bad at all. Eat the lot, Pet. We don't know when we will next get food,' Tom smiled, his mouth full of fries.

'Oh right, yeah, Mr Sparrow Appetite over there telling me to eat; that's not ironic, right,' Pet said with sarcasm dripping from her voice.

They ate in silence, both focusing on the task ahead. Tom felt calm and composed; even though the odds were heavily stacked against them, they had the element of surprise. He was used to the odds being stacked against him, right from being an orphaned Bosnian refugee to now.

Suddenly, Pet cocked her ear to one side. 'He's moving. Lots of noise and I just heard a door slam. I'd say he's on his way.'

'Right, then. Let's finish up here and get ready to go. I want to get as close to him as possible, wherever he is going.'

Tom stood and deposited some banknotes on the table, then picked up his rucksack and headed for the bathroom. He used the tap to fill the bladder in his rucksack. He would never consider deploying on an operation without water if he could possibly avoid it.

When he returned, Pet was stood looking at her phone, a cardboard box in her hand. She smiled as Tom approached.

'Thelma is very pleased with our tip. And look,' she angled the cardboard box towards Tom with a smile, 'apple pie to go.'

'Awesome. Any movement on the car?'

'Not yet, but he's out on the street. I'm certain of it.

'Let's go,' Tom said, and they headed out and got back into their car. Pet switched the feed from Cerović's phone to the external speaker on her laptop.

There was an unmistakable *"thunk"* of a car door being slammed, followed by Cerović coughing. There was a brief pause.

'He's dialling Babić now,' she said, her face a mask of concentration.

'Yeah Babić, I'm leaving now. Be there in thirty.'

After a pause, he spoke again. 'Yep, the cells are perfect. I'm ready to fit them right now. Okay, dude, see you real soon.'

'Call has finished,' Pet said.

'Jeez, what an asshole,' Cerović's voice came over the speakers. The sound of an engine starting and then moving was audible.

'Okay. He's moving, heading south.'

'Right. I'm moving up, closer to the main road. Let's see which way he goes next before we move.'

'Still moving. He's west along the M5 at the moment. If he turns south now along the M18 then he is coming towards us.'

'Okay. We stick here, keep talking to me.' Tom drove along the track towards the road, his face set in a mix of extreme focus and determination. Pet had seen that face before, and it normally preceded something bad.

*

'Where is he?' Tom asked, his eyes focused on the road ahead. They were still static in a small turn-off, but with a view of the main road at Krupac.

'Now heading south on the M18 towards us.'

'What's the next major point of deviation?'

'A short way ahead of us. If he stays on the M18 where it bends left for him, he will head briefly east before the road straightens due south again. If he turns by Krupac he will come straight past us.'

Tom squinted at the map open on Pet's laptop, 'Okay, we will hold here until we know what he is doing. If he continues on the M18, we will follow. I want to get an eyeball on him,' Tom began to immediately slip into the surveillance vernacular that was as natural to him as breathing after years of experience of covert surveillance in both the military and the police.

'He's just passing Vojkovici on his right.'

'Offside, you mean,' Tom said with a slight hint of a smile.

'Pardon?' Pet asked, sensing some pedantry was coming.

'We always refer to nearside and offside. If you say left or right, I can't know whose left or right you are talking to, offside and nearside will always be the same. Surveillance glossary, Pet. Important stuff.'

'Wow. I bet the long, winter evenings must just fly in your house,'

Tom said nothing, but just chuckled.

'Two clicks from us now, approximately,' said Pet. 'He is probably less than two minutes away from our location. If he comes this way, he will drive right past us.'

'I'll back up just a touch. I don't want to give him a free look at us if he heads this way; the roads are too quiet.' Tom engaged reverse and pulled the Skoda away from the junction until it was behind a treeline. They wouldn't be visible unless he actually turned into the track they were parked on.

Pet continued to stare at the screen. 'One click, Tom. Any time. Standby.'

'Don't say standby.'

'Eh?'

'Only say standby for the first lift of the day when he is leaving a premises.'

'Jesus Christ, and to think you have the temerity to call me a nerd,' Pet shook her head, but couldn't stop the hint of smile creeping across her face.

'Important details, Pet.'

'*Boring* details. No wonder you are single. Right, he has passed, he is remaining on the M18 towards Kijevo.' Pet said, all business-like and the epitome of efficiency. Tom could tell that she had done this before.

He engaged gear and took off at speed, turning left towards the M18. Coming to the main junction, he accelerated into the flow of the traffic, which was becoming a little busier. 'Next point of deviation, Pet?'

'About four clicks on the nearside, deviation towards Klanac,' Pet emphasised the word "nearside" with dripping sarcasm. Tom smiled as he drove, his attention fully on the road in front of him.

'Anything from the phone?' Tom asked.

'Just some music.'

'How far ahead is he?'

'Just about a click but bear in mind that GPS has a margin for error. Both phone and GPS dog tag have him around a click.'

'Okay, that's fine, I want enough distance so it will be completely clear when he has turned off. I'd hate for him to turn off and we go flying past him.'

'Nope, he's driving steady, I'd estimate he is driving at about sixty KPH, or thereabouts.'

Tom checked his own speedo and adjusted their speed to match that of Cerović. He wanted to maintain the current distance and let the GPS do the work for them. Much as he would have liked to get a view of the Land-Cruiser that Cerović was driving, he also didn't want to get too close. Surveillance would usually involve a number of vehicles, including at least one motorcycle, with the benefit that if one of the cars got too close, they could be pulled right back, or dropped out of the follow altogether. They didn't have that luxury. If Cerović noticed them, it was all over.

'Okay, he's approaching the junction for Klanac.' Pet paused intently concentrating on the screen. 'He's continuing on the M18.'

'Next point of deviation?' Tom said.

'Kijevo, in a click on your nearside.'

'Right. Are there farms around there?'

'Difficult to say from the map. It's a mix of forestry and dwellings from what I can see, but some of the terrain looks cultivated. Two hundred metres, to deviation. One hundred. Fifty. And he is committed again.'

'Good skills, Pet. Make a surveillance operative of you yet.'

She said nothing, just pulled a sarcastic face.

'Next deviation?'

'Less than a click, it's an unnamed road leading to what look like farm buildings with partially-cultivated land and some outbuildings. Five hundred metres.'

'Received,' Tom said, automatically.

'You know you aren't speaking on a radio, right?'

'Force of habit. How far?'

Two hundred, one hundred. Wait a second. Slow up, slow up we are gaining on him.' She stared at the screen intently, zooming the map into the blue pulsing marker. 'He's turned in towards the small buildings. Slow right up. You wanna follow him in? It looks real quiet.'

'No. Are there no exits beyond?'

'No. It extends in for just over a click, with tracks branching off leading to dwellings that all seem to have outbuildings.'

Tom slowed the car as they approached the exit. 'Any suggestions? How far in has he gone?'

Pet looked and clicked the distance-measuring feature. 'He is about three hundred metres in right now and is still moving. East. There is a small dead end just as you round the corner, go in, go in.' Pet pointed at a junction shrouded by pine trees on all sides.

Tom turned into the small road, which was made of a rough tarmac that jolted the Skoda's ageing springs. As they rounded the corner there was a small track that led partly into the forestry block that led up to an abandoned and, it seemed, unused electricity substation. Tom stopped the car and looked at the screen that Pet had open. They both watched with fascination as the blue dot inched across the screen before coming to a halt.

'Where's that?' Tom asked.

'Well, I'm only going from Google Maps' satellite images, but it looks like a reasonable-sized central dwelling with three outbuildings. It also looks like there is an agricultural polytunnel there. Bear in mind though that Google Maps are usually way out of date.'

'Can you find anything out about it online?'

'My access levels are way lower than normal; I'm assuming you don't want me to take any risks of hitting any flags that may be being deployed on the computer?'

'Definitely not. Surprise is the only advantage we have.'

'Okay, then I am relying on publicly available resources. It will take me a while, and we don't even know for sure which of the dwellings he is in. Without more information, I am stuck.'

'Well, I'll have to get you some more information, then.'

'How?'

'The old-fashioned way. I am going to have a skulk about and see what I can find out. Can you forward me a screenshot of that map with the dot on it?'

'Sure. But what are you gonna do? It's still daylight,' Pet asked.

'I'll be careful and I'll take a pistol. Once I identify the property, I will take a brief look if I can and then come back after dark. We only have a few hours of light left.'

Without waiting for an answer, Tom got out of the Skoda, leaving the keys in the ignition, and moved to the back of the car. Locating the pistol, he unclipped the holster from the webbing straps that affixed it to the MP5 magazine pouches. He clipped the concealed carry holster to the inside of his belt at the rear and rearranged his hoodie so it was invisible. He also grabbed the binoculars and slung them around his neck. He hefted the rucksack onto his back and then bent down, tucking his trouser bottoms into the socks, exposing his walking boots he had been wearing.

He opened Pet's door. 'Right, my cover story is that I am a birdwatcher getting ready to look for owls after dark. It's thin and won't be any use if I'm challenged by anyone, but it may be enough to keep any neighbours off our case.' He squatted by the door and looked at the screen of the laptop. Tracing the route he realised that, if he took a route through the forestry block and walked south-west for about five hundred metres, he would emerge at the rear of the property that Cerović had stopped by.

'Okay,' said Pet. 'What should I do?'

'Move away from here and hole up somewhere as close as you can reasonably be without attracting too much attention. Then monitor Cerović's phone, recording any conversations, and see if you can dig anything up about wherever he is. Be ready to get back here if I shout. I don't intend on being long, I just want to see where he has gone in daylight so I can plan for after dark.'

'Well wear this then.' Pet handed over a small, compact Bluetooth earpiece that she had dug out of her voluminous bag.

'Good idea,' Tom said, switching it on and quickly pairing it with his phone.

'Be careful, Tom.'

'You know me, Pet,' Tom smiled and turned away, heading for the forestry block.

*

Tom advanced into the pine forest, which was fairly dense and clearly hadn't been thinned for some time. Once in the forestry block, he was instantly transported back to his childhood home in the Scottish Highlands on the edge of the Cairngorm mountain range. It felt familiar and almost comforting as the smells of moss, pine, and damp earth assailed his nostrils. He breathed the scent in deeply and found it had an almost cathartic effect on him. It felt like his turf. This was the environment he had grown up in, and he could move through forestry such as this like a ghost, having done it years ago whilst watching for owls at night, or red squirrels during the day.

He quickly found the compass app on his phone and took a bearing south-west. If his calculations were right, he figured that a solid five hundred metres would bring him to the rear of the property he had seen on the Google satellite image.

He moved quickly but quietly through the forest, always keeping his eyes ahead to be sure he was on the correct bearing to get him to his destination, whilst being aware enough not to trip on the forest floor litter.

After about ten minutes he saw that the trees were beginning to thin, as he approached a clearing where the trees had been felled: clearly some time ago judging by the regrowth and the amount of gorse that was now beginning to creep into the spaces that the trees had left behind.

He slowed his pace as he approached a fence and found some cover behind a thick gorse bush. He painfully crawled through the thick, spiky bush, aware that a little discomfort was a small price to pay for maintaining his cover and obtaining a good spot to be able to observe the property. He was in his element: he wasn't just having a look, he was performing a close target reconnaissance. This was as familiar to him as walking, after all his years in the Royal Marines and SRR. His confidence was high; they'd never spot him.

As slowly as he could he inched through the bush, nestling himself as close to the ground as possible, all his senses alive to the smells, sights, and sounds of the forest. A faint sound carried to him on the soft breeze that was scented by pine and just a touch of woodsmoke. The noise was a dull repetitive beat with a hint of static to it, and it didn't fit with the tranquil woodland setting. He moved just a few more inches into a position where he could observe the clearing before him.

About a hundred metres in front of him sat a small, squat

farmhouse in the middle of the clearing. It was whitewashed with a dull red slate roof and a wisp of smoke drifting from the chimney. A smile spread across his face as he saw the two cars parked at the front of the farmhouse on a compacted mud parking area. One was a large Ford SUV, the other was Cerović's dark Land Cruiser. *Bingo*, thought Tom: this was the place.

Just to the left of the farmhouse was a wooden outbuilding about the size of a large garage, probably big enough to house a tractor and a couple of cars, or farm machinery. It was comprised of wooden timbers and had a corrugated iron roof that was painted red oxide.

Directly next to the wooden outbuilding was a smaller building that looked like what would often be described as a static caravan, or mobile home: the type of thing that would be found on American trailer parks. It had windows front and rear and seemed to be in a poor state of repair, with peeling paint and filthy windows.

As the breeze picked up, a little more of the dull, repetitive fast beat of a music track became more audible. He strained his ears, trying to identify the sound, recognising it after a few seconds: The Prodigy, a frenetic British hard-core dance band. As he listened, he recognised the track as *"Voodoo People"*, which he often listened to when working out. He smiled a little wider, now knowing that, not only was Mike in that outbuilding, but he was alive.

Moving achingly slowly, he got his mobile phone out and briefly took a few photos of the scene before dialling Pet.

'Tom, you okay?' her voice crackled in the Bluetooth earpiece.

'Yeah, I'm good. Cerović's Land Cruiser is here out the front. There is a farmhouse and two outbuildings. Mike is in one of them.' He spoke in a low whisper.

'How can you possibly know that?'

'Just trust me, okay?'

'Okay. Thank Christ for that. What next?'

'I go in after dark and get him out.'

'On your own? That's suicide. We should call this in.'

'No, we can't. We call this in, Mike dies immediately. If they

169

are subjecting him to TQ he is going to be uncomfortable, but he is alive, and he will be kept alive for a while yet. We have an advantage; they'll never see me coming. Anything coming in from Cerović's phone?'

'Yeah, he's gone inside and has been shooting the shit with Babić, who is speaking to him like something he just scraped off his shoe. He has told him to get on with getting the weapons tested and ready to move. They want them outta there urgently. Cerović asked him how many of the others were there, and I'm fairly sure that Babić replied something about twins being there. Cerović certainly replied: "Just the twins then, right?"'

'Okay. Is this all recorded?'

'Of course.'

'Any other voices?'

'No. Just Babić and Cerović.'

'Okay, I'll review it when I get back. I don't need to stay exposed here any longer than this. We know Mike is there and getting him out is all that matters. I will come back when it's dark and we worry about the weapons after that. I'll call you when I get back to where I got out of the car, okay?'

'Sure thing. Be careful.'

'Always,' Tom hung up and pocketed his phone.

He was about to begin to reverse course out of the gorse when a movement at the door of the farmhouse made him freeze. Cerović emerged, closely followed by a short, stocky male dressed in dark jeans and a leather jacket. They both walked over to the Land Cruiser and opened the rear cab door. Slowly, Tom raised the binoculars to his eyes, focusing them on the new male. He took in the rough features, hard eyes, and vertical, white scar that bisected the man's forehead. Davud Babić seemed to be staring straight at him, causing Tom to freeze like a rabbit caught in headlights.

Babić turned to Cerović and the moment was broken. He seemed to be speaking tersely to the other man and the set of his face made it clear who was in charge. Both men began to unload the batteries from the back of the Land Cruiser and, one by one, they transported them into the static caravan. Tom noted that nobody else came out to assist with the task of moving the heavy batteries. Once the task was complete, Babić turned away and went back into the farmhouse, leaving Cerović in the static caravan.

Tom decided that he had seen enough. There was no need to remain in such an exposed position during daylight hours. He looked at his watch, estimating that there were probably two hours of light left. He slowly reversed out of the gorse bush, wincing as the prickles scratched and dug in through his thin clothes. It wasn't the worst pain in the world; like all ex-Marines he was used to a gorse rash, having been forced to crawl around Woodbury Common in Devon during training. It had even been named as "Woodbury rash," it was so common.

Once clear and out of sight of the farmhouse, he turned and jogged back towards where Pet was, a plan forming in his head.

*

Tom jumped into the passenger seat of the Skoda. 'Let's get a little out of the way. Head back the way we came and take the first left. We'll find somewhere to hole up for a bit.'

'Cool. Everything okay?'

'Yeah, I think so. I'm sure they are holding Mike in a wooden barn by the house. There is seriously loud music going on, so my view is they are looking to break him down before really going to work on him.'

'How can you be so sure?' Pet replied as she turned right back onto the M18.

Tom shook his head, 'Cerović is working in a beaten-up looking static caravan and the music is coming from a large garage or barn type structure. There is no reason for that music otherwise, and I just don't see that they have the manpower to have Mike elsewhere when they are trying to break him with TQ. Also, Babić is there and he is the boss on the ground.'

'Fair enough. So what now?'

'We wait till last light in a couple of hours, keep an ear on what Cerović is up to via the phone, then I go in and get Mike. I don't think there will be too many people there. I only saw Babić and Cerović and what you heard on the phone certainly suggests that there are only another two. I don't know how many are in the house but bearing in mind only Babić came out to help move the batteries, my guess is that there is most likely a total of four.'

'Still, four against one: still bad odds. Especially as these people are badasses.'

'Cerović is a pussy, and they won't know I'm coming, so to me that's only three against one.'

'Still outnumbered; especially as they have guns.'

'You're forgetting something, Pet.'

'What?

'I can also be really mean too.'

Pet opened her mouth to speak, but the words died in her throat. There was nothing to say. Tom's face was fixed, his jaw tight and his eyes dead ahead.

'You want to hear what Cerović and Babić said?' she asked as they pulled off the main road and pulled over into a small layby on the quiet carriageway.

'Give me the summary. I want to make sure that we are ready for whatever comes over the phone.'

'Cerović tried to ingratiate himself about sourcing the batteries, but Babić was dismissive and just made it clear how important it was that they worked properly as they needed the weapons tested, packed away, and ready to go as soon as possible. All kinda threatening, and Cerović is clearly shit-scared.'

Tom paused; his eyes fixed on the windscreen. 'Okay. Then we wait until last light. We can't afford any more delay; I have a nasty feeling that, once the weapons are moved, their reasons for holding Mike start to get less pressing. I suspect that once they realise that they can't break him down they will just kill him and bury him where he will never be found. That's not going to happen, Pet. Not on my watch.'

28

Cerović was happy; he had to admit it, despite his anxiety about the psychos he was currently working with. He knew that Babić hated him and would probably cheerfully put a bullet in his head at a moment's notice. He was thankful that, for the time being at least, they needed him. They needed him to make these things work as they were all too fucking stupid to do it themselves.

Operating them was different. Any idiot could use them with a little bit of practice, and Babić had made it clear that they had enough operatives ready to deploy them, once they were all built. The six units that lay on the floor of the mobile home now were all ready and assembled, each with the e-weapons circuitry wired into the mechanism. It was now simply a case of integrating the batteries to give the additional power beyond that which the integrated power cells would give. These six were intended to be the first tranche of what was to be a whole raft of attacks that would be taking place in various countries over the next few months. He hadn't yet been told of the targets, though. Babić was a secretive bastard.

There was a rhythmic pumping of loud and fast music from the small barn in the yard, something which Cerović had found a little odd when he had heard it on arrival. Some of Babić's men were serious muscle-heads and he just assumed that they were working out in some kind of makeshift gym. The thrash metal was a little distracting but, as his work was simple, it wasn't such a problem.

All he now needed to do was load up the new cells and he was ready to rock and roll. He had tested all the batteries, and each was carrying a good level of charge, although he planned to use the field charger on each as soon as they got to wherever the deployment was going to be.

These six weapons, if correctly targeted and deployed, would cause chaos. Cerović had no idea what type of chaos they would cause, as Babić had blanked him when he asked what the targets would be. In reality, he didn't really care; as long as he was paid. He was going to be rich, and that was all he was bothered about. No more of the daily grind of work, just serious money in Bitcoin hidden away and ready to support him in luxury for the rest of his life.

The door banged open and Babić burst in. 'Cerović, I hope you have good news?' Babić said quietly in his deep, resonant voice, staring intently at him with those cruel, nasty eyes.

Cerović was frightened of Babić when he had first met him and today, if anything he was closer to terrified than scared. Cerović knew that if these weapons didn't work, then they would have no hesitation in shooting him dead.

'Y—yes. I've tested and I am certain the new power cells work correctly,' Cerović's voice trembled as he spoke.

'Calm, my friend. Calm.' Babić's smile was anything but reassuring. 'As long as these work as you have assured me, then all will be well, Stefan, and you will be a very rich young man.'

'Thank you.'

'Once the devices are in theatre, how quickly can you have them ready for deployment?'

'A few hours only to charge and integrate all the batteries. Sir, may I ask a question?'

'That depends, Stefan.'

Cerović nervously cleared his throat once more and ran his hands through his greasy, tangled hair. 'About my fee?' he left the word hanging.

'You have done well, my friend. I will arrange for the first instalment of your fee to be transferred in accordance with your instructions, yes?'

'Thank you, sir.'

'Just remember, Stefan. We don't tolerate failure in my organisation. The consequences of failure will be severe. Do you understand?'

'Of course, sir. I have not let you down yet, have I?'

'Of course not, of course not,' Babić guffawed just a little, but there was little mirth in the sound. 'Come, walk with me a moment. You have worked hard and maybe some coffee before you proceed to packing these away ready for transportation. There is an aircraft fuelled and ready to transport them to theatre, and you will be accompanying them to ensure their safe arrival. Come, now.'

Babić turned on his heels and strode out into the yard, Cerović following obediently. Cerović began to veer towards the farmhouse where there was a small kitchen, but Babić stomped off towards the barn.

'We have a flask of coffee in here, no need to brew fresh,' Babić said without looking backwards as he made his way to the barn door. The volume of the music increased as they got closer.

Babić threw the door open and strode in, whereupon the music promptly stopped.

The sudden silence was palpable and cloying. A fetid stench of shit and piss assailed Cerović's nostrils as he went into the dimly lit space. Two masked men, dressed in black wearing ski masks, stood either side of a naked, hooded man who was kneeling on the thin layer of straw, his manacled hands held limply aloft. He was shaking and trembling uncontrollably as the pain and pressure of the position he was in clearly took control of his muscles.

Cerović's mouth opened in shock at the sight of the pathetic individual. He had never witnessed someone being tortured before. The vivid red weals and seeping blood on his torso told a story, as did his blood-soaked neck and upper chest.

Babić nodded at one of the guards, who walked up to the bedraggled figure and ripped the hood from his head. The face beneath was covered in dried blood that had clearly come from a poorly dressed head wound on the man's temple. He had dirty blond blood-stained hair, and his face was bruised and swollen.

He blinked painfully as the light assaulted his eyes, his breathing was shallow and rapid, and he looked utterly shattered. He looked up, realisation on his face as he looked at the unmasked Babić, for the first time.

'Mr Brogan, how are you?' Babić said, a cruel smile spreading across his face. He walked across the barn where he picked up a silver thermos flask from the floor. He unscrewed the top and poured the steaming liquid into a tin mug, sipping it briefly before screwing up his face.

'Milan, this coffee is terrible. Still, wet, and warm, as my father used to say. Stefan, can I offer you a cup?' he said, offering the chipped enamelled mug to Cerović, who just stared at the scene before him, open mouthed.

29

As Babić's words came through the speaker, Tom jolted upright. 'Activate Cerović's camera.'

'Tom?'

'You said you could activate his phone's camera; do it.'

'Tom, if I activate it, I can't say if it will be apparent to anyone looking at the phone. Are you okay?'

'Do it. Do it now. I need to see what Cerović is seeing. He always wears his phone on his belt, so we should be able to see what's going on.'

'You sure?'

'Pet, just do it. Do it now,' he spat every word with a forcefulness that Pet had not heard from Tom before. She felt a chill down her spine and a wave of fear and concern wash over her.

Her fingers tapped at the screen. 'Okay, I am activating his camera now.'

A video image appeared on the screen and static erupted from the speakers. The screen flickered to reveal a pin-sharp image of the inside of a wooden structure. Rough wooden beams were supporting timber walls, and the floor was covered in straw. A rusting bicycle was leaning against the wall next to a powerful-looking portable music player, presumably the source of the pounding music. The image shifted as Cerović moved a few degrees to the left, revealing the bedraggled and naked figure of Mike Brogan kneeling on the floor: his arms shackled, his face and neck a mask of blood, and a crudely-affixed dressing to his temple. There were bruises and weals on his torso but, overall, he didn't look as bad as Tom had feared.

'Holy shit, it's Mike. He's injured,' Pet gasped.

'He's okay. Look at his eyes: he is still with us. They've not broken him yet.' Tom spoke reassuringly, but his face remained grim and his eyes never left the screen.

A voice boomed from the speakers, rich and resonant, and Tom's stomach lurched as Babić spoke.

'You see, Stefan, this man Mr Brogan has been meddling in affairs that do not concern him. He is an American agent, Stefan, and he has been interfering in our business which is not a desirable state of affairs. Now, Mr Brogan, you have very few more opportunities to tell us the truth. My men have been very patient with you and your mistruths up until now. This nasty business of interrogation is really unnecessary, so I would like to give you the opportunity now of enlightening me, the leader of this organisation, with your reason for being in Sarajevo. I hope that you choose not to tell me, as I have some wonderful plans of how I will deliver the, shall we say, stimulus? Yes... stimulus... of ensuring that you tell me what I want to know. Now then, anything new to add?' The question hung in the air, but Cerović's camera phone remained trained on Mike.

Mike simply shook his head, 'I told your men everything,' his voice was parched and cracked.

Suddenly and violently one of the masked guards appeared in front of the camera bearing a length of hosepipe which he whipped with terrible force across the torso of the kneeling Mike. It connected with a sharp crack and Mike fell back and screamed, a howling, animal noise that came from his very core.

Pet let out a muffled yelp, but Tom stared impassively at the screen, a rising sense of dread in his chest.

The picture shifted, as if Cerović was turning away from the violence, just as a further crack followed by a scream as the hosepipe struck Mike once more.

'Continue as before until you hear from me. I will speak to him again in a few hours,' Babić barked as he marched out of the barn.

'Cut the camera, Pet.' Tom said, his voice displaying a quality that Pet had not heard from him before.

They sat in silence for a full minute before Tom spoke once again. 'We are getting Mike out. We are getting him out, now.'

'Tom, it's so dangerous. They are fully armed and look like serious people. We need backup.'

Tom didn't speak. He just sat staring at the dash, his face a blank mask. As he breathed slowly in through his nose then released it slow and controlled through his mouth, an image entered his mind. His foster father's face, hard and lined. A soldier's face, a warrior's features, but at the same time, with twinkling and kind eyes. The image seemed to speak to him in that soft, Highland brogue that he knew so well. *'Tom, my boy. This is a shite situation right enough, but you can make it right. You have to make it right, boy. You know what to do, Tom. You always know, just do right, boy and everything will be good.'* The rhythmic quality of the words washed over him and he felt the turmoil begin to subside, his mind beginning to clear. He had a job to do. Mike needed him and, by God, he was getting him out of there. He would kill every single fucking one of them if necessary, but he was getting Mike out.

'Tom, you okay?'

'I'm sure. Drive back to where you dropped me off. I'm getting Mike out.'

'But Tom…'

Tom interrupted her, abruptly. 'No buts, Pet. I'm going up now; the light is fading fast and I'm getting Mike out now, as soon as it's the right time to do it.'

'I can guess,' Pet sighed. She knew that the determination and blank, frankly terrifying, look in Tom's eyes meant only one thing.

'Because it is the right thing to do, Pet. You know me as well as anyone, you know my character flaws and you know that the only thing stopping me going fucking mad is what my foster father taught me. Let's go.'

'Tom?'

'Pet, no. We don't have the luxury of debating my mental state. I'd love to have the time to consider it but, right now, Mike is being tortured and pretty soon he is going to get a bullet in the head. Let's go.'

Pet opened her mouth but, sensing the inevitable, closed it without saying anything else. She started the Skoda and drove back towards the farmhouse.

30

Babić was pleased. The weapons looked good and, despite his unusual character, Cerović seemed to have done a good job with them. He had watched as Cerović had assembled them over the past few weeks with help from Risto. He was confident that they would work following the testing that he had just witnessed.

His contact in the Embassy had given him due warning of the arrival of Mike Brogan, described as the senior agency "trouble-shooter". His capture had been all too easy, but it was proving difficult to get him to talk.

He was looking forward to getting this operation over with. The move from militia to crime had been simple and seamless and, for a long time, he had operated throughout the Balkans importing and distributing drugs and whatever other opportunities came his way. His brief incarceration in Belgrade had been nothing more than an inconvenience—he had still been able to cut deals and run things just as easily inside as out—but this was the big hit.

He looked outside the farmhouse and for a few minutes watched Cerović stacking the crates containing the weapons, ready for the transport that was on its way. It was all looking good. All down to his organisation skills, of course. Well, that and the finances supplied to him by the investors.

Looking at his watch, he realised that he needed to message his contact to let him know of their current status. The investors shied away from any direct contact; in fact, he had never physically met or seen any of them, apart from the late Zelenko, in a meeting just before he had been jailed. He had been worried about that, but contact had been re-established almost immediately on his release through the secure channels and they were continuing, almost without a skipped beat.

Opening his tablet, he selected the secure communication app. There was no video capacity, just a distorted voice that crackled out of the small speaker.

'Report?' The voice was again flat and mechanical, altered by voice-disguising software. He thought he could detect a trace of American, but he couldn't be sure.

'Good news: we are ready to proceed. The devices are all tested and operational. I have seen this myself. Cerović has done a good job.'

'Excellent news. What are your timescales?'

'The transport is on its way to collect the weapons and transport them to the airfield. The onwards journey is all planned and I do not anticipate any problems.'

'We need to be ready to strike within the next four days. I take it that this is achievable, yes?'

'Of course. We will fly across Europe and our final approach will be by sea to the operational theatre. I have lots of experience with these smuggling routes, as I am sure you are aware.' He hardened his tone, just a little; it didn't hurt to remind these faceless plutocrats that they weren't dealing with an amateur.

'It is why Zelenko assured us that you were the correct individual for this role. Unfortunately for him, his enemies were many and his profile in the Ukraine was just too overt.'

'Have your investigations revealed anything of his murder?'

'A reprisal attack is the intelligence that we are hearing from our sources in Ukrainian government and law-enforcement. He had upset many over his business dealings with the Russians. A lesson to all, perhaps.'

'Clearly. We will not fail.'

'Are your men aware of the final destination?'

'Only I know the final country; my men will only know once appropriate. They are fully trained, and I have six operatives on the ground already. Operational security is tight, you can be assured.'

'Excellent. Once you are in place and ready for the final orders you will call me. Only then will the objectives be revealed to you.'

'Understood. But we will require exact GPS coordinates and, once in theatre, we will need at the very least twelve hours' notice. I assume a precisely coordinated strike is required.'

'You will be informed when appropriate.' The voice was flat and dismissive.

'It would be very useful to know the strike order in advance so that Cerović can accurately plan and programme. He tells me that it may be important.'

'This is still subject to change. Remain flexible. Just make sure that your men are ready. This operation will wreak havoc that we need to be ready to exploit. Timings are crucial. We need the objectives to be struck hard to create the maximum chaos.'

'It will be. You have my word, we will destroy the objective.'

'I have told you this before: fear is a strong weapon amongst the public. The perception and fear of destruction is more powerful than the reality. People will be terrified and large organisations will be finished, which will allow for maximum profitability.'

'And I will share in this profit. You remember our deal.'

'Naturally. You will become a very rich man. Enough small talk. Carry on as agreed.' There was a click, indicating that the call was over.

Babić sat back in his chair and poured a large measure of vodka into a small glass and swallowed it in one. He smiled. They were ready.

His phone buzzed on the table. It was Yuri, the driver of his transport.

'30 minutes to arrival.'

Quickly he stood and walked out into the courtyard. He shoved the static caravan door open and stepped in to where Cerović was sealing the final crate.

'Cerović, we need to be ready to move in thirty minutes. Transport is on its way, we fly very soon.' Without waiting for a reply, he turned and crossed over to the barn where he nodded at

Risto and then beckoned him outside.

'The transport is thirty minutes away. Cerović and I will be taking the weapons to the departure point.'

'And if Brogan continues his current line?'

'After twelve hours, clear this place out completely. Not a trace of our presence to remain, understand? Kill Brogan. Put him in the pig swill and let the swine have a good meal for once.'

31

Tom kept very low as he crawled through the gorse bush, inching into the same position he had adopted just a few hours before. His black clothing and dark balaclava were perfect camouflage as the night drew in. There was very little ambient light in this rural area, and he was confident that even if anyone stared directly at his location, he wouldn't be seen.

Moving slowly, he lifted the image-intensifying night vision binoculars and looked at the farmhouse in front of him. A figure came out of the static and walked across the yard. Focusing on the face he recognised the stocky body, dark beard and scarred face of Babić walk up to the barn. The door opened and Babić spoke briefly to the masked guard before turning and walking back to the farmhouse.

The tinny thumping of the hard-core dance music was still blaring from the barn. Whilst he appreciated how unpleasant it would have been for Mike having his ears assaulted by the relentless cacophony, it was perfect for his purposes. He wouldn't need to be overly stealthy in his approach, as the only thing that anyone in the farmhouse or barn would hear would be the relentless din from inside the building.

Scanning the farmhouse, he saw a pile of large, square wooden crates now stacked outside the static caravan, clearly waiting to be moved.

This wasn't good. Despite his desire to get Mike out urgently, there was no point rushing in until he had some intelligence as to what he was facing. Going into the unknown now would be just as likely to get them both killed.

Neil Lancaster

His phone buzzed in his pocket and he answered it by pressing the button on his Bluetooth headset.

'Pet?' he whispered, even though he didn't need to.

'Babić has told Cerović to be ready to move the weapons in thirty minutes. There is transport on its way.'

'Christ, they are moving fast. Anything on where?'

'Nothing. He just told him to be ready to fly soon.'

'Anything on Mike?'

'Didn't say anything.'

Tom paused, turning the ramifications of this over. 'Once they've left the country, they have no further need for Mike. I can't get Mike out until I know who is in there. At least once those two have gone I can be sure I am shortening the odds. Thanks, Pet. Keep listening.'

'Sure thing. Be careful.'

'You know me, Pet.' Tom pressed the earpiece again and it went dead.

He felt a little bad about how abrupt he had been with Pet before leaving; it wasn't her fault and even he could tell that she had looked a little scared of him. He had wordlessly prepared his kit, checked the MP5 and, once she had driven him into the forest, set off without a backwards glance, the butt of the weapon in his shoulder, in full patrol mode.

The yard outside the buildings was quiet, with just the pile of boxes stacked and ready to go. A thought occurred to Tom. If he waited for the boxes to be loaded onto the transport and leave the yard, it was likely that they would never see them again. He couldn't rely on the malware on Cerović's phone, that was for sure. There was no guarantee he would take it and, if they were flying, it would be switched off in any case.

He scanned his surroundings once more; it was almost dark now, with some shafts of light escaping from the barn and a small glimmer from the farmhouse. Quickly, and before he could talk himself out of it, he made a decision.

He stood and advanced towards the buildings; moving stealthily as if patrolling, stopping and using the low-light sight on the MP5 as he advanced. He swiftly covered the distance between his laying-up point and the edge of the barn. Hugging the building line, he made his way around the wooden walls until he was on the edge of the hard standing where all the vehicles were stood.

Suddenly a shaft of light erupted from the door of the barn, flaring the low light sight. The volume of the pounding music increased. Tom moved his head back and flattened himself against the wall, his finger reaching for the trigger of the MP5. A dark clad figure wearing a camouflage jacket exited the building, an MP5 casually slung around his back. He pulled a balaclava up away from his face as he walked to the edge of the car parking area and reached for his fly. He then stood lighting a cigarette as he simultaneously began to take a piss, puffing away as the stream of urine splashed against the wall of the static. Zipping his fly back up, he turned and walked up to the crates, peering at the boxes in a half-interested fashion as he smoked his cigarette.

Tom stood as still as a statue, ready to fire at a second's notice, his breathing easy and controlled as he watched the guard puffing away. After a minute, the other man tossed the cigarette to the floor and ground it with his boot, before returning to the barn and slamming the door shut as he went back in, thankfully dulling the noise from within once more.

Tom realised that this could be his last opportunity and so, making no attempt at stealth, he walked straight up to Cerović's Land Cruiser and opened the door, ignoring the internal light that came on as he did so. He figured that anyone looking out at that particular moment would assume it was one of the other guards, and anyway: speed was everything. He quickly reached under the seat and pulled out the GPS dog tracker he had planted there hours earlier. Again, making little attempt at stealth, he slammed the car door shut.

Moving to the pile of crates he tried the lid of the nearest one. He swore as he noted that it was secured by a single screw at each corner. He reached down to his waistband and pulled out his

Gerber multi-tool, extending the Phillips screwdriver attachment.

Fortunately, the screws were not overly long so it was only a minute's work to unscrew each and soon he was lifting the lid. A mass of bubble wrap and polystyrene chips filled the box so Tom felt deeper, trying to get a sense of what was inside.

Something wasn't right. Whatever was in the crate did not in any way feel like the weapon described as being involved in the prison van break in Belgrade. Matte black tubular metal arms were folded inwards towards what felt like a bulky core in the centre of the box. It didn't feel like any type of weapon whatsoever, and certainly nothing like what they were expecting.

He looked around briefly, checking for any watchers. He needed to see what was inside the box. He raised the MP5 up, using the torch on the stock to illuminate the contents. Parting the polystyrene chips, he saw the tubular arms, a central unit with the words *"Agrispray 200"* emblazoned on it, and a cylindrical metal object with wiring and a mobile phone clamped into place at the top of the dark metal.

Tom extinguished the light on the MP5. It was a drone. He was certain and, if the brand name was anything to go by, it could be assumed it was an agricultural type, probably capable of carrying serious weight. The tubular arms were folded inwards, but he could see where the propellers would be mounted, and there was a powerful-looking central motor core with one of the Saft batteries that he had supplied to Cerović just a few hours ago strapped to the underside of the unit.

It was clearly a heavily adapted drone, with a mobile phone attached and a military grade battery powering it. It had to be a bomb, there was no other explanation; but how, and why? If it was a bomb of some kind, why was Cerović, an electronics expert, building it when a group of ex-military criminals would almost certainly have that experience amongst their number? Tom also wondered how this fitted in with the schematics that Pet had retrieved from Cerović's computer. They needed to know more.

He quickly decided that this changed nothing at this particular moment; he had to plant the tracker and get moving. Mike was still in that barn a few feet away getting tortured.

He quickly examined the wooden lid and found that it was polystyrene-lined, a three-inch slab of the white protective packing material stuck onto the underside. Taking out the blade on his Gerber he made a small incision in the side of the material, cutting it into a letter box shape. Quickly and efficiently he widened this hole, digging out the interior until he was able to slot the GPS tag inside. He then took the blade and cut the end of the section he had removed to make a rudimentary lid that he jammed in next to the tracker. The hole was now almost invisible, and all the debris he had created had fallen into the crate with the loose chips.

Tom replaced the lid and began screwing the fixings back in place. He was screwing the final one in when he heard the rumble of an approaching vehicle. He sped up, as calmly as he could, as the lights of the vehicle swung into the yard. A little over an inch of the screw was still proud of the surface of the lid.

The front door of the farmhouse opened, a shaft of light piercing the darkness. Tom completed the last two turns of the screw and then dropped out of sight behind the crates, breathing heavily.

Over the sound of the music he could hear the faint crunch of feet on gravel walking towards his location. He shuffled onto his front and leopard-crawled to the side of the static caravan, breathing heavily. *That was too damn close*, he thought, hoping that it would be worth it. It seemed that the drones would be leaving very soon, but he couldn't be any further distracted by that: his prime and only objective right now was getting Mike out.

He continued along the floor, noting with a wrinkling nose that he was probably crawling through the guard's piss.

Out of sight from the farmhouse, he circled around until he found an observation point behind a large, felled pine stump. Nestling in behind it, he eased into a viewing position once more. Pulling the MP5 sight to his eye, he used the optic to view the scene around him. It wasn't as good as a proper night sight, but with the lights from the truck and the open house door it was more than sufficient.

The truck was a small removal van, unmarked and scruffy looking. The driver, who was dressed in overalls, stood talking with Cerović and Babić by the crates.

After a minute they began to load the crates onto the back of the truck via the hydraulic tail-lift and within ten minutes the roller shutter at the back was closed and the six drones, and Tom's GPS tracker, were on the move once again out of the yard. Tom couldn't help but note that each of the crates were identical in size and shape. Was there a single drone in each, he wondered?

Cerović and Babić returned to the farmhouse and the door slammed shut behind them. Tom started to move once again along the building line of the barn, trying to see if there was anywhere he could get a peek inside the windowless building. He circumnavigated it looking for weaknesses, but the building was secure, and the timbers were new and stout with nowhere to look inside. He would need another method of ingress to rescue Mike. The most important task would be to find out how many opponents there would be once Cerović and Babić left. With those two still on site, Tom had less of a chance: they were all well-armed and there would be at least four of them. At the very least there would be two people undertaking the TQ of Mike: possibly more, bearing in mind one had felt secure enough to come outside for a cigarette and a piss. He would have to wait; there was no other option. Backing away he retreated to his earlier observation point by the tree stump and nestled in behind it once more.

Pulling his phone out, he dialled Pet.

'What gives, Detective?'

'A lorry has just come, and they've loaded up the crates and it's moved off. I'll tell you something, though, Pet. They aren't what we think inside them. The one I looked at had a bloody drone inside. A really heavy agricultural looking one with one of the batteries strapped onto it. It also has a bloody mobile phone attached. If I was a betting man, I'd say they were drone-mounted bombs of some variety in those crates.'

'Jesus! Are you sure?' said Pet.

'The one I looked in definitely had a drone in it, with what looked like some sort of improvised device underneath. I don't like the look of it at all. I've managed to secrete the GPS tag into one of the crates, so can you start tracking it?'

'How the hell did you manage that?' she asked.

'Just took the opportunity. Anything on Cerović's phone?'

'Nothing beyond the fact that Babić has just told them that they are moving imminently and that they will be flying. They are all going in Cerović's vehicle, Cerović has asked him for mission details but Babić just curtly told him to shut the fuck up, so he's not one for small talk I guess.'

'Right. Okay. Stay tuned, speak soon.' Tom hung up.

The door opened again and both men left the farmhouse, Babić leading the way. They walked up to Cerović's Land Cruiser and got in, the engine started, and the large SUV roared away.

Tom dialled once again. 'Pet, they're under way. Keep listening. I'm giving it ten minutes, then I'm going in. Be ready to bring the car up if I shout, okay?'

'You know what I am going to say next right?'

'Always careful, Pet.'

32

Risto and his brother Milan looked down with disdain at their prisoner as he lay on his side, quivering in pain after the last six blows that had been delivered to his naked form with the hosepipe.

Despite his frustration, Risto couldn't help but feel a grudging respect for the American agent. Not many men could have stood up to the hours of sensory deprivation, stress positions and occasional beatings that they had delivered, but he had remained resolute in spite of it all. He scratched his face; the ski mask was as itchy as hell, but Babić had been clear in his orders that they remained masked at all times. Good for intimidation, he had told them. It had seemed ridiculous, especially as Brogan was hooded as well.

'I think he will crack soon, Milan. He is weakening,' he bellowed in Serb into the ear of his twin brother.

'He is a strong one. Normally they break earlier than this, brother. How much longer?'

'Babić said twelve hours and to try some questions after every four. If nothing after that we kill him and dispose of him. Once they are out of the country it matters not what the American knows. That's what Babić said, anyway.'

'I'm getting tired of this, brother. Why don't we just kill him now?'

'You want to be the one to disobey Babić's orders? I know I don't; I've seen what he is capable of. I once saw him rip the skin off someone who displeased him.' Risto shook his head. His brother was a fierce warrior, but he was as stupid as a mule sometimes.

'I guess so. What happens after he is disposed of?'

'We call Babić and wait for instructions. We have to be ready to leave the country to support the operation, or they may want us to remain in Sarajevo. You know Babić, he doesn't share information.'

Over the din of the loud, pounding music the wail of a car alarm penetrated the wall of sound coming from outside the barn doors.

Risto scowled. He thought the others had all gone, so what had caused the vehicle alarm? As far as he was aware it was just the two of them left to continue Brogan's questioning.

'Milan, go and see what is happening.'

'I thought we were to stay together?'

'Never mind that; check it out and be careful. Weapon in the shoulder, brother, yes?'

Milan didn't answer, he just nodded and left the barn, shutting the door behind him. Risto turned back to Brogan's pathetic form on the floor, his nose wrinkling at the all-pervading stench of piss and shit. Checking his watch, he saw that they still had eleven hours left of this unrelenting, pounding music to suffer and, even with the small ear defenders he had tucked in his ear canal, it was still really draining.

All of a sudden the wailing car alarm stopped. That was good, he thought. Car alarms were often unreliable, and more hassle than they were worth. It wasn't as if they, as a dangerous criminal gang, were at a great deal of risk of car theft. Anyone who tried to steal from them soon found out that crime didn't pay.

Risto glanced back at the door, swinging his MP5 to point at whoever would come through it. He was feeling fairly relaxed, even more so when his twin's combat-jacketed and ski-masked form returned through the door, his own MP5 held in front of him, thumb raised in greeting. Instantly Risto relaxed: all, it seemed, was okay.

He turned his attention back to Brogan, who was shifting positions on the floor. Risto scowled; this was not permitted. He stepped forward, picked up the hosepipe, and delivered another hard blow across Brogan's legs. He was rewarded with a hiss of pain in response.

'No move. No move one fucking bit, American,' Risto shouted in English at the pathetic form.

Suddenly the pounding music stopped, only to be replaced with an all-consuming silence.

He turned back towards his brother, who was stood watching him, impassively. It was only then he noticed the blood on Milan's black-and-white combat jacket. The front was drenched in a dark bib of bright red blood.

'Brother, what happened? Whose blood is that on your jacket?'

The man before him seemed to smile behind the ski-mask and, in a quiet, almost amused tone said two words: 'Your brother's.'

Suddenly all was clear. Risto began to swing his MP5 upwards in an arc to engage the imposter but he realised, immediately, that he was too late. Far too late.

The imposter moved with impossible speed as he brought his own MP5 to bear, the report from the silenced weapon no more than a mechanical thunk.

The first low velocity 9mm parabellum struck Risto in the left side of his chest. It felt like he had been kicked by a mule, the bullet smashing into his thorax and carving a big hole in his lungs before deflecting off his spine. The second followed a millisecond later, smashing into his jaw and ricocheting upwards into his cranium. The low velocity characteristics of the projectile meant that it didn't exit his skull, as much of its kinetic energy had been dissipated by the initial impact. Instead it bounced about, destroying his brain completely. Risto dropped as if his legs had suddenly disappeared, dead before he hit the floor.

*

Tom tore off the ski-mask and ditched it on the floor before hastily unbuttoning the blood-soaked combat jacket.

It had been childishly simple after the guard had come out to investigate the car alarm. Tom had leaped on the man's back, locking his legs around his body, where they then both collapsed on the floor, Tom in complete control. It was then a simple matter of drawing the razor-sharp blade on his Gerber across the guard's throat and neck, slicing the windpipe open and cutting the carotid artery. This rendered his victim unable to scream, no matter how much he had wanted to. Tom had then released him and watched, as the guard had clutched at his ruined throat, trying pointlessly to stem the arterial bleed arcing from his destroyed carotid. He was dead within a minute with no blood reaching his brain and no air hitting his lungs.

Tom had watched impassively as the man had thrashed and struggled with panic in his flashing eyes. Tom felt nothing beyond a cold acknowledgement that he had done what needed to be done to save Mike. He would worry about anything else another time.

It was then a simple case of stripping the combat jacket— all wet and sticky with copper-smelling blood—from the corpse and slipping it on, replacing his own balaclava with the man's ski mask. He had barely looked at the man's face as he removed the mask, instead focused on what he needed to do.

The next guard had presented no difficulties, the element of surprise being wholly in Tom's favour.

Tom wiped the Gerber's blade on the corpse's combat jacket, closed the blade, and slipped it back into its case. He was silently thankful that he hadn't used Pet's treasured Leatherman for the gruesome task.

He approached Mike, who was still naked and shivering on the floor with his face hooded. Tom squatted down, and gently removed the hood from Mike's head.

'I'm getting a bit used to pulling your backside out of the fire, Mike,' he said gently and without sarcasm.

Mike blinked painfully as the light assaulted his eyes, 'Tom? Tom is that you?' His face was a mask of pain and confusion as the realisation began to hit home.

'I'm here, man. I'm here, you're safe,' Tom knelt down, hesitant as to how to deal with his friend. He lay an awkward reassuring hand on his shoulder. 'Look at me, buddy, look at me now.' Tom's voice was gentle and reassuring, almost soothing.

'Tom?' Mike said again and shook his head to clear the fog. The smell surrounding him was terrible, but as his eyes became accustomed to the light. Tom could see the familiar spark of intelligence was still alive in there.

'Yeah, it's Tom. It's all sorted, you're safe,' Tom said, hoping it was true, and acutely aware that he still needed to clear the rest of the buildings. He had no idea if anyone else was there, although he considered it unlikely.

'Thank fuck for that. Thank fuck.' Mike closed his eyes, once again, his body visibly relaxing as the reality hit home that he was safe.

'Mike, I need you to listen to me. Okay?'

Mike sat up, suddenly aware of his nakedness. 'Are my clothes here?'

Tom looked at the corner of the room and saw a pile of clothes on a chair.

'Yeah, they're over there, man, but I need you to listen. I need to check out the rest of the buildings to make sure no one is still here.' Tom picked up the pile of clothes and dropped them by Mike's feet. 'Get dressed. There is some water in a jerrycan over there; use it to clean up while I clear the rest of the place.'

Tom walked up to the guard he had just shot and released his MP5 from the clip. He checked that it was loaded and then placed it on the floor by Mike's feet.

'It's loaded, Mike. I am going to check out the rest of the place. I will knock three times when I return, understand?'

'Yeah,' Mike said, his voice more together and resolute, the efficient CIA agent in him slowly rising to the surface.

'Repeat what I just said,' Tom said. He needed to be sure that Mike was ready for this. The last thing he needed was Mike shooting him as he came back.

'You'll knock three times when you come back. I'm good Tom. Go.' He opened his eyes fully and Tom could see comprehension and understanding flooding back. Tom allowed himself a brief smile. *Jesus*, he thought. *Just how tough is this guy?*

'Good. Right, we don't have time to waste. I am going to call Pet and get her to come up as soon as we are clear, and then we are getting the fuck out of here. Okay?'

'Sure. I just need a minute to clear up. The bastards wouldn't let me take a shit or a piss.'

'You're all good, Mike. I'll be back soon.'

Tom left the barn, the butt of the MP5 nestled into his shoulder. He quickly ran to the cover of the SUV he had used for the diversion. He squatted down and used the low-light optic to survey the farmhouse, which was still in total darkness. Turning, he could see that the static caravan was in a similar state. Being the closest and smallest, he decided to clear the caravan first.

Slowly, carefully, he inched the door open, peeking through the crack. Then he suddenly and forcefully burst through the door, the sure-fire torch emitting a blinding beam from the front of the MP5. The room was empty, beyond a workbench that was littered with electronic detritus.

Tom left and quickly crossed to the farmhouse. He efficiently gained entry and, room by room, cleared the building without any dramas. The building was almost completely empty, beyond a couple of camp beds and a fridge stocked with beer and ready meals. A microwave oven seemed to be the only method of cooking, and a few rudimentary utensils and a couple of plates sat in the sink, covered in congealed food. The property had, it seemed, just been used for the storage and modification of the drones and for holding Mike. There was nothing Tom could immediately see that would be worth taking or investigating further, although something told him that there may be some value in revisiting the caravan where Cerović had worked.

He dialled Pet.

'Tom?' she said, the concern in her voice unmistakable.

'Mike is safe and the property is clear. Come round with the car now, okay?'

'On my way.'

Returning to the barn, Tom knocked three times as agreed, before standing to one side of the door and inching it open, just slightly.

'Mike, it's Tom. I am about to come back in; the property is clear. Repeat, it's Tom. Please don't shoot me.' The last thing he needed was a confused and itchy trigger fingered Mike, emptying a magazine of 9mm parabellums at him.

'It's cool. I'm fine,' Mike's voice was clear and business-like.

Tom gently pushed the door open before walking slowly in, his hands held in front of him and the MP5 hanging loosely on its sling.

Mike was fully dressed and was searching through the deceased guard's pockets, eventually standing with the man's mobile phone, a large and almost empty bottle of mineral water in his other hand.

'You okay?' Tom asked.

'Apart from being beaten with a hosepipe, held in stress positions for hours and having shit myself… I'm cool, buddy.' Tom was amazed to see a broad smile spread across his friend's face. Despite a face that was registering pain and discomfort, Tom could see that Mike Brogan, senior CIA trouble shooter, was back; if a little damaged.

'Seriously: any injuries?'

'My head is cut and I am sore as a bejesus from all the stress positions, but I'm surprisingly fine. I never want to hear thrash metal again, though. In their defence, they run a fairly tight tactical questioning routine. I only probably had another twenty-four hours left in me, and I would have had to move on from the cover story. I am also really hungry.'

'Cool. Well, Pet will be here any moment. We need to get out of here urgently; we have no idea if anyone else is likely to show. They may be considering a clear-up operation.'

'Agreed. Anything in the house?'

'No. Not that I could see; I think it was just a flop-house.'

There was the sound of a car from outside and alarm flashed in Mike's eyes. Tom hefted the MP5 and moved to the door, peering outside. 'It's Pet. Relax, man.'

'Seriously, I'm cool. I just need a little time to adjust.' His eyes didn't totally reflect his assurances. He looked exhausted, his face lined and drawn.

'You'll be f—'

'Tom?' Mike interrupted.

'Yeah?'

'Thanks, man. This is becoming a habit.' Mike approached and hugged Tom, fleetingly and brusquely. He broke off, and then it was back to business. 'Right, anything we need to check before we get out of here?'

'Need to check the other guard, and I want Pet to look quickly at Cerović's workbench in the static caravan. This isn't what we think it is, Mike; the weapons are not like the Belgrade job. There are bombs of some type, mounted on big, agricultural spec drones.'

'What?'

'Drones, Mike. Big powerful drones, they look like crop sprayer types—the brand name was *Agrispray*—all with some kind of improvised weapon strapped to them.'

'Jesus. Where are they now?'

'Gone on their way somewhere, but I managed to get a tracker in there. We will fill you in when we get away.'

Mike's eyes flashed with respect. 'Well done, bud. Right, let's get moving.'

'Mike?' Tom said, his eyes not leaving Mike's. 'Are you going to tell us the whole story about why we are here?'

Mike stopped and returned Tom's gaze, 'Let's get out of here, then I'll tell you everything, Tom, I promise.'

33

They quickly dealt with everything that remained at the property, Tom rapidly locating the other dead guard's mobile phone. They threw the MP5s in the boot of the car; as they were American-issued weapons, Mike wanted them to be available for further examination.

Pet had briefly hugged Mike with relief, before they all moved into their instinctive professional roles.

As Tom drove the Skoda away, he brought Mike up to speed on everything that had happened since meeting Cerović. Mike listened wordlessly.

When Tom had finished, Mike took a deep breath. 'So, at the very least we have one, and possibly six, drones with some type of weapon attached. Jesus, this could be worse than we thought, guys. Do we have anything to suggest what type of weapons? Explosives, nuclear, EMP, biological? We know nothing. Thankfully, Pet, your malware on Cerović's phone has given us half a chance,' he rubbed his face with frustration and obvious fatigue.

'I have a few screenshots I managed to save from Cerović's computer download,' said Pet, scrolling through a tablet computer. 'One of them was some kind of technical specification: electrical circuit diagram or something. I couldn't make anything of it, and just assumed it was some project, bearing in mind we thought we were looking for weapons similar to the one in Belgrade. Here,' she passed the tablet to Mike who looked at it, briefly. His face was blank as he studied the computer-generated diagram.

'Was this all there was?' he asked.

'Pretty much, the auto-destruct programme was as powerful as any I have seen. I only screenshotted that as something to look at later, as it looked like it may be relevant.'

'I'm glad you did, although I'm not sure what this actually is. I'm not an electronics man.' Mike was silent again as he studied the screen, his face giving nothing away. 'I need to get this to someone. I need to get this to someone fast, but I don't know who right now. Jesus, I just don't know who to trust enough with this, but we badly need to know what we are dealing with.'

'What do you think it is?' said Pet.

'It's a weapon of some sort, of that I am sure, but exactly what I have no idea. Do you guys know anyone who may be able to help?'

'Not exactly,' said Tom, 'but I know someone who pretty much knows everyone. I'd be surprised if he didn't know who to call, especially if this is an improvised weapon of some type.'

'Who?' asked Mike.

'An old friend of mine; he knows everyone in military and law enforcement circles. He would definitely know who to show this to.'

'Can you trust him?'

'I trust him more than I trust anyone in the world, Mike,' said Tom, seriously.

'Then do it. We need a break, but stress to him that he should not reach out to any US contacts.'

Tom nodded, 'Pet, can you get me a usable and disposable email account and then upload this schematic into the draft folder.'

Pet nodded and began busying herself on her laptop whilst Tom dialled.

'Hello, who is that bothering me on this fine morning?' a booming, sing-song Devonian accent reverberated in Tom's ear.

'Stan, you okay to speak?' said Tom.

'Tommy boy! Yes, all fine. I'm at home and it's just me and the dog, so fire away, Royal. What you up to? I heard a whisper that you are helping our transatlantic cousins out.'

'Just possibly. As always, I am wondering how you know this; I thought only the big boss knew about it,' Tom smiled. Stan was an old family friend and legendary ex-Royal Marine Regimental Sergeant Major. He now worked as an office clerk at Kilburn police station, but for reasons that nobody really understood he was one of the most influential men Tom had ever met. Stan knew everyone.

'You know me, old son: finger on the pulse. I am assuming that, as always this isn't a social call.' His voice reverberated with the rich tones of Devon delivered with the power of Brian Blessed.

'I am going to give you an email address and password. In the draft folder there will be a screen shot of an electronics schematic. I think it is a weapon of some kind. Can you quietly and discreetly speak to one of your contacts and see if anyone has an idea as to what it is?'

'As it happens, old son, I may have someone in mind. She's ex-military bomb disposal but is now one of the leading experts in IEDs at Fort Halstead. If she doesn't know, she will know someone who does. Can you give me a clue what this is about, although I suspect I know the answer to that question already.' There was a distinct touch of amusement in the booming baritone.

'Sorry, Stan. It's really urgent, mate, like turbo-urgent,' said Tom slipping into the Marine slang, where *"turbo"* was a generic term used to replace *"very"*.

'Roger that, old chap. I'm on it like a car bonnet.'

'Cheers, mate. I will message you the link and password now.'

'Excellent. Now, whatever is going on, be careful, Royal.'

'You know me, Royal.' Tom hung up smiling at the ex-Royal Marines' habit of often referring to each other as *"Royal"*.

'Pet can you send the address and password via secure message to Stan's phone? He uses *WhatsApp*, so at least it will be protected in transit.' He handed his phone over to Pet with the number displayed.

'Sure thing. He sounds a character.'

'He is. If anyone knows who to show this to, it's Stan.'

'So, what next?' asked Pet.

'Mike, we need answers,' said Tom. 'I came out here to help you with this job, and I was happy to do so, but we need to know all the reasons you brought us into this. It's been a really tough couple of days.'

Mike nodded. 'Are you still tracking them, Pet?'

'Cerović's cell phone is still switched on right now, but they aren't really talking, apart from Babić telling him to shut up. The GPS tracker Tom put on one of the crates has them stationary at Visoko, about an hour north of here,' she said.

'Any clues as to where they are going?'

'No. It was made clear that no one would be told until the last moment, but we understand they are flying.'

'Where is the nearest airport?' Mike asked.

'Sarajevo,' Pet answered.

'Not international; they could never get these through a major airport.'

'Lqvi is close to them, but that is tiny,' said Pet, looking at her computer.

'That's where they will be leaving from, then. Nothing else makes sense.'

'Then we call this in, right?' Tom asked.

'Not yet. We can't yet.'

'Why not, for Christ's sake?' Tom was astonished. 'We have stayed totally off-radar so we could get you out. There is clearly someone dirty close to all this but, now you're safe, we have to call this in, surely?'

'Guys, you trust me, right?

'Of course, but this seems like madness,' Tom shook his head.

'I will tell you everything, I promise, just give me a moment to get my head around where we are. Anything from Cerović's bench?'

'Not much: mostly wiring and a few basic components. I suspect the main bulk of the devices were built elsewhere and the caravan was just used to integrate the batteries. I did find these, however.' She passed over a couple of plastic blister packs that contained brand-new SIM cards.

Mike touched the packets briefly. 'Thoughts?'

'The drones are using mobile phones; possibly as detonators, maybe for their GPS,' said Pet.

'Possibly. Don't do anything on the CIA systems just yet.'

'Dare I ask why?' Tom asked.

'Burger.'

'Pardon?' said Tom.

'I want a burger. Let's find a take-out joint and then a hotel. We need a base to plan our next move.

*

Mike, Tom, and Pet all sat in a small room in an anonymous hotel on the outskirts of Sarajevo, the remains of a takeaway meal spread on the floor.

'Still no movement on the GPS tag. Same location, but there still seems to be an awkward silence in the car between Babić and Cerović,' said Pet.

Mike paused for a second before taking a deep breath. 'Okay. For some time now we have been concerned about a high-level leak in the Balkan region. Firstly, we lost a couple of assets in what the police decided were "gangland hits". Both of the individuals had been providing intelligence on the destabilisation being caused by some of the ex-militia groups increasing their grip in the region. They had been using tactics designed to sow distrust in the governments of the Ukraine and other countries in the region that remain susceptible to Russian interference. Much of this disquiet was being propagated by the desire to prompt significant fiscal instability, in order that a particular organisation can look to profit from the chaos. Have you heard of "disaster capitalism"?'

'It came up recently,' Tom said.

'Of course: Mr Zelenko and his neo-Nazi ideals. Yes, that was an interesting concept, that failed thanks to your intervention. We have been hearing rumours of a group of wealthy individuals investing heavily in these types of projects. Their intention seems to be to propagate serious financial instability by causing major unrest, or by causing a huge loss of faith in multinational corporations. The assessment is that they are becoming a serious threat to the interests of the United States and her allies.'

'I can see the potential.'

'It gets worse. Imagine a major multinational company is essentially rendered useless. Can you imagine what would happen to their nearest competitor?'

'Share prices would rocket, right?'

'Absolutely.'

'This I understand,' said Tom. 'So, we stop them?'

'Here is where we have a problem,' said Mike. 'Firstly, we have no idea what they are actually planning, and secondly: as I said, we think we have a mole in this region.' Mike paused a moment. 'The reason you succeeded with Zelenko is that, to coin a phrase, you went a little rogue and the mole would have been as unaware as everyone else about what you were up to.'

'So, what do we do?' asked Pet.

'We take out the mole. Now. Then we stop their plot in whatever form it takes. It's as simple as that.'

'I take it you have a plan?' said Tom

'We have a plan, guys. Us. You have given us the opportunity to follow the drones, but we need access to the infrastructure and resources of the CIA, police, and security services: wherever they are planning to deploy the drones. We will do this together.' Mike paused to let this sink in.

'Okay,' Pet said. 'But I don't have enough database access levels at present without putting myself on the CIA map.'

'Pet, I have been in this job a very long time. Organisationally I have no idea who to trust, but I know some individuals who I would trust with my life. I will make some calls and get you full system access. Then we will announce ourselves as being alive and well. To coin an old English phrase, we will toss a stone in a pond and watch the ripples.'

*

Early the following morning, Mike, Tom, and Pet all sat in the hotel room sipping coffee. They had all snatched a little sleep which, given the urgency of the situation, had seemed a little odd. Mike had been adamant, however, that they all needed rest if they were to be effective.

Mike had made some furtive phone calls which had resulted in him handing Pet a slip of paper containing a username and a password. Within seconds she was back online, with all the intelligence databases of the largest and most powerful intelligence agency at her fingertips.

'Are you ready to make the call?' Pet asked Mike.

'Yep. Can we disguise the origin?'

'Of course. I'm routing via Voice Over IP on a VPN which will show as an unregistered pre-pay number hitting a cell mast in central Sarajevo.'

'Who are you going to call?' asked Tom.

'Rudy O'Shea. He would be the natural person to call, being the ranking officer for this region. He should then make arrangements to have me brought in.'

'How about us?' Pet asked.

'Let's keep you off the radar, guys. If anyone is checking, let's make them think you are still somewhere in the Schengen zone.

'So, we make the call. Then what?'

'We watch the ripples, Pet,' Mike smiled, picking up the phone and dialling. His call was answered with a curt, 'O'Shea,' Rudy's voice booming over the speaker.

'Rudy?'

'Mike?'

'Yeah. I need to be brought in. Urgent. I am in the foyer at the Hotel Bistrik.'

'Man, where the hell have you been? People having been going mad,' the agent sounded shocked to hear his old friend's voice.

'Not over the phone, I need a full team to come get me. Keep this tight, Rudy; I don't know who I can trust. Are you at the Embassy?'

'No, I'm at home. Why?'

'Don't go to the Embassy, okay?'

'But, Mike, where have you been?'

'Not over the phone. Hotel Bistrik, ASAP. I gotta go,' Mike hung up, smiled, and made the motion of tossing a stone with his arm.

34

Babić sat in Cerović's car in a small car park adjacent to the only terminal of the small domestic airfield thirty minutes north of Sarajevo. They were almost ready to fly. Cerović yawned loudly in the seat next to him

Babić's contact in Italy had assured them that they couldn't fly until 9am the next morning. Apparently, they needed to arrive at the correct time to ensure that a friendly customs officer would be there to meet them. They could hardly allow the cargo to be searched, with six fully operational explosive devices all neatly packaged for onwards travel.

Babić looked at his watch: it was 8:30am. He was thoroughly sick of sitting in this wretched car, next to that flatulent fool Cerović. The idiot had initially talked endlessly about his plans for the money once they were finished with the operation, and it had taken all of Babić's resolve not to snap his skinny fucking neck. A few choice words with an underlying threat had soon shut him up, however.

Babić's phone buzzed in his pocket. Looking at the screen he recognised the number as being his American contact. He frowned, this was unexpected; the contact was normally so careful about calling and always used Wickr. It must be important, but it was unsafe.

He answered with a curt, 'Why are you calling me? You know our arrangement: calls can be listened to. Hang up and send Wickr.'

'This can't wait, Babić. Brogan has escaped. He has just called in, what the fuck is happening? I thought you were sorting this?'

Babić was shocked; how the fuck had the American escaped?

This meant only one thing: the twins were dead.

'He was secure when we left.' He covered the handset with his palm, 'Call Milan. Brogan has escaped.' Cerović pulled out his phone and began to dial.

'Well he is fucking out now. He has just called it in. I have no other information, but he wants picking up now.' The rich American accented voice sounded panicky.

'Where is he?'

'He wants collecting from the foyer of the Hotel Bistrik straight away. They are scrambling a team to collect him. You're lucky that the team is not immediately ready and will take a little time to get there,'

'How long do I have?'

'Thirty minutes, at the very most.'

'Leave it with me.'

'You need to find out how this fucking happened. If Brogan is out, we are all at risk. When are you flying?'

'You don't need to know when we fly. Why would we tell you this? Don't make the mistake of thinking we share information with you,' barked Babić. He hated the American fool. He was useful, but he seemed to sometimes think they were partners.

'You need to get to Brogan, fast, Babić, or we are all finished. You will never get out of Bosnia if Brogan is brought in. He will know far too much.'

'I said I will take care of it. They can't stop us now; we are ready to deploy and nobody knows anything of our plans.' Babić could feel his hackles rising, he wasn't used to being challenged like this.

'Your processes are bullshit. Brogan has escaped. Why isn't he fucking dead?'

'I said I will deal. Delay the team, somehow.'

'How the fuck am I meant to do that?'

'Your problem. Make it happen or you are finished,' he said.

'Jesus, this could be bad,' the American said.

'Who else knows about this?' Babić said, ominously.

'Why?'

'You know why? We have to close this down. Look, I need to go now, and too much has been said on the phone. Message me urgently with anyone else we should worry about,' Babić hung up.

'Nothing from either of the twins, phones both dead. What is happening?' asked Cerović.

Ignoring Cerović, Babić glanced at his watch. They only had twenty minutes to go, but they needed to move now; everything hung on getting the weapons out of Bosnia. Once they were out of the country, none of it mattered. They couldn't be stopped.

'What's going on?' Cerović asked, nervously.

'Nothing to concern you. We fly in a few minutes. Phones are now off; we are in mission mode.'

The Wickr app buzzed on his handset. He opened the message bubble and stared at the message from the American. Just a name and an address.

Without a word he got out of the car dialling as he did. He knew who to call; fortunately, a man with his contacts was always able to call on people ready to inflict violence for money. He smiled. This was soon going to all be in hand, once again.

35

'Talk to me, Pet,' said Mike, looking over Pet's shoulder as she tapped at the keys of her laptop on the hotel room's small desk. The half a conversation they had heard between Babić and the mole, picked up via the tap on Cerović's phone, had been illuminating to say the least. It had only taken minutes from Mike's call into Rudy for the news to hit Babić. That spoke volumes as to how well placed the mole was.

'The GPS tag has just disappeared,' said Pet. 'Literally just now; last activation right on the airfield runway.'

'That's not ideal, but inevitable, I guess. Plane acting as a Faraday cage once the doors are all shut. It matters not, Pet. Keep monitoring and, once they land wherever they are going, I will be able to call whatever resources we need to support. We can do nothing until we flush our mole, or it will either blow up in our faces or they will go to ground only to spring back whenever and we have to face it all again. We close them down for good, all of them and now. How about their cell phones?'

'Cerović's phone is now off, so I am running all the phones that we know about for instant activations following your call to Rudy. Babić is making a cell call now. Hold up.'

'He is calling another cell number. I'm running this one too. It's a burner, hitting a cell tower in central Sarajevo.'

'That will be the cavalry coming for me then,' Mike smiled.

'What numbers feature in Babić's historic data?' Tom asked,

'Not many. Only Cerović, the two numbers for the twin guards and this one, which hasn't featured anywhere else.' She pointed at the screen.

'Looks like they are using mission-specific burners that they can ditch quickly,' said Tom.

'Unsurprising. Check out that number, and the most recent phone number into it,' said Mike.

Pet nodded, her fingers tapping the keys once more, 'Burner. Very few calls in or out, just Babić. Which called into it just a few minutes ago.'

'That's your mole. Cell site for it, Pet?' Tom said, already pretty confident of what the answer would be.

There was more tapping from Pet, then a slow smile crept across her face. Rather than answering she turned the screen to show Tom and Mike. A map of central Sarajevo filled the screen, a shaded blue wedge showing the direction and strength of the signal emanating out from the location of the cell site mast. The blue area covered the US Embassy, perfectly.

Mike Brogan smiled. 'Hello, my corrupt little friend. I am coming to get you very soon.' He had an expression on his face that neither Tom nor Pet had seen before. It was grim determination. 'Pet, bring up the CCTV feed at the Bistrik, I suspect they are getting some visitors very soon.'

One reason that they had selected the Bistrik Hotel is that Mike had stayed there on a previous occasion and had noticed that they had an extensive CCTV system in place, with a bank of monitors behind the reception desk. It had only taken Pet a few minutes' tapping away on her laptop before she had the live feed displayed, showing four camera views. One of the outside on the street, one of the rear entrance, one of the lift lobby, and one showing the foyer and bar area. The foyer was fairly busy with guests passing through towards the restaurant and others checking out ready for a day's sightseeing or business meetings. The CCTV was of a high quality with pin-sharp images.

'Watch out: here come your reception party, Mike,' Pet said, pointing at the screen.

All three crowded around the screen, watching as a powerful-looking Honda motorcycle pulled up outside the hotel, with a dark-clad rider and pillion passenger. The passenger stepped off the bike and strode towards the hotel with purpose, his hand reaching to his waistband as he entered the foyer, clutching what they all assumed was a pistol. He paused, scanning all around at each of the occupants of the open-plan space. He checked the couples enjoying an early coffee, or reading newspapers, his tinted visor still obscuring his face.

Seeing no one, he exited the foyer and shrugged at his rider. Something then seemed to spook him and he cocked his head to one side and then made a hand gesture. Looking around urgently, he turned back and looked at the interior of the hotel, through the full-length glass. The rider pointed to his ear and then beckoned his passenger to re-join him. The man quickly jogged across, threw his leg onto the motorcycle behind the driver, and they sped off.

They all continued to watch the screen for a few moments more. 'Did something spook them?' asked Pet.

'There,' Tom pointed as a police car sped past, its warning lights strobing. 'The local constabulary scared them off. Nice one.'

'What now?' asked Pet.

'I need to speak to Rudy. Face to face.' Mike said, a blank look on his face.

'Are you sure that's wise, Mike? There is a very good chance he is the mole. You have only spoken to *him* since we broke you out,' said Tom gently.

'I'm aware of that. I've known Rudy for many years, he is a good man, but I want to look him in the eyes and ask him myself. If he's the mole, I'll bring him in. Where is his phone, Pet?'

Pet busied herself at her keyboard for a few moments. 'Hitting the same mast as the mole's phone, but that would also cover the Embassy properties on Omera Stupca,' she said.

'Monitor the phone traffic. I imagine that Babić will be getting a call letting him know of your no-show, Mike.'

Mike shrugged, a half-smile on his face. His eyes were red-rimmed and he looked drained as he rubbed his ribs, a grimace on his face, 'Let's see what ripples start from this, then we need to go proactive and do a little hunting of our own.'

'Boom!' grinned Pet. 'Someone is trying to contact Babić now, although the call is being diverted to a voicemail. It's the same number that he called once they learned you weren't dead, Mike.'

'Check all the numbers, Pet. Let's see what our friends are doing,' Mike said, stifling a deep yawn, his eyes half closing. He looked absolutely shattered.

'All switched off, as we suspected they would be. They must be airborne,' she said.

'How much battery life is there on your tag, Tom?' Mike asked, forcing his eyes to open fully.

'It was fully charged when I put it on. Hopefully another couple of days at least but, as I've not tested, I can't be sure.'

'Right. Pet, can you stay here? Stay tuned for any activations. Tom, you come with me. We're going to see Rudy.'

36

Mike and Tom pulled fifty metres along the road from the Embassy on Omera Stupca, close to where Mike had been snatched. They were sat in front of a sizeable building, which was set back from the road behind wrought iron railings and a small parking area.

'Is this Rudy's place?' asked Tom.

'Yeah. I met him here just after I arrived in Sarajevo. He gets sole use of the place, as they don't like the CIA men sharing with the oily rags. It's designed to be occupied by a family, but Rudy's wife and kids have stayed back in the US.'

'How do you want to play this?'

'You armed?'

'Yep. Beretta in my waistband,' Tom patted his belt line.

'We go in soft. I want to ask him first; it may not be him, and I want to give him the chance to convince me.'

'The phones don't help us. Either one could be here, or at the Embassy, as the cell mast covers both these areas. It's a shame we can't access the GPS to tie it down further,' said Tom.

'Not without access to the handset first, well, not in the timescales we have. We are where we are. Let's go.'

They walked casually along the road towards the property, even if Mike's casual stroll was beset with the trace of a limp.

'You okay, bud, you look sore?' Tom asked.

'Been better, been worse, man. Now's not the time, game on,' Mike tried to smile, but it came across as something more akin to a grimace.

An anonymous car sat on the driveway and the front room

curtains were drawn. They crossed the drive and ascended the few steps to the heavy-looking door. Mike went to push the bell, but something made Tom gently grab his arm.

'Is this Rudy's car?'

'It was here when I was last here.'

'Something is wrong, Mike.'

'What? I see nothing.'

'The curtains: why are they shut? And look at the car window: it's open. Something's not right, Mike, I'm telling you.' The lizard portion of Tom's brain was itching in an almost primeval way with the arrival of these potential combat indicators.

Tom gently rested his elbow against the black painted door and eased his weight forward. It swung noiselessly open on well-oiled hinges. He moved to one side of the opening and indicated that Mike should do the same. He raised his finger to his lips and reached into his waistband, pulling out the Beretta that he held low, in two hands. Nodding, Tom peeped around the door jamb, seeing an empty expanse of tiled hallway leading to an impressive looking staircase.

'What is in the front room?' he mouthed at Mike, pointing at the window.

'Office,' came back the whispered response.

Tom eased into the hallway with soft footsteps, his trainers making no sounds on the shiny surface. The smell hit him straight away. The coppery tang of blood, metallic and cloying mixing with the smell of cordite from a recently fired gun.

Tom moved fast and, in a fluid motion, swept into the office with his pistol extended, ready to engage.

Rudy O'Shea was slumped at his desk, a smashed bottle of some kind of spirit on the floor. His head was bowed forward, touching the desk, a neat bloody hole in his temple. A small pistol was in his hand, extended on the tabletop. The wall beyond was spattered with blood and the thick, greyish brain matter where the exit wound had destroyed the side of his head.

Tom edged forward and put out a hand to feel the dead agent's cheek.

'Still warm. I need to clear the rest of the place,' said Tom, his mind racing with the tactical options.

Mike just stood, a blank look on his face as he surveyed the scene before him. He remained like that for what seemed an age. 'Ah, man,' he finally said, sadly but with no shock. 'Rudy, Rudy, Rudy. What have you done?'

'It's bullshit, Mike. Total bullshit. This is staged; no way did he kill himself. It's a crude attempt to make it look like it, that's all,' said Tom in a low, even voice.

'Tom, we have to move. Bad guys could still be here, and cops could be on the way. There's nothing we can do for him now, but he is not the mole, I know it.'

Tom stopped and looked at Mike, 'how do you know, Mike, honestly?'

'I just know, Tom. I know and you'll have to trust me. The mole is still out there; we need to go, and we need to go now.' Mike spoke quietly but urgently, his handsome face lined, his blue eyes clouded with exhaustion.

Mike stared at the body slumped on the teak desk for a full thirty seconds. 'Too many deaths, Tom. Too many. I'm tired of this, man.' He lowered his head for a few moments, almost in a silent prayer, before straightening up, once more decisive. 'Right, let's go. I'll call this in later. We may need to keep this away from the local police. There is a fucking mole out there and I am going to find them and, when I do, I've a hellhole of a black site with their fucking name on it. Let's go.'

*

The short journey back to the hotel took place in total silence, Mike seemingly in another world, his eyes half-closed as he sat awkwardly, trying to take the pressure away from his sore ribs.

Tom had solemnly brought Pet up to speed on events, and what was most shocking was that she was not shocked. Tom realised that the consequences of their actions over the past few weeks had left their mark.

'Thoughts?' said Mike simply.

'We have an advantage which we need to press home, quickly,' said Tom.

'I'm listening.'

'We have the mole's number. He doesn't know we have it, and he also doesn't know that we have the number for Babić and that they use Wickr to communicate. Also, I'm betting that the mole doesn't know that Babić has just flown,' said Tom.

'How can we be sure of that?' asked Mike.

'One way to find out,' Tom smiled.

'So?' said Pet.

'We bring the mole into the open. Pet, can you make it look as though the message we send to the mole has come from the secure app on Babić's phone?'

'Sure, that's a two-bit fraudsters trick. I can have it ready to go in minutes,' Pet said, already typing.

'Keep going,' Mike said to Tom.

'We need him to relax, so we tell him that you were intercepted outside the hotel and are no longer a problem.'

'I can see the value in that,' said Mike, his interest clearly rising.

'Then we message him again and insist we need to meet. Once he is in the open, we have him.'

'Will he buy it? He just used a voice call; will he respond to a message?' said Mike.

'He'll buy it; you heard Babić bollock him for not using Wickr. He has no choice, does he? Babić talked to him like he was something he had stepped in. He is scared, Mike. He'll meet him.'

Mike sat and stared at the wall, turning it all over in his mind. 'Send the message.'

Tom picked up the phone. 'Ready, Pet?'

'Yep,' she nodded.

Tom composed a message, '*We have package. My men intercepted and it is secure. We need to meet, now.*"

The reply was almost instant, *'That's a relief. Why do we need to meet?'*

Tom tapped out a follow-up message, *'We need to talk. I have something you need to see, that package was carrying. You are at risk of exposure. Bibi Centar. One hour.'*

'I can't get there in that time.'

'You must.'

The screen remained blank for a full minute before the familiar blue script popped up, *"typing"* across the screen.

'Okay, one hour. Send full location.'

'Message when you are at Bibi,' Tom replied. 'Bingo,' he smiled at the others.

37

Tom and Pet sat in the small sandwich shop on the first floor of the Bibi Centar. Predictably, Pet was stuffing her face with a large sandwich, whereas Tom had satisfied himself with a coffee. Tom felt relaxed and ready for what came next; they just needed to wait. They had a perfect view of the level below, including the chain coffee shop that had a few tables scattered outside for a slightly more alfresco experience.

Tom checked his watch. 'Ready?'

Pet's cheeks bulged as she crammed the last of her sandwich in her mouth, but she nodded as she looked at her computer screen.

'Are you ready?' asked Tom again.

'Yep,' she managed. 'Interface is up, and your phone is porting via Bluetooth.'

Tom glanced back at his watch; exactly one hour had passed since the last message from the mole. The phone buzzed on the table

I'm here, where are you?' popped up on the app.

Picking up the phone, Tom began to type. *'Come into the centre and sit at one of the tables at Cordoba coffee on ground floor.'*

Tom looked up at Pet. 'Is he here?'

She nodded. 'Yep. Hitting a mast real close by.'

Tom nodded, took a sip of his coffee and watched. He had positioned himself so that, from his current position, he could look down through the glass barrier into a large plate mirror in a clothing shop window that gave a perfect view of the tables outside the coffee shop without making himself an obvious watcher by peering down over the barrier. This was meat-and-drink to Tom after years of surveillance in the military and police; he was utterly relaxed and comfortable.

Suddenly Tom spotted a tall, middle-aged male walking towards the café. His view, whilst adequate, was not good enough to see the face clearly, but he was confident that this was their man. His gait and demeanour were halting, staccato, and full of nervous energy. He faltered by the tables, looking around furtively. Tom shook his head. Thank God that the man was not a surveillance officer: everything about his demeanour was that of someone not relaxed in the environment. He eventually sat down, looking around jerkily and radiating nerves and discomfort.

'You see him?' Tom asked Pet.

She removed her glasses from her face and squinted, 'Yeah, grey-haired dude, skinny, looks kinda smart and like he doesn't belong.'

'Recognise him?'

'Can't say I do. You?'

'I can't see his face properly. Hold up.'

Tom quickly composed another short message and pressed send. *'You here?'*

The man jumped just a little and scrambled for his pocket, standing up hurriedly and knocking the chair over in his haste as he looked at his phone.

Tom decided that now was the moment and stood, looking straight at the smart, lean, grey-haired figure of Colonel John Havers, the Defence and Military Attaché at the Embassy of The United States of America, who was stood, looking panicky and harassed.

A slow smile stretched across Tom's face and he tapped at his phone again. *'Not here. Go back to car. You are clear, I will meet you there.'*

Tom stood as he watched Havers walking away before dialling Mike. 'Tell me something I want to hear, Tom,' said Mike's voice after a second.

'A friend of yours is on the way back to his car. You may want to say hi.'

38

Colonel Havers was pissed off; properly pissed off after being messed about by Babić. He was too exposed, anyone could see him in the shopping centre, and now he had to go back to his car to wait for the stupid fucking Serb. He was sick of this region with the overly macho culture, poor food, and high crime. He stomped down the stairs to the bottom level of the car park where he had left his pool car: a crappy VW Passat that he had signed out just half an hour ago.

So his mood was sour when he arrived back at the car, pressing the fob on the key to open the door. He frowned, the lights hadn't flashed and there was no unlocking noise when he pressed. Pressing again elicited nothing, once more. Seeing that the internal knob was still proud of the door trim, he realised that he must have left it unlocked. *Lucky not to have got the thing stolen in this city*, he thought as he climbed back into the driver's seat and slammed the door. He sighed a deep exhale of frustration and then his eyes flicked up to the rear-view mirror. Mike Brogan stared back at him, a half-smile on his face as he lounged in the Passat's worn seats. Havers flinched and let out a half-cry of alarm.

'Hello John.' Brogan said, his smile broadening, although without even a trace of humour.

Havers almost jumped out of his skin, his hand reaching instinctively for the driver's door, in a mix of panic and fear. A shadow fell across the driver's door window and, looking up, he saw the looming figure of a tall, lithe-looking man stood by the door, smiling. The smile was odd, like a teacher who was mildly amused by an errant child. But the eyes were deep, deep brown, almost black, and they seemed unfathomable, like a shark's. He realised with a jolt that he recognised him as the man who had been with Brogan and the female freelancer a few days ago.

'Oh, John. What have you been doing?' Mike's voice from behind him was low and gentle, like a nursery teacher calmly reasoning with an errant child. The edge of pure steel was unmistakable.

'Jesus fucking Christ, Mike! What the hell? I thought you…' he suddenly checked himself and closed his mouth. His heart was pounding in his chest, and he was breathing so hard with the shock he was almost hyperventilating.

Brogan interrupted. 'Sorry, carry on. You were saying?'

Havers said nothing, just opened his mouth, unable to formulate a sentence.

Brogan let out a small chuckle. 'Let me finish your sentence. You thought I was dead. You served me up to Babić and his henchmen and I have just had to endure hours of being tortured and beaten, so, John, it's fair to say that I am pretty motherfucking pissed at you right now.'

'Mike, I promise, I knew nothing…'

'Shut up, Havers. Just shut up.' Brogan didn't sound particularly angry; rather he projected an air of disappointment. 'You probably know enough about me to know that I have a fair bit of autonomy within the CIA and that I can, really easily, have you on a small plane, within hours, and on your way to a black site where you will experience much worse than what I have just been subjected to. So, Colonel. We are heading back to the Embassy now, where you are gonna tell me everything.'

The car door flew open and Havers was dragged out by the unsmiling dark-haired freelancer, who expertly secured him in an arm-lock and propelled him towards the back of the car as easily as if he was a child. Brogan stepped out of the car, the boot lid already swinging open. A pair of cable ties were quickly and expertly passed around Havers's wrists and zipped tight, securing his hands behind his back.

'In,' commanded the dark-haired man, his voice managing to

combine being both soft and menacing, and Havers was unable to resist. He had enough common sense to realise that Brogan and the unsmiling freelancer were in no mood to be messed about. Brogan had a fearsome reputation in the Service and, despite his clubbable manner, he was widely feared and respected as a ruthless operator.

Havers submissively climbed into the boot of the Passat and curled up into the foetal position, just as the lid slammed down plunging him into utter blackness.

*

Colonel John Havers sat alone in a windowless room in the depths of the Embassy. It wasn't a cell, but the absence of any door handles on the inside of the heavy wooden door meant it may as well have been. A bolted-down table occupied the centre of the room with similarly secured chairs on both sides.

The journey had been short and uncomfortable, and he had been assertively removed from the trunk of the car by two wordless Marines in the underground car park in the bowels of the Embassy building. From there he had been silently escorted from the car to the holding room, where he had been thoroughly and efficiently searched and his wallet, coins, phone and belt removed. The door had then slammed shut, leaving him alone in the room. Looking around the spartan space he couldn't help but notice the blinking red light on the small camera in the top corner of the room.

He was nervous. In fact, he was terrified. He had effectively been caught with his hands firmly in the till, and he dreaded to think what that bastard Brogan had in store for him. He shut his eyes tightly and tried to breathe deeply and evenly to calm his nerves. He wasn't successful. In fact, his fears grew with each passing minute. Not for the first time he cursed the "liaison" with Dalia, the impossibly young, impossibly pretty girl he had met at an Embassy event that led to a torrid affair. This had later led to an introduction to her brother, Milan, a nasty, ruthless criminal.

From then on, he was trapped. Forced to provide intelligence and support, for fear of his wife being told all the gory details. Of course, once that line had been crossed, there was no going back, ever.

Havers stood and began to pace the small, airless room, trying to organise his thoughts. What cards did he have to play? He had an idea of what Babić was planning, but his main problem was that he really didn't know too many specifics. One thing he knew for sure is that Brogan wouldn't play by any official "rulebook." He decided then and there that he had no cards to play, whatsoever, and the only way of staying out of some putrid black site in Europe somewhere was to make sure that Brogan needed him. He had to capitulate, completely. He was terrified of Babić, but he was even more scared of Brogan.

The rattle of keys in the door dragged him from his self-pitying reflection, and he was disturbed to see the frightening-looking freelancer walk into the room, an unfathomable look on his face as he stared at him with those dark eyes. He was closely followed by Brogan, who had a more transparent look etched across his exhausted-looking features. He looked fucking furious.

The door was slammed shut, causing him to jump, and silence enveloped the small room.

Mike didn't say a word but simply removed his jacket and threw it on the back of the empty chair on the other side of the cheap, laminate-topped table.

Still silent, Mike lifted his polo-shirt to display his lean torso. Havers was initially a little puzzled, but when he saw the state of Mike's chest and abdomen, his intentions became clear. There were vivid red weals all across his pale flesh, angry and weeping, clearly the result of a recent whipping of some kind.

'Oh, Jesus, Mike. I didn't know…'

Mike said nothing, but simply lifted his finger to his lips and sat back in his chair. He silently contemplated Havers for a full minute, his blue eyes—normally so friendly and bright—were a little clouded through fatigue and pain. There was also something else within them. Determination and ruthlessness.

'Rudy O'Shea is dead,' Mike said blankly and unemotionally.

The shock hit Havers like an express train. Rudy was dead?

He gasped, overfilling his lungs with a sudden onrush of air. He began to hyperventilate, his heart pounding in his chest and tears sprang from his eyes. 'Jesus. Oh man. No, no, no, no, no.' He violently scrubbed his face with his hands. 'Mike, I had nothing to do with it, you have to believe me. You have to believe me; Rudy was my friend. Oh, man, no, no, no.'

Mike stared at him, dispassionately. 'What did you tell Babić?'

'Just who else knew you were free,' Havers babbled. 'Rudy told me as it would be my Marines that brought you in. Nothing else, I promise. I didn't know that he would kill Rudy, Mike. I promise.'

'Pull yourself together, John. Calm down. You can make this right, but you only have one chance. Rudy is dead. I know you didn't kill him, but I also know that you know who did kill him.' Mike's voice was calm, despite the subject matter.

'How?' Havers asked between sobs.

'Someone shot him. Tried to make it look like suicide.'

'Oh man. Poor Rudy. Jesus, these motherfuckers. Mike you gotta help me, Mike, you gotta help me…'

Mike interrupted him. 'Okay, John. Here is how this is gonna go. No negotiations. You tell me everything you know, right now. Everything you know about this plot, everything about the investors, the whole shebang. If I even suspect, vaguely, that you are holding the smallest detail back—and I am making the sincerest promise here—I will pick up my phone and call a contact of mine. Once I make that call, we walk out of this room, and you won't see either of us again. The next humans you see will be the Marines that come to escort you to Sarajevo Airport, where a small jet is waiting to take you to a...' He paused for just a heartbeat, as if considering his next choice of words. 'Shall we say *"facility"*, Tom?' Mike paused to look at the man leaning in the corner of the room, who was still contemplating Havers, silently.

'I think that's one description,' he said, his face blank.

'Okay. *"Facility"* it is. Now, John, I take it you have heard of the influence I have, right?'

Havers was beginning to sweat and a bead of ice-cold moisture ran down the centre of his back, making him shudder. He briefly nodded.

'So you know I'm not bluffing, then. Don't bother shouting for a lawyer, either. There is only me, John. I am your only friend. You tell me everything. Now.' Mike sat back in his chair, his eyes boring into Haver's.

Havers sucked in a gasp of air, nodding rapidly. 'I'll tell you everything I know, all of it, I promise. But what then?'

'Oh, John,' Mike clucked with his tongue, shaking his head, sadly. 'It's over for you. All over. Your career is gone, you are going to jail. But there are jails and there are *"facilities"*: your choice is which type. Cooperate properly, and you will be held in a decent military facility with a reasonable regime. You will be able to look forward to maybe getting out one day. You have to pay for what you've done, but how you pay is up to you.'

Havers realised he had no choice. Jail was one thing, but a black site in some hellhole was another. He knew, at that moment, he had no cards left to play.

'I'll tell you everything, everything I know. But I don't know that much about the drone plot, honestly. I've taken kickbacks from arms dealers and I have top-sliced from some budgets, I'll tell you all about those. I will show you where the money is, offshore, I will tell you everythi—'

Mike halted his outburst with a raised hand.

'One thing at a time, John. You will tell us everything. I mean all of it, the whole lot, starting with your relationship with your girlfriend, Dalia: sister of Milan and Risto. That, I assume, was what got you snared into this plot. I'm sure your wife would not be so happy about that part of it.'

Havers almost jumped at the mention of Dalia. How the hell had Brogan found out about that so quickly? Seeing his reaction, Mike smiled.

'John, you should be more careful with your sexual proclivities. Your cell phone has been most illuminating, and don't think that using Wickr will stop us finding everything out.' Mike held up Havers's smart phone in a thumb and forefinger. 'You should know that deleting messages doesn't get rid of them, and I have people who can retrieve all of them. The photographs, the videos. All rather distasteful for a man of your age. What is she, twenty? Imagine these images in lurid colour at your trial?'

Havers said nothing, just closed his eyes. It was all over; Brogan had everything.

'Tell me about Pavlović,' said Mike.

Havers took a deep breath. 'Arms dealer. He mostly sells stolen Eastern European weapons to criminals across the region.'

'Type?'

'Mostly small arms, although he has moved explosives and I did hear he has acquired and sold mortars, grenades, and anti-tank weapons as well.'

'What about the American weapons stolen from the store a while back: the MP5s and Berettas?'

'I received word they were being stored there, on their way to be used by Bosnian law enforcement, so I told Pavlović without telling Babić. Pavlović sold them to Babić and we shared the profits, but Babić found out and was frigging pissed. He thought he was being double-crossed. Pavlović wanted out. He is a bad guy himself, but Babić has Sarajevo sewn up and has people everywhere.'

'Is that why you supplied him with the US passport? To protect yourself and get him away from Babić?'

Havers just nodded.

'Shame Babić had him killed first, right?'

Havers said nothing, just sighed and closed his eyes.

'That was a message to me, as much as anything. Just to show me that no one was safe from them; they'd have killed me as quickly as they would have killed anyone. I just got dragged in, Mike. Soon I was in over my head, with no way out.'

'What about the investors?' Mike said, ignoring him.

'I know barely anything about the investors. I don't think many do; not even Babić knows who they are. He only communicates with them through a secure channel.'

'Not good enough,'

'I promise, Mike. All I know is that they are a group of very rich people funding these plots, but everyone I have had contact with fears them and their influence. They have people all over: CEOs of multinationals, people in governments, law enforcement, intelligence, and military. Babić made it abundantly clear that they have people in the CIA, FBI and all layers of government and law-enforcement in many countries. Secrecy is everything to them. They want to cause turmoil, destroying companies and crashing currencies so that they can profit from it. I know nothing of who or where they are. Any money from them comes via Babić into my offshore.'

'What are they planning with the drones?'

'All I know is what Babić told me. I don't understand the science behind it, but he told me that they were going to use heavy-lift agricultural drones to deliver EMP surges to infrastructure targets. I don't know how they work, though, Babić never told me. They want to crash stock prices and short currency. I don't understand how; that's all he told me.'

'What's the target? There are six drones that we know of. What are they going to hit and where?'

'I don't know, I promise. I don't even think Babić knows the target. He kept saying that the investors are extremely secretive and won't give him the target until the last moment.'

'Come on, Havers. You must have a clue. Your future depends on you giving me enough to stop this,' Mike's calm persona slipped, as he stood and loomed over him, his face brick red with sudden fury as he bellowed at him.

Havers flinched at the sudden verbal onslaught. 'I don't know, Mike, honestly. I was kept in the dark; I just got paid for the information I supplied.'

'If we don't stop this, Havers, I am not going to be able to resist the pressure to have you sent back to the States. You will find yourself in some super-max facility that would make one of my irregular facilities look fucking luxurious. They will treat this as espionage, treason. Fancy a lethal injection, John?' Mike was shouting now, his face a picture of sheer, naked rage.

'Okay, okay, look. All I know is what he said in passing. I didn't think too much about it at the time, but it's all I have.'

Mike said nothing again, instead just standing over Havers, his hands rested against the desk, glaring at him.

Havers gulped twice, the fear shining from his eyes. 'Just one throwaway comment, almost. He said that the key to chaos is public fear and panic. His words were "When the lights go out and the shelves are empty, the people will riot within hours, not days." I remember it perfectly.'

'Which city?' Mike spoke in barely a whisper.

'I don't know. I promise I don't know, but I know one thing. It will be in Europe.'

'How do you know?'

'I thought it was just him being hyperbolic, at first. "Today Europe, tomorrow, the world".'

39

The small jet kissed the tarmac on the runway at Auxerre Branches Aerodrome, a small facility two hours south of Paris. Babić yawned deeply. He had managed to get some sleep on the flight from Sarajevo. It was fortunate that his expertise in moving contraband through Europe was so well-practised that it was easy to get an official to rubber stamp them in without even a glance inside the aircraft. This was a good thing, bearing in mind that the plane held six crates each containing a converted drone with an EMP device strapped to it.

From there, it was a quick refuel at a small, anonymous airfield and then a further flight which led them to the small, commercial airstrip. Travelling from one Schengen Country to another meant that there was no requirement for any customs checks.

A large van was waiting on the aircraft pan as the small plane shuddered to a halt. A stocky, shaven-headed driver stood waiting by the side of the van.

'Unload the crates, you two,' said Babić. 'I need to speak to our paymasters. How far to the pickup point for the sea crossing?'

'Four hours, or so,' the driver said, stretching.

'Be quick, we need to get moving,' Babić barked before opening his iPad and opening the secure communication app.

'Progress report?' the distorted voice demanded.

'We have landed in France; the devices are being unloaded now. We travel to the collection point and cross tonight.'

'Very good. Any complications?'

'None. The arrangements were as expected.'

'Excellent. And so they should, enough money was spent to

ensure this. We understand that Brogan is presenting something of a problem.'

'This has now been taken care of. I despatched teams to deal with Brogan and the other American from the Embassy.'

'I think not, Babić. I am hearing that he was not present and is now at the Embassy. Our sources also inform us that the Defence Attaché has been arrested by the Americans. Two bodies—twins, I understand—were found at the farm. Your men?' The mechanical voice still managed to sound accusatory.

'Yes. Risto and Milan.' Babić reeled internally at this. Jesus, how had Brogan got out and killed the twins? He couldn't think of anything further to say, so he said nothing more.

'This is inconvenient, Babić. What do they know of our plans?'

'Almost nothing. But Brogan could present a problem. Do we continue?'

'Of course, this is an inconvenience, nothing more. The timings are crucial. This is why we require such security measures that we insist upon. We were always going to encounter unexpected situations.'

'Well, as I do not even know the location of the strike, there is no chance that anyone else does. This does not set us back.'

'Of course not. What do you know of the freelancers who were with Brogan?'

'As I understand it, they left Bosnia and were last tracked on a ferry to Italy.'

'It seems you are mistaken. Our investigations have shown that they both returned back into Bosnia within a few hours. I would surmise that they are the reason that Brogan was freed and your men killed. It is fortunate that you had moved the devices away prior to this.'

'Indeed. Do we know anything about them?'

'Not yet. But they managed to obtain new passports, different from the ones they travelled into the country with. Unless they came in with multiple passports, which would be an unnecessary risk. They used German passports that, it seems, are genuine. I am sending screenshots of both.'

An icon flashed up on the screen before Babić. Opening the document, he found scanned black-and-white images of two passports' biodata pages: one in the name Greta Schmidt, the other in the name Hans Graumann. The girl was bespectacled, pretty, and young. The man was older, lean, and tough-looking with deep-set dark eyes and a fixed stare

'Do you recognise either?' The voice pierced his subconsciousness as he studied the images.

'I'd need to see a better quality picture, but I don't think so.'

'It is the only copy we have, it was from a passport scan, and it has degraded as it has been copied. Do you have any idea how they came up with fake German passports in a matter of hours in Sarajevo?'

'I may have.' In fact, Babić knew full well where these passports had come from, but he chose not to admit it at this particular time. There was only one person in Sarajevo who could come up with such documents at short notice.

'Well it matters not for now, but this is perhaps something for you to look into in due course. You will instruct your people in Bosnia to be on the lookout for this pair, and we will make our own enquiries. Do we need to discuss anything else?'

'No. Understood. When will I receive the full orders for the mission?'

'After you arrive at your next location.'

'Can I at least ask where we are going to next?'

'It will be obvious to you now, in any case. You cross to the United Kingdom tonight. The captain of the vessel is aware of where to take you and you will be met there. From there you will head north towards Yorkshire. Timing is crucial. Contact us at 9:30 tomorrow morning for further instructions. It must be done at the exact time to coincide with many other moving parts to make this operation a success.'

'Understood.'

A click, followed by a burst of static from the iPad, indicated that the call was over.

Babić sat for a moment in the uncomfortable seat. He couldn't shake the image of the dark-eyed man from his mind.

Delving into his bag he pulled out a burner phone he had brought to be used once they hit Europe, and slotted in a new SIM card. He quickly dialled one of his contacts in Sarajevo.

'Yes?' the voice, a rough-sounding Sarajevo accented man answered.

'Peter, my friend. It is Davud. I need a favour, do you know Braslav?'

'Of course, doesn't everybody?'

'I need you to pay him a little visit.'

40

'So where are we then?' Mike asked, sipping a strong coffee in a windowless room in the Embassy.

Pet was the first to speak. 'No cell activations from any of the phones we know about; it seems that they are practising good COMSEC at the moment. I have an alert to trigger should any of them hit a cell mast anywhere.'

'GPS tag?'

'Still working, I think, but it seems to be having a problem locating a satellite. I have been online trying to get it to handshake with me but it isn't playing.'

'That's not great. I thought that would be our key to tracking the drones all the way,' Tom said.

'Tom, it was a cheap GPS tag meant for a dog's collar, not international travel,' Pet shrugged.

'How about the flight from Lqvi? Anything on the online records?' Mike asked.

'Very little known. A flight plan was filed to a small airfield in Italy, but nothing has been seen of it since that I can find out,' said Pet.

'So, they could have flown onwards from there, or moved to travel by road, right?' said Tom.

'But we have actually no idea as to where. All we suspect is that the attack will be in Europe, and there's no guarantee of that, either. That is just from Havers, and he knows nothing, really.' Mike closed his eyes and sighed.

'It's in Europe, definitely,' Tom said.

'What makes you so sure?' Mike asked.

'Think about it. They have to transport six fully assembled drones with EMP weapons attached. No way are they doing this outside Europe. They entered the Schengen Zone so that we lose track of them as they won't flag on the borders. They could drive by road to anywhere in the whole of the EU without coming across a single barrier. Why would they take the short hop from Sarajevo to Italy if they were going on to America or Asia? It just doesn't make sense.'

'I agree,' said Pet, looking at her screen.

Both men looked at her expectantly.

'Those two SIM cards we found in his workshop at the farm. They are European, meaning they get the best data connectivity and price plans across the EU. If they went to Asia or the US, for instance, they would burn through the data in a very short time. They get the same rates throughout the EU with a European SIM. If they are using the GPS and data to navigate the drones, they won't want the phones to stop working because they've run out of data, right?'

'That makes complete sense, Pet.'

'I think so. You want to know something else?'

'Go on,' said Mike.

'I have traced where he bought the six missing SIMs, how much he paid for them, and the numbers attributed to them.'

'What? You're telling us this only now?' Tom said, his voice a mix of admiration and incredulity.

'I only recently found out. They were bought as part of the batch of eight at the nickel-and-dime he lives above. I figured he's a lazy son of a bitch so would get them close to where he lived. They are unregistered, but he was so lazy he used his own bank account to pay for them, which is very sloppy. But, bearing in mind he's a junkie, it's unsurprising.'

'Well that's really great, but it doesn't help us right now,' said Tom.

'What it does mean, Detective, is that when the drones are activated, I will know about it.'

Mike paused for a minute. 'Will we be able to take control of the drones?'

'No. I'd need to get access to the actual phones, like I did with Cerović's phone. I can't plant malware remotely; I need the device in my hand. The advantage, granted not immediately, is that we will be able to track the drones once they are in flight, at least between masts. It's not perfect, but it's a whole lot better than we had before.'

Tom smiled. 'As always, Pet, I am amazed at your abilities. But, right here and right now, we don't know where they are?'

'Nope. I have alerts should they use phones, spark up the drones, or use any of their known bank accounts. Basically, we need them to make another mistake, or I need your pooch tag to start working again.'

Mike looked thoughtful for a moment. 'You know what else doesn't make sense to me?'

'There are many things, Mike, so why not add to the list of confusing things?' said Tom.

'Everything I have read about EMP delivery, certainly ones that could be built by non-government organisations, is that they lack the power. Even with military spec batteries, I can't see they would knock out anything big enough to damage infrastructure. The US has tried to make effective weapons to harness EMP, but they have always been underpowered. I'm no expert, I admit, but I just can't see it. We are missing something.'

'Can you reach out to any US experts? NSA, DSA, surely someone has looked into it?' said Tom.

'You heard what Havers said. Babić is claiming that they have people in governments and law-enforcement all over. It could be bullshit, but do we take the risk. Can we be sure that if I make these enquiries right now, it won't get back to the wrong kind of people?'

'You know better than us, Mike,' said Tom.

'Until I can properly do a damage assessment from what Havers has told us I can't assess the risks of reaching out. I've had suspicions about some government departments for some time, guys, and I don't want to ruin this operation by risking that what we know gets to the wrong people. We could lose the advantage we now have. We should wait for your contact to come back. Can we rely on him?'

'Stan is the man I trust more than anyone, Mike.'

'Then we wait.'

41

The journey from Auxerre in the large panel van that had met them from the aircraft had been smooth. Cerović had sat alongside the taciturn driver, a rough and ready Croat who lived and worked in Paris. Babić had travelled separately in a Range Rover. The driver of that vehicle, a jovial Serb, had hugged Babić as he exited the plane before they had jumped in and the Range Rover had roared off.

A five hour journey had found them all parked in a small farmyard outside Étaples, a small port on the coast, south of Boulogne-sur-Mer.

Cerović went into the back of the panel van and went to one of the crates. He felt he should check the drones, just to ensure that the bumpy flight and onward journey had not caused any damage. He unscrewed the lid of the nearest box and removed it, placing it on the van floor.

'What are you doing?' Babić said from behind him.

'Just checking the drones. I want to make sure the journey hasn't damaged them at all.'

'You'd better hope they aren't damaged; you were responsible for packing them securely,' Babić growled, turning away, and disappearing out of sight.

Cerović removed some of the polystyrene chips from the box, placing them on top of the lid, and then stripped away the bubble wrap that had been piled on top. He had removed the rotor arms when packaging, but he wanted to check that the circuitry was still firing. The control panel was on the top of the frame: a rudimentarily assembled plastic board with circuitry beneath it and the mobile phone strapped into place alongside. It had been an absolute genius idea of his to utilise mobile phone tech alongside the drones' own guidance systems. It gave him a backup in case of failure and also meant that he could remotely send the detonate signal to the EMP device. He also had a timer function, so he could lock in the coordinates and then simply send the phone a timer signal which would initiate the electrical fuse embedded in the explosive to detonate the device.

He powered the machine up and the LED lights began to flash green. The small, cheap Huawei smartphone also burst into life, its small screen lighting up inside the tough case he had fitted it in to protect against any weather. He had thought of everything; no wonder they were going to pay him so well.

Satisfied, Cerović powered the drone down, the lights all blinking off one at a time and the phone powering down. He would only need twenty minutes for each drone to be made operationally ready. He smiled. This was going to be a cinch.

Babić appeared at his shoulder. 'Close it up. We are leaving very soon.'

'Where are we going?'

'The UK. Now shut up and get that fucking box secured again; we cannot afford any failures.'

42

Pet, Tom, and Mike were sat in the nondescript office in the bowels of the Embassy sipping bad coffee. Mike's eyes were closed, the fatigue etched on his face.

A muffled *"ping"* erupted from Pet's computer. She sat up, settled her glasses on her nose, and looked at the screen.

'We have an activation on one of the drone SIMs,' she said with rising excitement in her voice. She tapped at her keyboard. 'Literally just now. It sent out a "handshake" signal onto the network which has hit a cell tower somewhere.'

'Where?' Mike said sitting up, suddenly awake.

'Hold up. I'm just looking.' There were a few more taps before she announced, 'It is hitting a cell mast in Northern France in Étaples.'

'Show me on a map,' Mike said, standing up and leaning over her shoulder as she tapped away.

'Here,' she said, pointing at a small inlet port on the English Channel.

'Is it still on the net?' Tom asked.

'No, literally on and off immediately. A test maybe?'

Mike stared at the map a little longer. 'Well, now we know.'

'What? Pet asked.

'The attack is going to be in Britain. There is no other plausible explanation.' Mike pulled his phone from his pocket and dialled.

'It's Brogan, Director. I need a plane urgently from Sarajevo to London. The attack is going to be there. Yeah, I'm sure. Right. Okay. I'll speak to Novak.' He tucked his phone away.

'Okay. Flight is being arranged. Pet, start packing your gear up but keep monitoring. Tom, who do you trust to help us?'

'You can't call your people, or your freelancers?'

'I can, but I'm worried about using normal channels until we can actively and properly assess the damage that Havers and others connected to him have caused. The UK is your turf, Tom. You know who you can trust and Havers says that the investors have people in the UK. You stand the best chance of making sure this is kept tight. We aren't fighting a big organisation here, and we have a lead, we just need people to be able to respond quickly. That puts the ball in your court. The director is making sure that the right people Stateside are calling the right people in the UK to make this happen.'

Tom paused, thinking. There was only one choice; it was time to call Jane Milligan.

Tom dialled the familiar number on his phone. 'Tom, long time no hear. How is life helping out our American cousins?' Jane's firm northern tones were comforting.

'Jane. Can you speak?'

'Sure. Everything okay?'

'We will need the whole team scrambled and ready to move at a second's notice. All capacities covered, right? You will be getting a call from someone very soon, okay?'

'I understand. Sounds intriguing. Anything else?'

'This is a big deal, Jane. A really big deal.'

'Okay, consider it done. Where are you now?'

'Not over the phone, Jane. Just to reiterate, we will need everything. Every resource we have and everybody that is available. Start making the calls and I will explain to you as soon as we get a secure line.' He hung up and his phone immediately vibrated in his hand, a message from Stan.

'Royal, forwarding you a message from my contact.'

The phone immediately buzzed once more with a forwarded message.

Tom read the message out. *'Stan, from what I can see, and doing a little research, the schematic is for an explosively-pumped flux* *compression device. We have researched these a little as part of a threat assessment, but so far no one thinks they could viably be built outside of government control. In short-order, a high-explosive, such as TNT/ RDX/Semtex could, theoretically, be used to generate an extremely high power EMP, far more than would be produced from one powered by a more conventional source. They are a single use weapon, as the explosion destroys them, but they are a very worrying concept. Our assessment was that an EPFCD could produce a Poynting vector sufficient to cause very serious damage to electrical circuits. A very short burst would result in a big derivative of magnetic flux and therefore big inductive voltages in devices. Also, it would result in a broad spectrum EMP (short time <=> broad spectrum). Chance is, some spectral components are able to penetrate shielding and hardening in infrastructure. If you find out more, I'd be fascinated to hear more. I would genuinely worry if a viable device built to these specifications was in the hands of anyone with ill intent. Thanks, Lucy x'*

'Jesus,' said Mike, his face registering shock. 'So, this really is a serious threat. Using a conventional explosion to massively exacerbate an EMP surge. I don't like this, guys. I don't like it one bit.'

'I'm taking it that flux compression has nothing to do with time travel?' asked Pet.

'It would appear not,' said Mike.

'Does it change anything?' Tom asked.

'No, the objective is the same. It just seems the stakes got higher.'

Mike was looking at him, phone in hand, 'I'm waiting for the Director. There will be a plane at Sarajevo airport in three hours. Get together everything we need, leave all the MP5s and other weaponry here along with any passports you may have. I have sorted diplomatic ones for us all to travel on to get through immigration channels as quickly as possible.'

'Three hours, you say? I need to visit someone quickly before I leave. That okay?'

'Okay. But I need you back here, ready to leave in ninety

minutes. I will be spending that time on the phone to DC, briefing those I need to make this happen, and to mitigate any of the damage caused by Havers. Pet, keep on with your monitoring.' Mike was now the picture of efficiency as he began what he was employed to do: troubleshoot.

Tom nodded and walked out of the office, his mind set on what he had to do next.

*

Tom pulled up in the Skoda outside the cab office. He sat there for a few minutes contemplating what he was going to say to Braslav. The hints that he had been given from the old fixer a few days ago were just not enough. He needed to know exactly who his father had been. There were just too many unanswered questions for him to leave it as it was.

He remembered the words that the man had said to him when he was just twelve. *"Maybe Yugoslavia won't survive, but we will make sure you do, Tomo Novak."* He owed Braslav a lot but, he thought, Braslav owed him a full explanation. The father he thought had died in the Balkan War was not who he thought he was. What did that mean to Tom today? Could it explain why he was as he was? Tom had always assumed that his turbulent childhood had been the cause of his particular issues around empathy, but now he wondered. Was it genetic? Tom had killed many times during his time as a commando and later as a cop, and he never felt any type of emotion. No elation, no horror, no regret. It had always perturbed him and caused much agonising and self-reflection. The realisation that his biological father was a ruthless killer perhaps made this confusion all the more redolent. Just who the fuck was he? Was he always destined to be a killer? He shook his head to clear these thoughts, now was not the time.

Tom pushed open the glass door and stepped into the small, scruffy office.

He knew immediately that something was wrong. Very, very

wrong. Like all police officers, he could smell death. Every cop throughout the world knew that death had a distinct smell, beginning at the exact moment that the spark of life left the body. And Tom could smell that right now.

He reached into his waistband and produced the Beretta pistol, holding it in both hands, even though he was certain that the offices were empty of life. He found Ema first. She was sprawled just the other side of the beaded curtain, her legs spread-eagled, one shoe discarded and half leaning against the wall. There was a single bullet hole in the middle of her forehead, her open and staring eyes devoid of the spark of life. There was no exit wound, indicating that the bullet that had killed her was a low velocity round. Tom carefully stepped over her prone form, looking ahead. Pistol extended in front of him, he turned into Braslav's office with an ominous sensation of dread at what he was about to find.

He was both right and wrong. Braslav was dead, that was indisputably true, but his method of death was not what Tom had expected.

Braslav was sat in his wooden chair, bolt upright and dead. His hands were secured to the chair's arms. Tied, Tom thought at first, but as he moved closer he was shocked to see the flash of a silver nail embedded in each palm. A *De-Walt* air-powered nail gun was discarded on the floor, a red smear of blood staining the bright yellow plastic.

Braslav was as dead as anyone he had seen. Looking at his chest his white shirt was stained with blooms of blood where the nails had pierced his sternum, clavicles, shoulders, and elbows. He had not died easily. The final nail had clearly gone so far into his skull that it wasn't protruding from the small, dark hole it had made in his forehead. A single trail of blood ran down his nose and had pooled into his lolling mouth.

Tom turned, replacing the pistol into his waistband, loathing and fury rising in his chest. They'd tortured Braslav, the man who had helped him flee the warzone all those years ago. He almost surprised himself by the strength of how he felt, as he was used to being the person who was normally so composed. He wanted something new. Not just *"doing what was right"*, as Cameron always talked of. He wanted something far more primeval.

Revenge.

43

Cerović felt nauseous as the small fishing boat pitched and rolled in the swell of the English Channel. 'How much longer?' he bellowed into Babić's ear over the roar of the wind and the boat's engine.

Babić looked at his watch. 'Soon. Check the lashings on the crates. If they end up in the sea, we are all fucked. You, in particular.' He sneered at Cerović.

Cerović swore under his breath as he staggered with the roll of the craft. The thick, canvas straps had done their job and the crates remained tightly secured against the deck. It had taken him and Babić a good thirty minutes to get them as he had wanted. They were delicate pieces of engineering, and he hated the thought of them pitching into the black, rolling waves.

The engine note changed just a little as the boat's captain increased power. Looking ahead into the inky blackness, Cerović could see a powerful torch flashing rhythmically, the bright beam briefly hitting the boat.

'Who is that?' Cerović shouted towards Babić.

'Our reception teams. White light means we are clear. Red would mean stay away,' Babić said, his eyes glued to a pair of compact binoculars. He continued watching for a few moments more before saying, 'Get ready. Three vehicles, two drones in the rear of each. Allow the reception party to unload: they are all much stronger than you and they have practised this many times. Stay out of the way. This is now a military operation, Cerović. You stay clear until I tell you it is your time.'

The fishing boat chugged in, the engine slowing as it eased

towards a small, dimly lit wooden jetty that thrust out into water from a small rocky outcrop. Three large SUVs were parked in the gloom. There was no one else to see anywhere, and the spot had clearly been well-researched.

There was a gentle bump as the fishing boat nudged against the jetty, and Babić threw the mooring rope to a powerful-looking man stood at the end of the jetty. Within a few moments the boat was secure against the jetty.

Babić was right. The reception party worked with military efficiency. The bonds were released from the crates and they were carried from the craft, one between two of the dark-clad individuals from the reception team. Within a few minutes all of the crates were off the craft and securely stored in the rear open cabins of the vehicles, all new-looking double cab Ford Rangers. Tarpaulins were securely strapped over the back of each of the vehicles, hiding the crates from sight, and the tailgates were slammed shut.

'You travel in the rear car with Leon and Yevgeny,' said Babić. 'I will be in the front vehicle. There is a long drive now, so use the time to get some rest. I will need you ready to operate once we get there.'

'Okay, I guess.'

'One bit of advice, Stefan. I wouldn't try too hard to engage Yevgeny and Leon in your usual conversation. They aren't the most patient types, and your incessant rambling may incur their displeasure.' Babić smiled, mostly to himself, and strode up to the front Ford, climbing into the rear cabin.

Stifling his hurt at Babić' verbal barb, Cerović angrily climbed into the Ford's rear cab, sitting behind two powerful, dark-clad figures, neither of whom turned to acknowledge his presence. The engines were started, and they all moved off in convoy along the deserted coast road.

'Hey guys,' Cerović said in an exploratory attempt at engaging the pair. The passenger, the larger of the two, turned to face him and Cerović couldn't help but notice the bulbous broken nose in the gloom. It was a rough and tough boxer's face.

'Cerović?'

'Yes?' he answered, a hopeful tone in his voice.

'No talking. You sleep, we drive for long time,' his accent was thick Russian.

Well this was going to be a fun few hours, thought Cerović. Hours in a car with two dangerous-looking and taciturn Russians. He yawned deeply, realising just how tired he was. Fumbling in his pocket he reached for his phone, thinking that maybe he could play some games to while away the time; but, looking at the hard, uncompromising figures in front of him, he didn't think that they would appreciate the light and sounds from his phone.

His fingers brushed against a scrap of paper which he pulled out and stared at, a little puzzled. Seeing the cell phone number and doodled heart, a smile stretched across his face as he recalled the busty blonde Alina from the club the other night, just before he got kicked out by the overly-aggressive bouncer. A little message couldn't hurt. All being well he would be returning to Sarajevo in a few days a very rich man. Using his jacket to shield the screen as the phone booted up, he composed a short message, *'Back in Sarajevo in a few days, babe. Big business deal just come off, celebrate with me, Steff x'.*

44

Mike, Tom, and Pet all sat on board the small twin-engine Learjet, sat on the taxi area at Sarajevo Airport waiting for the all-clear to proceed. The inside of the aircraft was functional and comfortable without being luxurious.

'No aircrew to bring us food?' Pet asked, predictably.

'I doubt it. We did well to get the jet ready in this timescale; I managed to pull a string or two and I think that the Director may have had something to do with it. I think our poor pilot wasn't expecting to be flying now, but I guess an exorbitant fee was paid.'

'Not one of yours then?' Tom asked in a dead voice. He had barely spoken since returning to the Embassy.

'You okay, Tom?' Pet asked, one eyebrow raised.

Tom closed his eyes, his mind swimming with the vision of the elderly, helpless Braslav nailed to his chair. He didn't want to talk about it, but he realised that they needed to know. He had no idea how much Braslav had revealed during the torture. He hadn't known much, but he knew who Tom was.

'No. In fact I am very far from being okay,' he said in a voice that was flat and unfathomable.

'What happened?' Mike asked.

Tom took a deep breath, closed his eyes, and then told them the whole story.

'Jesus Christ, the fucking animals,' Pet said, 'They nailed him to the chair?'

'Yes.'

'Why?' she was aghast.

'Braslav was a good man, but he was a fixer. He knew everyone, and I imagine everyone knew him. If they found out that we had procured false passports in a matter of hours, the first person they would have visited would have been Braslav. I got him killed for no good reason; we could have achieved what we have without those passports,' Tom's eyes were dark pools and Pet could not read them even a little.

'You don't know that, buddy,' said Mike.

Tom said nothing. His eyes were just blank, his face unreadable.

'Whatever,' said Mike calmly. 'It's happened, and nothing can change it. We need to move on and get prepared for what comes next. Retribution will come, Tom. Remember what I always say: bad things happen to bad people.'

Tom closed his eyes, inhaled the stale, recirculated air and then exhaled. His eyes suddenly opened wide. 'You're right, of course. You always are, Mike. We have to sort this out once and for all. No disruption, no letting them escape, nothing. They pay for what they have done.'

'Agreed,' Mike said, and Pet nodded her head in agreement.

'Okay, where are we?' Tom said, once again all businesslike and efficient.

'Director has called who he needs to call. You get the picture, but the upshot is that your boss should have received a call from the Commissioner by now and, hopefully, she will be assembling your team ready to go to work as soon as we land.'

'She will have, I can guarantee it. Pet, anything?'

'Yep,' Pet said, staring at her now open laptop, 'Our friend Cerović switched his phone on a while ago, probably whilst we were going through security. He sent a WhatsApp message to a Bosnian number,' Pet read out the text sent by Cerović to Alina. 'He switched it off as soon as the message went, but his phone's GPS signal put him close to Whitstable, right by the sea. It looks like they've crossed the Channel.'

'Mike do you have a sat-phone?' Tom asked.

'Sure.' Mike tossed over a chunky looking phone with a stubby, fold out aerial. Tom dialled a number from memory; it was answered immediately.

'Milligan,' the curt northern tones rang in his ear.

'Jane, we are four hours away from City Airport.'

'Hello to you too, Tom. I heard this a few minutes ago. Buster will meet you. What do you need?'

'Is Tiny with you?'

'Not yet, but he is responding like everyone else. He will be in the office pretty soon, I guess.'

'Okay, that's great. As soon as he arrives, we need him to be looking for possible maritime incursions on the south coast. Last we knew they were at Faversham Road by Whitstable. They would have needed a craft big enough to accommodate at least six largish crates and they will need a large vehicle or multiple vehicles to move the contraband.'

'Contraband?'

'Six crated agricultural drones that are carrying powerful EMP weapons. I will brief you fully when we arrive, but I will have a friend of mine email some specs. This is a really big deal, Jane. We all need to bring our A-game here.'

'Understood. Anything else for now?'

'No. Just team assembled, ready for surveillance deployments with a full complement of vehicles, a bike and covert van. We also need everyone firearms-authorised-to-carry to be armed with Glocks and Sigs.'

'Consider it done. And Tom?'

'Boss?'

'Be careful, right?'

'Always, boss.' He tossed the phone back to Mike.

'All good?' Mike asked.

'Yeah. Jane is very good; she will have everything sorted for when we get there.'

*

Their passage through the diplomatic channels at London City was smooth and uncomplicated, and they emerged into the arrivals terminal.

Tom immediately saw the grinning face of his old friend and colleague, Pete "Buster" Rhymes, stood by the barrier.

'Oh, blimey. If I'd known you were coming, Pet, I'd have got someone else to pick this reprobate up,' Buster said in his rapid-fire cockney accent whilst hugging her. 'How ya been, mate?'

'Good, Buster, apart from your best friend bringing his usual bad luck.'

'He's a bleeding liability, mate, it's why I avoid him at all costs. How you doing, Borat?'

Buster was Tom's oldest friend. They'd both served together in the Special Reconnaissance Regiment and now were police colleagues. Buster presented as a fast-talking cockney wide boy of limited intellect, whereas the reality was that he was one of the sharpest operators Tom had ever encountered, despite the bluster.

'All good, Buster. Well, pretty shit, to be honest. But you know?'

'Why am I not surprised, mate.' Buster smiled, clapping him on the shoulder. 'Now, if I'm not mistaken, and my almost photographic memory serves me well, it's Mike, right? Basra, about 2005,' Buster offered his hand to Mike, who shook it warmly.

'Hey, Buster. Yeah, I remember you well. Are we ready?'

'Yes, mate. Car is full of gas and is ready to get us to the office. The whole team is ready to go and all rubbing their hands at the amount of overtime we are all going to cane on this one. Let's go.'

Buster turned on his heels and walked quickly out to the terminal where Tom saw a BMW 5-Series estate parked in a bay marked *"Police"*, next to a marked car. The dawn had gone, and the early morning sun was soon to rise; the sky was a pale, cobalt blue and it looked like it was going to be a beautiful day.

They all climbed in, Tom in the front seat, Pet and Mike in the back. Buster gunned the engine and they pulled off. Buster flicked a switch on the dash and a siren began to wail and the reflection of concealed, strobing lights began to pulse on the building walls as Buster started the powerful BMW.

'Hang on to your hats: blue light run ahead,' said Buster, a huge smile across his face as he sped off.

*

Rush hour had not really started yet, but Buster's use of the blue lights and sirens made short work of the ever-increasing traffic, and within forty minutes they were walking into the team's headquarters.

The team's HQ was a non-descript, low-slung building on a small industrial estate on the outskirts of Colindale in the far reaches of North London. It was a completely covert building that was posing as an import / export company headquarters with no police signage or anything that would lead the casual observer to believe that it was a law enforcement building.

That assumption, however, was as far wrong as it was possible to be. The building housed a team of experienced detectives, analysts, and financial experts, all at the top of their game and with one aim: to go after the most serious criminals that normal police units couldn't or wouldn't touch, for whatever reason. Corrupt public officials were their main fare but, when particularly difficult policing problems occurred, it was likely that the phone would ring in the control room at the anonymous offices. The team was covert in nature, it didn't exist on paper, but when serious issues needed tackling there was a good chance that they would be deployed.

Jane stood at the entrance to the building as Tom, Pet, and Mike walked in.

'Tom, you okay? You look shattered,' she said, smiling but with a touch of concern in her voice.

'I'm all good. This is my friend, Mike, who is something in American law-enforcement. I'll be honest, I've no idea about your actual title, Mike, but this is my boss, Detective Superintendent Jane Milligan.'

Mike chuckled. 'Pleased to meet you. I'm not sure I have a title, but I work for the US government and I understand that we have been assured of your cooperation.'

'Hi Mike. I have been instructed by the Commissioner that I am to offer every courtesy and every resource I have. You can be sure that that's what I'm going to do,' her and Mike shook hands, warmly.

'Glad to hear it. This is an associate of mine, Pet; she helps me out in situations like this.' Mike nodded at Pet who just smiled and waved.

'Do you want to be briefed on your own first, Jane?' Tom asked.

'No. Let's get on with it; no point telling the story twice. Tiny has some specs that your friend here sent him on the devices. I get the seriousness of the situation and we will do whatever we can to stop them deploying any drones on British soil.'

They walked through the corridor past the empty open plan offices, towards the briefing room.

The briefing room was packed, every single member of the team sat in there, waiting. There was a palpable sense of anticipation in the air, despite the fact that no one knew anything about what was to come.

It was a large room with plenty of seating and a large screen at the front that was lit with the words *"Covert Policing Advice Unit"*. This was the cover title for the team, which they used if forced to communicate with outside law enforcement agencies, but in reality it was rarely used. Buster had been desperate for the team to have a sexy name, but despite his suggestions of *"Viper Squad"*, this had been scoffed at and they remained, simply, *"the Team"*.

'Okay, guys, Tom is back from his travels, swanning it about somewhere in five-star hotels. Stood over there is Mike and Pet, who are here as advisers from the US government. I have to say that we are working under the highest classification of secrecy, do we all understand?'

There were nods all around the room.

'Right. Tom, over to you.'

Tom moved to the centre of the room so everyone could see him. He cleared his throat and stared at the occupants, many of them good friends of his. He needed them. He needed their experience and enthusiasm. So much had happened in the past few days, he barely knew where to begin. So he began at the start.

He told them everything, the lot in chronological order using the old Met Police acronym, IIMARCH. Information, Intention, Method, Administration, Risk Assessment, Communications, and Human Rights. It was second nature, so he didn't see any reason to use any other method. He displayed photographs of Babić and Cerović on the screen with names written underneath in bold typeface.

'So, are we all clear. We use whatever techniques that Tiny and Pet can come up with to trace the drones, then we intercept them and arrest anyone we find with them.'

Tiny spoke up from the back of a room. He was a huge man, over six-five, and everything about him was enormous. He was the Team's computer expert, with skills to almost match Pet's. 'The GPS dog tag, you say it's dead, right?'

'I didn't say dead, I said we can't get it to connect or find a satellite. Is that right, Pet?' Tom said.

'It is on the system, and it isn't showing as battery dead, but it won't find a signal. I think it lost it during the flight, probably owing to the metal of the plane acting as a Faraday cage and it hasn't managed to relocate since,' Pet said, shyly.

'I may have an idea,' Tiny said. 'Jane, can I take Pet and we can see if we can do something? It may be we can force a full reset remotely that may make it search for a satellite. If we can connect it back up, we are game on, right?'

Pet looked at Mike, who nodded.

'Good idea, Tiny. Maybe you two can share ideas on the phones and the GPS tag. It seems to me that if we can get a proper signal, we can progress fast and hopefully contain this,' Jane said.

Pet and Tiny left the office, Pet lugging her heavy shoulder bag.

'Can I say something, please Jane?' Mike asked, quietly.

'Be my guest,' Jane said.

'People, I can't stress too much the seriousness of what we are dealing with here. Our calculations are that, with the upscaling they've done and the fact that they have six drones, they could cause significant damage to infrastructure. The financial and the human costs would be significant. We are all relying on you to help us stop this plot. These people are dangerous, they are amoral, and won't hesitate to kill any one of us if it will further their objective.' Mike seemed to manage to catch the eye of each and every person in the room.

The room was silent as the gravity of what they were facing sank in, a silence which seemed to last an age until a shout from the open plan office was quickly followed by Tiny's massive head poking around the briefing room door.

'GPS tag is back online. We managed to get hold of the manufacturers; they have forced a full reset on a different frequency, and it is now hitting a satellite. It is on the A1 heading north, just south of York.'

Pet appeared at his side. She caught Tom's eye and raised her eyes to the ceiling, clearly a little ashamed that it had been so simple for the big Mancunian to get the device back online so quickly.

There was an outburst of muttering in the room and Jane raised her voice above the hubbub. 'Okay people, let's get kitted up and get moving. All with your partners in the cars, full surveillance kit, everyone in body armour. I want both bikes on this job as well. Let's get ready fast people, get armed up for all possibilities. Let's get going. Bikers, I want you leaving now, full speed: make up as much ground as you can and stay in touch. Don't crash, right? I want us all out of here in twenty minutes.'

Everyone leaped to their feet and began moving out of the briefing room, chatting animatedly, ready to go.

As they left the room Tom raised his voice, 'Shotguns in each car, okay? They may be the only way we can down a drone if we are too late.'

The Team members all filtered out of the room, leaving Jane behind with Tom, Mike, and Buster.

'Any clues as to where they are going?' asked Jane.

'North, to a major infrastructure centre is all we can be sure of,' said Tom. 'They have a good head start on us, but I'm fairly confident we don't have to break our necks to get to them.'

'Really?' Jane asked, 'I'd have thought urgency was the key here.'

'It is, but it's only 9am now. They have a, say, two and a half hour head start on us, but I don't think they will do anything until after dark. Why would they? Why risk people visually being able to see the drones? And for impact they need everywhere to be plunged into the dark once they strike. Remember: Havers said the lights would go out.'

'I have to say, Jane. This makes total sense to me,' said Mike. 'Six drones all heading in the same direction, as far as we can tell. This will be a co-ordinated strike, otherwise why would they do it this way?'

No one spoke, as it seemed no one had an answer to the partially rhetorical question. The silence in the room was palpable as each person thought.

The silence was broken as Pet burst into the room, 'We have them on ANPR, just short of Leeds. Three vehicles, all Ford Rangers, we are waiting for the photos to come through, Tiny has just made the call to the ANPR management centre, they just need retrospective authorisation from you, Jane, to release them; you just need to reply *"authorised"* to the email you have in your inbox, now.' Pet's eyes shone with excitement; it seemed that working with Tiny had fired her competitive spirit.

'Consider it done,' said Jane, picking up her phone from the desk and swiping to her email account.

'Brilliant, how did you manage that?' Buster asked.

'Her idea,' Tiny appeared at the door, his huge bulk almost blotting out the light from outside. 'I should have thought about it. But she realised that, if we tie the GPS movement of the tag with the ANPR stations, it would just be a simple case of filtering the vehicles that passed through at the exact moment the GPS put them in the firing line. We then just cross-checked to the ANPR cameras in Kent where the drones came ashore. The same three vehicles came through ANPR cameras on the M2 in Kent that have just hit the camera in Leeds. We have three Ford Rangers, in convoy, one behind the other. I'm betting that's our guys.'

'What does PNC show?'

'Sod all to work with. All are registered to Ford Rangers, but from different parts of the UK and listed to private individuals. We haven't checked yet, but I suspect they are cloned plates.'

'Good work, guys. Get it circulated to the team and let's keep working at this. I want to see images of these vehicles and let's keep looking for CCTV opportunities if they stop anywhere. Okay?'

'On it, boss,' Tiny said, turning away.

'This is good work, Jane. You have a good team,' Mike said.

'Thanks, but we aren't out of the woods yet.'

'But at least we know which woods we are in, right? We know what they have, we know what direction they're travelling in, and we know at least some of the vehicles that they are in. I'm thinking that three Ford Rangers, with capacious flat backs, will accommodate the six crates I saw at the farm, right?' said Tom.

'I reckon so. They're big bastard cars, either driven by farmers, or wankers who think they are,' Buster piped up in his normal, eloquent manner.

'Excuse DC Rhymes, Mike. He has a certain way of putting things,' Jane said, eyeballing Buster.

Mike chuckled a little, 'so, we pack up and get up there and wait for the right opportunity? We have to take them all out. It's all or nothing, guys, right?'

There were nods around the room.

'Okay. Saddle up and get going,' said Jane

45

Babić sat in the rear cab of the Ford Ranger as it continued its journey north, the motorway flashing by outside. He took little notice of the countryside, despite it becoming more scenic as they headed north. The driver and front seat passenger had been silent, which was fine by him as he needed to think and plan.

He would be receiving his final instructions and the identity of the final target from the investors very soon. He hated working in the dark, but his shadowy paymasters were almost maniacal about their identities being secret. They worked in silos, with each knowing nothing about the other members. He understood it; but having been in control of his own destiny, very successfully, it was hard not to be the prime decision maker. Still, the million dollars US that were currently sitting in his offshore bank account in the Cayman Islands made it easier to stomach. On successful completion of the mission he was due a further two million dollars, almost immediately. He smiled at the prospect.

But first he had to ensure this operation went smoothly. He checked his watch which showed 9:25am. It was almost time, but he wanted to make another call first.

He pulled out his burner phone, removed the battery, and plucked out the old SIM. Cracking the window a fraction, he tossed it out of the speeding car before quickly slotting a new SIM into the phone and snapping the battery back in. He dialled from memory, listening to the single tone as it rang.

'Yes?' the familiar voice at the end of the line.

'You have news of Braslav?'

'Yes. He supplied the passports to a lone man who paid cash.

The individual supplied the two pictures: one of him, one a female.'

'Is that it?'

'Yes. What else did you expect?'

'Why they needed them. Identity of the man, does he know him? Come on, this is poor work.'

'He didn't know any more,' the voice said, uncertainly.

'How can you be sure? Braslav is a tricky customer, he has survived in this world for years. He wouldn't have told you the truth without persuasion.'

'We were very persuasive. He resisted a little while, but we encouraged him to see the error of his ways,' the voice took on a slightly nastier edge.

'Meaning?'

'I'm sure you can guess, but he wouldn't expand. I think he told the truth.'

'Nonsense,' blasted Babić. 'Go and see him again. He will know more, trust me. I know Braslav and he would never tell you the whole truth.'

'We can't.'

'What do you mean? Who do you think pays you?'

'No, Babić: we can't. He didn't survive the interrogation,' there was abject fear in the voice that was detectable even over the crackly line.

'You fucking fool. You will live to regret this.' He hung up, fuming at the incompetence. He didn't care that Braslav was dead: not a bit. But this was heat he didn't need; Braslav had been influential and hugely popular, with many friends across Bosnia and further afield.

Babić reached for his iPad and opened the secure app, securing earbuds in his ears.

'Update?' the distorted voice demanded.

'We are all secure and are proceeding as anticipated.'

'Good. Are you satisfied with the six operatives? Our contact in the UK assures us they are experienced.'

'As far as I can tell. '

'Yes. They are all experienced in piloting drones, their targets are simple with minimal security, and Cerović will be able to brief them on the devices, yes?'

'Of course.'

'Very well. Proceed to Berwick-Upon-Tweed, to the coordinates I am about to send you. Lay up until we are ready to give final instructions. It is a small farm that will be clear of anyone, so you will have no problems. Have Cerović brief the others on the peculiarities of the devices. They must all be ready to fly and detonate them at the precise moment we order, is that understood?'

'Of course.'

'You will be joined by two further vehicles at the farm with four men in two vehicles. They can be trusted and will require briefing as well, although they too are experienced in these matters. When you get your final instructions, you and Cerović will deploy close to the prime target, whereas all the other vehicles will deploy at other locations. These will be sent to you at our next call, understood?'

'Has the package been delivered?' asked Babić.

'Yes. It is with the operatives who will be at the farm.'

'Understood.'

'Secrecy is vital, Babić. This is still your operation on the ground but this way, if anyone is captured, they will have little to reveal. Simple OpSec, Babić, you understand this, surely?'

'Of course, I understand, but I am working with people I have not verified or vetted personally.'

'They are all more than capable, and their tasks are relatively simple. Once you receive the final targets you will select your teams of two, each with a vehicle and a drone to deploy. You and Cerović plus two others will then deploy two drones at the main target once the others are ready. Understood?'

'Yes.'

There were no goodbyes, the line simply went dead to be replaced by a mail icon. Opening it, Babić saw a set of coordinates that he barked out to the passenger, who in turn input them into the satnav.

46

It was close to 10:30 in the morning before the team were all organised and kitted up with firearms, the statutory warnings issued to each officer who signed for their personal Glock 17m. Each car crew also signed for a carbine or submachine gun, depending on their recent qualifications. Half took Sig Sauer MCX carbines; half had Heckler and Koch MP5 A3, very similar to those that Pavlović had supplied, but the unsilenced variety. Each of the cars also took a Remington 870 pump-action shotgun. This was normally used as a door-breeching weapon or, in some cases when loaded with a wax and zinc powder Hatton round, for taking out car tyres. All the weaponry apart from the Glocks were locked in a secure safe in the boot of each car, the pistols worn on concealed carry holsters. All the team wore covert radios in harnesses, with concealed earpieces and discreet body armour.

Tom travelled with Buster in the BMW estate with Pet sat in the rear, her laptop and iPad open on the back seat, plugged into the twelve-volt socket. They drove north on the A1 at speed, the wail of the siren moving the heavy traffic to the side of the carriageway as the team made progress north in convoy. On the approach to any roundabout the lead vehicle would block all traffic on the roundabout to allow the convoy of six cars to pass through without halting. The lead car, therefore, regularly switched. It required maximum concentration from all the drivers as they sped north, towards the blue pulsing dot of the GPS signal on Pet's iPad screen.

Jane, Mike, and Tiny had stayed back at HQ, ready to liaise as necessary with their various chains of command. This was now a British-led operation, and politically it could be very difficult for Mike, as a CIA chief, to be directly involved. Tiny was at his terminal looking to eke out any advantage from the intelligence they had, as well as to monitor the GPS tags in each of the surveillance cars and the two motorcycles, with the latter having rocketed ahead to get closer to their objective.

'I have the photos of the three Fords here, guys,' said Pet. 'Tiny has just emailed them to me. All are new-looking, dark colours, all double cabs. Window tints are too dark to see inside.'

'Cheers. They'll still be easy to spot, three of them bastards in a row will look like a total dickhead convoy,' Buster said, looking at the iPad on his lap where the blue dot of the objective pulsed.

'How far?' Tom asked.

'GPS signal for the tag is north of Harrogate, we are at the very least three hours behind them. In fact, looking at this map, they are close to Darlington, at least I think Darlington. Christ, they are flying, the bastards.' Buster said.

'Blimey, a little clarity would be nice, I know you think the UK stops at Watford.'

'Fuck knows, mate. Map's all over the gaff. Suffice to say they are somewhere in northern monkey land.'

'I could do with a little more accuracy, Buster, genuinely,' Tom sighed, shaking his head.

'What, you want a bleeding grid reference or something?'

'Just an accurate assessment, will suffice.'

'Fucking hell, you are such a geek. All right, they are just approaching Scotch Corner, a big bastard of a roundabout about nine clicks outside of Darlington. That accurate enough, you pernickety twat?'

'Perfect. Thank you, DC Rhymes,' said Tom, sarcastically.

'Can I ask a question?' said Buster.

'Of course, fire away.'

'Why aren't we pushing this onto a local surveillance team close to where they are now? We could have one on them quickly if they redeploy them urgently. There is always a team working somewhere.'

'Put simply, Buster, we have reason to believe that the people organising this have contacts all over. There would be a whole heap of briefings required and authority levels obtained which would mean the intelligence being repeated to individuals we can't trust. If the organisers of this get a sniff that we are close behind them, they will disappear, and we will have lost them.'

'Fucking hell, we can't fail then.'

'Nope. How about the bikes, are they making decent progress?'

'Yep, they are about an hour ahead of us, not close enough, though and they'll need to refuel about every twenty minutes on those beast bikes.' Buster was referring to the powerful 1000cc motorcycles ridden by the lead bikers, whose job was simply to make as much ground as humanly possible so they were within a shot of getting eyes on the bad guys and accurately calling the rest of the team in. Tom looked at the clock on the display as he drove. They needed to make good ground, but he remained confident that nothing would happen until after dark. As they had about nine hours of light left, he was confident that they could catch them up before any action began. Tom checked his mirrors and increased his speed, as he was lead vehicle, all the following cars matched him mph for mph. Game on.

*

'They've stopped. Definitely stationary and it's not a refuel,' Pet exclaimed from the rear of the car.

'Where?' Tom asked.

'A couple of hours north of here; they left the freeway at Berwick-Upon Tweed and it looks to me like they are stopped in a remote area a short way inland. Hold up, I am zooming in.'

Buster repeated this update on the radio as the car sped along. Jane's voice sparked up over the vehicle's speakers.

'Got it here as well, Tiny is researching now. Wait for an update but keep running.'

'Four-two, how far away from Berwick are you?' Tom asked into the radio.

'At least ninety minutes, we had to refuel again,' the voice was faint against the howl of the engine.

'Fucking typical,' Buster muttered, almost to himself.

'Eyes on, Pet. If they're all stationary, we go in. We could get the fucking lot in one go and this plot dies in one fell swoop,' Tom said accelerating away. This could be it, thought Tom. If they were using a remote area for a lay-up-point until after dark, then this could be the break they need. 'Jane, are you receiving?' he said into the covert mike secreted in the car.

'Yes, go ahead,' she said.

'My advice for this is we approach to their current point as soon as we can. If Jim and Harry get on scene on the bikes, they deploy in close on foot to see if we have all six crates on site. If that is a positive, we contain and then go in. We will need some local back up; can you get them on stand-by?'

There was a brief pause and Tom could imagine Jane assessing all the options. 'Interim and dynamic plan is approved, I will liaise with the Northumberland Police; I won't be revealing the nature of the mission, as we remain covert at this stage, understood? All units acknowledge.' Jane barked her orders clearly, and she was now waiting for each of the units to affirm that they had received and understood.

After each unit had acknowledged, Jane continued, 'Control back to you, Tom. I am going to liaise with the strategic firearms adviser. I will come back to you soon.'

'Give me an RVP, Buster,' Tom said. They needed a place to meet to quickly plan the operation. If the bad guys and the drones were still on site when they arrived, they would need a speedy and dynamic plan to assault the farm and secure the drones. He knew for a fact that these guys would be fully armed, so they would have to be on the top of their game. Tom felt the adrenaline surge in his body as he drove fast and straight up the A1.

After a few moments studying the map on the tablet in front of him, Buster said, 'Best option, Borat, is Asda car park just outside Berwick. Just ten minutes away and we won't show out like a bulldog's testicles there. It's really quiet around the farm.'

'Fair enough. Radio it out to the team, mate. I need to concentrate.'

Tom zoned out for a second, lost in his thoughts as Buster relayed the message out to the team. This was a big and dangerous operation now, with an unknown number of well-armed, well-trained individuals intent on deploying the drones. This was a situation he could never have imagined. His mind whirled and his thoughts were turbulent.

47

The three Rangers had all pulled up alongside two new looking pickup trucks: a dark, mud spattered Mitsubishi and a silver Nissan which had a tarpaulin-covered object in the rear, securely lashed down. As they stopped, four large men stepped out of the front of the vehicles, watching the new arrivals. To Cerović they all looked to be carbon-copies of the guys that picked them up from the fishing boat. They were all Slavic-looking, well-built, and morose; military, tough, and dangerous. They paid him scant attention and seemed to want to know absolutely nothing about him.

Babić briefly addressed all the men, including the four newcomers, before it was time for the drones to be tested.

The farmyard was now a hive of activity. Each of the drones had been removed from its crate, the flight arms extended and rotors attached. The operators all seemed pretty familiar with the basic functions of the drones and Cerović felt pretty confident in their abilities.

He explained the processes for arming the EMP weapon and how to power up the devices.

'Why the mobile phone?' asked one of the operators, a smaller, wiry man with a scarred face and sleeve tattoos on both arms.

'I integrated the phone as it affords some control over each unit that the standard control system doesn't allow. It means I can remotely track each of the drones when they're in flight to ensure everything is synchronised. Also, if one of the GPS systems fails, we have a backup. The biggest reason is that, once we get coordinates for each target, I can individually enter these into the phone and utilise their map system. If the course is locked in, even if the cell phone 4G system fails, the drone will go to its target and can be remotely deployed by me using the phone linkup. Useful if one of you gets killed.'

'Nice to know,' the man said, flatly.

'Okay, everyone power their drone up, I want to be sure each is ready to go. Just go to a low hover, no flying about as I don't have time to fix any damage if you crash.'

In a few moments there was the familiar deep buzz of six drones as the rotors whirred loudly. Each operator had a black, ruggedized control unit that looked like a typical remote-control unit but with a hi-definition screen in the centre. It seemed that all the operators were completely comfortable and within a few seconds there were six drones in a low hover stirring up a small dust cloud.

'Okay, cut them off,' Cerović shouted, drawing his finger across his throat.

All the drones were gently settled back on the ground and the motors were silenced.

Babić stepped out into the courtyard watching the scene before him. 'Everything working okay?'

'All looking good, we are ready,' Cerović nodded.

Babić went over to the Nissan truck, put his kit in the cab and then went round to the flat bed at the rear. He lifted the tarpaulin, smiling when he saw what lay beneath, a feeling of familiarity flooding through him. A muffled ping erupted from his pocket: it was time. He returned to the farmhouse to hear a pinging sound coming from his iPad on the table. Opening the secure app, the familiar mechanical voice spoke. 'Are you ready to receive instructions?'

'Yes. Proceed.'

'I am sending three sets of coordinates to you now. These are to be input into three of the drones and the operatives for each are to proceed to a safe laying-up point close to the target destination and wait. Each target is a major electricity sub-station surrounding Edinburgh. Understood?'

'Yes, continue,' Babić said, brusquely.

'Each team at the three substations will have their drones, in the hover, at forty metres above the facility. And at precisely 2300 hours they will detonate their devices, is that understood? The drones are to be powered up at precisely 2230 hours in order that we can be assured via our remote monitoring that they are set and ready to deploy. There is to be no other communication between the teams, yes?'

'Yes, continue.'

'The next screen will have a further two sets of coordinates, very close to each other, but it is imperative that each drone goes to these coordinates precisely, is that clear? It must be inch perfect and they must hover at one hundred metres before deploying the EMP device; is that clear? In a similar fashion, the two drones will be powered up at 2300 hours in order that we can monitor these remotely as well. Understood?'

'Yes.'

'These drones must then detonate at precisely 2315 hours. It is vital that you are as far away from this facility as you feel comfortable before detonation, is this clear?'

'What is the target?'

'The target, Commander, is Torness nuclear power plant in Dunbar. First your men will destroy the power grid, then you will strike fear into the hearts of the country by disabling a nuclear power plant. In a few hours, much of Scotland will be dark.'

'And the final drone?' Babić asked.

'This is for the contingency plan which we discussed some time ago, Babić.'

48

The team continued driving along the A1 at speed, ever narrowing the distance between them and the drones. The bikers had just radioed in saying they were about thirty minutes away from the GPS location.

Tiny had researched the location and identified it as Jarrow Farm, a smallholding with unclear ownership or residence details. The property showed no accounts, and the relevant authorities seemed to know very little about it.

Pet shouted from the back of the car. 'I have multiple drone activations. Four, five, hold-up. Six. Six drones are on and I am getting signals. All are hitting a cell mast close to Berwick. They are hooked into the 4G system.'

'What does this mean? Are they deploying now?' Buster asked.

'In daylight?' said Tom. 'I can't see it. Why would they?'

'No idea, Detective, but the SIMs that we have attributed to the phones in the devices are active right now.'

'Jane, are you receiving?'

'Go ahead, Buster,' Jane's northern tones crackled through the speakers.

'Multiple drone activations. Is Tiny seeing this?'

'Yeah I'm watching. Hold up, we've just lost one. In fact, there goes another, just four on now.' The big Mancunian spoke briskly.

Pet sighed. 'That's all of them now silent again. So, what was that all about?'

'A test,' said Tom. 'That's the only thing that makes sense. They are all military, or ex-military at least. All soldiers test their kit before a battle.'

'Does this change anything?' asked Pet.

'Nothing. We keep going. We are about an hour out; the bikes will be on scene very soon. We reassess then. Alpha seven, Alpha eight, proceed as before, inform us when you are on scene. Acknowledge, over.'

'Alpha eight, all received.'

'Alpha seven, all received.'

The distinctive roar of the bikes made the voices hard to hear. Tom felt for the guys on the bikes, riding at that speed for that length of time was seriously hard work and, once on scene, they would have to stealthily recce the farmhouse. Everything depended on what they found.

The convoy continued on, not letting up for the next twenty-five minutes. Tom spoke to Jane, who had liaised with the strategic firearms commander. The advice was for the Team to conduct a control and containment exercise if the crates and suspects were present. They were then to call on a local SFO team, currently on standby at Berwick-Upon Tweed with a tactical firearms controller.

The radio crackled in the car as they sped along. 'Alpha eight, now on scene, with Alpha seven. We are securing the bikes nearby and we will advance and get a visual on the property. We'll report back as soon as we have something to tell you.' The confident voice of Harry—callsign Alpha eight—rang over the airways.

'Alpha eight, all received. No engagement unless fired upon. Visual confirmation only.'

'All received.'

There was a heavy silence in the car as Tom imagined the two officers attempting to get a view on the farmhouse. Buster had an iPad open with a zoomed in, blurred aerial photograph displayed. It was a smallish farm with a main house and a few outbuildings. The boundary seemed to be a poorly kept hedgerow, which would have afforded a good view of the parking area at the front of the farmhouse.

'I know: it's Google satellite, mate and could be well out of date, but it looks piss-easy to recce, loads of cover, and not a great deal of distance.' Buster said studying the image.

'If I know Harry,' Tom said, 'he will have looked at that before he moved up. Hopefully we will hear soon. What's the GPS saying, Pet?'

'No change. Still a strong signal, putting it right in the middle of the farmyard.'

The radio crackled with static and Harry's whispered voice filled the car. 'Alpha seven, in position. Have a visual on the farmhouse and the parking area at the front. No cars present. Repeat, no cars present. No signs of life at the property at all.'

There was a brief silence in the car whilst Tom digested this. He pressed the transmit button on his radio. 'Have you a visual on all of the farmhouse?'

'From Alpha eight, yes. All sides are clear.'

'Fuck!' blasted Buster. 'Are they in the right fucking place?'

'They sure are,' said Pet. 'I'm tracking the GPS in their radios. Two signals, one north and one south side of the property. The GPS you put in the crate is still showing in the middle.'

'Alpha seven and eight. Proceed with caution but move in closer. Retreat if confronted and still only engage if life threatened. We have a GPS in the middle of the plot.'

'Yeah moving up now. Wait.'

There was another turgid silence for a further minute that was almost deafening in its intensity.

'Alpha seven, the property is clear. Someone has been here recently, there is some still warm burnt debris in the fireplace in the farmhouse. There is also a heap of open wooden crates in the barn. Looks like they've unloaded the drones and moved.'

The only sound in the car was the roar of the engine as they continued north.

'Is now a good time to ask where the GPS tag was?' said Buster.

Tom's face gave nothing away; it was a blank mask as he considered his options.

'Right, we continue to the RVP and reassess. I need some clear thinking and suggestions from everyone.' Tom paused as he pressed the transmit switch. 'All units, drones have gone. Repeat, drones have gone. Jane, they have unpacked the drones and left the crates. The GPS tag was secreted in one of the crates. We now don't have a live link to where they are,'

Jane's tone was calm and collected, as expected. 'Received here. I will despatch CSIs to the farmhouse to retrieve any evidence. What are our options?'

'Can Tiny keep on with ANPR?'

'Consider it done,' Tiny's voice boomed out of the speakers.

'I'm open to suggestions, guys,' Tom said to Buster and Pet.

'Fuck knows, mate,' said Buster. 'I ain't here for my brains or looks. We need to catch a break. We are hot on their heels so we need to look for any high value targets that may be vulnerable to EMP. Is that a start?'

'It is actually a very good suggestion, but there must be loads of potentials: water, power, internet, GPS systems, dams, wind farms. The list goes on.'

'There must be something,' said Buster.

A thought flashed through Tom's mind; something Havers had said.

'Fear,' Tom exclaimed.

'Pardon?' said Pet.

'Havers, the bent bloke at the US Embassy. When we were interrogating him, he talked about fear, almost as if it was a weapon in itself. He said that the intention was for the lights to go out and spread fear among the population when the supermarket shelves empty. It's a power station, or power stations. It has to be. They are wanting to turn the lights out, that's what they want. What major power infrastructure facilities do we have nearby, Pet?'

Pet began tapping at her computer. 'North of here we have plenty of active substations, major pylons crossing the country. There are hydro dams and a significant amount of windfarms both on- and offshore. We have Torness power station half an hour up the coast road in Dunbar and Hartlepool almost two hours south of us. There is—'

'Hold up, say that again.' Tom shouted, looking in the mirror at Pet.

'Torness power station.' Pet looked puzzled.

'That's it. That's fucking it. Don't you see? It's the Chernobyl effect, right?'

'Tom, what the pissing hell are you going on about?' Buster said.

'Torness is a nuclear power station. It has two reactors. I remember it from a few years ago: jellyfish gummed up the cooling water intakes and they had to shut the reactor down. People were terrified thinking that that part of Scotland was going to be reduced to a nuclear wasteland. It would be ten times worse now with social media how it is, irrespective of whether it's feasible or not. People would panic; this is exactly what the investors want.' Tom's eyes were shining.

'Holy shit! What the fuck would a couple of big bastard drones do to a nuke power station?' Buster had a rare ability to deploy old English oaths, and he excelled himself often, but right now, they both shared his sentiments.

'I really have no idea, Buster. Whichever, the fear of a meltdown is what they are after. I need to speak to Jane on the phone, I'm not putting this on the net. Pet keep monitoring for any drone activity; that is still our best bet but, once they are up, unless we are close enough, it's too late,' Tom said pulling over to the side of the road, 'Take over driving, Buster, we still RVP in Berwick.'

*

Jane put the phone down with a sense of dread. A nuclear power station, as much as she wanted it to not be true, she had to admit that it certainly seemed to be the most likely target.

Mike looked at her as she recounted Tom's hypotheses and his reasoning for it.

'I have to say, I see Tom's way of thinking. Havers did use the analogy of fear being the strongest weapon, lights out and empty shelves. You want to know something pretty secret?'

'That depends, Mike.'

'The threat assessment for EMP is really high in the States. The president has allocated huge resources into research and development of infrastructure protection against EMP from terrorist or rogue nation strikes. The nuclear energy industry has made some overt claims that an EMP strike on a nuclear power plant would not be overly worrisome, but you know something else?'

'I suspect you're going to tell me.'

'It's considered to be bullshit by some experts. The reality is that nobody has a clue what would happen to a nuclear power station if struck by a serious EMP microwave burst.'

'I need to speak to someone at the Civil Nuclear Constabulary, we can't keep this under wraps with them, they will need to beef their security up massively.'

*

Jane sat with Mike in front of the large screen, waiting for the video conference which had quickly been arranged by the Commissioner's staff officer.

The tone that emitted through the speakers indicated that all parties were now ready to begin. Two figures appeared on a split screen, one wearing the blue uniform with insignia of the Civil Nuclear Constabulary, the other in casual clothing.

'Good evening, gentlemen. Thank you for agreeing to this video conference, which I accept is slightly irregular, but I hope we can agree that in the circumstances is necessary. I must apologise for the Commissioner's absence, but she is briefing COBRA as we speak. Introductions first: I am DCS Jane Milligan from Covert Policing Advice, this is Mike Brogan from the US Embassy.' Mike nodded at the introduction.

'I am Assistant Chief Constable William Donaldson, Civil Nuclear Police.'

'Professor David Gillam; I am the CEO of the Atomic Energy Authority,' the other man spoke in a soft Scottish accent and had the look of a scientist about him, his rumpled cardigan, scruffy hair and bushy moustache giving him an intellectual appearance.

'Thank you, gentlemen. We have identified what we believe to be a significant threat against somewhere in Scotland, probably Torness power plant. We have good intelligence that there are six heavy-capacity drones, with extended range built into them all, carrying a powerful weapon capable of delivering a powerful EMP burst. We do not know exactly what the target is, but we strongly suspect that a nuclear power plant is the most likely.' Jane spoke quickly and efficiently, using her words sparingly and wisely.

There was a pause as both men digested the information.

'Can I ask how reliable this intelligence is?' Donaldson asked.

'Very. We have had an operator visibly see the drones and, until very recently, we were tracking them until we lost the signal a while ago, somewhere close to Berwick-Upon-Tweed. We have had intelligence facilities deployed and we have no doubt that the devices are viable.'

'How can you be sure that Torness is the intended target?' Donaldson asked.

'We can't, in short. The proximity of Torness and the nature of their journey makes it our primary concern, but we also accept that we have other nuclear sites within a few hours, and at present we cannot track the devices or the operators.'

'This is our problem, Jane. We have other power stations within a few hours of Berwick. Hunterston B and Hartlepool are all within easy striking distance. Why Torness?'

'My operative on the ground strongly feels that that is by far the most likely, as the drones were clearly being prepared for flight close by at a remote facility, and it seems they are all now active and ready for deployment. It seems unlikely to us that they would undertake this preparation if they were to travel any further than necessary.'

'Is there no way of tracking them?' Professor Gillam asked.

'Only once they power them up and they begin flying. They are using mobile phone SIMs as part of their navigation system. We have the facility to track them, once active, but it is not accurate, and we don't know the extent of it. Our feeling is that it is a backup system.'

'Then we will have some advance warning, at least?'

'Well, yes, but we won't have GPS data, just cell sites which will only give approximate locations.'

The ACC crossed his legs and cleared his throat before speaking again. 'Jane, if I'm honest, I am not worrying about this. At the moment, nothing you have said so far causes me any great angst. A recent risk assessment by experts concluded that any drone threat was minimal. Our facilities are extremely secure, and the limited range and payload capacity is so small that it would be akin to a small boy using a peashooter to attack a fort. I will raise the threat level at all our facilities, and we will have expert armed officers on standby. Any drones that come close will be shot out of the sky,' his smile was as insincere as it was arrogant.

'Well I am worried, Bill,' Professor Gillam said. 'Is this an explosively pumped flux weapon?'

'Yes,' said Jane. 'We have good intelligence to support this.'

'Do we know a potential power output?'

'No, we don't have that information.'

'I have to say, this makes me very uncomfortable.' Professor Gillam wiped his brow.

'But David. The core is under massive amounts of concrete, all the control systems are secure, I can't see how it will threaten the facility,' the ACC seemed a bit less certain than before.

'Well, I'm afraid that I do not share your confidence. I am not completely sure of the effect that a well-directed EMP blast will cause. If it stops the water pump, disables security, destroys diesel generators and control systems, the system could overheat, and we won't be able to enable a safe shut down. I can't be sure—I have no idea, in fact—but it may cause a meltdown, it may not. We are in unknown territory here.'

'David, can you be sure?' The ACC looked distinctively uncomfortable now.

'I can't be sure of a single thing. This is unprecedented, Bill. It may not make a scratch, or it may cause a full safety emergency with a nuclear escape. Whatever you have to do to beef security or stop this threat, I suggest you do it. And do it fast.'

49

Tom, Buster, and Pet sat in their car waiting. Just waiting. None of them particularly knew exactly what they were waiting for, so the feeling of impotence was strong. Tom had made the call an hour ago that he would be better served splitting his resources, so he had despatched his teams so he had a unit West of Edinburgh and the remainder, including the bikes, close by. They had edged further north, closing the distance between them and Torness. He remained convinced that the last location, when the drones were removed from the crates, indicated that the targets would be close by.

'Can we play *I Spy*?' said Buster, sarcastically.

'Only if you want a punch in the face,' Tom replied.

'I Spy sucks,' added Pet, and the car returned to its previous silence.

Jane had just recently called with the news that the leading expert on nuclear power plants was distinctly worried about the consequences of an EMP strike on a power station. COBRA was being briefed and were currently deliberating. Tom looked at his watch and saw that it was nearly twenty-past ten. He could imagine the political hand-wringing that would be going on at that moment.

Pressing his radio switch, he said, 'Alpha three are you in position?'

'Yes, yes. West of Edinburgh, just off M9.'

'All other units hold close by my location and wait for updates.'

Tom only half listened as the acknowledgements came in.

There was nothing else they could do. It was like being in the military again. Holding up, bored, waiting for what could be a short, sharp, and highly dangerous mission.

'Coffee?' Buster asked.

'Oh yeah, I could do coffee,' Pet said, brightening.

'Go on, then. There was a garage just a couple of miles back,' Tom said.

'You're buying, Borat. The amount of fucking overtime you must have pulled in in the last few days,' Buster started the car and pulled out of their layby, back towards the all-night garage they had passed a while ago.

Jane's voice popped up on the radio. 'Tom, COBRA have met and an SAS team from Hereford are being briefed but will need some response time and then travelling time to get to you.'

'Yes, all received. No ETA, I take it.'

'No, but it will be hours even if they are flying; stay alert, people.'

'Typical Hereford; top blokes but I've a nasty feeling they'll be a bit late for this party,' said Buster, shaking his head.

Pulling into the garage Tom said, 'My shout then.' He got out of the car and crossed the forecourt to the brightly lit shop, jamming his earpiece in as he did.

Once inside he used the coffee machine and began the process of dispensing three coffees into the large paper cups. Screwing the lids on, he walked up to the cashier and paid, yawning as he did so. He really needed the caffeine, barely having slept for a few days.

Suddenly Pet's voice crackled in his ear. 'We have an activation. Drone has just come online, hitting a cell mast in Falkirk. Hold up, another activation: three are now online, the other two close by.'

Leaving the coffees with the perplexed-looking cashier, Tom ran out and jogged over to the car.

'Show me,' he said as he climbed in. Pet turned the screen towards him: pulsating blue dots were positioned to the north and west, with two fairly close to their location.

'Only three. Can you overlay with any potential targets? Power stations, dams, hospitals, anything?'

Tiny's voice came over the net. 'I've been messing about in maps at your location and we have a number of potentials, guys. The model I have lists a number of priorities. I'm mirroring them over to you, but you have three major power substations right slap bang in the centre of each of the cell activation areas. I've narrowed them down as much as I can and applied the azimuth. I am sure the targets are the power substations at SP Energy near Falkirk, Crystal Rig and Dunbar close to your location. We need to get people there, pronto.' Tiny didn't get excited much, so his words had impact.

'Agreed. Alpha three to SP Energy, Alpha four to Dunbar and five to Crystal Rig. Alphas six, seven and eight remain with us, all units acknowledge.' Tom's voice was calm.

As the acknowledgements came through one by one Buster spoke, quietly, almost anticipating the answer.

'How about us, Tom?'

'There are still three drones out there, mate. I think we can guess where they are going to be targeting.'

A deep, cloying silence enveloped the car. Things were about to get very lively.

'Buster, let's move up closer. Head north towards Thorntonloch, there's a caravan site there by the beach,' said Tom as he studied the map on the iPad.

Buster said nothing, just shifted the gear stick and pulled away.

50

Babić stepped out of the Nissan that had just pulled up on the beach and took a deep breath of the sea air as a Ranger pulled up alongside. The two huge Russians stepped out of the front of the Nissan, joined by the two from the Ranger all cradling their submachine guns and surveying the scene around them.

The waves lapped gently in the gloom and the warm, balmy evening was quiet and peaceful. He looked ahead where he could see the harsh arc lights from their objective: the nuclear power plant in the distance. He wondered with a smile how much longer the lights would be operational for. Looking at his watch he saw that it was only five minutes before eleven; all the drones had shown on Cerović's map, so it was also safe to assume that they were ready to deploy. Any time now, he thought. Then he would be a rich man and he could escape all this crap.

Cerović was outside of the car, unfolding the struts on the two drones and attaching the rotors carefully, tightening all the fastenings.

Babić walked across the sand to Cerović. 'All in order?'

'All looking good. Ready to power up at 2300, as you said.'

'Not a moment before.' He looked at his iPad, noting the three pulses at each electricity substation. Soon they would be up and flying, ready to snuff out the power and plunge Edinburgh into darkness. A feeling of prickling anticipation coursed through his veins. The money was a driving force, but he had to admit, the power over other humans was intoxicating.

He continued to stare at his watch, the digital numbers turning over as the time eased closer to 11pm. When the digits shifted to read 23:00 he smiled and simply said, 'Power up, Cerović. Input the GPS coordinates and be ready on my mark.'

'Ready when you are, man,' replied Cerović.

'Lock in the course and set the detonation sequence.'

'Done.'

A muffled ping came from Babić's pocket. The investors. His brow furrowed; this was unexpected.

He stepped into the Nissan and opened the secure messaging app.

'Yes. This is a bad time. We are about to strike on Torness.'

'Babić, you have a final target. Leave Cerović with two of your men and a vehicle. Take one man, the final drone, and your equipment and head to the coordinates I am sending you now.' The mechanical voice was suddenly gone, and a set of coordinates popped up on the screen. He clicked on the icon and looked at the map. A slow smile spread across his face.

51

'We have an activation on the final two drones. Hold up, I'm trying to isolate,' Pet almost shouted.

'Tiny are you getting this?' Tom asked over the radio.

'Yes, just applying triangulation and azimuth,' his voice came over the net.

'Pet, I want you to force Cerović's phone to power up. He is with those two drones. They are going to strike Torness and he will definitely be there.'

'Are you sure? It will be obvious, it will be visible, and it may be seen.'

'Do it. We need GPS coordinates; a cell site isn't enough, and I am certain that all their attention will be on the drones. Do it now.'

'Okay I'm forcing it now. Hold up. Powering now. Jesus, Tom they'll see this.'

'No, they won't.' Tom's voice was flat and eerily calm.

There was an interminable pause that felt like an hour but, in reality, was probably less than a minute.

'Bingo. GPS. Wait a second,' Pet tapped furiously at the keys, desperately trying to isolate the signal.

All of a sudden, there was chaos over the net, from the other units at the substations.

'Drone sighted, drone sighted, hold up, contact.' The bellowing voice of Lin, one of the team members, came over the net followed by the boom of a shotgun and the rattle of automatic gunfire.

More units were shouting but Tom tuned them out. There was nothing he could do; he knew Jane and Tiny would be listening and directing local resources. He had to focus on what was immediate and what was now.

'Got them,' Pet screamed. 'Half a click away, north on the beach. Back onto the A1 and go south. We will run parallel with them; you will then have to cross the field to intercept.'

Buster spun the wheel and sped off, directed by Pet. They drove parallel to the coast until Pet shouted, 'Here now! They are three hundred metres in that direction.'

Looking at his map with the neon pulsing dot of Cerović's phone dead central on the beach, Tom shouted into the radio over the howl of the BMW's engine. 'Remaining units close in, I'm sharing location now on your screens. Alpha six move south of the signal, we will come in from the north. Stealthy approach, shotguns ready to engage. Don't let those drones get off the fucking ground.'

When they were adjacent to the signal, Buster pulled off the road bouncing onto the soft verge grass.

'They're straight there, Tom. Three hundred metres.'

Tom and Buster dived out of the car and went to the boot, opening it and unlocking the vehicle safe. Tom pulled out the Sig Sauer MTX carbine whilst Buster grabbed the Remington 870 and racked the action, injecting a shell into the barrel. Tom slapped a magazine into the Sig and cocked it. He stuffed a further couple of magazines into his patch pocket on his combats and buttoned it up, securely.

He smiled at Buster. 'Ready?'

'No, am I fuck. You always get me in these shit situations you twat,' he grinned widely back. 'Let's do this.'

'Pet, monitor the computers. Straight in if anything crops up.'

'You got it. Be careful.'

Buster and Tom turned and began jogging along the rutted, ploughed field between the A1 and the beach. As they moved everything went just a shade darker, as all the lights in the houses nearby and the distant town lights all went off simultaneously. Suddenly it was almost pitch black, apart from the nearly full moon and the distant glow from Torness with its independent power supply.

'Looks like some of the drones hit home at least.' Buster said, over the continued chatter on the radios. Some reports were beginning to filter in, but it was hard to make any sense of them and concentrate on the task in hand. Jane's steadying presence on the net was comforting as she directed resources. One positive was that neither man had heard the fatal words, *'Officer down'*, yet.

As they closed towards the beach Tom saw the dark outline of a large pickup truck casting a shadow against the moon's reflection in the sea. He pointed at his eyes and then pointed at the truck and Buster nodded. Both men dropped to their knees and took cover against a scraggy gorse bush.

'Alpha six report?' Tom whispered.

'Just south of the signal,' came the hoarse reply.

'Okay, we are moving up now. Three figures by the Ford, parked on the beach. Do you have it?'

'Yes, yes. We are moving up.'

'Received. Wait for my signal.'

'What will your signal be?'

'Lots of big bangs,' Tom said. Now wasn't the time to piss about. Those drones could not leave the ground.

'You ready Buster?'

'I'm always ready, you twat. But I am gonna stop hanging around with you.'

'Let's go.'

They ran at a crouch, getting to within forty metres of the truck where they ducked down by the scant cover of a small depression in the ground.

A deep, intense buzz and humming sound suddenly became audible despite the breeze in their faces. Suddenly two bright torches flashed on in front of them, illuminating the two drones that sat on the beach, their blades whirring and blowing the coarse sand in all directions.

Out of nowhere what had been a background hum became a loud roar as a helicopter roared into view overhead from behind them at a perilously low altitude. The words *"Police"* could easily be read, being emblazoned on the underside in white writing. The side door of the helicopter was open, and a lone uniformed officer was sat in the doorway clutching a long-barrelled firearm of some variety. The dark figures extinguished the torches and darted out of sight ducking down behind the side of the pickup. The helicopter flew low over the truck, moving out so it was in a low hover over the sea, the jet wash chopping up swirling waves in the still water. A powerful nightsun spotlight burst into life and bathed the truck in blinding, white light as the marksman brought his weapon to bear on the pickup.

One of the figures on the ground darted to the rear of the pickup and emerged clutching what looked like a long, bulky weapon which he hefted onto his shoulder.

Tom's blood ran cold. 'No, no, no! Police helicopter, back off, back off, suspects in possession of an energy weapon. Back off back off,' he yelled against the deafening roar from the helicopter.

A solitary spark was the first evidence of any effect; just a small, lone spark that was visible through the open door. All of the sudden, the nightsun exploded in a hail of sparks. The helicopter then went into complete darkness, all electrical circuits fried by the powerful blast of electromagnetic waves. The engine cut out, as dead as if a cut-out switch had been flicked. It spun wildly out of control before rearing onto its side and hitting the water with a resounding and deafening crash, where it disintegrated in a swirling foam of black water.

'Crash, crash. The helo has crashed, we need all emergency services, now. Multiple casualties,' Tom bellowed into his radio. His earpiece burst into life in his ear in response.

A crackle of gunfire and muzzle flashes erupted from the rear of the pickup, and the sand at their feet danced with the impact of nine-millimetre parabellums. There was hardly any noise from the silenced weapons as Tom and Buster dived to take cover. Tom crawled into a firing position, shouldering the Sig. The pickup was still in total darkness, all torches extinguished, as Tom stared down the optic which fortunately had a low-light capacity which intensified the bright moon. He fired a strafing burst at the vehicle, the loud cracking report from the Sig announcing firmly that there was a new player in this game.

The lead drone lurched into the air unsteadily hovering close to the sand as it skirted away from the pickup. A hail of withering automatic fire forced both Tom and Buster to shrink into the depression they were using as cover.

'The drone, Buster. Don't let it get away,' Tom shouted.

'Fucking hell, Borat, I'm gonna make you pay for this shit! Cover me,'

Tom aimed at the muzzle flashes and let out a further long burst of the high velocity ammunition, Buster jumped onto his haunches and fired a deafening blast from the Remington. The shot smashed into the skimming drone making mincemeat of the rotors. It bucked and rolled and crashed into the sand in a tangle of twisted metal, useless and destroyed.

'Good shot. Just one more to go, Buster.'

'I can count, you cheeky bastard. Get ready,' Buster said pumping another slug into the Remington. Three MP5s opened up on them simultaneously, the sand almost seemed to come alive as the bullets peppered all around them.

'Jesus fucking Christ!' Buster shouted as he tried to clear his eyes from the sand that had been blown into them. 'This is the least fun ever!'

The sharp, high-pitched wail of the remaining drone erupted from behind the pickup, and it suddenly shot upwards at a remarkable speed. Tom could only watch as it climbed rapidly. Buster pointed the Remington upwards and let loose a barrage of shots, semi blindly, but the drone glided away, untouched, upwards at a staggeringly fast rate and out of their range.

'Shit!' said Tom. 'Shit.'

A stocky figure stood up at the rear of the pickup, his MP5 raised to his cheek, and began firing wildly at them. A sharp crack of a Sig came from further down the beach and struck the man square in the centre of his chest, knocking him backwards with a cry. Tom knelt up and peppered the pickup with a further long burst of automatic fire as Buster rushed forward, racking the Remington as he went. A tall and powerful looking man emerged from the back of the pickup firing wildly at Tom. Buster paused and fired the Remington, catching the man full on from just twenty metres. The man flew back, blasted to bits by the terrible force of the heavy shot, landing in the sand in a crumpled heap.

Tony from Alpha six appeared south of the pickup, a Sig in his shoulder, screaming, 'Armed police! Put your hands up!' as he advanced.

Tom also began to advance, weapon in shoulder, towards the pickup. He, Buster, and Tony circled the pickup. Cerović was lying on the floor moaning and holding his leg.

'I've been shot, I've been fucking shot, help me,' Cerović wailed. Two other figures were in the sand nearby. Tom advanced carefully, but both men lay absolutely still, clearly dead or dying.

'From Alpha one, ambulance required, multiple casualties.'

'Alpha one, received. Locals are on way,' Jane's voice was calm, as normal.

'We have one drone away and currently heading towards Torness; please advise those on site,' Tom said.

'Acknowledged. Security is on site,' she said, icy calm.

Two smashed remote-control units lay broken and useless on the sand, both a twist of plastic and mangled circuitry.

'I'm hit, man. It hurts so much,' Cerović moaned from his position on the sand.

'Shut up Cerović, you have a flesh wound,' Tom said. 'How do we stop that drone?'

'You can't,' Cerović replied. 'The course, altitude, and detonation are locked in. Babić smashed the controllers and then he drove off, he just abandoned us. I can't do anything now; you need to get us away from here.' He paused and blinked up at Tom. 'Why the fuck are you here?' His face was fixed in a mask of confusion and pain. 'You're a cop? You're a fucking cop. I thought you were an arms dealer. Ah man, no, no, no,' Cerović began to wail, understanding flooding in.

Tom stared at him. 'Buster, lock him up.'

'Fine, but what are you going to do?'

Tom picked up the EMP weapon that had been used to down the helicopter. It was heavy and cumbersome. He hefted it into the back of the Ranger, climbed into the driver's seat and gunned the engine. 'I'm going to try to take down that drone before it explodes. You and the others sort this out, I'll be back soon.' He slammed the door and roared off along the sand towards the power plant.

52

Tom drove as fast as the sand would allow in the big truck, the engine roaring. He bounced up onto the adjacent field and within a minute was back on the A1, heading north.

Pressing his transmit button, he spoke. 'Jane, I need to get into the site, urgently. I am travelling along the A1 and I will be at the main gate in about two minutes. I am in a dark Ford pickup. I have something that may be able to disable it. The same thing they took the helo out with.'

'I have the ACC on the conference line; we are following this together. Hold up.'

'Hurry, this thing has its course locked in and it is set to auto-detonate any time. We have no idea what it will do.'

'Okay, the ACC is calling Torness now; you should be able to access as soon as you get there. Will this weapon work?'

'I have no idea, Jane, but it took a great big helicopter out, so we have to be in with a chance.' Tom accelerated as fast as the heavy Ford would allow. As he surged up to the plant's entrance, the gates were already opening in front of him, like the parting of the Red Sea. Two uniformed constables at the gates, armed with Heckler and Koch G36 assault weapons, waved him on. He drove straight through the still-moving gates and into a clearing, in between a group of heavily fortified buildings and a large steel shipping container.

An impossibly young-looking uniformed sergeant, also clutching a G36, ran up to meet him. 'DS Novak?'

'Yes, have you seen it?' Tom said, getting out of the Ford.

'Yes, it's hovering at about one hundred metres straight above us now. It's too far for shotguns to be effective. Can it cause damage?' He pointed upwards, and the red, flashing light was clearly visible: as he had said, about one hundred metres above them, its high-pitched buzzing clearly audible.

'What's your name, mate?'

'Jerome,' he said, looking puzzled.

'Well, Jerome, to be perfectly honest, I don't have a clue. But the alternative is we sit here and wait for it to go off. Now, I have no idea what will happen once I use this thing. Get all your people to take cover somewhere and you may want to think about finding somewhere to hide as well.'

Tom hefted the heavy weapon out of the truck as Jerome busied himself on his radio, relaying Tom's message.

The weapon was about a metre long and had a roughly fabricated, hard vulcanised plastic covering, giving it the shape and feel of a large, bulky firearm. It had a crudely fashioned trigger assembly that led out to a long barrel with what looked like a black spotlight at the end. There was a rudimentary sight mechanism, with an optic that seemed to have been made using a monocular that had been bolted on to the side of the unit. Tom heaved it onto his shoulder and fixed his eye to the eyepiece. There was some image enhancement on the monocular and, as he raised it to the sky, the stars beamed brighter than normal as the low light capacity harvested all the available ambient light. He began scanning the sky above him. He saw it immediately: the small flashing light from the mobile phone shining brightly enhanced by the night vision.

Looking to his side he saw Jerome staring open-mouthed at him. 'What the fuck is that?'

Ignoring him, Tom depressed the trigger, which moved easily with a satisfying clunk. The whole unit vibrated with suppressed electrical energy, and Tom's hair felt like it was standing on end. He felt a distinct and palpable heat emanating from the weapon, but there was no beam, no flash: nothing. Just a humming and a feeling that the very air around them was being positively charged.

Tom's eye stayed glued to the hovering drone. A small spark emanated from the form, akin to a small firework, and the drone bucked in the air. The buzzing of the beating rotors suddenly stopped and they were enveloped with an all-encompassing, deafening silence.

'Fuck, it's worked,' said Jerome, wonder in his voice.

The drone began to fall, like a stone from the sky. Tom ditched the weapon and shouted at Jerome, 'Take cover! It's coming down, fast!' They both ran and dived behind a short, squat concrete building.

There was a further millisecond of absolute silence and then a mangled crash as the drone hit the ground. Looking tentatively from their hiding place Tom saw a twisted pile of metal thirty metres away from the truck. There was no smoke, no beeps, no noise. Just dead, inert metal and wires, devoid of power.

Tom walked hesitantly up to the destroyed drone. It was dead. No lights, no noise, just a pile of metal and circuitry. Tom had enough knowledge of explosives from his military days to know that an electrical detonator required a power source to initiate. Without that, it was safe.

He breathed a heavy sigh of relief.

'Is it okay, I mean is it going to blow up?' Jerome asked, tentatively.

'I hope not. The fuse is an electronic one activated by a mobile phone electric current. No electricity, no detonation. It's over.'

'Fucking hell, mate. Good skills,' Jerome said, a trace of wonder in his voice.

'Call it in, Jerome. I can't guarantee how safe it is. It contains explosives, so there is still a chance it may blow up,' said Tom.

'Erm, yeah sure. I will call it in as a Hazmat incident; the world and their wife will be here soon.'

'Awesome. Nice to meet you, Jerome. Good job.' Tom shook the man's hand and jogged over to the Ford. He heaved the energy weapon back into the truck and climbed in. The big V8 engine roared as he drove out of the site and back towards the beach, his radio earpiece still buzzing with reports and directions flooding in.

As he drove, Tom couldn't help but feel that something was wrong. It all felt too easy, and Babić had clearly fled the scene. It just felt wrong. He shook his head and headed back to the beach.

53

The scene at the beach had developed since he had left. There were two ambulances, two fire tenders, and what seemed like dozens of police cars along with a coastguard rescue vehicle. Strobing blue lights everywhere; it was a scene of utter chaos and confusion.

A lifeboat was trawling the area where the helicopter had ditched into the sea, the crewmen looking forlornly into the black water.

Tom got out of the Ford and approached the clutch of uniformed police officers. Buster and Tony were stood talking to a uniformed inspector, a middle-aged woman who looked a little overwhelmed at the catastrophe that she was at the centre of.

Tom approached the small group wearily, a wave of total and utter exhaustion beginning to overwhelm him.

'DS Novak?' The inspector said, panic etched across her features.

'That's me,' Tom said.

'I'm Inspector Fraser, duty officer. DC Rhymes has updated me, but can you confirm that the weapon at Torness has been disabled?' she had a soft Edinburgh accent and her eyes were wide with concern.

'Yes, Ma'am: the nuclear site is safe as far as I can be sure, but CNC are calling it all in and they are implementing their Hazmat procedures now. I think you can leave it to them. My team are going to adjourn to a police station that has power and wait for the relevant Police Complaints Authority. We are now in a post incident procedure and we will be preparing our witness statements in order that an investigative team can deal with the aftermath.' Tom turned to Buster. 'Any news of the team, Buster? Any casualties?'

'No, mate. One of the drones hit home, the others were disabled. Two of the bad guys were taken out by one of our units, two arrested, and two are on their toes.'

'Thank you mate. Get the team organised and ready to go.'

Inspector Fraser clearly wasn't satisfied with Tom's explanation. 'Detective sergeant, I need to establish what has happened here. I need answers, right now. We have two dead bodies, a prisoner with a gunshot wound, and a helicopter that has been shot down.'

Pet was suddenly at Tom's shoulder, clutching her tablet computer. 'Tom. We have another drone activation.'

'What?' said Tom turning to her, a sinking feeling in his chest.

'South of here, about five miles and moving fast, hugging the coast,' said Pet, looking at the screen.

'What, *away* from Torness?' Tom asked.

'Yes, away from Torness.'

'Any possible targets there?' he asked.

'Not that I can see.'

Tom picked out his phone and called Jane.

'Tom, well done, nice w—' Jane began, before Tom interrupted her.

'Jane, we have another drone activation. Five miles south of here.'

'What? What on earth can it be targeting?'

'Do you still have a direct line to the nuclear power people?'

'Yes, they are still on the conference line. Hold on, I will relay to them.' There was a pause for a full, agonising minute before Jane's voice came back on the line, sounding urgent.

'Tom, there are nuclear flasks on the move. They left the sidings at Skateraw just before this all happened. They halted the train briefly while the incident was playing out, but they have resumed the journey and are south of you now, en-route to Sellafield. They are on one of the regular journeys with the nuclear waste.'

'Is EMP a threat to the train?'

'The scientists think it may stop the train, but the flasks are impregnable. They are shielded by a massive amount of armour. EMP will do nothing to them.'

'Is the train being tracked?' asked Tom, something in his memory starting to scratch at him. Why would an EMP drone take out a nuclear waste train? He recalled a video he had seen on the internet of a train hitting a flask in an experiment. The train was a write-off, but the nuclear flask was undamaged.

'Yes, the train is permanently tracked. What are you thinking, Tom?'

'Babić is going to strike at the train, I'm sure of it. I need to move, I'll call soon. Pet, Buster, let's go.' Tom shouted.

He went to the back of the ambulance where Cerović was being attended to in the rear, his face a mask of pain.

'Cerović, the sixth drone is up. Babić is controlling it. Where are they?'

'I don't know, man. I didn't know about this.' he groaned.

'Come on, you must have an idea. If he succeeds in what he is trying to do the consequences will be bad for all, especially you. Do the right thing, Cerović.'

Cerović paused and took a rasping breath. 'iPad in the back of the Ranger. The drone's GPS is being tracked. It will be on there.' he grimaced once more.

Tom went to the big Ford and ripped the door open. An iPad sat on the driver's seat, a map application open with a single pulsing blue dot visible south of their location.

Realisation hit Tom like a truck. He knew what they were planning; they needed to move fast.

54

Tom, Pet, and Buster jumped into the big bullet damaged Ford, their assault weapons in the footwell by Tom's boots. Buster gunned the engine and roared off along the A1 heading south as Tom updated the team.

'Where, Pet?'

'Seven clicks south, train track follows the coast, live progress of the train is being shared with me by CNC. It's still moving south, so not been struck yet.'

'Who is with us, Borat?' asked Buster.

'All the team are either too far away or are holding the prisoners. We are on our own apart from local support. Firearms teams from local forces are closing, but who knows how long. We need to get there, now, guys.'

'Why so urgent, Tom? I thought these nuke flasks could survive anything,' said Buster over the howl of the big V8 engine.

'Something I heard in Sarajevo just occurred to me. Where is the drone, Pet?'

Pet studied Cerović's iPad and looked at the blue dot. 'It's now stationary, two clicks ahead of us. The train is just north of it, moving south towards the signal. It's directly over the train track. If what I am seeing is correct, the train will pass under any moment.'

'Jesus, we will be too late,' said Tom flatly.

'Too late for what, Borat? Talk to me for fuck's sake,' said Buster.

'The drone is going to take the train out. Then, if I'm right—and I hope to God I am not—Babić will be waiting with an anti-tank weapon.' Tom's voice remained level as he reached down into the footwell and detached one of the low light sights from the Sig

Sauer.

'What?' said Buster, incredulously.

'It's the only thing that makes sense. The attack at Torness is just a bloody diversion designed to cause chaos and attract all the cops to it. This is the real danger. If they have what I think they have, it is easily powerful enough to pierce the armour on a nuclear waste flask. This area will be ruined for ever.'

'Fucking hell. What do you think they have?'

'Their weapons supplier was suspected of having and selling a Bumbar anti-tank rocket,' said Tom, strapping his seatbelt into place. 'Seatbelts, both of you,' he added.

'A Bumbar. That's the Serb version of the Milan, right? Fucking hell,' said Buster snapping his belt into place.

'Even worse, it's resistant to electrical counter-measures: the operator has to manually steer it onto the target. Fire-and-forget rockets like the Javelin could be affected by the EMP. We have to stop Babić firing.'

'Almost there, just around the next bend, guys,' said Pet.

'Okay, guys. We ready?' said Tom, racking the slide on his MP5.

'No. I fucking hate you and I am not hanging out with you any more you fucking shit-magnet,' yelled Buster over the screaming engine.

'Lights off Buster,' said Tom and Buster extinguished the headlights on the car as they rounded the bend, just using the light cast by the bright moon to find their way. Suddenly there was a loud, dull explosion. There was no fireball and no flash; there never was without a secondary explosion from fuel or gas. Well not outside the movies, anyway.

'Fuck, they've detonated the drone!' shouted Buster as they rounded the final bend.

The train was about five hundred metres from the road and it was totally stationary. Completely dead, devoid of any lights with debris from the explosion raining down on it. It was heavily laden with two trailers, both carrying the innocuous-looking beige flasks that resembled stout square shipping containers with the characteristic cooling fins. The two locomotives that had been towing the deadly cargo were stationary and dead.

Parked on the grass verge at the side of the road was a large open-backed Nissan, its load bay facing the train. There were two figures in the back attending to a distinctive-shaped weapon mounted on a tripod. Tom lifted the night scope to his eye and surveyed the vehicle. 'It's Babić and one other, they're preparing to fire the Bumbar. Ram them, Buster; ram the bastards!'

'What?' shouted Buster.

'Do it! Do it now, Buster, it's the only way. Ram the back end and they won't hit the train. Ram them now!' Tom yelled.

'I fucking hate you, Borat. Hold on!' Buster yelled as the Ford closed on the Nissan, thirty metres, twenty metres, ten metres. There was a flash as the missile ignited, causing a back-blast of flames from the rear of the weapon. In almost slow motion, the missile left the launch tube, its control wire trailing behind, still attached to the control unit.

Pet screamed as they closed, the Ford smashing into the rear of the Nissan's cargo area and lurching it violently sideways, throwing Babić and his man off the back of the vehicle, tumbling onto the soft earth of the field at the side of the road.

Without an operator to control it, the missile spun out of control and lurched upwards, climbing as it roared at terrific velocity towards the train before flying straight over the top and heading harmlessly towards the sea. Without the control system, its range was soon exhausted and it simply died and splashed down into the North Sea.

The airbags exploded, but the seatbelts stopped them from being thrown forward. Tom was shaking himself free and diving from the truck before the big car had even fully come to a stop, his MP5 ready to engage.

Babić's friend loomed out from the other side of the Nissan, firing wildly with a pistol, but his aim was poor after being violently thrown from the vehicle. Tom dropped him with a quick double tap from the MP5, and he went down in a heap on the floor.

A flash came from the other side of the Nissan and Tom felt the buzz and disturbed air of a bullet flying past his ear as Babić homed into view, his hand bucking as he fired with his own pistol, wildly and blindly in Tom's direction. Tom dived to the side and rolled on the floor, attempting to bring the MP5 to bear on the Serb, whose face was a mask of hate as he screamed in fury as he advanced.

Tom raised the MP5 and levelled at the centre mass of the advancing Babić and squeezed the trigger. The MP5 just clicked; a dead man's click.

Babić smiled as he levelled the pistol at Tom, sensing victory.

Suddenly Buster, appeared at speed, his bloodied face a mask of pure, naked aggression and threw himself at Babić, driving his shoulder into the Serb's ribcage and propelling him forwards with tremendous force, where he landed in a heap on the ploughed soil.

In a flash Tom was on top of Babić, his arm encircling his neck and locked into place against his other arm. The perfect rear naked choke. Tom had won many Jiu-Jitsu bouts with this choke, and he had also killed with it. Once applied in that way, it would never be escaped from. Tom smiled with a small sense of satisfaction as he squeezed tighter. Babić began to buck and thrash as his throat was constricted and the blood supply was interrupted thanks to the compression of his carotid arteries. Babić's struggles were of no use, it was game over.

'Tom stop,' Buster said, breathing heavily as he stood over Tom. 'Not now, not here, mate. You can't kill him. We take him in, we do this right, mate. No killing, not now.'

'He deserves to die, Buster. He has caused so many people to die. He killed my friend.'

'Tom, please stop,' said Pet, who had appeared from the mangled Ford, a cut to her face and her eyes full of fear. The sound of wailing sirens entered Tom's consciousness and the strobe of blue lights began to be visible as their backup arrived.

Tom tightened his grip, just slightly, as Babić's thrashing began to subside.

'Tom, mate, please don't. It won't help you or anyone else,

mate. You'll put Pet and me in a horrible position as well. Don't kill him; we'll take him in. He can rot in jail.' Buster's normal rapid fire, sarcastic Cockney banter had become much softer.

Tom exhaled, defeated, and relaxed his grip on Babić. The Serb took in a deep rasping breath. 'You win, Buster. Lock him up.' He stood and strode off to meet the oncoming backup, dialling Jane on his phone.

'Tom?' Jane's voice sounded worried.

'It's over.'

55

The three-hour trip up the A9 to Carrbridge was undertaken in comfortable silence, mostly because Pet slept like a baby. Tom drove the big BMW through the Cairngorms feeling the tingle of anticipation as the softly rolling Perthshire hills morphed into the rising jagged peaks of the Cairngorm mountain range.

There had been a big team debrief at the police station in Edinburgh that had lasted all night and into the following morning before they were all dismissed. They all had given their statements, and Jane had told them all to take a day in Edinburgh to recover. The counter-terror team had accepted responsibility for the investigation and all the prisoners were being interviewed at various police stations. There would be more interviews at a later date, but Jane had been resolute that her team, and Tom in particular, needed a short break before anything else happened.

Tom hadn't wanted to go to hotels with the rest of the team. He had a powerful urge to see his foster family and, being so close, it made sense. On a whim he had asked Pet if she'd like to come with him, and she jumped at the chance.

Pet woke up as they left the A9 and took the winding mountain roads through pine forests and towards his foster family's home in the shadow of the towering Bynack Mhor.

'This place reminds me of Bavaria. It's beautiful,' Pet said, admiring the scenery.

'It's home Pet. I'll come back here to live one day.'

They drove up the rutted track and parked the BMW next to Cameron's battered old Land Rover Defender. A flash of barking black fur came tearing out of the house, tail thrashing and tongue lolling as the little spaniel tore up to greet the newcomers. Tom opened the door of the car and the little black dog leaped in and onto his lap, showering him with slobbery, wet licks.

'Blimey, Peggy,' Tom laughed as the dog's backside wriggled side to side, trying to counterbalance her whizzing tail. 'This is Peggy,' he said to Pet. 'Whatever you do, don't call her a cocker spaniel to Shona, she's sensitive about it. They paid a premium for a cockapoo, but it ended up being all cocker and no poo.' Tom laughed as the thrashing dog leaped across him, knocking the indicator switches and sounding the horn with her leg, as she leaped on Pet, transferring all her affections to the newcomer.

'Woah, friendly doggy,' Pet said ruffling her ears trying to fight off the slobbery attack.

Cameron appeared from the back of the house, his overalls stained with a mix of mud and paint.

'Tommy-boy! You never said you were coming,' he said, a beaming smile over his lined, cracked face, his bright blue eyes shining with delight.

Tom and Cameron hugged warmly.

'I was in Edinburgh and had some time. Cameron, this is a good friend of mine, Pet. Pet, this is Cameron, my foster-dad.'

'Pleased to know you, love. Peggy leave her alone. Sorry, Pet, she's a grand dog, just loves people a little too much.'

Shona appeared from the back of the house, a huge smile forming on her face. 'Tom, what a lovely surprise,' she delightedly threw her arms around him and they hugged.

'Shona, this is my friend, Pet. We kind of work together. Pet, this is Shona, my foster mum.'

Pet managed to extricate herself from Peggy and got out of the car, smiling.

'Pleased to meet you both, Tom has told me lots about you.' She hugged Cameron and Shona in turn, warmly.

'Well come on inside, lassie. I've got the kettle on, time for tea.'

They all walked inside the farmhouse and soon were all drinking tea from weathered mugs around the kitchen table. Pet's eyes were immediately drawn to a freshly baked batch of golden-brown scones sat on a cooling rack.

'You want a scone, Pet?'

'Sure, they smell awesome, Shona,' she said picking one up and taking a big bite.

'Pet loves her food, I've never seen anyone eat so much,' Tom said, smiling as Pet chewed.

'News has been crazy, Tom, anything to do with you?'

'Maybe, but you know the score. I can't say, Cameron.'

'Fair enough, but at least answer me one thing, you know, put my mind at rest?'

'Go on.'

'Is everything okay? It's just not like you to pitch up out of nowhere, like this, and with the news, and all...' His words faltered, but there was no doubting the concern in his voice.

Tom paused to sip his tea, before softly speaking. 'The last few days have made me reflect on a few things, and I learned a little bit more about my father, much of it not good. I don't think he was as good a man as perhaps I once thought. Don't ask me for any more details, but it has made me realise that you guys mean everything to me, so, I just really needed to come and see you.' Tom was surprised to feel an unusual swell of emotion envelop him. Was this what normal people felt?

There was a long pause in the room before Cameron spoke, his face split with a wide grin, 'Ach, don't go getting all soppy and sentimental on us now, boy, I'm not used to it and you'll have me blubbing in front of your pal, here.'

'I know, I'll stop now, but sometimes, I just need to see you guys, and smell the Highland air, you know how it is?'

'Aye man, course I do. Now, bugger tea and scones. How about a beer?'

56

Six Weeks Later

Johnson Cyrus Higginson sat at his huge teak desk in the middle of an enormous office that occupied a corner of the huge stucco house in the most fashionable part of Boston, Massachusetts. He was excited about what he was about to do.

The operation in Scotland, despite police thwarting the attack, was considered to have been a huge success. It would have been even better had the incompetents managed to detonate the drones and render Torness useless, but the panic it had caused had still plunged the stock prices of Tru-Gen, the international power company that owned and operated the nuclear plant, to new lows. It had been beautiful to watch the price plummet, especially as he and the rest of the investors had shorted all their shares before the incident. He was planning to advise that once they hit their lowest point that they selectively buy again whilst the price was on the floor. The addition of the anti-tank attack on the waste train had been an inspired idea. People were horrified about just how regularly toxic waste was transported across the country by train, and the attack had just highlighted this risk.

The sudden overnight dip in the price of both sterling and the euro had meant that their short positions on the currencies had made a massive profit for them. The web of investment companies that he controlled was wide and complicated, and would be totally unfathomable to anyone else. They were home and dry, and all he had to do was return the money back to the investors, which he was now all set to do. Checking his watch, he logged in to the secure messaging app on his tablet computer and clicked on the conference function. One by one the eight icons appeared on the display, confirming that each member was online.

'Proceed, please.'

'Thank you, Mr Chairman. Ladies and gents, thank you for joining me. I have very good news for all of you,' he boomed in his Boston Brahmin accent.

The chairman spoke first; Higginson assumed he was a man, but the voice-changing software made it impossible to know. 'We wait to hear with interest. We all were concerned, as much of the operation was—what one may consider—unsuccessful, no?'

'Mr Chairman, despite law enforcement thwarting the attacks at Torness and the majority of the sub-stations, the loss of public confidence in Tru-Gen has been significant. The share price dropped heavily, as I am sure you have monitored, and our short position in those shares through the multiple investment companies made very pleasing profits. Allied to that there was, as you will all be aware, a significant dip in the value of the pound and the euro, which was simple to exploit as well.' Higginson could not help but sound extremely pleased with himself.

A new voice, also disguised, spoke. 'Yes, we have been following closely. Your decision to also heavily invest in the green energy companies was inspired. Ever since the Scottish First Minister announced that they would continue to seek independence on the basis of, and I quote, "Removing the scourge of nuclear power and nuclear weapons from Scotland", many investors are now seeing the green energy sector as being highly investable.'

Higginson smiled, placed a fat cigar between his lips and applied a flame, puffing at the fragrant smoke with extreme pleasure.

'Trust me, my friends, I have ensured that we have profited heavily from this as well. The prices had slipped somewhat, so the purchase price was low; owing to the social media frenzy we managed to precipitate in the weeks before the attack. Also, our bot farms managed to exploit the failed attack beautifully by spreading more and more public unease about nuclear power. *#NoNuclear* was trending for days. Together with targeted advertising on several social media platforms, we have probably hastened the demise of fossil and nuclear fuel by many years and we will profit wonderfully.

'Anyway, to business. I am delighted to inform you all that I have managed to realise a significant return on your original investment which I am now ready to transfer to you. I have set the transactions in place as you have all requested, but please note that, as I have utilised many different methods of transferring the funds, they may arrive from multiple sources.'

Higginson began to tap at the keyboard in front of him, beginning the processes that would enable eleven billion dollars to be transferred from multiple accounts, unit trusts, shell corporations, and law firms to other multiple financial institutions. All untraceable and all totally out of reach of anyone in law enforcement in multiple non-reporting jurisdictions. As ever, the richest people in the world were about to become richer.

After a final keystroke, Higginson declared, 'It is done. Congratulations, investors. Here is to our continued success.'

There was a long pause, and Higginson took another deep, satisfying pull on his Cuban cigar. He reached across to the cut-glass decanter and poured a healthy measure of thirty-year-old, single malt whisky into a tumbler and sat back in his leather chair.

'How long?' came a voice from the tablet.

'Imminently, my friend. These are complex transactions and sometimes the funds take a moment or two.' Higginson tried to sound convincing, but a little trace of concern began to take hold. He had tested this method just yesterday, which had resulted in an almost immediate arrival of the funds. He checked his terminal; the final command had definitely gone, the funds should have been there by now. His face began to flush red and he swallowed the whisky in a single gulp.

'How long, Higginson?' a voice said, making him jump. He

had no idea that anyone in the investors knew his actual name.

'Imminent, imminent. Just a glitch,' he stammered as he tapped furiously at the keyboard. Suddenly, the screen went totally blank: a deep, impenetrable black. He tapped at the keys and checked the power cable. It was securely in the power port and the plug was in the wall.

Panic began to rise in his chest. Something was wrong.

'Where is my fucking money?' came a deep, growling voice from the tablet.

'Where my money?' came another which had an oriental sound to it despite the voice disguiser.

All of a sudden eight distorted voices were shouting and demanding, each cancelling each other out so it just sounded like a wall of static sound. Higginson scrubbed his face with his hands and tapped at the keys, uselessly, once more.

Suddenly the screen burst into life, but not with the rows of figures that he had been hoping to see. An image of a Jolly Roger flag filled the screen, fluttering gently in a breeze. The skull had a cigar in its mouth and seemed to be smiling. The speakers burst into life with a raucous, cackling laugh that drowned out the distorted demands for the missing billions of dollars now floating round, lost in the electronic ether.

57

One Month Later

Tom and Buster left the farmhouse in Carrbridge with Peggy streaking ahead of them, making a beeline for Cameron's battered old Defender. She launched herself into the back of the old car, her tail thrashing in delight. They had both travelled up the previous day to finally get the fishing trip they had been promising themselves.

Soft Highland rain fell from the sky in a fine mist, but despite this a weak outline of the sun was trying to make inroads into the clouds.

Tom carried a tackle box and two rods, which he slipped into the back of the Defender and slammed the tailgate shut, being careful to avoid the blurring black tail that was thrashing away, joyfully.

'This better not be boring, Borat. You keep telling me fishing is cool, but the last time we went in Ukraine it was boring as bollocks, and some bastard ended up pulling my fucking fingernail out.'

'Buster, it's fun. We can catch our supper.'

'What a salmon?'

'No, not a salmon, brown trout.'

'Brown fucking trout? Trout sucks, I want salmon.'

'We can't get a salmon.'

'Why?'

'Wrong time of year.'

'See, boring already. Will there be beer?'

'I've a few cans in the tackle box,' Tom smiled. They'd come up for a few days once all the evidence had been stacked up and a full review of the recent operation had been completed.

The journey was only about ten minutes, and soon they were descending a steep hill that led to a river that Tom assured Buster was good for trout.

Peggy dashed off ahead as soon as they pulled the Defender over at the top of the hill. As they trudged down the slippery bank, they saw that they were not alone. Peggy had charged up to the fisherman, her tail thrashing as she greeted the new wader-clad human. Her boundless enthusiasm and love for everyone and everything was a constant source of pleasure for Tom.

'That dog is a fucking nutjob, Tom. Look at her hassling that poor fisherman; she'll be scaring the shit out of all the fish!'

'Peggy, come on,' called Tom, but her delight at meeting a stranger had rendered her temporarily deaf.

As they got closer, Tom called more sternly and she turned and trotted back to them, 'Sorry, pal,' Tom said to the fisherman's back.

'No worries, dude,' said a familiar voice. Mike Brogan turned, a big smile across his face.

'Why am I not surprised that it's you?' Tom said, shaking his head.

'Hey, can't a guy do a bit of fishing? Coincidence, man.'

'Oh blimey. Yanks in town, that don't bode well. Every time you show up the world gets a bit more shooty and dangerous,' said Buster, trying to hide the wide grin that was spreading across his face.

'Yeah, right. Beer?' said Tom.

'Now I'm *really* glad you're here,' Mike said catching the tin of IPA that Tom tossed at him. He popped the can. 'Cheers,' he said, taking a deep swig. 'It's good beer,' he said, smacking his lips.

'Cromarty beer. Nice little place on the Black Isle.'

'Hmm, I need more of this.'

'Mike, much as I am delighted to see you, you didn't come here for either the fishing or the beer,' said Tom cracking open another can and tossing one to Buster.

'I just thought that we could share some learning following recent events; a bit of quid pro quo.'

'Surely you have been briefed?'

'Only official briefs. Nice to hear the other stuff,' said Mike, taking another swig.

'It is what it is, Mike. Cerović is singing like a canary and blaming everyone else. Babić is saying nothing at all, not even a little bit. Foreign agencies are queueing up wanting to see him. His is one of the most wanted men in Europe. The other prisoners were all ex-military freelancers. All charged, but none of them are talking. Professionals, I guess. Evidence is all bang to rights and CTC, who are preparing the case, are very confident.'

'Any problems for you and the undercover stuff in Sarajevo?'

Tom shrugged. 'No one seems to think it's a problem. The whole case is being based purely on what happened up at Torness. They've dropped the Chinese wall on everything before that.'

Mike looked puzzled. 'Chinese wall?'

'The case is being based purely on what happened that can be directly evidenced by the cops whilst they were in the UK. There is shit loads of evidence, the helicopter was filming them, and it survived the crash. There are tons of forensics, all over the drones and in the cars and guns. They are both going away forever, I'd say. Anything other than that will be other side of the Chinese wall and will be subject to public interest immunity. Judge has already ruled on it on national security grounds. I may have to give evidence, but the judge has already said he will allow all of us to do it from behind a screen under cover names.'

'All cool then.'

'Yeah, how about Havers?' Tom asked.

'He's in military prison. He is already trying to plea bargain and is squealing like crazy. He has already snitched on a couple of rogue military officers. I'd say all loose ends are tied up.'

'Really? How about those that financed it all?'

'The investors? No need to worry about them, Tom. I heard you use a saying once: "There is more than one way to shoe a horse".'

'I may have said it once or twice; it's an old Serb saying.'

'Sounds like a shit version of "More than one way to skin a cat",' Buster grumbled.

'I think the Serb one came first, Buster,' said Tom.

'Whatever. Still sounds crap.'

Mike didn't answer, instead tossing his smart phone to Tom.

'Swipe left,' said Mike.

The first image was a screen grab from a news site, with the headline, *"BOSTON INVESTMENT BANKER COMMITS SUICIDE".* There was a picture of a well fleshed man and a short story about how his investment company had gone bust with massive losses and he had thrown himself out of a window.

Tom swiped again, this time it was a similar screen grab from a North Korean news feed, fortunately translated. *"DEAR LEADER'S MINISTER OF FINANCE EXECUTED AFTER EMBEZZLEMENT".*

Another swipe, *"MINISTER RESIGNS AFTER DECLARING BACKRUPTCY AFTER MULTI MILLION INVESTMENT LOSS. POLICE INVESTIGATING MONEY LAUNDERING ALLEGATIONS".*

Another swipe, *"RUSSIAN GAS TYCOON GUNNED DOWN IN MOSCOW ATTACK".*

"INDIAN STEEL MAGNATE CHARGED WITH FRAUD".

'I take it there are a few of these?'

'Yeah, one or two, and we have it on very good authority that the investors suffered a multi-billion loss after some hackers managed to intercept multiple electronic transmissions. As I understand it, they are no longer operational and are blaming each other for their losses.' Mike smiled and took another long draught of the beer.

'I wondered why I'd not heard from Pet for a while?' said Tom smiling.

'I always said Pet was a clever bugger,' said Buster admiringly.

'I think she called in some help from her geek squad of hackers.

They love a challenge,' said Mike.

'I guess you hit the nail on the head a while ago,' said Tom.

'What's that?'

'Bad shit happens to bad people.'

'You know it, buddy.' The three men touched beer cans, picked up their rods, and began to fish.

THE END

Did You Enjoy This Book?

If so, you can make a HUGE difference

For any author, the single most important way we have of getting our books noticed is a really simple one—and one which you can help with.

Yes, you.

Us indie authors and publishers don't have the financial muscle of the big guys to take out full-page ads in the newspaper or put posters on the subway.

But we do have something much more powerful and effective than that, and it's something that those big publishers would kill to get their hands on.

A committed and loyal bunch of readers.

Honest reviews of our books help bring them to the attention of other readers.

If you've enjoyed this book I would be really grateful if you could spend just a couple of minutes leaving a review (it can be as short as you like) on this book's page on your favourite store and website.

Thank you so much—you're awesome, each and every one of you!

Warm regards

Neil

Acknowledgements

As always, when I come to the end of a book, I am once again reminded that whilst writing a book is a solitary endeavour, publishing a book isn't, and therefore I'd like to say thanks to a few fabulous people.

To my boys, Alec, Richard, and Ollie, for all the laughs and reminding me why I do this stuff.

To my super beta readers who help me iron out the lingering (thousands) of typos and can spot a plot hole at a thousand yards. Jacqueline Beard, Nikki Hounsell, Karen Campbell, Clare Lancaster, Andreas Rausch and Fi Phillips: you have my undying gratitude.

A big mention goes to Colin Scott for his tremendously erudite advice, patient coaching, and shits and giggles.

I am enormously grateful to the continuing mine of advice from the crime writing community who have helped me navigate this journey from cop to writer. There are lots, but special mentions go to Denzil Meyrick, Lin Anderson, Margaret Kirk, Mike Walters, and Tony Parsons.

I have to mention someone who I can't mention for some very interesting insights into stuff I can't talk about. It was fun talking.

To Pete and Si at Burning Chair, for turning the semi-literate gibberish I serve up into something resembling a book. It's fun and I'm glad you don't take my foot stamping histrionics seriously.

As always, I want to mention all my former colleagues in blue from across the UK. The criticism being levelled at the police is shocking and distressing for me to observe from the side-lines, and it is undeserved. These guys put themselves in harm's way, every day, 24/7 and they do it for us. Give them a break; you'll miss them if they go, trust me.

Of course, a final word must go to you, dear reader. Thanks for taking a chance on a washed-up ex-cop who loves slinging words on a page and hoping they make a story, without you, I'm just shouting into a void.

Peace,
Neil

About the Author

Neil Lancaster served over thirty years in law enforcement in the both military and Metropolitan Police, working in a number of detective roles investigating serious and organised crime. During his career he chased murderers, human traffickers, fraudsters and drug dealers.

Neil now lives in the Scottish Highlands where he spends his time writing crime fiction, influenced by his experiences.

You can follow him at www.neillancastercrime.co.uk

Or on Twitter - @NeilLancaster66

About Burning Chair

Burning Chair is an independent publishing company based in the UK, but covering readers and authors around the globe. We are passionate about both writing and reading books and, at our core, we just want to get great books out to the world.

Our aim is to offer something exciting; something innovative; something that puts the author and their book first. From first class editing to cutting edge marketing and promotion, we provide the care and attention that makes sure every book fulfils its potential.

We are:

- Different
- Passionate
- Nimble and cutting edge
- Invested in our authors' success

If you're an **author** and would like to know more about our submissions requirements and receive our free guide to book publishing, visit:

www.burningchairpublishing.com

If you're a **reader** and are interested in hearing more about our books, being the first to hear about our new releases or great offers, or becoming a beta reader for us, again please visit:

www.burningchairpublishing.com

Other Books by Burning Chair Publishing

The Tom Novak series, by Neil Lancaster
Going Dark
Going Rogue

10:59, by N R Baker

Love Is Dead(ly), by Gene Kendall

A Life Eternal, by Richard Ayre

Haven Wakes, by Fi Phillips

Beyond, by Georgia Springate

Burning, An Anthology of Short Thrillers, edited by Simon Finnie and Peter Oxley

The Infernal Aether series, by Peter Oxley
The Infernal Aether
A Christmas Aether
The Demon Inside
Beyond the Aether
The Old Lady of the Skies: 1: Plague

The Wedding Speech Manual: The Complete Guide to Preparing,

Going Back

Writing and Performing Your Wedding Speech, by Peter Oxley

www.burningchairpublishing.com

Neil Lancaster

Going Back

Neil Lancaster

Made in the USA
Coppell, TX
17 November 2021

65925763R00184